By Connie Willis

Terra Incognita
A Lot Like Christmas
Crosstalk
The Best of Connie Willis
All About Emily
All Clear
Blackout
All Seated on the Ground
D.A.
Inside Job
Passage
To Say Nothing of the Dog
Bellwether
Uncharted Territory
Remake
Impossible Things
Doomsday Book
Lincoln's Dreams
Fire Watch

THE ROAD TO ROSWELL

THE ROAD TO ROSWELL

A Novel

CONNIE WILLIS

DEL
REY

NEW YORK

Copyright © 2023 by Connie Willis

All rights reserved.

Published in the United States by Del Rey,
an imprint of Random House, a division of
Penguin Random House LLC, New York.

DEL REY is a registered trademark and the CIRCLE colophon
is a trademark of Penguin Random House LLC.

Hardback ISBN 978-0-593-49985-6
Ebook ISBN 978-0-593-49986-3

Printed in the United States of America on acid-free paper

randomhousebooks.com

2 4 6 8 9 7 5 3 1

First Edition

Book design by Elizabeth A. D. Eno

To Eleanor Cameron, Robert A. Heinlein, Ray Bradbury, John Wyndham, Damon Knight, and all the other science fiction authors who first sparked my interest in aliens.

And to Jack Williamson and Frederik Pohl, who took one look at the Roswell crash and said, "It's a weather balloon."

The surest sign that intelligent life exists elsewhere in the universe is that it has never tried to contact us.

—Bill Watterson

Be hospitable to strangers.

—The Code of the West

"Let me ask you something. If you were an alien—you can go anywhere in the world—would you pick Roswell?"

—*Roswell*

THE ROAD TO ROSWELL

CHAPTER ONE

Paul: Yeah, well, you're killin' yourself. A friend
can't be worth that.

Hogy: Well now, how would you know? Did you
ever have one?

—*The Virginian*

Serena wasn't in the airport waiting area when Francie got off
the plane in Albuquerque, but a man carrying a sign reading
FIRST CONTACT COMMITTEE—WELCOME TO THE UFO FESTIVAL
was.

UFO Festival? Serena hadn't said anything about a UFO festival
going on at the same time as her wedding. *Maybe it's not in Roswell,*
Francie thought hopefully. But of course it was. Where else would a
UFO festival be?

And as if to confirm that, here came two guys in Star Trek uniforms and Spock ears, hurrying up to greet a third in a silver unitard
and a gray alien mask with large black almond-shaped eyes and no
nose.

*Thank goodness I didn't succeed in talking Ted into being my
plus-one for this wedding,* she thought. *Or worse, Graham.* She'd
tried to talk somebody, anybody, from work into coming with her

so Serena wouldn't try to fix her up with someone, but when she'd told them where the wedding was, they'd all said no.

"Roswell?" Graham had said. "The place with all the UFO nut jobs?"

"Why is it in Roswell?" Ted had asked. "Does your friend live there?"

"No, she lives in Phoenix. They're just having the wedding in Roswell."

"*Why?*" Graham said. "Why would anyone in their right mind go to *Roswell?*" and she'd been forced to tell them that Serena was marrying one of those selfsame UFO nut jobs, at which point both of them had not only refused to be her plus-one but told her she was crazy for going herself.

"I have to," she'd told them. "Serena asked me to be her maid of honor, and she's one of my very best friends. She was my freshman roommate in college. We have a special bond."

"A special bond?" Graham had said. "What are you, Sisters of the Traveling Pants or something?"

"No," she'd said defensively, "but I owe her a lot. She saved my life when I was a freshman," and tried to explain how, when she'd arrived at college in Tucson, knowing no one, homesick for New England, and shocked by the heat and barrenness of the Southwest, Serena had kept her from getting on the first plane home. She'd shown her around campus, introduced her to people, taught her what tumbleweeds and javelinas and saguaros were, and convinced her there weren't any rattlesnakes on campus (which would definitely have sent Francie screaming back to Connecticut). And when Francie's high school boyfriend had broken up with her two weeks later, Serena'd sat with her while she'd sobbed, told her "he wasn't right for you at all," and generally patched her back together.

"She's been a terrific friend," Francie said. "Sympathetic, funny, and—"

"And out of her mind if she believes all this aliens-from-outer-space garbage," Graham had said. "I don't know about you, but it's my policy to avoid nut jobs, old roommates or not."

Ted nodded. "I had a roommate my sophomore year who believed birds were spying on him. You don't catch me going to *his* wedding."

"She isn't a nut job," Francie protested. "She's just a little . . . ditzy, and inclined to go along with what her boyfriends think."

And she has terrible taste in men, Francie added silently. Worse than terrible. When Francie first met her, Serena had been dating a kamikaze BASE jumper who'd wanted her to dive headfirst into the Grand Canyon with him, and her taste hadn't improved since then. She'd dated a gun-stockpiling survivalist and a breatharian, who believed you could survive on air and positive thinking, and been engaged to a soul shaman and a stormchaser.

"All the more reason not to go," Graham had said. "You'll just be condoning her marrying this guy."

Ted had nodded. "Definitely complicit. Unless you're going because you want to talk her out of it," and Graham had pounced.

"That's it, isn't it? You're going out there to pull one of those dramatic 'speak now or forever hold your peace' numbers, aren't you?"

She'd insisted she wasn't, but they hadn't believed her and had refused to listen when she'd tried to explain that she wouldn't have to talk Serena out of it—that Serena always came to her senses and started having second thoughts herself. That's what had happened with the stormchaser. "He thinks tornadoes are an *adventure,* like *The Wizard of Oz* or something," she'd told Francie, "but they're dangerous! And he expects me to drive straight into them with him!"

All Francie'd had to do was stand there while Serena talked herself out of it and called the wedding off. But to have that happen, Francie had to be there to listen to her doubts and assure her she was doing the right thing. Serena counted on Francie to be her sounding board and her backup, to rescue her from making a terrible decision just like she'd rescued Francie so many times. "Friends are supposed to help each other, aren't they?" Francie had asked Ted and Graham.

"Yeah, but there are limits," Ted had said. "What if next time she decides to marry a serial killer and you talk her out of it and he comes after *you*?"

"She is *not* going to marry a serial killer."

"My advice is to tell her something came up and you can't come," Graham said.

"Yeah, tell her you broke your leg or something," Ted added.

"I can't do that. I can't just *abandon* her. She needs me."

"Okay," they'd said, "but don't come crying to us if this turns out to be a complete disaster."

Which it very well might, she thought, looking around the waiting area. *Where* was Serena? She'd specifically said she'd be at the airport to drive Francie down to Roswell. "That way we'll have a chance to talk," she'd said, and Francie had taken that as a sign Serena was already having second thoughts. *So where* is *she?*

Francie texted, Where R U?

No answer. *Maybe she thinks we were supposed to meet at baggage claim,* Francie thought, shouldered her carry-on, and went down the escalator to see if Serena was there.

She wasn't, but a number of people going to the UFO Festival were, and yes, the festival *was* in Roswell, because their T-shirts all said so, and as if that wasn't enough, they were all talking about a UFO sighting that had happened on Monday night.

"Where?" a woman in a silver minidress and green body makeup asked.

"West of Roswell. Just outside Hondo, near those big red-rock buttes," one of the T-shirt guys said.

"I don't remember any red-rock buttes near Hondo," the green woman said.

"I don't know, that's just what they said. It was on UfosAreReal .net."

Francie texted Serena again, checked the other luggage carousels, and then walked outside to see if she might be waiting in her car.

She wasn't. Francie went back inside to the baggage carousel in case she'd missed her somehow, checked her texts, and then called Serena. "Where *are* you?" she said when Serena answered.

"In Roswell," Serena said, sounding harried. "I'm so sorry about this. I intended to be there to meet you, but we've had all kinds of problems, and I still have to pick up your dress, and it's a complete *zoo* here with the festival and the town getting ready for the Fourth of July and everything, so I asked Russell's best man to pick you up. His name's Larry. He's *perfect* for you."

I doubt that, Francie thought. Serena's taste in guys for Francie was as bad as her own choices in boyfriends. At her almost-wedding to the stormchaser, she'd tried to fix Francie up with a ghosthunter who spent his time in ghost towns with an EMF detector, looking for the ghosts of outlaws and claiming he'd collected their ectoplasm. Which was why Francie had been so desperate to bring a plus-one with her.

"Larry's totally hot," Serena was saying. "He's six foot two and really interesting to talk to. He's had three close encounters and been abducted twice. He wrote a book about it—*The Survivor's Guide to Alien Abduction.*"

"So where's he supposed to meet me?" Francie said, scanning the baggage claim for someone tall, dark, and handsome, but the only people waiting for their luggage were three teenagers in Star Trek uniforms and Spock ears. "He wasn't abducted again, was he?"

"No," Serena said, "but there was a possible sighting two nights ago that he had to go check out."

Oh my God, I am so glad Graham and Ted refused to come, Francie thought. *I would never hear the end of it.*

"I'm afraid you're going to have to rent a car and drive down. I'm *really* sorry."

I'm not, Francie thought. Three hours in a car with a nut giving you tips on how not to get beamed up and probed by aliens was the last thing she needed. "It's fine. I'll go rent one right now. Hang on," she said, walking across to the car rental area as she talked.

Apparently everyone in Albuquerque was also renting a car. The line was really long. But at least the people in it looked relatively normal. She got into the line behind a grandmotherly-looking woman and said to Serena, "Okay, I'm in line. How do I get to Roswell?"

"You take I-40 east out of Albuquerque to— What?" Serena said, obviously talking to someone else. "Why not?"

There was a pause, and then Serena said, "Francie? Sorry. Can I call you back?"

"Yes," Francie said, and added silently, looking at the length of the line, *I have a feeling I'm going to be here awhile.*

"Okay, bye," Serena said, and hung up.

The woman in line ahead of her turned around. "I couldn't help hearing you asking how to get to Roswell. Are you going to the UFO Festival, too?"

"No," Francie said, "I—"

"Oh, you should," the grandmotherly woman said. "They hold it every year on the weekend closest to the anniversary of the crash— July the eighth."

"That's wrong. They didn't crash on the eighth," a middle-aged man in front of her said. "They crashed on the sixth. It was reported in the newspaper on the eighth."

"The festival has all sorts of speakers and panels," the grandmother went on, "and a hospital gurney race with aliens strapped to the gurneys—not real ones, of course."

Of course, Francie thought, cursing Serena for consigning her to this line. And to who knew what else?

"There are fireworks at the fairgrounds," the man said, "and tours out to the J. B. Foster ranch where the saucer crashed."

"And the government covered it up," someone else in line put in.

The man nodded. "So many people attended it last year they had to add an extra day. This year's theme is Alien Abductions."

"My grandson was abducted," the grandmother said. "He was driving to Truth or Consequences one night when he heard this strange whooshing noise and then saw this strange light. It paralyzed him so he couldn't resist and beamed him up out of his car and into the ship. They stuck a needle up his nose and implanted a chip in his brain."

The man nodded. "My neighbor was abducted, too. He has a scar where they implanted a chip into his leg."

Francie looked longingly at the front of the line, but it hadn't moved at all.

"You *must* come to the festival," the grandmother said. "I'd be happy to show you around."

"I'm afraid I can't," Francie said. "I'm here for a wedding. I'm the maid of honor."

"Oh, how nice!" she said, and a woman farther ahead in the line piped up, "My niece got married at the festival last year. All her attendants were dressed as Grays."

"Grays?" Francie said blankly.

"E.T.s. Aliens."

"There are three kinds of extraterrestrials," the man explained. "Grays—those are the ones you see in the movies with the silver skin, big heads, and almond-shaped eyes—and Reptilians—they're worse than the Grays, they want to take over Earth—and Venusians. They're tall and blond and look outwardly human, but you can tell they're aliens because they just *feel* wrong. The sight of them makes your skin crawl."

"That's because we're hardwired to be afraid of anything from another planet," the second woman said knowledgeably. "It's called exo-xenophobia. We automatically feel terror and loathing when we're in the presence of something from another planet."

"Is everyone going to be in costume for your wedding?" the grandmother cut in to ask.

"No," Francie said, and then remembered Serena had only said, "You'll love your dress," which didn't preclude a bizarre headdress. Or an alien mask.

"My niece's wedding was at the UFO museum," the woman was saying, "in front of the flying saucer."

"Do you know how long the drive to Roswell takes?" Francie asked to change the subject.

"Three hours," the man with the abducted neighbor said.

"You're not driving down by yourself, are you?" the grandmother asked nervously. "Over half of all abductions happen to people when they're alone in their cars."

"And there was a sighting the night before last," the wedding woman said. "They got a video of it," and the first man immediately pulled out his phone and began typing.

"You're not driving down after dark, are you?" the grandmother asked Francie.

That depends on how long this line takes, Francie thought. "No. I'm leaving as soon as I get my car. But I really don't think there's any reason to worry—"

"Then you should look at this," the man said and thrust the phone at her.

The video had obviously been shot from a partly rolled-down car window. It showed darkness and then a momentary blur of light that was definitely a UFO. Or an airplane. Or a passing headlight. Or a kid with a flashlight.

But the others were all very impressed with it. "It looks just like the sighting the last day of the festival last year," the wedding woman said, and the man who'd described the categories of aliens nodded sagely.

"They always show up during the festival. They sense when we're thinking about them," he said. "They're telepathic, you know."

"That's not a UFO," a lank-haired guy standing in front of the wedding woman said, coming up to look over her shoulder at the video.

Thank goodness, Francie thought. *A ray of sanity.*

"It doesn't look *anything* like the one that abducted me," he said. "Mine had these round red lights all around it."

"What did the aliens do to you?" the first woman asked.

"I don't know. I was driving down to Las Cruces one night around midnight, and all of a sudden my car died, just like that. I thought I must be out of gas, but the gas gauge said half-full, and it wasn't just the car's engine; the lights and my cellphone died, too. And then I saw these giant glowing red orbs. And that's the last thing I remember."

Thank goodness for that, Francie said to herself, looking hopefully at the line, which was finally moving.

"The next thing I know," the guy went on, "it's morning, and my pickup's in a ditch. And when I contacted MUFON—that's the Mutual UFO Network," he explained for Francie's benefit, "they said it definitely fit the pattern. The aliens almost always abduct people driving alone."

The woman turned triumphantly to Francie. "You see? Maybe you'd better forget about renting a car and ride down with one of us."

Over my dead body, Francie thought. "Thank you," she said. "That's very nice of you, but I'm going to need a car when I get there. And that reminds me, I promised I'd call my friend back. Can you hold my place in line for me?"

"Of course," the grandmother said, and Francie went over to a corner to call Serena.

"You haven't started down yet, have you?" Serena asked when she got her.

"No, I'm still in line at the rental car counter. I'm not going to be wearing some sort of costume for this wedding, am I?"

"Costume?" Serena said blankly.

Oh, thank goodness, Francie thought.

"Speaking of which, when you get here, you need to try on your dress in case it needs any last-minute alterations. I can't wait for you to see it. It's absolutely gorgeous."

Yes, well, that was what she'd said about Francie's maid-of-honor dress when she'd nearly married the stormchaser, and that had turned out to be a tie-dyed nightmare with eight-inch-long fringe. But at least Serena'd confirmed it wasn't a costume.

"I'll be there as soon as I can," Francie said. "There's a really long line for rental cars, but I'll leave the minute I get it and—"

"About that," Serena said.

Uh-oh, Francie thought.

"Russell was wondering if you could pick up another guest first. Russell was going to come get him, but he's waiting to hear from Larry, and since you're already there, I thought . . . He's flying in from D.C., and his plane's due at one forty-two, so it shouldn't delay you that long. His name's Henry Hastings and he's on Delta flight number—"

"This isn't another one of your setups, is it?" Francie interrupted.

"With *Henry*?" Serena said. "*No*. He works for the FBI. He's this grim, always-wears-a-suit type. Russell met him when he was researching how the government covered up the Roswell crash because they're secretly working with the aliens."

"And this Henry person told Russell they were?"

"*No*," Serena said. "He told Russell the whole thing's ridiculous, that there aren't any aliens, and the only cover-up was of a Cold War project the Air Force was conducting."

No wonder Serena didn't consider him matchmaking material. He sounded entirely too sane and sensible.

"Russell says that the fact that he's denying it proves he's part of the cover-up, so he invited him to the wedding to try to worm the truth out of him."

And Henry is stupid enough to come? Francie thought, her opinion of him dropping. Until she remembered she had no room to talk.

"I'll be glad to pick him up," she said. At least she could save him three hours of being trapped in a car with Russell grilling him about government cover-ups. "What's his flight number?"

"It's 429, and his cellphone number is—"

"Hang on till I find something to write with," Francie said, hurrying back to the line. She pantomimed writing, and the grandmother handed her a pen and a flyer for the UFO Festival.

"Thanks," she murmured. "Okay, Serena. Go ahead."

"He's on Delta flight 429 from D.C. It comes in at one forty-two. His cellphone number is 202— What?"

Francie could hear a muffled male voice, and then Serena saying, "But surely that doesn't include *flowers*!"

More muffled talk, and then Serena came back on the phone. "I need to go," she said. "Call me as soon as you've connected with Henry. Bye."

"Wait!" Francie said. "I need his cellphone number."

"Oh, right." Serena told her the number and then hung up.

Francie scrawled the number on the back of the flyer and then entered it in her phone and handed the flyer back to the grandmother. "No, no, you keep it," she said, "in case you find time to go to the festival. I really wish you'd change your mind and drive down with one of us."

Luckily, at that point it was the grandmother's turn at the counter, and before the others could start up again about abductions and UFO sightings, a second agent appeared and Francie went up to the counter.

They were all out of cars in the compact, small, midsize, and full-size categories. "You should have made a reservation," the agent said reprovingly. "We're really busy because of it being the Fourth of July weekend and the UFO convention and all."

"How about a flying saucer, then?" Francie asked.

"No, we don't have any of those," the agent said seriously. "All we have left is a Lexus LS at $385.00 a day or a Mercedes-Benz G 550 at $432.00 a day. The Mercedes has heated seats."

Just what I need in Albuquerque in July, Francie thought. Besides which, she couldn't afford either one. "Don't you have anything less expensive?"

"I told you, you should have made a reservation," the agent said, typing. "Oh, wait, we have a Jeep Wrangler that was just turned in. It's $51.00 a day."

"I'll take it," she said, and handed the agent her ID and credit card. "Is there any way I can expedite this? I have to meet someone coming in on another flight."

"Of course," the agent said, and produced forms for Francie to sign for accident, liability, and key replacement insurance, roadside assistance coverage, and buying a tank of gas up front. Francie signed them and produced her credit card, and the agent handed her a receipt to sign and a road map of New Mexico.

"That's okay," Francie said. "I have my phone."

"You'd better take the map," the agent said. "There are a lot of places in New Mexico without coverage."

I'm not going anywhere but Roswell, Francie thought. But any-thing to speed things up. She took the map.

There were still four more forms to sign, and by the time the clerk handed her the keys, it was nearly one forty-five, and she de-cided she'd better meet Henry Hastings before she picked up the car. She grabbed her bag and went back upstairs to check the departures-and-arrivals board to see if his flight had landed.

It hadn't. The flight was flashing DELAYED and showed a new ar-rival time of two fifteen. Of course.

But it was only half an hour late, and that would give her a chance to grab something to eat. She hadn't eaten since having a stale bagel and coffee at LaGuardia. She texted Serena the new arrival time and then went upstairs to the cafe, asked for a table for one, and looked at the flautas, carne asada, and chimichangas on the menu, none of which she'd heard of when she first arrived at college. Serena had taught her what they were—and introduced her to Dos Equis and sangria, either of which would have helped while she was in that line, but which she'd better not have now since she was going to be driving and she had a feeling most of those alien abductions were alcohol-fueled.

She ordered chicken tacos and iced tea and then called Serena to tell her the flight had been delayed.

"Oh, dear," Serena said. "I really need to talk to you."

"About what?" Francie asked, hoping she'd say, *I've decided Russell's crazy and I can't marry him,* but all Serena said was "Don't worry. I guess it can wait till you get here."

"I'll be there as soon as I can," Francie promised. "I'll pick up Russell's friend and we'll start down to Roswell immediately."

She hung up and ran out to check the board again. The flight now said two thirty-five. She went back to her table, where her tacos were just arriving.

So was the woman from the next table. "I couldn't help over-hearing you say you were going to Roswell," she said. "Are you going to the festival, too?"

"No," Francie said, and bit into a taco, hoping that would give the woman a hint.

"Oh, you should." The woman sat down at Francie's table. "W. Chambers Knoedler is going to be there. He wrote *Invaders in Our Midst*. It's about how there are extraterrestrials among us right here, right now."

And they've disguised themselves as UFO nuts, Francie thought, gobbling down her tacos so she could leave.

"They're the advance guard of the invasion. The aliens are planning to take over the world and enslave all of us. Knoedler thinks they plan to time the invasion to coincide with the festival, when all the UFO investigators are busy and won't realize what's happening."

"Mmm," Francie said. "This is all really interesting, but I need to go check the arrivals board to see if my friend's flight has arrived yet."

"You don't have to do that. I've got it all right here on my phone. Which airline and flight?"

Francie couldn't think of a good reason not to tell her. "Delta," she said. "Flight 429."

The woman tapped at her phone. "It's not coming in till three thirty-two," she said, "which means there's plenty of time for me to tell you about the UFO sighting west of Roswell. It happened Monday night. Knoedler thinks it was the first wave."

She began tapping at her phone again while Francie looked around in vain for the waitress so she could get her check.

"Here's the video Knoedler took," the woman said. She showed it to Francie. This time it looked like a picture of the moon rising, which it no doubt was. "This is only a scout ship, of course. Not a battle cruiser. Those are disguised to look like planes."

The waitress was nowhere in sight. Francie pulled a twenty and a five from her purse, put them on the table, grabbed her bag, told the woman, "It's been nice talking to you," and fled out to the waiting area and over to the arrivals board.

Flight 429 was now delayed to five forty-five. She called Serena. "The flight's been delayed again," she said. "It doesn't get in till five forty-five. Do you still want me to wait?"

"No, I was just going to call you. Henry just texted Russell. He had something come up at work, so he's taking a later flight. A red-eye. So he said not to pick him up, that he'll rent a car."

That's what he thinks, Francie thought.

"So you can come straight down," Serena said, "and help me figure out what to do."

"About what?" Francie said. *Please say, "About Russell."*

"About the wedding venue." She lowered her voice. "Russell's really excited about it, and I know we were lucky to get it, but . . . oh, well, I'm sure you'll know what to do. So get here as soon as you can. Bye."

"Wait," Francie said. "You haven't told me where you are."

"Oh," Serena said. "We're at the UFO museum."

CHAPTER TWO

ROSWELL OR BUST.

—*Bumper sticker*

The lines for the car rental shuttle and then to get out of the lot were almost as long as the one at the car rental desk, and it was after three before Francie actually left the airport. *And it'll probably take me an hour to get out of Albuquerque,* she thought.

But she was out of the city and on her way up into the scrub-covered Sandia Mountains within minutes. Serena had said it was three hours to Roswell. *Good,* Francie thought, crossing the narrow range of arid mountains. *I should be there by six.* At the crest, she pulled over and texted Serena to tell her that, and then started down out of the mountains, the plains opening out below her as she did.

She'd forgotten how far you could see out here in the West. The ochre-brown desert, barred with long indigo shadows, stretched out for miles and miles, all the way to a line of blue mountains to the north and a low buff-colored ridge to the east. And she'd forgotten how beautiful the midsummer skies could be—dotted with white Georgia O'Keeffe clouds or streaked with miles-long vapor trails, or, like today, a clear, cloudless expanse of azure blue.

The monsoons must not have started yet, she thought. Which was too bad. She'd always loved the towering thunderstorms they brought. But as she recalled, those didn't start till the end of July. And in the meantime, there wasn't a sign of a cloud. *Or a UFO.*

But as she turned south toward Roswell, she saw a huge cloud off to the west. It didn't have the flat, sheared-off anvil top of a thunderhead yet—it was still growing—but it had the billowing white cloud-masses of one. It looked like a clipper ship sailing the blue ocean of sky. And it looked like it was headed straight for the road to Roswell.

I hope not, she thought. Beautiful as they were to look at, the downpour they produced could be hard to drive through and she was already late. And that blur of gray she could see below the cloud definitely meant rain.

But luck was with her. A few miles later, the road angled sharply east, and by the time she went through the tiny town of Vaughn, the storm was far to the west of her, so far that when she passed a wind farm, with its tall white sentinel-like columns and airplane-propeller blades, the blades were barely moving.

The road turned south again, but as she came even with the thunderstorm, it was still a long way west, and thunderstorms only moved—what? Twenty miles an hour? And there weren't any other storms she could see. The sky ahead was completely clear. The road went down a long, straight hill covered with junipers and scrub oak, and then leveled out onto a plain dotted with dry grass and sword-leafed yuccas, cut by an occasional dry gulch or a rutted dirt road.

The roads didn't look like they led anywhere, and there wasn't anyone on them—or on the highway. There was no traffic at all except for once in a while a bone-white dried tumbleweed blowing across the road—and no signs of human habitation except for an infrequent fence or cattle gate.

She passed signs for Tomahawk Ranch and Cottonwood Draw and Dry Wash Road. There was still no one on the highway, and Francie decided it was safe to call Serena while she drove. "Where *are* you?" Serena wailed. "I thought you'd be here by now."

"I just passed Dry Wash Road," she said.

"Oh, good, that means you're getting close. Now, when you get into town, just stay on 285. It turns into Main Street. You follow it— What? Hang on a sec," she said, and Francie heard someone talking and another voice, a man's, say, "No, not till nine A.M. tomorrow."

Serena came back on. "Main Street's blocked off for the festival, but Russell says it doesn't close till tomorrow morning. Follow Main Street till you get to the downtown area. I'm at the UFO museum, making arrangements for the wedding. The museum's on the right side of the street, and it's got a big blue sign like a movie marquee out front. You can't miss it. It's got a giant head of an alien on it. Just tell them at the entrance that you're with the wedding, and you won't have to pay to get in— What?" she said. "Hang on a second," and Francie heard her say, "Well, is there any way you could move it to some other place?"

She came back on the line. "Sorry. Anyway, I need you to get here as soon as you can." She lowered her voice. "I'm having some trouble with the museum people. And Reverend Buckley's going to be here from five to six to go over the service and work out where we're going to stand and everything, and I want you to meet him."

Reverend Buckley, Francie thought. That sounded reassuringly normal.

"He's a high priest in the Church of Galactic Truth," Serena said. "He's been in telepathic contact with entities from Venus, Saturn, and Aetherium Six, and he's really interesting."

I'll bet.

"I've told him all about you, and he can't wait to meet you."

Graham and Ted were right. I shouldn't have come, Francie thought, and wondered if it was too late to say she'd gotten an emergency call from the office and had to fly back immediately.

Or maybe I could tell Serena I was abducted by aliens, she thought. The people in line had said they usually kidnapped people driving alone on deserted roads. And after the wedding she could tell her she'd seen a blinding white light and that was the last thing she remembered.

And Serena would end up married to a guy who believed all this claptrap. No, Francie couldn't abandon her, not after she'd kept Francie from giving up that first week of college *and* had rescued her from that creep she'd dated her junior year.

"Well, then, could you cover it up?" Serena was saying to someone. "Francie, listen, I've got to go. I'll see you at six."

But Serena hadn't taken into account the congestion the UFO Festival created. As Francie got closer to Roswell, the traffic picked up, and by the time she passed the town's official sign, it was bumper to bumper. The sign read ROSWELL—DAIRY CENTER OF THE SOUTHWEST, as if the town fondly hoped that was what it was famous for.

I don't think so, Francie thought, and apparently the townspeople agreed because a hundred yards on there was another sign with an alien and a crashed spaceship on it that read WELCOME TO ROSWELL—UFO CAPITAL OF THE WORLD and, as she came into town, a giant purple-and-green banner was strung across the highway, proclaiming WELCOME TO ROSWELL'S UFO FESTIVAL! THURSDAY THROUGH SUNDAY! THE TRUTH IS RIGHT HERE!

She was stuck behind a semi carrying the pieces of a carnival ride, and in the lane next to her were a food truck and a pickup full of inflatable green aliens and black Mylar balloons emblazoned with TRUST NO ONE.

The street was lined with what Francie'd expected in a Western town—gas stations, fast-food places, a Walmart—but they were all decked out for the festival. The McDonald's sign proclaimed OUR BIG MACS ARE OUT OF THIS WORLD! Starbucks was advertising a Cosmic Caramel Frappuccino, and Taco Bell's sign read ALIENS WELCOME. Walmart announced it was YOUR CLOSE ENCOUNTERS HEADQUARTERS—EVERYTHING YOU NEED FOR FIRST CONTACT, and

the Shell station reminded people to FUEL UP HERE FOR YOUR TRIP
TO OUTER SPACE.

There were signs touting crash site tours, a UFO Spacewalk, and
an Extraterrestrial Pet Parade, and others saying TOUR THE PLACE
WHERE IT HAPPENED! VISIT THE J. B. FOSTER RANCH, and TAKE A
SELFIE WITH AN ACTUAL ALIEN. And as she got closer to downtown,
the oval-shaped lamps on the lampposts that lined the street had
black almond-shaped eyes on them.

Serena had been half-right. Main Street wasn't closed, but one
lane had been blocked off, and people were busy setting up tents and
booths in the middle of it: ALIEN FACE PAINTING, EXTRATERRESTRIAL
BASEBALL CAPS, LITTLE GREEN MEN GREEN CHILE BURRITOS, ALIEN
INVASION RESPONSE TEAM HEADQUARTERS.

She found the UFO museum, which, in addition to its movie-
marquee sign proclaiming INTERNATIONAL UFO MUSEUM AND
RESEARCH CENTER and its giant green alien head, had clusters of
alien balloons tethered everywhere, but there was nowhere to park.
She drove several more blocks and then circled back and followed
the Public Parking signs to the municipal parking lot, but it was
full, too.

By the time she found a parking place on a residential street several blocks over, down the street from a church whose sign read
WORSHIP SERVICE 11 A.M. SUNDAY'S SERMON: UFOS ARE PILOTED BY
SATAN'S DEMONS, it was nearly six thirty. She debated leaving her
bag in the car, but if they were going on from the museum to dinner
or something, she'd have to hike all the way back to get it.

She slung the bag over her shoulder and was immediately sorry.
She'd forgotten how hot early evening in July in the Southwest could
be. By the time she reached Main Street, lugging the bag, she was
parched and perspiring.

Main Street was jammed with people setting up kiosks and ban-
ners reading GET YOUR ALIEN TATTOOS HERE, SPACE BURGERS, and
E.T. SUNRISES—EXTRA TEQUILA, and setting out racks of alien repel-
lent, UFO key chains, bumper stickers, magnets, mouse pads, coffee
mugs, cookie jars, Beanie Babies, baseball caps, NEW MEXICO—LAND

OF ABDUCTIONS and WHAT HAPPENS IN ROSWELL GETS SHIPPED TO AREA 51 T-shirts, and vile-looking fluorescent green snow cones and cotton candy.

There was a line outside the museum waiting to get in, and another one inside, and when Francie finally worked her way to the front and explained that she was with the wedding, the ticket seller (wearing a THE TRUTH IS OUT THERE T-shirt) had to check with a supervisor before giving her a yellow sticker to put on her blouse and saying, "They're in the back."

Francie put the sticker on and started toward the rear, working her way past framed newspaper clippings, photos of crop circles, a display of the wreckage from the 1947 UFO crash (which looked suspiciously like fragments of a weather balloon), an alien floating in a Plexiglas tube full of green liquid (which looked suspiciously like the one in *Independence Day*), and a U.S. map of UFO sightings, to a large open space with a cement floor.

There was a diorama of an alien autopsy on one side, a wall full of sci-fi movie posters on the other, and a life-size crashed flying saucer in the front. Next to the flying saucer stood four silver aliens. They had large heads, skinny elongated limbs, and aluminum foil collars, and the whole thing looked like something a fourth-grader might have made, but the people standing in front of it didn't seem to care. They were oohing and ahhing over it—one woman said, "It looks *just* like the real thing!"—and taking pictures with their phones, and when the saucer's top suddenly opened and emitted a hissing burst of steam, they jumped as if they expected a real alien to emerge.

Serena wasn't part of the crowd, and Francie wondered if there was another room behind this. She started for the back, but halfway across, Serena and a man emerged from a door marked No Admittance. The man had a bushy beard and was wearing a KEEP CALM AND PROBE ON T-shirt. Serena was talking intently to him, and it looked like they were arguing.

Please don't let that be Reverend Buckley, Francie thought. "Serena!" she called, and Serena shrieked and flung herself at Francie.

"Finally! I was about to give up hope! What happened? I kept

Reverend Buckley here as long as I could, but he had a lecture to give on Communicating with Extraterrestrials."

"I'm sorry," Francie said, but Serena wasn't listening.

She was asking, "Did you have trouble finding the museum? Where did you park?"

"I—" Francie began, but Serena'd already turned to the bearded Keep Calm and Probe On guy and said, "This is Francie, who I told you about."

Oh, no, Francie thought. *This is her fiancé?* "You must be Russell," she said, putting on a smile and stepping forward to shake hands with him.

"No, this is P.D., the person in charge of weddings here at the museum," Serena said. "Russell just stepped outside to take a call. He couldn't hear for the steam from the flying saucer," she explained, looking past the crowd toward the front of the museum. "I can't wait for you to meet him! Oh, good, here he is." She hurried over to greet a tall, extremely good-looking man. Which explained what Serena saw in him.

"Francie, this is Russell," Serena said, linking her arm in his and looking up at him adoringly.

So, no, not coming to her senses yet, Francie thought, her heart sinking.

"Russell, this is Francie . . ."

"It's great to meet you, Francie," he said. "Serena's told me what a good friend you've been."

Which sounded comfortingly normal. Maybe he wasn't as bad as she'd thought.

"Look, Serena, I can't stay," he said, turning back to her. "That was Larry on the phone. There's been another UFO sighting out west of town. Near Hondo. I've *got* to go check it out."

And there went that hope.

"Oh, do you have to go right now? Can't Larry check it out for you?" Serena said. "The decorations—"

"You don't understand," Russell said. "Two sightings in one week! And this one was in almost the same place as the first one."

The bearded man nodded sagely. "They always come around the

anniversary," he said. "To spy on us. Did they get video?" he asked Russell.

"I don't know. That's what I need to check out." He turned to Serena. "I'll be back as soon as I can, and we'll all go to dinner. Okay?" He kissed her on the cheek, said, "Nice to meet you, Francie," and ran toward the front of the museum.

"Bring Larry with you," Serena called after him. She turned back to Francie. "I really want you to meet Larry. He'd be perfect for you. He's an expert on UFO landings, like Russell. They're writing a book together."

"I'm writing a book, too," the bearded guy said. *"They're Here: Alien Landings in Roswell and Why They've Come to Earth."*

"Why *have* they come to Earth?" Francie asked curiously.

"To kill us all," he said cheerfully, "and turn us into zombies, and—"

Serena cut in. "You said it would be all right for us to use lights as decorations?"

"It depends on the kind of lights. I've got some in back," he said and slouched off through the door marked No Admittance.

The moment he was gone, Serena grabbed Francie's arm and said, "I'm *so* glad you're here. I *have* to talk to you."

"About what?" Francie said, hope stirring in her again.

"About *this.*" Serena waved a hand at the alien autopsy diorama. "Look at it! I don't want to get married surrounded by aliens! Especially dead ones." She walked over to it. Two department store mannequins dressed as a lab-coated doctor and a businessman in a black suit and fedora, both wearing surgical masks, stood looking down at a wizened gray alien on a gurney.

"Who's that supposed to be?" Francie asked, pointing at the businessman in the suit.

"One of the Men in Black," Serena said as if that explained everything. "I can't get married with *that* staring at me," she said, pointing at the alien.

"Could you put a screen in front of it or something?"

Serena shook her head. "I already asked. P.D. said it's in the contract Russell signed, that we can't cover it up. He said all the other weddings have loved it, that some of them have even incorporated it into their service. He said one bride placed her bouquet in the alien corpse's hands instead of throwing it. But that seems really—"

"Ghoulish?" Francie said.

"Yes! And that's not all. The museum says we can't take down the posters," Serena said, gesturing at the posters for *Them!* and *The Thing from Another World* and *Mars Attacks!* "Or cover up anything. We can't even stop the flying saucer from spurting steam during the service. I didn't have a chance to drive out here to see the venue beforehand, but Russell assured me it would be perfect, and now look at this place! And the museum says we can't make any alterations to the space without their approval—not even having flowers at the altar, because P.D. says they block the view of the flying saucer! And it's too late to find another venue. The wedding's Saturday—that's three days from now—and everything else in town is booked because of the festival. What am I going to do, Francie? I'm counting on you to get me out of this mess!"

As usual, Francie thought.

"Could you postpone the wedding till after the festival?" she asked. *Or, better yet, call it off altogether?*

"No, Russell says it's critical that we get married on the third. That's when the saucer crashed."

"I thought it crashed on the sixth," Francie said, remembering what the people at the airport had told her.

"No, that's when they found the wreckage. It actually crashed and killed the aliens inside on the third."

Of course it did, Francie thought. "Well, how about having the wedding outside?"

Serena shook her head. "Russell originally wanted to have it out at the crash site, but I told him no because of you being so deathly afraid of rattlesnakes."

"There are rattlesnakes out there?" Francie said, shivering at the mere thought of the slithering reptiles.

"Russell says no, there haven't been any rattlers at the crash site since 1947. He said they sense the aliens' presence and won't go near the place. And he said even if they did, they're more afraid of you than you are of them."

That's not possible, Francie thought.

"But then it turned out we couldn't get it anyway. It's booked solid with tours the whole festival."

"I was thinking more along the lines of a park," Francie ventured.

Serena shook her head. "Russell says UFOs generate thunderstorms. There was a thunderstorm the night of the first Roswell crash *and* the night of the Socorro crash."

I'm glad I didn't tell Russell about the thunderstorm I saw, Francie thought, *or he'd be sure that sighting he just heard about is real.*

She consulted her phone. "The Weather Channel's forecast for Saturday is clear and sunny. No chance of thunderstorms." She handed the phone to Serena so she could see it.

Serena handed it back. "That's because the Weather Channel doesn't believe in aliens."

Let's hope not, Francie thought.

"And if there was a storm, my dress would get ruined—oh, that reminds me, you haven't seen your maid-of-honor dress yet!"

She darted into the back and returned carrying a pair of high-heeled silver sandals and a garment bag. "You're going to *love* it," she said, laying the bag down on top of the dead alien on the gurney and unzipping it. "It's really special. It's absinthe shimmer."

Francie held her breath, praying, *Just in case Serena actually goes through with this, please, please, don't let it be hideous,* but except for the fact that "absinthe shimmer" was another word for the same neon green as the snow cones and cotton candy, it wasn't as bad as she'd expected. No hoop, no ruffles, no rosettes. It was a simple princess-style dress with a scoop neck and a long flowing skirt.

"And it has pockets!" Serena said happily, showing off the slit pockets set into the skirt. "So you can carry your phone or your lipstick or car keys or whatever. Go on, try it on," and Serena sent her off to the bathroom.

Except for the skirt being too long, it fit perfectly, and the pockets *were* large enough for her phone. She stuck it in the right-hand pocket, jammed the T-shirt and jeans she'd been wearing into her bag, and came out to show Serena. "It's a little too long . . ."

"That's because you're wearing Skechers," Serena said and made her sit down on the edge of the flying saucer diorama to put on the high-heeled sandals.

"See, it's perfect," Serena said when Francie stood up. "And that's not the best part. When you start down the aisle—" She stopped talking as music came from somewhere. It was the theme from *The X-Files.*

"Sorry, it's my phone," Serena said, pulling it out of her pocket and looking at it. "It's Russell." She put the phone up to her ear. "What? . . . You're kidding! There's definitely been a landing west of town close to where the original crash was!" she told Francie excitedly. "Three different people caught it on video. What—?" she said to Russell. "Channel 5 has footage! They think this one crashed, too!" she told Francie, and listened again. "Oh, but I hoped we could all have dinner together. And I need you to talk to the museum people about the wedding arrangements. They—"

There was another pause, and then Serena said defensively, "Of course I realize how important this is!"

She listened again, and Francie could hear Russell shouting, "This is our chance to get incontrovertible proof! But only if we get there before the government does! If we don't, they'll cover the whole thing up just like they did the first time!"

Francie wasn't the only one who could hear him. The people taking pictures of the crashed UFO diorama had come over and were listening—and whispering: "Where did she say it was?" and typing on their phones and showing each other what they'd found.

"But I can't just abandon Francie," Serena said. "I've got to take her over to the motel. And if I don't get the wedding arrangements sorted out now, there might not be time—"

One of the people consulting their phones said, "Twenty-four miles west of Roswell on U.S. 70," and there was a general exodus.

By the time Serena got off the phone, she and Francie were the only ones left in the room.

"If you need to go," Francie said, "I'm sure I can find the motel myself and—"

"No," Serena said firmly. "I'm not going anywhere till I've figured out how to make this place look presentable for a wedding," and started toward the No Admittance door to get P.D.

He was just coming out, carrying a black light bulb and a handful of fluorescent light sticks. "How about these?"

"No, no, no," Serena said. "I meant twinkle lights."

"Twinkle lights?" P.D. said blankly.

"Yes, you know, like those strings of lights they put on Christmas trees. I want to hang them across the ceiling"—she showed him—"and around the doors and the flying saucer."

"I'd have to see them first," P.D. said doubtfully. "The museum has to approve any alterations to the space. We have to preserve the museum's integrity."

You have a dead alien being cut open on a gurney, Francie thought, *and you're worried about integrity?*

"Do you have them with you?" P.D. asked. "I can't approve—"

"They're in my car," Serena said. "I can go get them."

"How long will it take?" P.D. said. "Because I need to close up the museum—"

And take off for the UFO landing site, no doubt, Francie thought. *And what do you bet when we come back with the lights, he'll already be gone?*

"I'll go get them, Serena," she said, "and you can stay here and talk to P.D. about the rest of the arrangements."

"Oh, would you, Francie?" Serena said. "*Thank* you!" and went to get her car keys.

Francie debated asking if she could change out of her maid-of-honor dress and high heels first, but P.D. was already looking at the E.T. clock on the wall and scowling impatiently.

"Where's your car?" she asked Serena, and then thought, *I hope it's not parked as far away as mine.*

"It's a block south of here and a block and a half east on the cross street," Serena said, handing Francie her car keys. "It's a black SUV, a Navigator. The lights are in the back seat. *Thank* you for doing this. You've saved my life! Again."

"That's what I'm here for," Francie said, and hurried through the museum and out to the street.

It was much cooler outside than it had been, now that the sun was starting to go down and the crowd of people that had jammed the street before had disappeared. There were only a couple of vendors left, finishing setting up their kiosks, and a small knot of tourists near the corner talking about—of course—the alleged UFO crash. "Are you going?" one of them asked.

"I don't know," a young woman answered. "I keep thinking of that scene in *War of the Worlds* where they all go out to see the spaceship and get fried."

"That doesn't worry me," an older guy wearing a Stetson said. "I've got my rifle. And my Smith and Wesson."

Francie hurried past them across the street, and down the next block, holding her long skirt up and wishing she'd at least taken the time to change back into her Skechers.

She started down the side street, looking at the diagonally parked cars. Every single one of them was a black SUV. She had to go out in the street and look at their rear ends to tell which was the Navigator.

There were *three* Navigators, all with bumper stickers that could have been put there by Serena—or Russell: TRUST NO ONE and I BRAKE FOR FLYING SAUCERS and WEAR YOUR SEATBELT—IT MAKES IT HARDER FOR THE ALIENS TO SUCK YOU OUT OF YOUR CAR. She had to click the key remote to tell which one was Serena's.

The blinking lights showed her it was the one at the end of the block, with the WE ARE NOT ALONE bumper sticker. Francie opened the back door and leaned in, looking for the plastic bag. It wasn't there, but Francie could see a tangle of white cords on the floor of the front passenger side.

If that's the twinkle lights, Francie thought, shutting the back door and opening the front door on the driver's side, *we'll never get them untangled.*

She leaned across the driver's seat. On second glance, it didn't look like a tangle of cords. It looked more like one of the tumble-weeds she'd seen on the way down here. *How did a tumbleweed get in Serena's car?* she wondered, and one of the tumbleweed's branches moved.

Oh my God, she thought, *you're an*— and before she could turn to run, a tentacle lashed out with the speed of light and whipped itself around her waist like a lasso.

CHAPTER THREE

"There are some things a man can't run away
from."

—*Stagecoach*

One moment she was opening the car door and gaping at the
alien, and the next its tentacles had lashed out with snake-
striking speed and wrapped around her feet, her knees, her
chest, her neck, and had deposited her into the driver's seat with
her hands clutching the steering wheel, unable to move.

Paralyzed, Francie thought, horrified. *That woman at the airport
was telling the truth about being abducted and not being able to
move,* and then realized that the reason she couldn't was that her
hands were bound to the steering wheel with something that looked
like twine.

But it wasn't. It was two of the vine-like tentacles of the alien—
sitting? standing?—next to her on the passenger seat. And there was
no question it was an alien, even though it didn't look at all like the
big-headed, black-almond-eyed extraterrestrials with childlike bodies in the UFO crash diorama.

It didn't even have eyes. Or a body. Just dozens and dozens of serpentlike tentacles radiating from a central point. *Like Medusa and her snakes,* Francie thought, though that wasn't the right comparison. If they'd been snakes and two of them had been wrapped around her wrists—or touching her at all—she'd already have died of fright.

They were more like branches, growing out of all sides of the tumbleweed, and the ones around her wrists looked like vines except that they weren't green. They were the same bone white as the tumbleweed. Except it wasn't a tumbleweed. This was an alien—though it didn't look at all like anything she'd seen in Roswell or anywhere else.

Which was how she knew it was really an alien. No human would ever have come up with an ordinary tumbleweed as an extraterrestrial. Well, that and the overwhelming sense that she was looking at something utterly foreign. Something from outer space. Which meant she should be feeling the exo-xenophobic horror the woman in the car rental line had claimed people felt.

She didn't. That didn't mean she wasn't terrified, though. She was. *Oh my God, I've been abducted by an alien!* she thought. *This can't be happening!*

But at the same time she was furious—livid because this meant aliens *did* exist, which meant Russell and all those other UFO nuts had been right, and outraged at being manhandled and kidnapped.

Because kidnapping was obviously what the alien had in mind. It—He?—pointed with one of its free vinelike tentacles at the steering wheel, at the back windshield, and back at her hands, clearly wanting her to back out of the parking space.

Which was the last thing she should do, even if she could. All the self-defense classes said never to go with a kidnapper—they just wanted to get you to some isolated spot, far from help. Which in this case might mean a flying saucer. Or another planet. Instead, you were supposed to throw your keys as far as you could to keep your abductor from getting them, or sling them out of reach under the car.

Only she had no idea where Serena's keys even were. *Hopefully I dropped them on the ground outside when the alien grabbed me,* she thought, and then remembered that, according to the woman at the airport, aliens were telepathic, and tried to put the idea of having dropped the keys out of her mind, but the alien gave no indication that he—it?—had heard her thoughts.

Good, she thought, and tried to remember what else you were supposed to do when you'd been kidnapped.

Call for help.

But the instant she opened her mouth to scream there was another tentacle-vine across her mouth, flattened to the width of duct tape and just as tight.

Oh my God, he's going to strangle me! she thought, and began to scream in earnest, but nothing came out but a muffled gurgle, and when she tried again, the gag began to tighten inexorably.

"I won't scream, I promise," she tried to say through the gag, which was the wrong thing to do. It grew even tighter.

She nodded to show the alien she understood and went perfectly silent, perfectly still.

What am I going to **do**? she thought frantically. She couldn't call for help, she couldn't run away, and she didn't think the alien was going to settle for her just sitting here waiting for Serena to start wondering what had happened and come to check. Especially since the alien was pointing with increasing frequency at the steering wheel, each time tightening the bonds around her wrists like a tourniquet. She had to do something before he cut off circulation altogether.

She tried to speak through the muffling gag, and, amazingly, the alien removed the tentacle from her mouth.

"You want me to drive you somewhere," she said as soon as he did, "but I can't unless you untie me."

The alien obviously didn't understand. He pointed at the windshield again and back at the steering wheel and tightened the tentacles around her wrists some more.

"No! If you want me to drive you, you have to untie me!" she shouted, and whether it was the tone of her voice—or her desperate attempts to free her hands—that did it, the tentacle unwound itself from her right wrist and hand and then pointed fiercely at the windshield, as if to say, *Now drive.*

"I *can't*," she said and pointed to the ignition on the side of the steering column, and pantomimed inserting a key in the slot. "No keys," she said, wondering what she was going to do if he didn't understand.

But he did. He used the tentacle he'd had around her wrist to fish around in the slot, the tentacle narrowing and disappearing inside it, and for an awful moment, she thought he was going to be able to use *it* as a key. But he pulled it out of the keyhole and set it—and half a dozen other tentacles—roaming over the floor, clearly searching for the keys.

One of her hands was already free. If she could convince the alien that the keys were outside and get him to go out to look, he might have to untie her other hand, and she could scramble out the passenger door.

"I think I dropped the keys when you grabbed me," she said, pointing out her side window, then at the ignition, then out the window again. "Outside," she repeated, and to her relief, he reached past her to open the door.

But it was just like when he'd grabbed her the first time—he had the door open, the tentacle through it and back inside holding the keys and the door shut before she'd even had time to move. The alien inserted a key in the ignition.

Let's hope that's the wrong one and that he can't find the right one, and that someone comes along to rescue me before he finds it, Francie thought, scanning the street in the rearview mirror, but the block was deserted, and the alien was now working his way through everything on the key ring, including Serena's flying-saucer key chain ornament.

He seemed to have forgotten all about Francie. When one of the keys didn't fit in the slot, he unwound the tentacle from her left hand and brought it over to help push.

And with both hands momentarily free, now was surely the time to make a break for it. Francie slid her hand silently down to the door handle, moved to push it open with her foot—and discovered what she should have noticed before: that her feet were bound tightly to the car's pedals, one to the gas and the other to the brake.

And he'd apparently found the right key. She heard it click into place. *Please don't let him figure out he needs to turn it to start the car,* she prayed, but she wasn't going to get that wish, either.

His tentacle turned it in the ignition. The engine roared to life, and he immediately rebound her left hand to the steering wheel, pointed firmly at the windshield and then at her.

He doesn't know I need to put it in gear, she thought, which meant as long as she didn't show him, they couldn't go, and the self-defense classes all said, "Under no circumstances go anywhere with the kidnapper," because once in an isolated place, you had no chance of rescue. If she showed him how to drive the car, he might decide he didn't need her anymore and let her go. Or he might wrap a tentacle around her neck, strangle her, and dump her body. So the best thing to do was just sit here.

But those self-defense teachers had obviously never been kidnapped by an alien. When she didn't move, he retied her right hand and began steadily tightening the bonds around both hands and her feet, and jabbed at her chest in a way that seemed to indicate he knew she was stalling and had no intention of putting up with it.

"I don't know how the car works," she told him. "It's not even my car. It's my friend's, and when he"—she'd decided *he* sounded more intimidating than *she*—"finds out you stole it, he's going to be really mad."

The tentacles continued to tighten.

"Okay, okay, but I have to put the car in reverse, and I can't do that when I'm tied up," she said, jiggling her right wrist and then her feet to illustrate, and the tentacles unwound from her right hand.

But only her right hand and her feet. He kept a tight grip on her left wrist. She pushed the gearshift into reverse and backed out of the parking space.

And now what? *Drive to Main Street,* she thought. There were bound to be people there. She put the car in gear and turned it toward Main Street.

She'd forgotten about the seatbelt alarm. The second she started to drive forward, it began to beep—an annoying high-pitched noise—and the alien went berserk.

She instantly jammed on the brake and stopped, but the sound continued. The alien's tentacles flailed wildly, curling in on themselves, like someone trying to put his hands over his ears, and for a second she thought this was her chance to get away. But in all his mad thrashing, he hadn't let go of her left wrist. His grip tightened so much she thought he was going to cut her hand completely off.

"Don't—it's only the seatbelt alarm," she shouted over the dinging and pulled the strap down across herself, wondering how she was going to get a seatbelt on him as well, but the alarm cut off the moment she clicked her seatbelt into the slot. Which meant either the alien was too light to trigger the seatbelt warning, or he was a figment of her imagination.

Though if he was, he was an extremely vivid one. When he stopped flailing and let go of her left wrist, there was a red mark on it.

She started toward Main Street again, and one of his tentacles immediately shot out and refastened itself around her right wrist, while a second began tapping frantically at the side window, telling her to go north instead.

"I can't go that way till we come to a street. We're in the middle of the block," Francie explained, and he stopped tapping and withdrew his tentacle from her right wrist. But Main Street was two blocks to the west. What would he do when she reached the first cross street and she didn't turn north?

He didn't seem to notice. His pointing tentacle was plastered against the passenger-side window and he was looking (she assumed) at something to the north.

She glanced that way and saw a flash of white light. *It's fireworks,* she thought. *At least I hope it is, and not another UFO landing.*

You're starting to sound as bad as Russell and those people at the airport, she told herself. *Of course it's fireworks. It's the Fourth of July weekend.* One of the men in the car rental line had said there was going to be a fireworks display at the fairgrounds.

Whatever it was, it kept the alien from noticing the alien-headed streetlamps as she turned onto Main Street, and the alien-bedecked signs on the festival's kiosks. But the kiosks—and the street—were completely deserted.

*Where **is** everybody?* Francie wondered. Had they been kidnapped like she had been and were now driving their aliens to wherever it was they wanted to go? Or had they all been vaporized?

No, there were no signs of a sudden disappearance—no open doors or cars abandoned in the middle of the street or scorch marks on the pavement, and the food trucks and kiosks she'd worked her way through before had all been carefully closed up, their hatches pulled up and/or their blinds pulled down. There was a Closed sign on the UFO museum.

They must all be at the fireworks display, she thought. *Or out west of town with Russell and his best man, looking for that crashed UFO and its occupant.*

He's right here, you idiots, she wanted to say.

Apparently the police were out there, too, because there wasn't a single cop car on the street—or even a car, for that matter. *Maybe they're all at the police station, fielding calls from people about the crash,* she thought, but when she tried to turn at the arrow pointing to the police station, a tentacle lashed out to circle her wrist and yank the wheel back straight.

"All right, all right," she said. "You want to stay on this street. Fine," and after a couple of minutes, "You could tell me where we're going, you know, instead of jerking me around like that."

For an answer, if it *was* an answer, he pointed ahead through the windshield to the north.

She continued up Main Street, past the brick courthouse and the UFO Festival banner and the McDonald's and the Shell station. She glanced down at the gas gauge, hoping it might be close to empty, but it was over a quarter full. What kind of mileage did Navigators get? Likely more than enough to get wherever it was he was taking her.

There was another flicker of white far ahead of them, and this one couldn't be fireworks, because there was the sign for the fairgrounds, and it pointed off to the east. So what was it? Flares that the alien's flying saucer was sending up to guide him to it? Or the signal that the invasion was about to begin?

Neither. A moment later, the light flickered again, and she saw it was a flash of lightning from a thunderstorm far to the north of town. *The one I saw this afternoon,* she thought, breathing a sigh of relief, and concentrated on trying to find someone, anyone, who could help her.

There was nobody, and they were rapidly reaching the northern edge of town. And the last thing she wanted to do was head into the countryside with him. It was *really* deserted. And in another half hour or so it would be dark.

I have to do something **now,** she thought as they passed a warehouse and then the ROSWELL—DAIRY CENTER OF THE SOUTHWEST sign. But what? Jerk the car to a stop, roll down the window, fling the keys out into the brush, and try to follow them? She'd never even get the window all the way down.

They were coming to an intersection. U.S. 380, it said. EAST—PORTALES, 90 MILES, the sign above the right lane read, and the left lane, WEST—HONDO, 55.

The UFO sighting had been west of town, so presumably that was where everyone was. It might also be where the alien's spaceship was, but at least there'd be people who might be able to help her. She pulled into the left-hand lane and put on her left-hand turn signal.

A tentacle lashed out, wrapped itself around her foot, and jammed it down hard on the brake pedal. The car stopped with a jarring lurch.

Which obviously meant he didn't want to go west. "Okay, then," she said. "Tell me which way you *do* want to go."

She expected him to point north, as he had the entire time they'd been in the car, but he didn't. His tentacle wavered, moving across the windshield to the passenger side and back. It bobbled along the back windows, wrapping around till it was on her side window, then coming back to the windshield again, clearly searching for something. What? Lights from the mother ship that was supposed to pick him up?

The only lights visible were another flicker of lightning from the distant thunderstorm, which, now that it was getting dark, lit up the whole inside of the cloud, and the red tail-lights of a pickup truck as it turned north from a side road ahead. Why, oh why, couldn't it have been headed this way? But at least it was a sign that there were other people on the road.

The alien must have seen the tail-lights because its pointer tentacle was back to the windshield and pointing in the direction the truck had gone.

She hesitated, thinking of all those miles of empty desert she'd come through on the way down here, and the alien tapped the windshield impatiently, pointed at the gearshift, and started for her hand.

"All right, I'm going," Francie said, put the car in gear, clicked the turn signal off, and headed north on 285, trying to remember how many miles it was to Vaughn and planning what she'd do if she met a car coming south. She'd flash her lights as soon as she saw it, pull into the oncoming lane, lean hard on the horn, and pray it could stop in time. And if it didn't, maybe the airbag would squish the alien flat.

It wasn't a great plan, but it might have worked—only, except for the pickup truck, whose tail-lights had nearly disappeared ahead of them, there wasn't a single car on the road.

"Where are you taking me?" she asked after several miles.

No response. The alien's tentacle remained glued to the windshield.

"If you'd tell me, I'd know where to go, and we could get there faster."

His tentacle tapped the windshield.

"No, I know that," Francie said. "I mean, where are you trying to end up? Albuquerque? Santa Fe? Your spaceship?"

Nothing.

"Did it crash and you bailed out, and now you're trying to get back to it?"

Still nothing.

"You won't get away with this, you know," Francie said. "My friends will be out looking for me. I told my friend Serena I'd be right back. She'll be worried sick. When I don't come back, she'll call the police," and then, thinking he might not know that word, added, "the government, the people in charge, the authorities."

But first she'll call me, she realized, thinking of the phone in her pocket. She'd prayed that Serena would call, but now she hoped fervently that she wouldn't. She didn't want the alien to know she had a phone. When and if they stopped somewhere, she might be able to call for help. But if Serena phoned now, and it rang . . .

It didn't, and they didn't encounter any more vehicles. Once she saw a red light she thought might be a tail-light, but within a couple of miles it became obvious it was only the blinking airplane warning light on top of a radio tower far to the north.

That and the occasional flicker of lightning from the thunderstorm, now low on the horizon, and a pink glow in the west as the sun set, were the only lights anywhere.

She slowed as a tumbleweed rolled across the road, and then wondered if it was an alien, too, but her alien paid no attention to it or to the occasional tumbleweeds beside the road, and they didn't lash out as she passed, so she decided they must be actual tumbleweeds.

She had no idea how far north she'd driven. She'd passed Dry Wash Road and Cottonwood Draw a while back, so she was at least forty-five minutes from Roswell, and Vaughn was at least an hour away.

We really are in the middle of nowhere, she thought, *and it's getting dark.* "You're in a lot of trouble," she said to the alien, which was a classic case of projection, if there ever was one. "Kidnapping's a federal crime, you know."

He didn't know, of course—and, in spite of his seeming to have responded to her words back when he'd first kidnapped her, she wasn't sure he understood a word she said. Or else he wasn't paying attention. His dashboard tentacle was roaming again, moving across the windshield to the passenger-side window and then back.

Could he have mistaken the red tail-lights for lights from his spaceship, and now that they were out of sight, didn't know which way to go?

No, he'd only been looking for the right spot. His tentacle shot out to bind her foot again, this time to slow her down rather than stop her, and a second tentacle pointed ahead to a narrow road off to the right.

It was a dirt road that wound through sagebrush to a low hill and out of sight behind it. *And if I take it, I'll be out of sight of the highway,* she thought, *and completely at his mercy.*

She jammed her foot down hard on the gas pedal to go past the road, but it didn't work. The alien deployed multiple tentacles to lift her foot off, push down on the one on the brake pedal and turn the steering wheel, and in the blink of an eye, they were on the dirt road and heading east.

"You can't do this!" she protested, and knew that sounded exactly like every other kidnapping victim right before they were murdered. "I need to be in a wedding!"

The alien wasn't impressed. He directed her over a cattle guard and, after several hundred yards, past an old-fashioned windmill and a rusted tank of water, which meant there were cattle nearby, though she couldn't see any.

Is that why he came this way? she wondered. *To mutilate some cows?* But half a mile later, when they passed several of them standing out in the sagebrush, the alien didn't make her stop or even slow down. He continued to point steadily ahead.

Maybe this is the road to a ranch, Francie thought, *and somebody there can help me.*

But after another mile, the dirt road turned into a track and then a pair of ruts. "Are you sure this is the way you want to go?" Francie asked the alien.

No response.

It was obvious no one had used this road in a year, if the height of the dry grass between the ruts was any indication. She could hear it scraping the undercarriage of the car as she drove over it. *They won't find my body for months,* she thought. *If ever.* "I don't think we're going the right way," she said.

Still nothing. His tentacle continued to point through the windshield, completely focused on the road ahead.

So focused that if she suddenly slammed on the brakes, might she be able to jump out and make a run for it before he could stop her? No, he'd lash out with those tentacles before she got a dozen yards and lasso her and haul her back.

But not if he can't find you, she said silently. That would mean waiting till it was dark enough that he couldn't see where she went, and it would have to be somewhere with bushes or rocks big enough to hide behind.

They were already too far from the highway for her to walk back, but she might be able to stay hidden long enough to be able to call Serena.

The alien was obviously on a deadline of some kind. Maybe, if she was able to hide well enough, he'd give up looking for her and take the car to wherever he was going, and then it would just be a matter of waiting till sunrise, then going back to the highway and getting help.

But there weren't any rocks. Or bushes. Just an unending landscape of grass and dirt and foot-high sagebrush, and it was really getting dark now. She reached to switch on the headlights, and a tendril lashed out to stop her.

"Ow!" she said. "Look, unless you've got a finger that lights up like E.T.'s to show us the way, I'm going to have to turn on the headlights."

No loosening of the tendril.

"All right, fine," she said, leaning forward to see the road through the darkness, "you'd better turn on your finger, then," and realized light was coming from inside the car.

Francie glanced over at him, expecting to see glowing tentacles, but he was just sitting there in the passenger seat, unchanged.

"What—?" she said, looking down, and saw to her horror that she was the one who was glowing.

For an awful instant, she thought the alien had done something to her, and then she realized that this was the "special" quality of her dress that Serena had been hinting at—it lit up. Well, not lit up, exactly, she thought, glancing down at it intermittently between bouts of peering at the difficult-to-see road, but it definitely gave off a phosphorescent glow. Which rendered her plan to get away from the car and hide somewhere impossible. Her dress was like a beacon. And there was no way she was going to take it off and try to make a break for it in her underwear, not with javelinas and coyotes out there. And cactus. And rattlesnakes. *Thanks a lot, Serena,* she thought.

The alien was tentatively touching the skirt of her glowing dress with the tip of one of his tentacles and then pulling it back quickly as if recoiling in horror.

"I know, it's hideous," she said. "Sorry for the crack about E.T.'s finger. I obviously have no room to talk."

He responded by sending out more tentacles to touch the fabric, and she took advantage of his preoccupation with the dress to turn the car's headlights on again. This time he didn't turn them off, and a good thing, too, because night had completely descended, and all she could see was the narrow tunnel of the ruts they lit—ruts that were gradually growing less discernable.

"I think the road's running out," Francie said and stopped the car.

The alien tapped the windshield impatiently, motioning her to go forward. "There's no road," she said, "and if I keep going we're liable to hit a rock or something and break an axle."

More pointing, and he fastened a tentacle around her wrist and made a move with a second toward her gas pedal foot.

"All right, all right, I'm going," she said, and inched carefully forward for another half mile or so before he motioned for her to stop for no reason she could see.

There was no flying saucer, no charred circle of where one might have been, and no red or blue or green lights flashing overhead.

There weren't even any cows for him to mutilate, just dirt and dry grass and a few scattered clumps of sagebrush for as far as the car's headlights reached.

As she'd driven, the alien had gradually loosened the tether from her wrist and then withdrawn it. She half expected him to reattach it now that they were stopped, but he didn't. *He knows I don't have anywhere to go,* she thought.

"Why are we stopping here?" she asked.

He tapped the ignition, motioning her to turn off the car.

"Listen, I brought you here," she said. "Now let me go. I won't tell anybody about you, I swear! Just let me go so I can go to the wedding," she pleaded. "My friend's counting on me."

The alien tapped the ignition again, violently, and when she didn't respond, took hold of the key and turned it off himself.

They were immediately plunged in impenetrable darkness—except for her dress, which continued to glow. But, unlike the fluorescent light stick it so closely resembled, it didn't give off any light to see by. All it did was keep her eyes from adjusting to the darkness. After a full minute, she still couldn't see anything—not even the steering wheel or the dashboard. Or the alien. *And if he lays a tentacle on me, I'll scream,* she thought, peering into the darkness where he should be.

But she didn't feel anything, and after a few more seconds, she heard the passenger-side door click open and a sort of thump as the alien rolled (or fell) out of the car. She didn't hear him shut the car door, and as her eyes adjusted a little to the darkness, she could see it standing open and make out his shape rolling slowly off to a spot fifty yards away from the car and then stopping.

How far did his tentacles reach? *They can't extend fifty yards,* she told herself, leaning across to pull the passenger door nearly shut and reaching to start the car.

But the ignition's key slot was empty. *He took the keys with him,* she thought bitterly. *Of course.*

She searched the car anyway, feeling on the passenger seat and the floor and under the seats, but they weren't there.

He has them, she thought, looking out to where he sat (stood?) motionless in the dirt. What was he doing? Readying the equipment to probe—or kill—her with? Or was he signaling the mother ship to come get them? If he was, he wasn't using any signal lights or flares or lasers that she could see, and his tentacles didn't seem to be moving.

She looked up through the windshield at the dark, star-studded sky, but there was no movement there, either—no blinking, darting lights, no star-obscuring shadow of a slow-moving spaceship, not even a falling star.

Her eyes had finally adjusted to the darkness, and she could make out the outlines of the landscape they were in. It was just like the one they'd come through—flat and broken only by sagebrush or an occasional tumbleweed or clump of dry grass. The storm and its lightning had disappeared, and the sky was clear in all directions and scattered with stars.

There was nowhere to run to, nowhere to hide, and no way to start the car except for hot-wiring it, which she had no idea how to do. Which left what?

Her phone. If there was any coverage out here.

Given the way her luck was running, probably not, but it was worth a try. She looked over at the rise where the alien had been sitting. He was still there, sitting motionless in the dirt. She slid her phone from her pocket, switched it to her left hand, and turned it on, holding it carefully down at her side so her body was between the light of its screen and the alien. It showed two bars.

Please let that be enough, she thought, peering over at the still unmoving alien and wishing she could tell which way he was looking. With the car door ajar, he was likely to see the light from her phone when she put it up to her ear or hear her talking. She needed to get somewhere where he couldn't see.

Behind the car, she thought. She slid her phone back in her pocket, undid her seatbelt, wincing at the click, and pushed her door cautiously open, keeping an eye on the alien.

He didn't move.

She eased the door a little farther open, waited a moment, got out, and then dropped down on her hands and knees and pushed the door nearly closed so it would look shut.

If the alien was even looking. *Maybe he's gone to sleep,* she thought hopefully, and felt her way slowly along the car's side to the rear, keeping low enough to be out of sight. When she reached the back of the car, she took a quick peek around the bumper to see if the alien was still there—he was, his motionless form silhouetted against the horizon—and then squatted down next to the rear tire and unlocked her phone. Now it showed only a single bar.

Please let **that** *be enough,* she prayed, and dialed 911, pressing the phone hard against her ear with both hands so the alien wouldn't hear it ring.

"911," a woman's voice said matter-of-factly, and Francie went limp with relief. The aliens hadn't invaded and vaporized everybody after all. "If this is not an emergency, hang up and call the police department."

Oh, it's definitely an emergency, Francie thought as the woman recited the number.

"What is the nature of your emergency?" the woman asked.

"I've been kidnapped," Francie whispered. "I—"

"I'm having difficulty hearing you," the dispatcher said. "Can you speak louder?"

"No," Francie whispered. "I've been *kidnapped.*"

"Is your kidnapper there with you?"

"No. He's off . . . I'm calling from behind the car, where he can't see me, but I'm afraid he—"

"Is there a safe place you can get to? A store? A gas station?"

"No, we're out in the middle of the desert north of Roswell, and anyway, he won't let me get away. He—"

"Roswell?" the dispatcher said, her tone changing slightly, and Francie could hear her speaking to someone else, though she couldn't hear most of what the dispatcher said. Francie caught the words "another one," and then the dispatcher came back on the line.

"Can you describe your kidnapper?"

"Yes, he looks like a tumbleweed, and he has these vines or tentacles or something that can lash out and—"

"Tentacles," the dispatcher said, and called to someone, "I *told* you it was another one."

"Christ," Francie heard a man's voice say. "This is the fifth one. I hate the UFO Festival."

"I'm not making this up," Francie whispered urgently. "I swear. This alien grabbed me and—"

"Abducted you," the dispatcher said. "I know. Are you aware that calling the police to make a false report is an indictable offense punishable by jail time and a fine of one thousand dollars?"

"It *isn't* a false report," Francie protested. "I know it sounds crazy, but I really have been—"

"And preventing a citizen from reporting an actual emergency by tying up police lines is a felony," the dispatcher said. "What if there'd been a *real* kidnapping," she asked, giving way to her anger, "and that person couldn't get through to us? Tell your friends that if they try this again, you're all going to spend the night in jail!" and hung up.

Well, of course she did, Francie thought. *What did you expect, telling her you'd been abducted by aliens? You should have told her it was a guy with a gun.*

Now what? Call them back? No, they'd recognize the number, and they were already mad. *And what makes you think they'll believe you a second time?*

Serena. She'd believe her—or at least Russell would. And maybe they could convince the police. Or, more likely, come roaring out to see the alien for themselves. Which would be fine. *At this point,* she thought, *I'll accept any help, no matter how loony.*

She crawled to the other side of the car and sneaked a look around it. The alien was still sitting in the same place. Good. She crept back to where she'd been and called Serena.

"Hi, Serena here," Serena said.

Oh, thank goodness. "Serena, this is Francie," she whispered. "I'm in trouble. I've been—"

"I'm not here right now. Leave a message after the beep."

Oh God, she must have gone out to look for the landing site after all, Francie thought, waiting an eternity for the beep.

When it did, she said, "Serena, this is Francie. I—"

"This mailbox is full," an automated voice said.

No-o-o! Francie thought, scrolling through her phone for Russell's number, though she was sure she didn't have it or the Highway Patrol's, and the people whose numbers she *did* have were two thousand miles away. But they could call the Roswell Police Department and convince them that she was telling the truth. She called Ted's number and he answered, but he was obviously at a bar because she could barely hear him over the music and laughter, and he couldn't hear her at all. "You were *what*?" he shouted. "Speak up. I can't—listen, I gotta go. Call you tomorrow," and hung up.

She called Graham. "Don't tell me," he said. "I warned you your trip was going to turn out to be a disaster."

That's one word for it, she thought. "Listen, Graham," she whispered urgently. "I've been kidnapped by an alien. I know it sounds insane, but it abducted me and made me drive it out to the middle of the desert. You've got to contact the authorities—"

"Exactly how much have you had to drink?" Graham said.

"Drink?" Francie said. "I haven't had anything to—"

"I'll bet," he said, laughing. "What, are you at some sort of bachelorette party with your crazy friend?"

"No! I'm serious. You have to help me—"

"I would, but my spaceship's in the shop. Have a good time. Say hello to E.T. for me!" he said, laughing, and hung up.

So what now? she thought. Who did you call when you'd been abducted by an alien? The First Contact Committee? Or the Church of Galactic Truth?

The FBI, she thought, and remembered the guy she'd been supposed to pick up at the airport, Henry Hastings. Serena'd said he was taking a red-eye, but if he hadn't left yet, he could call the FBI and have them contact the office out here. Thank goodness she'd put his number in her phone. She typed in his name and hit Call.

His phone rang. And rang. *He's already in the air,* Francie thought.

And even if he answered, this was pointless. It wasn't as if this was *The X-Files*. The FBI wouldn't believe her any more than the police had. And Serena had said he didn't believe in aliens.

It doesn't matter, she thought. *When he gets here and finds out from Serena that I'm missing, he'll realize* **something** *happened and that he needs to call the authorities. And his being with the FBI means he's in a perfect position to institute a search.*

If Serena knew she was missing. What if she was still out at the so-called landing site with Russell?

But surely by the time he arrived, Serena would've come back. And she didn't have anyone else to call. If he didn't answer . . .

"Hello," a businesslike male voice said.

Oh, thank goodness, Francie thought. "Hello! This is—"

"You have reached the phone of Henry Hastings. Please leave a message."

Leave a message, she thought bitterly. *By the time you get this it'll be too late. I'll have been probed and mutilated or dragged off to another planet.*

But she had to try. *And please don't let his mailbox be full,* she thought and, as soon as the beep came, launched into her story.

"This is Francie Driscoll. I'm a friend of Serena's. I came out to Roswell for her wedding, and I've been kidnapped by a space alien. I know it sounds completely insane, but he grabbed me when I went to get something from Serena's car and forced me into the car and made me drive him out to the middle of the desert," she whispered, speaking quickly to get it all in before the message cut off.

"The car's a black Navigator, license plate"—she crept around to the back of the car to peer at it—"New Mexico CJE-500. We're north of—"

A tentacle came flashing out of nowhere with blinding speed to encircle her wrist, another to wrap itself around her waist, and a third to grasp the phone.

"Don't—" she said, but the alien had already sent it spinning far out into the darkness.

CHAPTER FOUR

"Well, it looks like you've got another passenger."
—The Ringo Kid, *Stagecoach*

And this is the part where the kidnapper kills you in a rage, Francie thought, watching her phone—and her last hope of rescue—spiraling out into the darkness where she would never be able to find it. She braced herself for what was coming.

But all that happened was that the alien grabbed her and bundled her into the car, just like last time. Only this time he tied her to the driver's seat, not the steering wheel, and his tentacles flattened out into bandages, wrapping her up like a prisoner bound to a chair.

The passenger-side door was still ajar, with the part of the tentacle that wasn't wrapped around her body trailing out of the car, onto the ground, and over to the alien, who was sitting serenely in the same place he'd been before, as if he hadn't moved at all.

She tried to see if she could wriggle out of the bandages, but they immediately tightened. She wasn't going anywhere.

And nobody was coming to rescue her. *I should have started by telling the FBI guy where I am,* she thought ruefully. Not that it mattered. He wouldn't have believed her any more than the dispatcher or Graham. And Serena didn't even know she was missing, and even if she did get back from trying to find the UFO crash site and found Francie gone and called the police, it took at least twenty-four hours for a person to be considered missing. By then, the alien would have . . .

Would have what? If he intended to kill her, he'd had plenty of opportunities already. Unless he was waiting till his superiors got here. Was that what he was doing sitting out there? Waiting for his boss to arrive with the mother ship?

The night wore on. She thought for a while about what she should have done and then about how she'd failed Serena. Not only was she not there to help Serena talk herself out of marrying Russell but if she *did* manage to get away, how could she tell Serena that his belief in aliens was crazy? *I don't exactly have a leg to stand on in that department. And the wedding's in three days.*

But Serena'd said she wouldn't consider getting married without Francie there. *Let's hope she meant that, and that she'll insist on the police coming and rescuing me.*

And what if **that's** *what we're doing here?* she thought suddenly. *What if he crashed his flying saucer and now* **he's** *waiting for rescue?*

She looked up at the sky, scanning it for moving lights, but there was nothing, and the alien was still sitting there motionless. *Maybe he's fallen asleep,* she thought and moved her hand.

The tentacle tightened instantly. So, no, still awake. Or maybe the tentacles tightened automatically, in which case she'd really better not try to free herself or she'd end up squeezed to death, like by a boa constrictor.

Or freezing to death. Desert nights, even in July, got really chilly, and the air from the partly open passenger door was cold. But the bandages wrapped around her were just like a blanket. She felt warm and drowsy.

That's just what he wants, she thought. *He's waiting for you to go to sleep so he can probe you or impregnate you or whatever it is they do.*

But that was plainly ridiculous. He could have done anything to her at any time, yet all he'd done was make her drive him here—and take away her phone. And so long as she didn't try to free herself from her bonds, it looked like he wasn't going to do anything in the near future, so she might as well try to sleep, at least till the mother ship arrived.

She must have succeeded because when she opened her eyes, it was morning. The desert was a pale brownish-purple in the early light and flat as far as the eye could see, with no ranch or fence in sight. And no signs of life anywhere.

Except for the alien, who still sat in the exact same place. *Whoever he's waiting for hasn't come,* she thought. But then again, neither had the police. Or the FBI.

So now what? she wondered. *Are we going to sit here all day?* She hoped not. She was hungry and cramped and had to go to the bathroom—and she couldn't even stretch, tied up like this.

Moments later, the tentacles loosened from around her and retracted, and the alien began rolling back toward the car. Francie leaned forward to look up at the sky, afraid she'd see a ship hovering above them, but she couldn't see anything but a line of feathery golden clouds off to the northwest.

The alien must have spotted something, though, or else gotten his bearings now that it was light, because he heaved himself into the passenger seat, used a tentacle to slam the door shut, and pointed peremptorily through the windshield.

"And good morning to you, too," Francie said.

He jabbed at the windshield again.

"I can't go anywhere without the keys," she said, pointing at the ignition, and in one of those quicker-than-the-eye-can-see movements, he produced them from somewhere, stuck the key in the ignition, and turned it. The engine started.

"Where to?" she asked.

He pointed out her window and then out the back.

"You want me to turn around?" she said, and when he repeated the pointings, she managed—in spite of some sagebrush and a couple of yucca plants—to get the SUV pointed back the way they'd come.

"Now where?" she said, hoping he'd take her back to the road they'd come on, and he did, directing her to where the ruts had ended and from there to the dirt road and back along it, past the windmill and the water tank, now surrounded with cattle, to the highway.

Francie started to turn south and was instantly stopped by a tentacle around her hand and the steering wheel and determined motions from a second tentacle pointing north.

"If you're looking for your spaceship, it's not that way," Francie said. "It's the other way." She pointed south. "My friends saw where it landed west of Roswell. I can show you."

The alien continued to point north and to tug at the steering wheel.

"I can't go north," she said, trying again. "I have to go back to Roswell. My friends will be worried about me," and when that had no effect, "You don't understand. I have to go to a wedding. Serena's counting on me. It's my duty."

That didn't work, either. His grip continued to tighten until she turned north, and he kept her tethered as she drove, in case she suddenly tried to make a U-turn.

"Where are you taking me now?" she said, knowing she wouldn't get an answer, and she didn't. "Wherever we're going, it had better not be very far. We're going to run out of gas soon."

That was a lie. The gas gauge said they still had three-eighths of a tank, but hopefully he wouldn't know that. "And I'm going to need a bathroom. And food. If I don't have food, I won't be able to drive you."

No response, but hopefully she would be rescued soon, now that they were back on an actual road. Even if the FBI guy hadn't gotten her message, Serena would have reported her disappearance to the

Roswell police, and they'd have put out an APB. Unless the aliens had launched a full-scale invasion last night, and there wasn't anyone left to rescue her.

But if that were the case, there'd have been Air Force jets racing overhead, plumes of smoke on the horizon, and the distant sound of explosions, wouldn't there?

Instead, the morning was soundless and clear, the sky a bright, non-smoky blue except for the puffy golden clouds she'd seen at dawn, now white on the northwestern horizon.

There weren't any signs of a town, either, though they had to come to one eventually, or to a roadside gas station or something. *And when we do,* she thought, *I'll plow into the building, and while he's trying to get free of the airbag, I'll run inside and tell them to call 911.*

But there was no town, no gas station, not even a dirt road leading off into the desert. They passed a sign with a picture of an airplane on it and the words THIS AREA PATROLLED BY AIRCRAFT, but there was no sign of a plane, either, though once she thought she heard a helicopter. She leaned forward, peering out the windshield, but she couldn't see anything.

Where *was* everybody? This part of the country was deserted, but there should be *some* cars on it. Or at least a flagman and a crew working on the highway. There was always road construction this time of year. You couldn't go ten miles without running into construction. She should have come across some by now. Unless every single person in New Mexico had been grabbed getting into their cars, forced to drive to the aliens' flying saucer, and been spirited off to their home planet—and for some reason her alien had forgotten where they'd parked.

No, that couldn't be it, because he clearly knew where he was going. They'd passed several possible roads to turn off onto, but he'd ignored them all and pointed steadily at the empty road ahead.

No, not quite empty. There was a guy up ahead by the side of the road. He was wearing jeans and a blue denim shirt and had a khaki duffel bag on the ground beside him. *Oh, thank God,* she thought. *There's someone left who hasn't been abducted.*

But he would be if she stopped. The alien would grab him just like he'd grabbed her, and then they'd both be hostages. And it wasn't like he'd be able to rescue her. He was all alone out here, in the middle of nowhere, with no vehicle in sight. A hitchhiker. He'd scrambled to his feet as soon as he saw her car, grabbed up the duffel bag, and put his hand out in the traditional gesture of thumbing a ride.

You don't want this ride. You really, really don't, she thought, glancing at the alien to see if he'd spotted the hitchhiker yet.

And how exactly would she know? It wasn't as if the alien had facial expressions. Or a face, for that matter. But his tentacle on the dashboard had given no indication he knew the guy was there. It was still pointing straight ahead.

Good, then she had a chance of driving right past the guy. She put her foot down hard on the gas pedal.

The guy was stepping out into the road. She glanced at the alien again, and when she glanced back at the scene ahead, saw that the guy was waving his arms wildly, flagging her down.

"Get out of the way!" she shouted. "Move!" But he was standing his ground.

There was no time to swerve. She jammed on the brakes, tumbling the alien onto the floor, and the car lurched to a stop so close to the guy she thought she'd hit him after all.

But he was grinning. He bent down to pick up his duffel bag, and Francie glanced anxiously down at the alien on the floor of the passenger seat. He wasn't moving. Had she knocked him out? Or accidentally killed him?

The guy was walking toward the car. She fumbled for the button to roll up the windows, but she wasn't fast enough. He was already leaning in at the open passenger-side window.

"Thanks," he said. "I thought for a minute you weren't going to stop. I don't know what I'd have done if you hadn't. I was starting to attract buzzards." He grinned again, and she saw that he wasn't any older than she was. He had a thatch of straw-colored hair and a sunburned nose.

"I really appreciate this," he said. "My name's Wade, by the way.

Wade Pierce." He reached for the door handle. "I was on my way to—"

"No! Don't—" She lunged across to lock the door, dropping her voice to a whisper to keep the alien from hearing. "I can't give you a ride. I'm sorry, you'll have to hitch a ride with somebody else."

"Somebody else? What do you mean, somebody else? There hasn't been a car past here all morning!"

She reached to put the car in gear.

"Do you know how *hot* it is out here?" he said, gripping the window frame. "I'll be dead from thirst before anybody else comes along! I wasn't kidding about those buzzards—"

The car wouldn't start. She must have killed the engine when she jammed on the brake.

"Look," he said, leaning in the car window, "if you're afraid I'm an escaped criminal or a serial killer or something, I'm not."

She turned the key, but the motor just turned over uselessly. *Come on, start,* she thought desperately, and tried again.

"And if you're worried about me making a pass at you, I won't, I promise." He let go of the window frame and held his hands up in a "hands off" gesture. "Just give me a ride to the next town."

"I *can't*," she said helplessly, and tried to start the car again.

"Look," he said, "I don't know why you don't want to give me a ride, but if you're engaged in something nefarious, like bringing in illegal immigrants from Mexico or something, I promise I won't tell."

Illegal immigrants, she thought wryly and glanced down at the still-motionless alien.

Mistake. In the split second of her looking down, Wade had reached in, unlocked the door, and started to open it.

"No!" she said, diving over to hold it shut against him. "Get away from the car! There's an alien in here. He'll—"

But he wasn't listening. He'd gotten the door open and was leaning in to put his duffel bag on the floor. On top of the alien.

"Stop! Don't! Run!" she cried, and several things happened at once. His duffel went flying into the back seat; Wade said, "What the—?" as he was yanked into the passenger seat; the door slammed shut; her foot involuntarily slammed down hard on the gas pedal; and the Navigator shot forward at eighty miles an hour.

For a couple of minutes it was all she could do to keep the car from going off the road, and when she was finally able to spare a glance for Wade, he was bound to the passenger seat like a spider's prey and shouting ineffectually because of the flattened-out tentacle across his mouth.

"I'm sorry, I tried to warn you," she said. "Don't try to get free. Or to run away. He's too fast."

He certainly was. This time she'd had a front-row seat (literally) to just how blindingly fast the alien could move. His tentacles had flashed out with the speed and snap of a whip, not only stuffing Wade into the car and tying him to the seat but rolling up the windows, starting the car, and pressing down on her gas pedal foot.

The seatbelt warning was beeping loudly, though the alien seemed to have adjusted somewhat to the sound; otherwise he'd probably have wrecked the car. But he was still disturbed by it, and as soon as Francie'd gotten the car slowed down to a reasonable speed and back in its own lane (though there still wasn't another car in sight), she glanced over at Wade to see if she could reach across him and fasten his seatbelt so the noise would stop, but the alien had bound him firmly to the back of the seat, using so many flattened tentacles that she couldn't even *see* the seatbelt slot. She'd just have to hope it was the kind of warning that shut itself off on its own eventually.

It wasn't. "That's the seatbelt warning," she said to the alien, even though there was no way he'd understand. "It's making that sound because Wade doesn't have his seatbelt on. You need to untie him so he can fasten it. And, Wade, stop trying to talk. He'll take your gag off if you shut up. Or at least that's what he did with me."

Wade nodded and went silent.

"Let him go," she said to the alien. "He won't try to get away," and after a minute the alien withdrew his tentacle.

"Like hell I won't try to get away," Wade muttered the moment the gag was off, and he turned on Francie. "Why didn't you warn me you had an *alien* in the car?"

"I did. You wouldn't listen!"

"You said you had an alien in the car, not an *alien*! Why didn't you shout 'Alien abduction!' or 'Martians!' or better yet, just drive on past?"

"Because you stepped in front of the car!" she said hotly. "What did you want me to do, run over you?"

"You could have driven around me. Or warned me something funny was going on."

"I did warn you. I told you to run."

"I didn't have time, what with Indiana Jones and his bullwhip here! Why didn't you at least mention that?"

"Because *I* didn't have time," she said, "and I wouldn't shout, if I were you, or he's liable to put that gag back on. And this time I may not try to talk him into untying you."

"He *didn't* untie me, in case you didn't notice," Wade said, struggling against his bonds.

"And I wouldn't do that, either," she told him. "Moving just makes them tighter."

"Fine," Wade said and let his body relax against the restraints. "Where's Indiana Jones here taking us?"

Francie looked at him in surprise. She'd thought he'd be as undone by being abducted as she had been, but he didn't sound freaked out or even frightened, just amused. "So, where's he taking us?" he repeated.

"I don't know."

"What do you mean, you don't know? You're the one driving."

"Would you *please* untie Wade so he can put on his seatbelt?" she shouted at the alien over the still-beeping seatbelt warning, and the tentacles promptly loosened and withdrew.

"Thanks," Wade said, rubbing his arms and legs. "He was starting to cut off my circulation." He peered through the windshield at the landscape. "So where do you think we're going? His flying saucer?"

"I don't know," she said. "He points, and I drive in that direction. Can you *please* buckle your seatbelt? That sound is driving me crazy."

"Sure," he said, reaching over to grab the belt. "Though I'd think you'd be more upset about being abducted by an alien." He slid the seatbelt buckle into the slot, and the beeping stopped. "He *is* an alien, right?"

"I think so," she said. "I mean, what else could he be?"

"I don't know," Wade said, turning to look speculatively at him. "An entry in the exotic vegetables category at the county fair? Or some kind of desert octopus maybe?"

Francie shook her head. "There's no such thing. Plus, octopuses only have eight tentacles. He's got at least fifty."

"Or more," Wade said, looking interestedly at him. "How about a Southwestern version of Medusa? Or a tumbleweed made out of snakes?"

"He's not made of snakes," Francie said firmly.

"How do you know?"

"Because I'm terrified of snakes. And the way his tentacles move isn't how a snake moves. It's more like the way a vine's tendrils move, except for the speed. I think that's why I wasn't afraid when he abducted me. I mean, I was afraid he was going to hurt me or kill me, but not—"

"Where were you when he abducted you?"

"In Roswell. I went to get something out of my friend's car, and he was hiding inside and grabbed me like he did you."

"Roswell," he muttered.

"Why did you say that? Do you know of something that's happened in Roswell?"

"No," he said. "But that's where I was headed when my car broke down. To the UFO Festival in Roswell."

"You were going to the festival?" she said. That explained why he hadn't been freaked out by the alien—he was a UFO nut, just like Russell.

"You mean was I attending it?" he said. "No, working it," and before she could ask "Doing what?" he asked, "Did anybody see you get grabbed?"

"No, there was nobody around. I tried to scream, but—"

"He clapped his tentacle over your mouth like he did me," Wade said, nodding. "Did he hurt you at all? Or molest you?"

"No."

"And you're sure you're okay?" he said, sounding genuinely concerned.

"I'm fine," she said. "He lassoed me and tied me up when I tried to run away, like he did you, and he tightened the tentacles on my wrists, but it wasn't to hurt me. He was just trying to get me to do what he wanted."

"Which was what?"

"Drive him north out of Roswell."

"Did anybody see this happening?"

She shook her head. "There was nobody on the streets." She told him about the UFO sighting west of town.

"What about once you were on the highway?" he asked. "Did anybody see you then?"

"Not a soul. You don't suppose everybody else has been abducted, too, do you?"

"No. I saw a bunch of cars on the road before I broke down, and there were people getting gas in Vaughn."

"Oh, good," she said, relieved. But if there hadn't been a full-scale invasion, then why weren't the police out looking for her? Serena *had* to have told them by now.

"So then what happened?" Wade asked. "Indy here's been making you drive around ever since?"

"No." She told him about the alien's making her stop and going off to contact his ship or whatever he'd been doing. "I had my phone in my pocket, and I tried to call 911, but the dispatcher didn't believe me, so I called this guy from the FBI—"

"And what, you just happened to have some FBI agent's number in your phone?"

"*No,*" she said. "Serena gave it to me."

"Who's Serena? Does she work for the FBI, too?"

"No, she's the friend I told you about, whose car I went to get something out of. This is her car."

"Oh. So you called this FBI guy. What did he say?"

"He wasn't there. I left a message, but he probably thought it was a crank call, too, like the dispatcher."

"Did you get in touch with anyone else? Family? Friends? Boyfriend?"

"I don't have a boyfriend. I called a couple of friends from work, but one couldn't hear me and the other one thought I was drunk. And I didn't have the chance to call anybody else. The alien saw what I was doing and jerked the phone out of my hand with that whip-tentacle thing of his, and it flew out into the middle of the desert somewhere."

"So he obviously didn't want you to get in touch with anyone," he said.

"If he knew that was what the phone was for. He might have thought it was a weapon." She hesitated, wanting to ask him if *he* had a phone, and then decided she'd better not. If the alien understood what they were saying, he might confiscate it, too.

"And you weren't able to contact anybody else before he did that?" Wade asked.

"No. I tried to call Serena, but she didn't answer, and her phone wouldn't let me leave a message."

"So effectively nobody knows you've been abducted."

"Right," she said, expecting him to be upset because the cavalry wasn't likely to swoop down and rescue them anytime soon, but he was off on another train of thought.

"Where do you think Indy's making you take him?" he asked, nodding at the alien. "Obviously not to his flying saucer since you said that landed west of town. So where else would he go?"

"I don't know. Maybe more than one UFO landed, and he's trying to contact the other ones, but he doesn't know where they are."

"Or maybe his ship crashed and he bailed out, so he doesn't know where it is," Wade said. "The question is, why kidnap you? Why not just steal a car and go look for his ship himself?"

"*I don't know.* I assumed it was because he didn't know how to drive. Maybe his tentacles aren't heavy enough to put pressure on the pedals or something."

"Or maybe—"

He stopped. The alien was tapping Francie's arm.

"What is it?" she asked.

The alien pointed at the windshield and then at the passenger-side window, causing Wade to rear back out of the tentacle's reach. "You want me to turn?" Francie asked. "Where?" There was a sign for a historical marker up ahead. "You want me to pull off at the marker?"

"Maybe he's here on vacation," Wade said. "If he's a tourist, he might want you to take him to Yellowstone or the Grand Canyon. Or—"

"Shh," Francie said as the alien tapped her arm again. "You want me to turn off right now? Into this field? I can't. There's a fence."

He tapped the windshield more determinedly.

"All right, all right, I'll turn. Wade, can you see somewhere I can turn off?"

"There's a dirt road up ahead," he said, pointing.

She made a right turn onto it, past a hand-lettered sign reading CIMARRON RANCH, 8 MI.

"So much for the Yellowstone theory," Wade said. "Maybe this road leads to where his UFO crashed," but after only a hundred yards, the alien motioned Francie to pull over to the side of the road at the top of a rise and stop the car.

It looked exactly like last night's field, only with more rocks and a better view. From up here, you could see for miles in all directions. Not that there was anything to see—no ranch house, no windmill, no other roads. Nothing but reddish-brown dirt and a vast expanse of sky. The clouds that had been on the horizon earlier had disappeared, and the sky was a bright, unmarred blue.

Francie stopped the car, and the alien immediately opened the passenger door, swarmed over Wade, and got out, tethering them securely to the steering wheel and the gearshift respectively as he did. He left the door open and rolled out into the field, to the high-

est point of the rise, and then stopped and stood/sat there motionless.

"What the hell's he doing?" Wade asked.

"I don't know," Francie said. "He did the same thing last night
and again this morning. I thought he might be trying to contact the
mother ship."

"Makes sense," he said, and she wondered again why he was
taking all this so calmly. He hadn't even been particularly upset at
having been trussed up like a turkey. "I wonder why he hasn't been
able to contact them."

"I don't know," Francie said. "Maybe they crashed, too. Or
maybe we're in a dead zone. You know, like with cellphones." She
lowered her voice. "You don't happen to have a phone in that duffel
bag of yours, do you?"

"Sorry. The only stuff in it," he said, reaching back for it with his
untethered hand and unzipping it, "is my dirty laundry. And these,"
he added, pulling out a sheaf of brochures.

"What are those?"

"Anti-abduction insurance policies," he said, handing her one.
"Five hundred thousand dollars' worth of coverage for the low, low
price of ten dollars."

Francie opened out the brochure. It looked like a real insurance
policy, with engraving around the edges and an embossed gold seal.
"Full coverage in the case of abduction, alien probing, tracking-
device implantation, and alien impregnation," she read. She looked
up at Wade. "In other words, you're a con man."

"Con man?" he said, stuffing the brochures back in the duffel bag
and zipping it up. "Absolutely not. That's a legitimate policy. I've
sold hundreds of them, and not a single policy holder has ever been
abducted by an alien."

"Till now," Francie said, pointing at the alien sitting on the hill.

"I didn't sell you a policy."

"So I take it you don't believe in all the UFO stuff," she said.

"That's a tough question under the circumstances," he said, nodding at Indy. "But no," and Francie felt a wave of relief.

"Anyway, sorry about not having a phone," he said, dropping the duffel bag back on the floor of the back seat, "but I doubt if there'd be any coverage out here." He looked over at the alien. "So you said last night he sat there like he's doing now. Was he looking up at the sky?"

"I don't know. I haven't even been able to figure out where his head is, let alone his eyes."

"But he can see."

"Yes," she said, thinking of how he'd responded to her dress when it lit up.

"Okay, so if he's trying to send a signal, nobody's answering." He watched Indy some more. "Has he tried to communicate with you?"

"Besides pointing, you mean?"

"Yeah, has he tried to talk to you? I don't necessarily mean in English. It might sound like Wookiee grunts or R2-D2 beeps. Or those musical notes in *Close Encounters*."

She shook her head. "He hasn't made any sounds at all."

"Really? But we know he's not deaf because he responds to what you say." He looked speculatively at the alien. "Maybe he *can't* talk. He doesn't have the equipment for it, like vocal cords."

"Or a mouth."

"Right," Wade said, frowning. "But he has to communicate somehow. All sentient creatures have a mode of communication."

"This woman I met said aliens are telepathic."

"There's no such thing as telepathy."

"Well, until an hour ago, I'm betting you'd have said there was no such thing as space aliens."

"That's completely different. So if he can't talk," Wade continued, "maybe he uses sign language. You don't happen to know American Sign Language, do you?"

"No, but I know what it looks like, and he hasn't done anything like that. All he's done is point."

"Maybe *that's* his way of communicating," Wade said. "Pointing. And his forcing you to drive is his way of saying, 'Take me to your leader.'"

"No," she said firmly. "Because he's the one telling *me* where to go, not the other way around."

"Maybe he just hasn't figured out how to talk to us yet," Wade said thoughtfully. "He definitely understands what you say to him, right?"

"I'm not sure. Sometimes he seems to, but other times he doesn't. When I told him he had to take me back to Roswell because I had to be in a wedding, he completely ignored me."

"A *wedding*?" he said. "That explains it. I was afraid maybe you dressed like that all the time."

"No," she said stiffly. "My friend Serena's getting married, and I'm her maid of honor. That's why I came out here to Roswell."

"Did you explain that to Indy?"

"I tried, but he didn't give any indication that he understood."

"Maybe he doesn't know what a maid of honor—or a wedding—is," Wade said.

"In which case what we should do is keep talking to him and explaining things, right?"

"Wrong," he said. "What we should do is figure out a way to get away from him."

"But—"

"Here's what I think we should do. When we come across a gas station, we say we're almost out of gas—"

"Which is true. I've only got a quarter of a tank."

"You do?" He leaned over to look at the gas gauge. "Great. That way, you won't be lying, in case by some bizarre chance he *is* telepathic. Anyway, we get him to stop to get gas and I'll distract him while you go inside and tell the clerk to call 911."

"What makes you think Indy would let me do that? You saw what he did when you tried to get away." *And when I tried last night,* she added silently. "And what about you? What if he grabs you and drives off?"

"Then you wait for the cops and tell them what happened and which direction we went."

"But why me? Why don't *I* distract him and you go in?"

"Because Indy trusts you more, which means he's less likely to lasso you and drag you back to the car. And if only one of us can get away, it should be you because *you* have to be in a wedding. You've got someplace you have to be, and I don't. Nobody's expecting me."

"All right," she said reluctantly. "But what if he won't let me go in? Or even stop?"

"We'll cross that bridge when we come to it. We've got to at least try, unless you want to run the risk of ending up on your way to Alpha Centauri, and this is the only plan we've got. And there's no time to come up with a different one."

"Why not?"

"Because he's coming back," he said, nodding at the hill, which Indy was rolling back from. "Apparently this place was a dead zone, too."

Indy rolled into the car, over Wade's lap to the center console, and pointed them back to the highway and then back south. "Maybe he's changed his mind about abducting you and has decided to take you back to Roswell," Wade said, but Indy almost immediately pointed off to a paved road leading northeast.

"So now what?" Francie said.

"Now we hope there's a gas station on this road. And in the meantime, we work on communicating. *Sprechen Sie Deutsch*, Indy?"

No response.

"*Parlez-vous français?*"

Nothing.

"*Klaatu barada nikto.*"

"What's *that*?" Francie asked.

"What the alien in *The Day the Earth Stood Still* said. It means 'Please don't destroy us.'"

"Oh, good," Francie said sarcastically.

He ignored that. "Do you know any languages besides English?"

"A little high school Spanish." She glanced away from the steering wheel for a moment. "Indy, *habla español?*" she asked, but he didn't respond to that, either.

"*A ty govorish po russki?*" Wade asked.

Still nothing.

"*My spaseny,*" Wade said.

"What movie's that from?" Francie asked.

"None," he said. "It's Russian. It means 'We're saved.'"

"We're saved?"

"Yep," he said, pointing ahead to a large faded yellow sign. "Because there's a gas station up ahead."

CHAPTER FIVE

"Don't say it's a fine morning or I'll shoot you."
—McLintock!

"All right," Wade whispered, glancing at Indy, whose attention seemed totally fixed on the road ahead, "you know the plan. You're gonna tell Indy you have to go to the bathroom and go inside, and I'll distract him while you have the clerk call 911. Tell him you were kidnapped, *not* abducted. Don't say a *word* about aliens—"

"I know," she said, thinking of the 911 dispatcher's response the night before.

"Tell him this escaped convict kidnapped you and you managed to get away from him, and the clerk needs to call the Highway Patrol."

"What if he thinks *you're* the kidnapper?" she asked. "Everybody out here carries guns, especially a clerk in an isolated convenience store. What if he tries to shoot you?"

"Somehow I don't think that'll be a problem," Wade whispered, nodding toward Indy, who still didn't seem to be paying any attention to their conversation.

"Except that we'll have another abductee."

"Not if you tell the clerk that you got away from your kidnapper a couple miles back and walked here, but you're afraid he'll come looking for you, and the clerk needs to get the cops out here ASAP."

"What if he doesn't believe my story?"

"Then call 911 yourself."

"I don't have any money. I didn't have my purse with me when he abducted me."

Wade dug in his jeans pocket and pulled out a handful of change. "Here."

"What if Indy won't let me—or the clerk—call?"

"Make the clerk lock the door before you make the call, and then you and the clerk lock yourselves in the walk-in freezer till the cops come."

But what if it's only a gas station and not a convenience store and there is no inside? she wondered, but when it came in sight a minute later, it was clearly both. Its windows were covered with ads for Coors and Marlboros and lottery tickets, and there were three gas pumps outside.

"Oh, look," Wade said loudly, "there's a gas station up ahead. Do we need gas?"

"Yes," she said. "We're nearly out. And I need to go to the bathroom. And get something to eat. I'm starving." Which was true.

"Then we'd better stop," Wade said, and Francie pulled cautiously off the road and in to the gas station, braced for Indy to grab the steering wheel and force her back on the road.

He didn't, and she pulled cautiously up to the first pump, noting with relief that there weren't any cars at the other pumps or parked in front of the building. At least stopping here wouldn't get anyone else abducted.

"No," Wade whispered, "go to the one that's farthest from the door. The last thing we need is for the clerk to spot Indy. Or for Indy to spot the clerk."

She nodded and drove on to the last pump, stopped the car, switched off the ignition, and reached down for the gas cap lever, sure that at any moment Indy would grab her wrist.

He didn't, but when Wade opened his door and started to get out, tentacles immediately shot out and clasped themselves around his waist, his hand, and his feet.

"Hey, hang on," Wade said. "Don't go all *Raiders of the Lost Ark* on me, Indy. I'm just getting gas. Gas," he repeated, pointing at the gas gauge on the dashboard. "Fuel. Without it, we can't get you wherever it is you're trying to go. Are you trying to get back to your spaceship so you can go home?" He pantomimed a spaceship shooting upward. "Whoosh! Your ship has to have gas, right? Fuel? Propellant? If it doesn't, it can't go, either."

More gestures, this time of a spaceship sputtering and falling back to Earth. "Fuel." He pointed at the car and then the gas pump. "Gas. So the car can go. Here, I'll show you how it works," and Indy must have understood at least some of that because he detached his tentacles and let Wade get out of the car, following him around it to the pump.

Wade glanced back at Francie as he went, mouthing, "Go," and Francie silently opened the door, slid out, and walked quickly toward the convenience store's glass doors.

"This is the gas cap," she heard Wade say as she reached the door. "You screw it off, and inside . . . no, don't screw it back on! You have to take it off to put in the gas."

She opened the glass door, praying there wasn't a buzzer. There wasn't, but there was a string of dangling bells, which tinkled wildly. She hastily shut the door and then looked for a lock she could turn. There wasn't any, just a slot for a key. She'd need to have the clerk lock it. She turned and hurried past the chips and soda pop and beef jerky and candy bars, trying not to think how hungry she was, and over to the counter.

There was no one behind it. "Hello?" she called, and then, more loudly, "Hello! Is anyone there?"

No answer. She leaned over the counter, trying to see into the back, but she couldn't see anyone, and there wasn't a back door visible. The clerk must be in the restroom.

She hurried over to the restrooms, but the doors to both the men's and ladies' rooms stood ajar. She knew she should look for the clerk, but this might be her only chance to use the bathroom. Any second Indy might realize she was gone and lash out with his tentacles to drag her back to the car, and the sight of the bathrooms had reminded her how badly she had to go.

She darted into the restroom, used it, and washed her hands, making the mistake of looking in the mirror over the sink. She definitely looked like a kidnap victim, her hair mussed and her mascara streaked. There were bruises and scratches on her arms from Indy's manhandling her into the car—twice—and the hem of her dress was dirty from her crouching in the dust beside the car. Wade should have known something was wrong just by looking at her.

So why didn't he? she wondered, dragging her fingers through her hair, wiping her face with a wet paper towel, and dabbing at the smudges on her dress—and then thought, *Maybe I shouldn't have done that.* She needed to convince the clerk she was in trouble so he'd call 911 for her.

If she could find him. He still wasn't back when she came out of the ladies' room, and she couldn't afford to wait. Wade couldn't distract Indy forever. It would have to be the payphone. If they had one.

They did, in the corner next to the front windows. With an OUT OF ORDER sign on it, and she could see why. There wasn't any receiver.

She peeked cautiously out between the beer and cigarette ads to see what the alien was doing. He was holding the nozzle from the gas pump, and Wade was trying to show him how to put it in the gas tank, but Indy kept hanging it back on the pump, so she was okay for the moment.

She went back over to the counter, calling, "Hello! Anyone there?"

No answer. *He must be out back smoking,* she thought, and looked to see where the back door was.

The bells on the front door began to jangle. Francie jerked around, thinking, *It's Indy!* but it wasn't. It was a short guy with a crew cut wearing a black T-shirt and cargo shorts. She could see his car pulled up outside. He walked over to the soft-drinks cooler without a glance at Francie, grabbing a bag of Doritos on the way.

Now that he was nearer, she could see his T-shirt had a drawing of a flying saucer and the words I BELIEVE. Which meant if she told him the real situation, he might actually take her seriously.

But I can't risk the possibility he might not. And Wade had told her not to say anything about aliens or abduction.

"Hi, I'm sorry to bother you," she said, "but could I borrow your phone? I've got to make a call. It's important," and when he looked wary, she added, "My name's Francie, by the way."

"Mine's Lyle, but I'm in kind of a hurry. Can't you ask to use the clerk's?"

"I can't find him. There wasn't anybody here when I arrived. I only need your phone for a minute. I promise I'll be fast."

He ignored her request. "Did you look in the back?"

"No," she said. "I shouted—"

He walked rapidly past her, his arms still full of his purchases, and went behind the counter and into the back, calling, "Anybody here?"

He came back. "He's not there," he said. "Did you look out the back door?"

"There isn't one."

"How strange! People don't just vanish into thin air like that, unless—" He gave her a sharp look. "Unless they were abducted. Did you see anything on your way here? Unusual lights in the sky? Or a strange object?"

"No," she said, but he wasn't listening.

"I *knew* it landed up here," he was saying excitedly. "Everybody was so sure the UFO landed out west near Hondo, but I knew that was just a diversion. They always land in secret, and last night I saw lights up this direction."

That was lightning, Francie said silently. *And if they land in se-*

cret, they wouldn't **have** *lights.* Aloud, she said, "What are you talking about?"

"I'm *talking* about the UFO that was sighted last night and that obviously abducted the clerk." He stopped and stared at her, seeming to take in her mussed dress and her disheveled hair for the first time. "Where did you get those scratches?"

"I—"

"I know where you got them. The aliens implanted a monitoring device in you. You were abducted, too, weren't you?"

And I was worried he might not believe me, she thought, but the knowledge that he obviously would wasn't particularly reassuring, especially when he said, "You had a close encounter of the fourth kind, didn't you?"

"A what?"

"On Hynek's scale," he said. "He made a scale for all the different levels of alien contact. The visual sighting of a UFO is an encounter of the first kind, physical evidence is the second kind, seeing an EBE is the third kind—"

"EBE?"

"Extraterrestrial biological entity," he said. "Abduction's the fourth kind, taking you up to their ship and interrogating you. You can find it all on my blog at AliensAmongUs.net. What did you tell them when they took you up to their ship? You didn't give away any secrets about our defense capabilities, did you?"

"No. I mean, I wasn't—"

"Did they ask you about our nuclear weapons? That's obviously why they're here. They want to get their hands on our nuclear arsenal so they can wipe us out and take over the Earth."

Oh my gosh, he's as crazy as Serena's fiancé, she thought. *And the last thing he needs to find out is that there's an alien out at the gas pump. There's no telling what he might do.*

"Look," she said, trying to calm him down, "nobody's taking over the Earth, and nobody's been abducted."

"Then where did you get those so-called scratches?" He didn't wait for an answer. "You don't remember, do you? You were driving along and all of a sudden you saw a strange light, and after that you don't remember anything till you found yourself here hours later, with no memory of what happened during the missing time."

Time. She'd already been in here far too long. Any second Indy might notice she was missing and come looking for her, and she still hadn't called 911.

"I didn't see a light," she said urgently. "I didn't see *anything.* I have no idea what you're talking about. If you could please just lend me your phone for one minute—"

"You think you didn't see anything because the aliens wiped your memory. They can control minds, you know, *and* time. They can expand time and collapse it so no time has passed between when you were abducted and when you were returned."

"That isn't—"

"Look at those incisions where the aliens implanted their monitoring and controlling devices." He pointed at her scratches. "They're proof—"

"No, they're not, and they're not incisions. I wasn't taken up to an alien spaceship. I was kidnapped! In my car. I managed to get away from him and walk here, and that's why I need your phone, to call the police."

He was smiling tolerantly at her. "That's just what you *think* happened. Look at what you're wearing. That's proof you were abducted. The color of that dress never originated on Earth. They took your clothes and stuck you on an operating table on board their ship and probed you. And then afterward they put that dress on you and left you by the side of the road.

"Come on," he said, transferring his Doritos and Coke to his left hand and grabbing Francie's arm with his right. "I need you to show me exactly where you were when you first saw the lights." He began propelling her toward the door.

"No!" she said, resisting. "You can't go out there!"

"Why not?" He whirled to face her. "They're out there right now, aren't they?" he said. "Oh my God! This is incredible!" He let go of her arm and pulled his phone out of a pocket of his cargo shorts. "This is my chance to see an alien! To have my own close encounter! What are they, Grays?"

"No. You don't understand, you can't—"

"Don't worry. I won't get close enough to their saucer to let them beam me up," he said, tapping his phone, "but I've got to get a picture. It's what we've been waiting for all these years—actual proof that they exist!" and before Francie could stop him, he'd pulled the door open, its bells jangling wildly, and held his phone up.

"Don't—" Francie said, but she was too late. Wade, now standing by the car with the nozzle in the gas tank, had already glanced nervously toward the door at the sound of the bells.

She saw him look down at Indy and make a grab for him, but he was too late. The door flashed open, the bells went wild, and the guy's phone spun out in an arc past the pumps and the road and into the weeds on the other side. The Doritos and Coke followed it, the bottle spewing brown foam everywhere.

Lyle yelped as multiple tentacles encircled him and Francie, opened the car doors, swept Lyle into the back seat and Francie into the front passenger seat, and slammed both their doors shut behind them.

Apparently Indy had yanked Wade into the car and wrapped his foot around the gas pedal at the same time, because Wade was already peeling out of the gas station onto the highway and heading north, tires screeching, seatbelt alarms beeping.

What happened to the gas pump hose? Francie wondered, afraid it was still on, writhing like a snake and spewing gasoline everywhere. She turned around in her seat to look back.

"It's off," Wade said, reading her mind. "Thank God for automatic shutoff, so at least we don't have to worry about burning the place down."

"Indy, let up!" he called into the back seat, where Indy had rolled to sit next to Lyle. "We're going too fast. You're going to get us all killed," and, amazingly, Indy loosened his grip on Wade's foot, and Wade was able to slow the car down to a less life-threatening speed, and Francie and Wade were able to get their seatbelts on.

That didn't stop the terrified whimpers coming from the back seat. Lyle was huddled in the far corner of the back seat as far away as he could get from Indy, gibbering, "Oh my God! This can't be happening! What *is* that thing?"

"An alien," Wade said.

"An *alien*? From outer *space*?" He scrabbled up the side of the car, trying to escape from him. "Oh my God!"

I thought you wanted to have a close encounter, Francie thought. "I wouldn't do that," she said aloud, remembering what Indy had done to Wade. Several of Indy's tentacles were already quivering. "Yelling upsets him."

But Lyle was beyond listening. "Get him away from me!" he screamed, scrabbling frantically up the side of the car. "It's going to eat me! Oh my God!"

"He's not going to eat you," Francie said.

"Yes, he is." He slapped wildly at Indy's tentacles.

"Don't," Francie said. "Indy will—"

The alien was already doing it, wrapping his tentacles around Lyle's arms to stop them from flailing and pinioning them to his sides.

"Oh my God!" Lyle cried. "He's wrapping me up in a cocoon, just like in *Invasion of the Body Snatchers*! He's going to turn me into a pod person!"

"He isn't going to turn you into a pod person," Francie said. "Just *please* stop screaming or Indy will—"

"Oh my God!" Lyle shrieked, his voice reaching a pitch capable of breaking glass. "He's wrapping up my head!"

He was indeed, slapping flattened tentacles across Lyle's mouth and chin and forehead till he looked like an Egyptian mummy, with only his nose and his eyes, wide with terror, left showing.

The bonds were so tight he couldn't even wriggle. He was still making muffled, high-pitched squeals, though.

"You need to stop screaming," Francie said. "You're just making it worse." She unbuckled her seatbelt, ignoring the beeping that that caused, and turned to kneel on the seat, facing Lyle. "Listen, you've got to calm down," she shouted over the alarm. "If you don't, he won't let you go. He won't hurt you. He's only doing this because the noise makes him nervous," but Lyle was apparently too far gone to understand her. His squeals got even louder—and higher.

"Jesus," Wade said. "How the hell am I supposed to drive with that caterwauling? Indy, can't you—?"

"Don't," Francie said. "Indy will—"

He'd already done it, flattening another tentacle over Lyle's mouth and muffling the sound to a whisper.

"*Thank* you, Indy," Wade said. "I couldn't hear myself think. So what happened back there? You were supposed to call 911 and then you two were supposed to hide in the walk-in freezer till the police came."

"There wasn't any walk-in freezer," she said, turning around and sitting back down. "Or any clerk."

She refastened her seatbelt so the alarm would stop and she wouldn't have to shout. "He's just a customer who came into the store while I was there. His name's Lyle. He was up here searching for the aliens who landed last night."

"Well, he found one," Wade said, glancing at him in the rearview mirror. "Were you at least able to get through to the police?"

"No. The payphone was broken, and when I asked Lyle if I could use his phone, he demanded to know what had happened to me, and when I told him I'd been kidnapped, he immediately concluded I'd been abducted and insisted on going outside to see if he could get a photo of the UFO—and you know the rest."

"What about his phone? Does he still have it?"

She shook her head. "Indy got it and threw it out of reach."

"Which means we're right back where we started, only with one more person to worry about. Did anyone see you and Lyle get snatched?"

She shook her head.

"Good."

Francie frowned. "I thought you *wanted* to notify the police."

"I wanted *you* to notify them, and for them to come pick you up.

You saw what happened to what's-his-name here." He gestured at the back seat. "If the Highway Patrol comes after us, Indy's likely to hog-tie 'em and throw 'em in the back seat, too, and we're already running out of room in here as it is. If this keeps up, we're gonna need a bigger boat."

Francie nodded. "Preferably one with a bathroom on board, since I somehow doubt if he'll let us stop at any more gas stations."

"Yeah, and one with a galley. I'm starving."

You're *starving?* Francie thought. *I'm the one who hasn't had anything to eat since yesterday afternoon.*

"I don't suppose you managed to snag some Slim Jims while you were in there?" Wade asked. "Or a couple of candy bars?"

"No," she said, but he'd stopped listening.

He was looking intently in the rearview mirror. "I don't see any-body behind us," he said after a minute, "and no flashing lights. And since the clerk didn't see anything—"

"But when he sees Lyle's car there with nobody in it and the gas pump nozzle on the ground," she protested, "he's bound to realize something's happened and call the police, and they'll put an APB out on Lyle."

Wade shook his head. "I doubt if he's going to want to admit he was MIA when he was supposed to be minding the store, so my guess is he won't do anything. So, unless Lyle told somebody where he was going . . . did you, Lyle?" he called into the back seat. "Tell anybody where you were going?"

"He can't answer you, remember?" Francie said. "He's got a gag over his mouth. But I'm pretty sure he didn't. He wanted to be the first one to find the UFO."

As she said this, the squeals from the back started again. "Indy, untie him," Wade said. "He's trying to tell us something."

Francie didn't really expect Indy to obey, but he withdrew the flattened tentacle across Lyle's mouth, leaving Lyle looking like he was going to start gibbering again.

"Don't scream," Wade said, eyeing him in the rearview mirror, "or he'll slap that tentacle right back over your mouth. You've got to speak calmly and quietly."

"He won't hurt you," Francie said.

"You don't know that!" Lyle yelped. "He might stick one of those tentacles of his down my throat like in *Alien* and then burst out of my chest—"

"He's not going to burst out of your chest," Francie said. And Wade said, "You've been watching too many movies," but Lyle wasn't listening.

"Get me out of here!" He wriggled wildly, struggling against his restraints. "Cut me loose! Don't either one of you have a knife?"

"No one's cutting—" Francie began.

"If you try to hurt Indy, you'll just make him mad," Wade said mildly, "and then he's really liable to turn the screws on you."

"But you have to do *something*!" Lyle yelped. "What about fire? Do either of you have any matches to burn him with? Or water? The aliens in *Signs* could be killed with water. It scalded their skin when it was poured on them."

"May I just point out that *Signs* was also a movie?" Wade said. "And a completely illogical one at that. I mean, why would a hydrophobic—and meltable—species pick a planet to invade that's three-fourths water?"

"That's why they landed in the Southwest," Lyle said triumphantly, "because there isn't any water here. Don't you have some water or Coke or something you can throw on him to at least see if it'd kill him?"

"No," Wade said. "And if I were you, I wouldn't talk about doing Indy bodily harm. He may very well understand what you're saying."

That possibility clearly hadn't occurred to Lyle. He shrank back against the seat, looking frightened.

"Good," Wade said. "Now that we've got that settled, Lyle, who knows you were heading this way?"

"Nobody," Lyle said, still watching Indy warily. "If I'd told them I'd seen UFO lights, they might have beat me to it."

"Lights?" Wade said. "What's he talking about?"

"He said he saw lights north of Roswell," Francie said, "but it was just the lightning."

"Oh, right," Lyle said sarcastically. "It was lightning or swamp gas or the planet Venus. That's what they always say. Obviously it was a UFO, since the alien's right here. And the clerk back there has obviously been abducted, too. They took him to their ship."

"How do you know?" Wade asked.

"Because that's what they do!" Lyle said, his voice rising in spite of Wade's warning. "They abduct people and take them up to the mother ship to perform horrible experiments on them. That's where he's taking us now, and when we get there, they're going to put us on an operating table and probe us—"

"Nobody's going to probe you," Francie said.

"You know, I've never understood the whole probing thing," Wade said. "I mean, why would an advanced civilization, capable of faster-than-light travel, come all the way across the galaxy just to sexually molest the natives?"

"*Because* they want to crossbreed aliens and humans." Unable to gesture, Lyle nodded toward Francie. "They want to impregnate her with their sperm and use her as a vessel for growing an alien-human hybrid and—"

"Gag him, Indy," Wade said, but Indy either didn't understand the word, or he was curious to hear more about alien-human hybrids, because he made no move to stop Lyle from talking.

"The hybrids look just like humans, but they're actually aliens sent here to spy on us and transmit information back to their home planet for the invasion."

"And you think that's why Indy's here?" Wade asked. "To invade Earth?"

"Of *course* that's why he's here. They're here to take over the planet, just like the aliens in *Independence Day*."

"Which is *also* a movie," Wade said. "Indy could have come here for lots of other reasons than taking over the planet."

"Name one."

"Okay. To see if there's intelligent life here. To monitor us to see if we're becoming a danger to the rest of the galaxy. To ask us to join the Galactic United Nations. To warn us against the dangers of nuclear war or global warming. To return a videotape they rented from Blockbuster the last time they were here. Why are you UFO guys always so fixated on invasion?"

"Because they've been working to invade Earth for at least seventy-five years that we know of," Lyle said. "They've been secretly watching us and abducting people and building bases—"

"And your proof for any of this is what?" Wade asked. "Have you ever actually seen one of these alien bases? Or a UFO, for that matter?"

"There are hundreds of photos—"

"All of which were faked. I'm talking about physical evidence."

"What about the UFO that crashed northwest of Roswell on J. B. Foster's ranch in 1947? We have the wreckage. The Air Force took it and the aliens to a secret government base at Area 51."

"That was a weather balloon," Wade said. "Or rather, a whole bunch of weather balloons taped together, with sonic detection equipment on top." He turned to look at Francie. "It was a secret Air Force Cold War project. They floated the balloons over the Soviet Union at high altitude to listen for aboveground nuclear testing. And they didn't want anyone to find out about it, so when one crashed, the Air Force covered it up and let people think it was a UFO."

"That's what they *want* you to believe," Lyle said. "It *was* a UFO, and there were aliens inside. The ranch hand who found the crash, Mac Brazel, saw them. And the mortician in Roswell testified that the Air Force called him right after the crash and asked him how many child-size coffins he had, and when he went out to the airfield to talk to them, he saw them performing an autopsy on one of the dead aliens."

So that's what that autopsy exhibit at the UFO museum was supposed to represent, Francie thought.

"I thought you said the Air Force took the aliens to Area 51," Wade said.

"They did," Lyle said. "*After* the mortician saw them performing the autopsy. He said it was definitely an alien."

"Yeah, well, he also said he didn't actually see the autopsy," Wade said, "that he was dating a nurse at the airfield who told him about it, and when the reporters said they wanted to interview her, he said she'd been killed in a plane crash over the Atlantic. And when they told him there hadn't *been* any such crashes in 1947, he told them she'd become a nun." He turned to Francie. "A nun who'd conveniently taken a vow of silence."

"That's because he couldn't tell them what had really happened, that the aliens had abducted her and taken her back to their home planet to be their slave. That's why they abduct people, to enslave them. They impregnate them first and then enslave them. And suck their blood."

"Which is from *The Thing*," Wade pointed out. "Also a movie."

"I thought you said they abducted people to impregnate them with alien-human hybrid babies," Francie said.

Lyle ignored that. "How can you ask me if I have any evidence of aliens when one's got me tied up like a mummy right now? *He's* your proof. The aliens are here, and we have to warn people!" he cried, his voice rising. "We have to tell them about the invasion before it's too late, before they kill us all!"

That was clearly too much for Indy. He whipped a gag across Lyle's mouth again, and when Lyle tried to free himself, wrapped another layer of tentacles around him.

"Indy!" Francie said. "Let him go!"

"Ignore her," Wade said, and when she glared at him, "We're better off this way."

He lowered his voice. "If Indy *is* here to decide whether we're a danger to the galaxy, then the less said about invading and enslaving and killing the better. We don't want to give him any ammunition for thinking we're a violent species."

"In which case you probably shouldn't be using the word 'ammunition,'" Francie said.

"True." Wade grinned at her. "And we shouldn't be giving him ideas about probing us and impregnating you. Or mutilating cows." He nodded toward a herd of cattle they were passing. "That's another thing that's never made sense. Why would an advanced civilization travel all the way across the galaxy to torture a harmless cow? Don't they have any innocent creatures of their own they could mutilate? And why come to Earth? We're in the middle of nowhere, cosmically speaking, all the way out on an insignificant arm of the galaxy that's about as populated as this part of the country is. There's just no reason for them to come to a backwater one-horse planet like Earth when they could go to the galactic equivalent of Tokyo. Or Paris."

"But they *did* come here," Francie said. "Or at least Indy did."

"Yeah," Wade said. "And the question is *why*."

Lyle emitted a muffled squeal from the back seat.

"And no, he's *not* an invader, Lyle," Wade said. "Or if he is, he's a really bad one. In the first place, he had to bum a ride to get where he's going, and, in the second place, he doesn't seem to know where that is. *And* he doesn't have any weapons."

Louder squeals from the back. "I don't think Lyle agrees with you," Francie said.

"Okay, you're right. He is armed, pardon the pun. But for snatching a few people, not for holding off an army. Or destroying the planet."

More squeals, which were easy to translate. Lyle was obviously saying, "You don't know that! He could have a death ray. Or a nuclear bomb."

Which Francie supposed was true, but she didn't think he was an invader, either.

But then why was he here? Not to warn the government or open trade relations with Earth. If he was, he'd have landed in Washington, D.C., or Munich or Beijing, not in New Mexico. And he'd be able to speak the language.

"Maybe he's looking for something," she said. "What's in New Mexico?"

"Roswell," Wade said promptly. "The UFO Festival, the UFO museum—"

"I'm serious."

"I don't know," he said. "Carlsbad Caverns? Chaco Canyon? The World's Largest Chili Pepper?"

The muffled sounds from the back seat had reached a hysterical pitch. "I think Lyle has an idea on the subject," Francie said. "Indy, let him go. We need to talk to him."

Indy undid Lyle's wrappings and then slowly withdrew the flattened tentacle and let it lie limply on the car seat next to him, but still flattened out, as if he were ready to slap it over Lyle's mouth again.

"All right, Lyle," Wade said, looking at him in the rearview mirror, "why do *you* think Indy's here?"

"To retrieve the UFO that crashed at Roswell in 1947," he said, eyeing the tentacle warily. "They've got it hidden at a secret government base inside Devils Tower."

"Devils *Tower*?" Wade said. "That's from *Close Encounters*. Which is also a movie. And I thought you said it was at Area 51."

"It was. They moved it. There's a secret base at Area 51, too. And there's one at Wright-Patterson Air Force Base. Under Hangar 18."

Francie looked at Indy to see if he was having any response to what Lyle was saying, but there was no indication he recognized the name of any of the places Lyle was talking about, or had even heard them.

"Devils Tower is in Wyoming and Wright-Patterson is in Ohio, and Indy landed in New Mexico," Wade said logically.

"But there are secret bases in New Mexico, too," Lyle said. "There's one in Aztec. A UFO landed there in 1948, bigger than the one in Roswell, and they found sixteen bodies in it."

"That was a hoax," Wade said.

"That's what they want you to think," Lyle said. "The government's been secretly working with aliens for over seventy years. That's what the Men in Black are all about. They're an ultrasecret government agency whose job is to keep the presence of aliens hidden from the public. They retrieve evidence so no one can prove their existence. Or they try to. But there were witnesses to the Aztec landing. Silas Newton and—"

"Leo A. GeBauer," Wade said, "who claimed they'd salvaged an alien metal from the UFO and made it into a device for finding oil and gold. The strange alien metal turned out to be aluminum, and the whole thing turned out to be a scam the two of them had cooked up."

"How do you happen to know so much about it?" Francie asked.

"I try to keep up with what all the other con men are doing so I can steal their ideas," Wade said with a grin. He looked in the rear-view mirror at Lyle. "You'll have to come up with something better than that."

"Fine," Lyle said grudgingly. "What about the Plains of San Augustin crash? *That* wasn't a hoax." He turned to Francie. "This rancher, Barney Barnett, was driving in his truck and he saw an alien with big black eyes and no ears standing by the road and picked him up, and it led him to a smashed UFO."

"It wasn't a UFO," Wade said. "It was a crashed AT-6, and Barney Barnett's account of the alien hitchhiker was thoroughly debunked. But even if it wasn't a hoax, it can't be where Indy's taking us, and neither can Aztec. They're in the wrong direction. Aztec's west of here and the Plains of San Augustin are south, and in case you haven't noticed, we're headed due north. So where might he be taking us? *Besides* his probing headquarters?"

"He might be taking us to one of their transfer points."

"Transfer points?" Francie asked.

"Places where the planet's ley lines cross—"

"Ley lines?"

"They're a made-up group of lines between historic structures like the Pyramids and Stonehenge," Wade said. "They're supposed to map 'Earth energies.' Totally bogus."

"They are *not*," Lyle said angrily. "They're real, and where they cross, they create a multidimensional zone where alien ships can pass from one dimension to another. That's why their ships are so hard to track on radar. There's one at Four Corners, where Colorado and New Mexico and Utah and Arizona meet."

"Well, that's not where he's taking us," Wade said.

"How do you know that?"

"Because this road just turned east."

It had, veering sharply to cross and then follow a set of railroad tracks that stretched east to the horizon. "What's east of here?" Wade asked.

"East . . . there's a base in Gulf Breeze, Florida."

"*Florida*?" Francie said.

"Yes, there have been *dozens* of saucer sightings there. They have photographs of one of them!"

"And the guy who took them turned out to have a two-foot mock-up of a saucer in his basement. Anyway, Florida's too far away. Tell me someplace a reasonable distance east of here. What's on this road?"

Nothing, Francie thought. They'd passed nothing at all since turning east, not a ranch, not a junction, and the only sign Francie'd seen had said ZOPILOTE, 28 MILES.

"There's Marfa, Texas," Lyle said. "You know, the Marfa lights?"

"No," Francie said. "What are they?"

"Car headlights," Wade said.

"They're mysterious lights that dance on the horizon east of Marfa," Lyle said, "moving in one direction and then another and then vanishing."

"Like I said, headlights, from cars going up the switchbacks on Chinati Peak."

"No, they're *spaceships*," Lyle said. "The aliens have a secret base underneath Chinati Peak, and that's where they disappear to."

"Marfa's too far away," Wade said. "Isn't there anything closer?"

Lyle thought a minute, and then said, "There was a famous sighting in Hobbs. Four guys were driving along this rural road at night when they saw a line of red lights, and then their car died. They thought it was out of gas, but when they got out of the car, they saw this UFO hovering above them."

"Speaking of out of gas," Wade said, "you know those devices I told you about that could supposedly find oil and gas and gold?"

"The ones that the Aztec crash con men were hawking?" Francie asked.

"Yep. We could sure use a real one right now."

"Why?" Francie said, alarmed. "What's wrong?"

He pointed at the gas gauge. The needle was on E.

"You were supposed to fill up the car while I was inside," Francie said.

"And you were supposed to call the police," Wade said. "I was busy keeping Indy here from realizing you were gone."

"But you were fueling up when we came out—"

"I'd just put the nozzle in. I only managed to get half a gallon in the tank before we took off, if that."

"How far do you think we can get before we run out of gas?"

"I don't know. In most cars when it's on empty, there's usually a little left, but I've never driven a Navigator. Ten or fifteen miles, maybe?"

Francie looked around at the landscape, which was empty desert as far as she could see, no houses, not even any dirt roads that might lead to a ranch. "The sign back there said Zopilote was twenty-eight miles," she said.

"We might be able to make it twenty of that," Wade said. "If we're lucky."

They weren't. A scant mile later, the engine coughed and died. Wade restarted it, and the car went a few more yards, during which time he was able to pull it off the highway and onto the side of the road, and then it died completely.

CHAPTER SIX

Be there for a friend when he needs you.

—*The Code of the West*

The moment the car died, Lyle made a grab for the back door handle and Indy made an even faster grab for Lyle's wrist.

"I wouldn't try to get away," Francie said. "He'll wrap you up again," and Lyle pulled his hand back as if he'd touched a hot stove.

Wade was still trying to restart the car, but nothing happened. "We're completely out of gas," he said.

"No, we're not," Lyle said nervously. "They're here." He turned to look out the back window at the sky. "Their saucers' magnetic fields shut off the car's electrical systems. That's what happened to Barney and Betty Hill. Their car stalled and their headlights and the lights on their dashboard went out, and then the aliens abducted them."

Wade said, "Well, we've already been abducted, so that can't be it."

"It happened to a lineman's truck, too—"

"That was in *Close Encounters*," Wade said. "You watch too many movies." He gestured at the sky through the windshield. "As you can see, not a flying saucer in sight."

"That's because they're using a cloaking device."

Francie looked up at the sky. It was an empty expanse of blue, without a single cloud in sight. And the place where they'd come to a stop was empty, too—no houses, no windmills, no road that might lead to a ranch, not even any fences, and no shade except for a scraggly desert willow, under which lay an empty whiskey bottle and a few beer cans.

Stretching away from the road was an expanse of reddish dirt and dry weeds, broken only by a sandy rise off to the left and, a hundred yards beyond it, a flat-topped outcropping of ochre-colored sandstone, crumbling below into a jumble of fallen rocks.

"Trust me, we're just out of gas," Wade said. "Gas," he said to Indy, who was pointing out the windshield at the road. "Fuel. Petrol. Go juice. The stuff I was trying to put in the car when you decided to grab everybody and go roaring off."

Indy tightened his grip on Wade's hand and dragged it to the ignition in a movement that clearly said, "Go."

"He can't," Francie said. "The car ran out of gas." She pointed at the fuel gauge and shook her head. "No gas."

Indy's tentacle squeezed tighter.

"Ow!" Wade said and turned the key in the ignition to show him. It made a sputtering sound. "See?" he said. "No gas."

Indy's grip tightened.

"Stop!" Francie said. "It's not Wade's fault. We're out of gas. Let *go*!" and surprisingly, Indy released Wade's hand, gave an overall wriggle that looked almost like a shrug, wrapped two tentacles around the door handle, opened the door, and rolled out.

"He's going to kill us!" Lyle wailed from the back seat. "He's going to vaporize us with his death ray because we didn't obey his orders!"

"He's not going to shoot us," Francie said, watching Indy roll off through the weeds.

"Then what's he doing?"

"He's calling Triple A to come bring us some gas," Wade said.

"No, he's not. He's contacting the mother ship," Lyle wailed, "so it can beam us up to their operating room and they can probe us."

Francie ignored him. She was watching Indy, who'd reached the top of the rise and was sitting down like he had before. "He rolled up a little hill last night, too," she said thoughtfully. "Could he be trying to spot his own ship?"

"Maybe," Wade said. "Or a landmark that might give him a clue as to where it is."

"That's not what he's doing!" Lyle shouted. "He's sending a signal! Look!" He scrambled out of the car and pointed up at the sky. "There it is! The mother ship!"

"That's a hawk," Wade said, getting out, too.

"Not the hawk! There!" Lyle said, pointing at a completely empty section of sky. "You can't see it because they're using a cloaking device! Do something!"

"What exactly would you suggest?" Wade asked him. "We're miles from civilization, and we're out of gas."

"What would I *suggest*?" Lyle said hysterically. "Try to escape! Flag down a car!"

"We haven't passed a single vehicle in the last thirty miles," Wade said, "and if one did pass us and we flagged it down, Indy would just abduct them, too. And the car's too crowded already."

"Then we have to escape on foot," Lyle said.

"On *foot*?" Wade said. "We're in the middle of nowhere—and, according to that sign we just passed, the next town's twenty-eight miles from here."

"I don't care," Lyle said. "I'm not staying here and waiting for the aliens to come and turn me into a science experiment. I'm getting out of here!" He stomped off down the highway.

"Wait!" Francie said, opening her car door and getting out.

"Shh," Wade said, glancing over at Indy, who was still sitting motionless on the rise. "Maybe he won't notice."

"But Lyle can't walk twenty-eight miles in this heat," Francie said. "Especially without water."

"No, but he can make it a couple before he figures that out and comes back, and in the meantime, we won't have to listen to him going on about death rays and killer aliens." Wade grabbed his duffel bag from the back seat, took it over to the desert willow, kicked the whiskey bottle and beer cans aside, and sat down on his bag under the tree. "Besides, I'd like to see how far Indy's reach extends." He watched interestedly as Lyle started down the road.

The answer was at least two hundred yards, at which point Indy, who hadn't moved at all from his spot on top of the rise, suddenly shot out a tentacle. It arced out like a cast fishing line, grabbed Lyle by both arms, and snapped him back to the car and inside. Indy slammed the car door shut on him, retracted his tentacle, and resumed sitting, motionless, on the rise.

"Wow!" Wade said admiringly. "There goes my plan to make a run for it and distract Indy while you two get away."

"True," Francie said. "So what *do* we do? We can't stay here. I don't know about you, but I'm starving. I haven't had anything to eat since yesterday afternoon, we don't have any food or water, and it doesn't look like it's going to rain anytime soon." She looked up at the cloudless blue sky where the hawk was still circling. "It's already hot. By this afternoon . . ."

"I know," he said. "We're going to need to get hold of some food and water somehow. Maybe the next vehicle to go by will be a food truck. Or a car with too many people to fit in the Navigator, and Indy will have to leave somebody behind, and you can flag down the *next* car—"

"And call the authorities?"

"And your friend Serena, and she could come get you so you don't miss her wedding."

"What makes you think Indy would be willing to leave me—or anybody else—behind? How do you know he wouldn't just tie the extra people to the top of the Navigator?"

"You're right," he said. "So what do you suggest?"

"I don't know. Make a sign that says 'Call Police'?"

Wade frowned. "With what?"

"I don't know. Maybe there's something in the car we can use,"

she said, starting back to the Navigator, and when Wade didn't follow her, she called back over her shoulder, "Besides, I need to make
sure Lyle's all right and open the windows for him. It's got to be
really hot in there."

"Fine," Wade said, staying where he was. "Maybe his little escape attempt has managed to knock some sense into him."

It hadn't. "Have you noticed anything funny about Wade?" he
called to her through the window when Francie got to the car.

Indy had locked the car doors and bound Lyle up even more
thoroughly than he had before, and sweat was dripping down Lyle's
face.

"Indy, unlock the doors!" Francie called to the alien. "And untie
Lyle!"

He did so without moving from his spot on the rise, though he
kept Lyle's wrist tethered to the door handle, which was probably
just as well.

Francie tried to turn on the car so she could open the windows
and then remembered they were out of gas and opened the three
doors Lyle wasn't tethered to instead.

"Do you want *your* door open?" she asked him.

"No." He leaned forward. "Have you noticed anything suspicious about Wade?"

"Like what?" Francie asked, looking on the floor of the back seat
for something they could use as a sign.

"Like maybe he's not what he seems. He's not afraid of being
abducted, and when he gives the alien orders, the alien obeys—"

"That's not quite—"

"*And* he knows all about Roswell and Aztec and the Marfa
lights, even though he *claims* not to believe in UFOs."

"Mmm," said Francie, checking under the front seats, but there
was nothing there except the twinkle lights Serena had sent her to
get.

"How did you meet him?" Lyle persisted. "Was he with you
when Indy abducted you?"

"No." She explained how Indy had grabbed her the night before
and Wade this morning. "He was hitchhiking."

"Don't you think it's strange that he just happened to be out there, in the middle of nowhere, when you came by?"

"His car had broken down."

"Did you actually *see* the car?"

"No."

"Then how do you know he was telling you the truth? How do you know he wasn't out there waiting for you and the alien to come by?"

"Waiting for—? Why?"

"Because"—he lowered his voice and leaned toward her conspiratorially—"he's one of the Men in Black."

You **do** *watch too many movies,* Francie thought. "He's not a—"

"Or else he's one of them. A Reptilian. They can disguise themselves to look like humans. You can't trust him!" Lyle said, and when Francie started to walk away, he called after her, "Trust no one! It's a conspiracy!"

"What's a conspiracy?" Wade asked her when she got back to the tree.

"Lyle thinks you're a Reptilian."

"Rats!" he said, snapping his fingers. "He's discovered my secret."

Francie looked out at Indy, who still sat motionless on the rise. "Any sign he's almost done with whatever he's doing?"

"Nope," Wade said. "You might as well sit down." He moved over to make room for her to sit beside him on the duffel bag. "We could be here awhile. I've been thinking," he said as she took a seat, "maybe it isn't his ship that he's looking for."

"You think it's one of Lyle's underground bases?"

"No, but he might be trying to rendezvous with somebody. Or maybe he came here to get something."

"I thought you said Earth didn't have anything aliens would want."

"Yeah, well, maybe I was wrong. Maybe whatever it is he came here to get doesn't exist on his planet."

"Like cows?" she said dryly.

"No, like a medicinal plant or a rare-earth element or something that's in short supply there. Here on Earth, we've got worldwide shortages of helium and scandium and neodymium. I can see us traveling to another planet to get them."

"Maybe," Francie said doubtfully, gazing at Indy. "I've been trying to put myself in his place and figure out what would make me act like he's acting."

"And?"

"If I found myself in a strange place and needed desperately to get someplace, but I couldn't communicate with the locals, and I didn't know how to operate their vehicles, I'd probably kidnap somebody and try to make them take me there, too."

"So you think he's desperate," Wade said. "Do you have a theory as to why?"

"No. Maybe he has to get back to his ship or wherever it is he's going by a certain time, or he's got some other kind of deadline, like his ship crash-landed here on the way to somewhere else, and one of the other crew members was injured and he's got to get medical help for them."

"Then you'd think he'd have hijacked a doctor, not a maid of honor." Wade frowned. "Maybe he's on the lam."

"On the lam? You mean you think he stole a ship or robbed a bank and the Galactic Police or somebody are after him?" Francie said, looking out at Indy, still sitting motionless in the sun. "He doesn't exactly look like a criminal."

"Yes, well, neither did Ted Bundy."

"Who, I recall, posed as a hitchhiker and talked young women into giving him a ride."

"Okay, so let's say he's not a criminal. But he could have witnessed a crime and the bad guys know it and now they're after him to shut him up."

"But in that case wouldn't he just want to get as far away as fast as possible instead of stopping all the time?"

"Well, technically, he wasn't the one who stopped this time," Wade said. "We ran out of gas, remember? But you're right—any bad guys would have caught up with us by now. So maybe your

theory's right, and he is desperate to get somewhere to help someone."

"Then shouldn't we help him instead of trying to get away or
calling the authorities?"

"*No*," he said firmly. "In the first place, desperate people do desperate things. We don't know what Indy might do if we can't get
him where he needs to go. And if it turns out he *is* being chased,
there's no telling what *they* might do to us. In the second place, we
have to get you back to your wedding. When is it?"

"Saturday," she said. "And it's really crucial that I be there."

"Then we've definitely got to see to it that you are."

"How?" Francie said. "We're out of gas, remember?"

"Oh, yeah." He grimaced. "And if we sit here much longer, we're
going to die of thirst. Or heatstroke. You didn't happen to see any
water in the car when you were looking for cardboard and Magic
Markers? In the back maybe?"

"I didn't look," she said, and returned to the car and checked the
back, just to make sure, but it was empty.

"I've already searched for tracking devices, if that's what you're
looking for," Lyle said.

"It's not," Francie said and lifted up the mat to look underneath,
but there was nothing there except a jack and a spare tire. She shut
the back and started toward Wade.

"Wait," Lyle said. "Come back," and when she did, he whispered, "I just saw him open his duffel bag and take something out.
Probably a Reptilian laser blaster. He's getting ready to kill us both."

She didn't even dignify that with an answer. She walked back
over to Wade. "There wasn't any water or food in the car," she said.

"There wasn't any in my duffel bag, either," he said. "I just
checked." He sat back down on it and squinted up at the hawk, still
circling overhead. "I sure hope that's not a buzzard."

"Oh my God!" Lyle cried, and they both looked over at the car.
Lyle was pointing wildly out the window. "He's coming back!"

Francie turned to look at Indy. He'd rolled off the rise, but he
wasn't returning to the car. "He's heading for that rock outcropping

farther out," she said. "The rise must not have been high enough for
him to see any landmarks from."

"Or signal the invasion fleet from," Lyle said.

"Well, whatever he's doing, I'm not sure he should be doing it on
those rocks," Wade said, shading his eyes with his hand. "Outcrop-
pings like that are usually full of rattlesnakes."

"Rattlesnakes?" Francie cried, a shiver running through her. She
automatically looked down at her feet.

"Yeah," Wade said. "They like to sun themselves on the rocks."

And Indy would never have seen a rattlesnake. He'd have no idea
they were dangerous. "Oh my God, he won't know they're poisonous," she cried. "He won't know they can kill him!"

"Great!" Lyle shouted from the car. "They'll kill him, and we'll
be able to get away!"

Francie ignored him. "Indy, don't go there!" she called. "Come
back!"

But the alien continued to roll toward the outcropping.

"We've got to warn him!" she cried and took off running.

"*Warn* him?" Lyle shouted from the car. "What are you doing?
He's the enemy!"

Indy had reached the outcropping. "Indy," Francie called, "get
off the rocks! There are poisonous snakes!" and realized he wouldn't
know what snakes *or* poisons were. "They look like your tentacles,
but they're dangerous!"

She was nearly to Indy, but he gave no indication that he heard
or saw her. "They have fangs," she shouted, and realized he wouldn't
know what fangs were, either. "Sharp, stabbing teeth that can kill
you! They—"and heard an ominous buzzing.

She stopped cold and looked down. There was a coiled snake
almost at her feet, nearly invisible against the brown dirt, its tail rattling a warning, its head raised. All the terror and loathing she
hadn't felt at the sight of Indy's tentacles poured over her, paralyzing
her.

"Wade—" she said tremulously.

"Don't move!" he ordered, running toward her. But he was too
far away.

The snake was already pulling back its head, and when it struck, it would be as fast as Indy's lashing tentacles—and as unstoppable. Her only hope was staying absolutely still. Any movement—

Oh, no, Indy was rolling toward her.

Don't! she wanted to shout, but that might only make the rattler strike. *Stay where you are,* she thought at him, praying that he was telepathic after all. *Keep perfectly still.*

But Indy continued to roll in her direction. "Stop!" she shouted, and the rattlesnake struck.

For a horrible second she thought she'd been bitten, and then she realized one of Indy's tentacles had brushed against her shin as he intercepted the rattler and caught it up in his tentacle.

"Don't!" she cried. "It'll bite you!" and saw that Indy had spread the end of his tentacle out, like he'd done to make a gag over Lyle's mouth, only this time he'd thinned it enough that it made a nearly transparent bubble, enclosing the snake completely. She saw it inside the bubble for an instant, and then Indy flung it, writhing, far out into the field and away from them.

"Are you all right?" she asked Indy, scooping him up and reaching for the tentacle that had done it.

"Get out of there, Francie!" Wade called, running toward her. "Where there's one rattler, there are others!"

She clutched Indy to her and looked down at the ground around her, but she couldn't see any snakes. Or hear any rattling.

Wade had reached her. "Are you okay?" he demanded. "Did the rattlesnake bite you?"

"No—"

"Are you sure?" he said, kneeling and pulling up her skirt to check her legs for puncture marks.

"It didn't bite me," she insisted. "It's Indy I'm worried about." She grabbed his tentacle and began to examine it. "Indy, did the snake bite you?"

"Ask him after we've gotten out of here," Wade said and hustled her back toward the car.

As soon as they were back on the dirt of the pullout, she handed Indy to Wade to hold while she examined his tentacles one by one, looking for signs of a puncture wound, but she couldn't see any marks—though she wasn't sure what she should be looking for. Swelling? Redness? Those were human signs of snakebite. An alien's symptoms might be completely different. But as she examined each tentacle in turn, she couldn't see any color change or alteration in Indy's manner, and he seemed unaffected.

"I don't think it had time to bite him," Wade said. "That snake didn't even know what hit him. Indy's fast!"

"I know," she said. *Thank heavens.* She took him back from Wade. "You saved my life, Indy."

"You saved his, too," Wade said. "He's fast, but if you hadn't warned him, a rattler could have bitten him before he even realized it was there, let alone dangerous."

"And then we wouldn't have had to worry about how to get away from him," Lyle called resentfully from the car.

Wade ignored him. "Indy, you owe Francie a debt of gratitude. She saved your bacon."

"And now that's what he'll turn us into," Lyle said. "If you ask me, you shouldn't have lifted a finger to help him."

Francie glared at him. "I'm not asking you, and if you say one more word, I'll tell Indy to gag you again," she said. "Indy, thank you for protecting me," and she would have kissed him on the top of his head if she could have figured out where his head was.

Indy wriggled to be let down, and when Francie put him back on the ground, he rolled toward the outcropping again. "He obviously didn't understand a word of that," Wade said.

"I know," Francie said, starting after him. "Indy, there might be other snakes!"

Wade stopped her. "He's proved he can take care of himself," he said, catching hold of her arm, and even as he spoke, she saw Indy fling a second snake, writhing, far out into the field, and then a third. "I think it's the rattlesnakes you should be warning."

Indy reached the top of the outcropping without disposing of any more snakes, sat for a couple of minutes, then rolled rapidly back to the car and motioned them inside. He got in himself, rolling over

Francie to his spot in the middle, shut the doors, and pointed through the windshield.

"Here we go again," Wade muttered.

"Indy, we can't go," Francie said. "I told you, we're out of gas." She pointed at the gas gauge. "See? Empty. No gas. Here, I'll show you. Wade, pull the gas tank release lever," and as he bent to do it, she got out of the car.

Indy immediately lashed out to pull her back in. "I'm not trying to run away," she said, silently cursing Lyle. "I want to show you something. Come on." She motioned to him, and he let go of her wrist and rolled out of the car after her.

She led him around to the driver's side, pulled the door to the gas tank all the way open, and unscrewed the gas cap. "This is the gas tank," she said. "Remember, Wade showed you at the gas station? You put gas—fuel—into it to make the car go. But we don't have any."

Indy stuck a tentacle tentatively into the hole and then all the way down.

"See?" Francie said. "No gas."

Indy withdrew his tentacle.

"The engine has to have gasoline to run. Fuel. It . . ." she began, and realized she had no idea how to explain what the gasoline did. "Wade! Can you explain to him how the car works?"

Wade obligingly got out of the car and put the hood up. "Okay, this is the cylinder. Inside it is a piston—"

"Don't tell him that!" Lyle called from the back seat of the car. "How do you know he's not here to steal our technology?"

"Somehow I doubt that an alien race which has mastered inter-galactic travel is here to steal the plans for the internal combustion engine," Wade said, and continued explaining how the car worked, but Indy gave no indication he was listening.

Instead, he poked randomly at the different parts of the engine—the spark plugs, the windshield wiper fluid tank, the intake manifold—winding his tentacles like vines under the crankcase and around the battery and the engine block.

"What's he doing?" Francie asked.

"I have no idea," Wade said.

"He's planting a tracking device," Lyle put his two cents in from the back seat, "so the mother ship can find us and target us for destruction."

"He's not planting a tracking device," Francie said, though it wasn't at all clear what he *was* doing. His tentacles slid rapidly, deftly, around the parts of the engine, exploring, and then he withdrew all but one of his tentacles, took the rod propping up the hood from its slot with it, lowered the hood, screwed the gas cap back on, motioned Wade and Francie back into the car, got in, and pointed at the ignition and then out the window at the road.

"Great," Wade muttered. "He didn't understand a word we said."

Indy wrapped a tentacle around Wade's wrist and guided it toward the keys.

"The car won't go, Indy," Francie said, frustrated. "We don't have any gas."

Indy tightened his grip on Wade's wrist.

"Ow!"

"We're going to have to show him again," Francie said.

"And let's hope he gets the message before he completely cuts off the circulation to my hand. Ow! Okay, okay," Wade said and turned the key in the ignition.

The car started.

Francie looked at Wade and then leaned over to look at the gas gauge. It still read empty.

Indy had detached his tentacle from Wade's wrist and was pointing insistently out the windshield.

"Could there have been a little gas left in the tank?" Francie asked.

"No," Wade said and put the car into drive. He pulled out onto the highway. "Okay, so maybe there was. In which case, we're going to go a quarter of a mile and then have to go through this whole rigamarole again."

But the car was still going when they reached Zopilote, twenty-eight miles on. It consisted of a fallen-in adobe building and an abandoned gas pump. "I'm not surprised," Wade said. "*Zopilote*'s Spanish for 'buzzard.'"

"Thank goodness we didn't have to walk here and then find out it was a ghost town," Francie said.

"You mean 'Thank Indy,'" he said. "He's the one who turned water into wine, or rather, air into gas."

"With his mind." Lyle leaned forward over the seat. "Aliens have telepathic powers. They can move objects with their minds."

Francie ignored him. "You mean you think Indy made some new kind of fuel?" she asked Wade.

"Or altered the engine so it would run without gas," Lyle said. "They can make people do whatever they say. They can even make them kill themselves if they try to stop the aliens."

"That was on *Roswell*," Wade said. "A *TV* show."

But Lyle went right on, "They can make their ships invisible and make people forget they were abducted. They can alter time at will."

Francie expected Wade to say, "You have definitely been watching too many movies," but he didn't. He was staring at the road ahead, lost in thought as he drove.

"Or," Lyle continued, "he could have connected the car to a tractor-beam, like in *Star Wars,* and it's pulling us toward their secret underground base."

"We are not being pulled by a tractor beam," Francie said.

"You only think that because you've been hypnotized by the chemtrails."

I refuse to ask him what chemtrails are, Francie thought, but she didn't need to. He went right ahead without her.

"The aliens drop hallucinogenic drugs from the sky to hypnotize us and keep us from being aware of their presence. You think they're just the contrails from airplanes, but—"

"Indy, shut Lyle up again," Francie said, and the alien immediately removed his pointer tentacle from the dashboard and slid it toward Lyle.

"Fine, if you don't want to know," Lyle said, and subsided, and they drove several miles in silence.

Then Wade said, "I've been thinking, based on what happened to Lyle back there—and that rattlesnake—that it's obvious we're *not* going to be able to escape from Indy. He's just too fast. And even if we did manage to contact the police, it'd end up with them being abducted, too. Or with all of us getting shot. And even if it didn't, and they believed us, which I doubt, they'd insist on calling in the FBI, and I think you're right, Indy's got a deadline of some kind, and if the authorities got involved, Indy would never make it in time."

"What happened to 'Desperate people do desperate things'" she asked, "and 'We don't know what Indy might do if we can't get him where he needs to go'?"

"We know he's not dangerous," Wade said. "He's proved that because, one, he saved your life, and, two, he hasn't killed Lyle, even though he's had more than enough reasons to."

"The only reason he saved your life was so he could plant a hybrid alien-human in you," Lyle said.

"See what I mean?" Wade said to Francie. "Indy's clearly got the patience of a saint. You were right that we should try and help him."

"*Help* him?" Lyle yelped from the back seat. "What if he's trying to invade Earth? Or destroy it? You're going to help him blow up the planet?"

"If we find out where it is he's trying to get," Wade went on imperturbably, "we can get him there in time to help his injured crewman or whatever he's trying to do, and he'll be so grateful he'll let us go."

"There's a word for people like you!" Lyle shouted. "It's 'traitor'!"

"And if the Feds show up, we can tell them what's going on and keep them from shooting Indy."

"You're traitors to your own planet!" Lyle shrieked. "To your own species!"

"Besides, we owe it to the little guy," Wade argued. "After all, he saved your life. And I'd want somebody to help me if *I* was in trouble."

"Mm-hmm," Francie said skeptically. "So you want to do this out of the goodness of your heart? It has nothing to do with the fact that this no-fuel thing of Indy's might revolutionize the car industry and make you a fortune?"

"Of course not," he said, turning wide eyes on her. "I can't believe you'd suspect me of such a thing. I want to do this purely to help Indy—and solve the climate change problem. But, hey, if I can make a little money on the side, what's wrong with that? After all, it's Indy's fault I wasn't able to get to Roswell to sell my anti-abduction insurance policies. And anyway, we don't really have a choice when it comes to turning him in. He's made it obvious he won't let us, *and* he won't let us get away. But if we help him, we might get this over faster and you might be able to make it to your wedding on time."

"There's just one thing wrong with your plan," she said. "Even if we don't try to alert the authorities, they'll still be looking for us. Serena will have definitely called the police by now. They'll have an APB out for us."

"We'll just have to stay out of their way, then."

"If Indy'll let us," she said doubtfully.

"Don't worry," he said. "So far he's taken back roads, and it's a big state, with thousands of miles of road for the Highway Patrol to cover."

"But Serena will have given them a description of her car and its license plate number."

"So the next time we stop, we change it."

"With what?"

"Mud, if we come across any water. Or duct tape if Indy lets us stop at another gas station, or preferably at someplace bigger, where there are lots of people and they won't be so likely to notice us. Especially you in that dress."

"You don't know the half of it," she said, and when he looked questioningly at her, "My dress lights up after dark."

He shook his head, laughing. "Of course it does. You might know—" he began, and stopped and then went on, "So then we really need to get you something else to wear. Maybe we can convince Indy to stop at one of those big trading posts that sell T-shirts and moccasins."

"I doubt if we can convince him to stop anywhere after what happened at the gas station," Francie said. "What were you going to say before, when you said, 'You might know'?"

"What? Oh, nothing. Just that you might know everything that could go wrong would. Like your dress. You couldn't possibly be wearing something ordinary that wouldn't stand out to the cops. And the clerk at that gas station couldn't possibly have been behind the counter like he was supposed to be."

"And Indy couldn't possibly stick to the back roads like you hoped," Francie said, pointing through the windshield at the highway entrance sign ahead.

"Maybe he just wants us to cross it," Wade said hopefully, but Indy's pointer tentacle ordered him to turn onto it.

"No, Indy," Francie said. "We need to stay on the little roads. If we go on the big road, the police will grab you and keep you from going where you want to go. We need to get off at the next exit," but her words didn't have any effect at all. He continued to point steadily west.

"It's okay," Wade said, getting on the highway. "We're more likely to find one of those big trading posts this way. See? What did I tell you?" He pointed at a yellow billboard that said STOP AT THUNDERBIRD TRADING POST 22 MILES AHEAD.

Francie wondered why he wasn't more concerned about taking the highway. There was lots of traffic, especially semis with CB radios to call the Highway Patrol with, and lots of them listened in on the police bands. They'd hear the APB that had to be out on Serena's car by now.

But all Wade seemed interested in was the line of Thunderbird Trading Post billboards. "Look at that!" he said, pointing at one with a picture of a silver necklace with blue-green stones and the words GENUINE TURQUOISE JEWELRY!

"What do you want with a turquoise necklace?" Francie said.

"Not the necklace," Wade said. "Underneath it." He jabbed his finger at the next sign, which read GENUINE INDIAN MOCCASINS! and had a picture of fringed and beaded slippers. "Look at the bottom."

"Seventeen miles ahead?"

"No. Next to that. 'Tour Buses Welcome.'"

"You're going to try to steal a tour bus?"

He looked at her incredulously. "*No*. Why would we steal a tour bus?"

"You said we needed a bigger vehicle."

"I didn't mean . . . no, the fact that tour buses are welcome means this trading post place is big, and there'll be lots of cars there, which means one more won't be noticeable."

It also means there'll be lots of people there for Indy to abduct, she thought, *and then we* **will** *need a bigger boat.*

"And if it's big, it'll have duct tape we can change the license plate with," he said. "And food."

"The alien won't let us stop," Lyle said from the back seat. "That's why he altered the engine, so we couldn't use stopping for gas as a way to escape!"

"Hush," Wade said. "Indy, there's a place up ahead where we need to stop. You know how Francie told you the car couldn't go without fuel? Well, humans need fuel, too."

"Don't tell him that!" Lyle said, agitated. "What if he does the same thing to our insides that he did to the engine? Or plants something in there? Like in *Alien*?"

"Indy's not going to plant anything inside us," Francie said.

"As I was saying," Wade went on to Indy, "humans need fuel, too. It's called food, and we can't function without it. See?" he said, taking his hand off the steering wheel to point at the next billboard, which showed a plate of bacon and eggs that made Francie salivate. "Food."

Indy's only response was to jab his tentacle at the windshield.

"You try, Francie," he said. "Tell him we need to stop at the trading post to get some food. Look, there's a billboard with an ice cream cone on it you can use."

"Yes, and it says 'Ice cream, 10¢,'" she said. "That sign's got to be fifty years old. How do you know this place is still open and not a ghost town like Zopilote?"

"It's not," Wade said, pointing at the next sign, which said FREE WI-FI. "It's still there."

"But what if it's empty like the gas station?" Lyle said. "What if the aliens have abducted everybody? Or killed them all, like in *War of the Worlds*?"

"Then we won't have to pay for the moccasins," Wade said, and to Francie, "Tell him it's imperative we stop. He seems to understand you better than he does me."

She wasn't at all sure of that, but she said, "Indy, if we don't get food, we can't help you. We can't drive you where you want to go." She pointed at the next sign, which had a hot dog on it. "People food."

No response.

"We *have* to stop. We need to get food," she said, hoping the next billboard would have a slice of pizza or something, but it didn't. It had a Navajo pot and read GENUINE INDIAN POTTERY, and the next one proclaimed FIREWORKS! followed by a succession of signs advertising Kachina dolls, cowboy boots, Route 66 souvenirs, and clean restrooms. They were only a mile from the trading post when she finally saw a sign with a picture of, thank goodness, a steaming cup of coffee. Coffee wasn't strictly food, but it would have to do.

"Food!" Francie said. "*Please* stop!" and when there was still no response from Indy, she went on, "We promise we won't try to escape or to contact anybody. We just need to get something to eat," and her desperation must have gotten through to him because Indy moved his tentacle to point to the turnoff to the trading post, flanked by a billboard with a giant arrow pointing to it and the words YOU'RE HERE!

Wade took the exit before Indy could change his mind. "You're a genius," he said, turning onto the road to the trading post. "I could kiss you! I didn't think he'd buy it."

He pulled into the parking lot, and he was right, the Thunderbird

Trading Post was big—a huge red building with a giant thunderbird kachina on its flat roof, a dozen gas pumps out front, and acres of parking marked Cars, RVs, and Tour Buses, where a bus emblazoned with CITIES OF GOLD CASINO was in the process of disgorging a number of elderly people.

But except for the bus, a semi getting gas, and a couple of cars parked out front, the huge lot was empty. Wade parked in front of the side door. "Do you think this is a good idea?" Francie said, pointing at the bus passengers, who looked like they were heading for the same door. "Indy might grab—"

"You're right," Wade said, and moved the car to a spot halfway between the door and the front of the building.

He shut it off. "Okay, now," he said, "I'll go in first and buy some food, and see if I can find you something to wear so you won't be so noticeable, and then you can go in and use the bathroom."

"I'm going with you," Lyle said, and when Wade objected, Lyle told him, "I've gotta use the bathroom, too."

"Fine. We'll both go in," Wade said. He looked down at the far end of the parking lot where the bus's passengers were approaching the building, and opened his door. "We'll be as fast as we can, Francie." He got out of the car.

A tentacle instantly shot out and pinioned his wrist.

CHAPTER SEVEN

"Welcome to Earth."

—*Independence Day*

"Now what?" Wade said, looking at Francie in dismay.

"He doesn't trust us after the gas station incident," she said. "Indy, you've got to let Wade go so he can go inside and get us food," but he kept the tentacle where it was.

"Wade won't try to escape," she said. "I promise."

The tentacle tightened.

"Maybe he'll let me go inside," Francie said.

Wade shook his head. "No way. That dress of yours is way too conspicuous. All right," he said to Indy, "you can come with me, but no yanking me back into the car and only one tentacle."

"And we can't leave the car door open," Francie said, and Indy let go of Wade's wrist, stuck the tentacle through the window, and refastened it on Wade's wrist, all with the speed of lightning. Francie expected Wade to start into the trading post, but he was looking thoughtfully at Indy. "He definitely understands what we're saying," he said. "Or at least what *you're* saying."

"Which means you'd better stop talking about probing people and disintegrating them, Lyle," Francie said.

Lyle got out of the car, and Indy immediately slid another tentacle through the window and clamped it around his wrist.

"Talk about *me* being too conspicuous," Francie called after them. "You can't go in there with alien tentacles around your wrists," but as they walked toward the side door, the tentacles narrowed to the circumference and invisibility of fishing line.

She wondered what would happen when they shut the door to the trading post behind them, but that apparently wasn't a problem. The fishing line was thin enough to fit under the door—and sturdy enough to withstand being stepped on by the senior citizens from the casino bus, who were now beginning to reach the door.

I hope they don't trip, she thought, but an elderly man with a walker went right over the tentacles without incident, and so did a large frizzy-haired woman.

She watched the others stream in after them: a thin balding man in a Hawaiian shirt, a man in a blue suit and an Astros baseball cap, a tiny white-haired woman in a print housedress and a straw hat emblazoned with a pair of sequined dice.

A tan-colored car with a government logo pulled into the parking lot, and a minute later two men in khaki uniforms and sunglasses got out and walked toward her.

Oh, no, Francie thought, pushing Indy down and ducking down herself as they went by her and in the side door. *The Highway Patrol. Or ICE agents,* and she was relieved to see Wade and Lyle coming out the side door with a yellow Thunderbird Trading Post bag, which Wade thrust at Francie.

"Here are your clothes," he said glumly.

"What's wrong?" Francie asked. "Didn't they have any duct tape to disguise the license plate with?"

"No," he said, "and I didn't get a map, either. The clerk didn't even know what I was talking about. She asked me why I didn't use my phone. The closest thing I could find was this kids' map, *Fun Things to Do in New Mexico*." He pulled it out of the bag.

"What about the food? They had food, didn't they?"

"Yes, but I couldn't get it, thanks to Lyle here. I caught him writing *Help! I've been abducted by aliens!* in soap on the men's room mirror and had to get him out of there before he did anything else." He shoved Lyle into the back seat.

"I'm not going to stand by and let aliens take over our planet!" Lyle said.

"Tie him up, Indy," Wade ordered the alien. "Francie, get changed." He pointed to the bag.

"Wait," she said. "I saw some police officers go inside just before you came out."

"I saw them," Wade said. "They're not cops. They're Border Patrol agents. They're looking for another kind of alien."

"But if there's an APB out on us, they'd have been notified, wouldn't they?"

"That's possible," Wade said, "which is why you need to get changed before they spot that bridesmaid's dress."

"Maid of honor," she said absently and opened the bag. Inside were a pair of denim short-shorts, a hot pink tank top, and a pair of beaded turquoise moccasins.

"The only other shoes they had were fishing waders and flip-flops," Wade said apologetically, "and I figured if we ended up in the desert again . . ."

She pulled out the tank top. It had a rhinestone-studded flying saucer on it and the words I WAS ABDUCTED BY ALIENS, AND ALL I GOT WAS THIS LOUSY TANK TOP.

"You thought this was less conspicuous than my dress?"

"Yeah. Nobody who'd actually been abducted would go around wearing that. I brought you a scarf, too, to tie back your hair with so you won't match the APB description," he said, and when she didn't start taking off her dress, he asked, "What are you waiting for? Get dressed."

"I'm not changing with you standing there gawking," she said. "Go get the food or something. And take Lyle with you."

"And let him start hollering 'Help!' to the Border Patrol? No way," and when Francie continued to look stubborn, he went on, "How about if I just have Indy blindfold him?"

"No. What if the Border Patrol comes out and sees him and then comes over to ask me what's going on?"

"Fine," Wade said. "But hurry. We need to get out of here. Indy, let Lyle go." He came around and opened Lyle's door. "And no more escape attempts, or I'll tell Indy to wrap you up for good." He yanked Lyle out of the car. Indy wound a tentacle around Lyle's wrist again, and Wade got a tight grip on his arm and marched him toward the side door.

As soon as their backs were turned, Francie reached back to undo her dress. She couldn't reach the zipper. It was too low on her neck to get to. She tried reaching around from the side, but it was still out of reach.

"Wade, wait!" she called through the open window. "I need you to unzip me." She twisted around on the seat as he returned so her back was to him and lifted her hair up off her neck.

Wade leaned in the window. "Don't get any ideas, Indy." He unzipped her. "There. Anything else I can help you with?"

"No," she said, letting her hair drop. "Go."

He grabbed Lyle by the arm again, and they disappeared through the side door, followed by several more passengers from the casino bus. Francie waited till they'd all hobbled inside and then gave a quick look around to make sure no other vehicles were pulling in, grabbed the tank top, and slipped her dress off her shoulders.

And was hit by a whirling tornado of tentacles beating at her shoulders and neck. She gasped at the sudden violence of the attack. "Indy! What are you—? Stop!" she said, instinctively putting up her hands to ward him off. "What are you *doing*?" but he was beyond hearing her.

He was lashing out wildly, blindly, his tentacles flying every which way, a whirling cloud of stinging whips. "Indy, what's wrong?" she cried, trying to shield her face and body from the whipping tentacles yanking at her dress.

No wonder abductees thought the aliens were probing them, she thought, grateful that Lyle wasn't here to see this.

"What *is* it?" she cried, trying to grab one of his tentacles to get his attention. "Tell me what's the matter. Are you sick? Are you hurt? Did you see something that scared you? It's all right! Nobody's going to hurt you!"

That produced even more frantic flailing, his tendrils wrapping around one another, tangling up, weaving together. He was literally tying himself in knots, poor thing. *Oh my God,* she thought. *He* **was** *bitten by the rattlesnake and now he's dying!*

"Did the snake hurt you? Where did he bite you?" she said, trying to get a look at the flying tentacles, then realized suddenly that his movements weren't random.

They were aimed at her chest, and at her dress. Indy was frantically trying to pull the top of it up over her, pushing the sides of the zipper together and, when they fell away, attempting to wrap tentacles around them to hold them in place.

He's trying to put my dress back on me, she thought, and then, a little hysterically, *Please don't tell me you like this awful dress. I thought you came from an advanced civilization.*

"Okay, okay, I'll put it back on," she said, but she couldn't because his frenetic movements were taking the bodice out of her hands as she tried to get her arm back in the armhole and pushing it against her.

"Indy, I can't get it back on if you don't let go of it," she said, tugging the bodice out of his grip.

His tentacles went wild, whipping everywhere, trying desperately to put the fabric back against her skin.

Oh my God! she thought, suddenly enlightened. *He thinks the dress is part of me.*

He'd never seen her except in the dress. He thought it was part of her body, that her skin was peeling off her. "No, Indy, no," she said. "It's not me. It's just a dress. Clothes. I'm not hurt. I'm fine. These are my *clothes.*"

He was still trying to reattach the bodice to her chest, winding tendrils around both sides and attempting to tie them together.

He must not ever have seen clothes, she thought. "Clothes. We wear them." She needed to show him. She held up the tank top and then the jean shorts. "See? Clothes."

No response. Indy's tentacles went on knotting themselves up into an impossible tangle in his distress at being unable to get the dress back on her.

He clearly didn't get the connection she was trying to make. And why should he? Neither the tank top nor the shorts looked anything like her dress. And she didn't have another dress to show him.

Wade's duffel bag. Maybe if she showed him a shirt like the one Wade was wearing, he'd recognize it as something Wade had worn and make the connection. She grabbed up the bag, unzipped it, and began rummaging through it.

Yes, he had a shirt, thank goodness, and it was just like the one he'd worn into the store. Francie pulled it out and, fending off Indy's flying tentacles, showed it to him. "See? Clothes. Not Wade. Clothes. They're not part of us. They're separate."

He didn't stop his whirling tentacles, but he did reach forward with a tendril to touch the shirt's sleeve, and his thrashing around seemed to slow a little.

"Yes, that's Wade's shirt. Clothes." She touched her skirt. "And this is my dress. My clothes. We wear them to protect—" *No, better not say "to protect us from getting hurt."*

"To cover our bodies," she finished. "And then we take them off because they're dirty," (though Wade's shirt looked perfectly clean) "or because we want to put on other clothes."

The flailing stopped, and Indy let go of the bodice and began fingering the tank top.

"We wear different clothes for different occasions," Francie said, pulling her dress down over her hips, wriggling out of it, and holding it up. "See, I'm not hurt. I'm fine. Body." She pointed at her bare midriff and then at her dress. "Clothes."

She took off her high-heeled sandals and pointed at them and then her bare feet. "Clothes. Body."

Which didn't cover the issue of underwear, but she didn't have time to get into that now. "These clothes," she said, holding the dress out to Indy, "are for going to a wedding, and these," she held up the tank top and shorts, "are for going in the car with you."

She pulled on the shorts, which were ridiculously short and tight. *No wonder Indy thinks clothes are skin,* she thought, reaching for the hot pink tank top. It was just as tight as the shorts and cut far too low. She wished she could put on Wade's shirt instead, but she didn't dare risk it, even though Indy had seemed to understand her explanation. Who knew what else he didn't understand? He might think she'd turned into Wade or eaten him or something.

She put Wade's shirt back in the duffel bag, reached for the moccasins, and then stopped. Indy's wild lashing had begun again.

Oh, now what? she thought, and then saw that now the flailing was an attempt to undo the knots he'd gotten his tentacles into while he was so upset, but it wasn't working. He was only making them worse.

"Don't," she said, putting the moccasins down and pulling him onto her lap. "Here, let me see."

His tentacles were in a hopeless snarl. "Let me untangle you. Hold still." She began working on the largest of the knots, gently untangling the tendrils. There was no question they were part of *his* body because he flinched occasionally when she tugged too hard. But he made no sound.

He must not be able to, Francie thought, because if he could, he'd definitely have cried out when she took off her dress. He'd clearly been hysterical at that point. But except for the whoosh of his whipping tentacles and the slap of them against her skin, he'd remained utterly silent. *So how on earth is he going to be able to communicate with us?*

It took her several minutes to finish undoing the knots. "There, all done," she said. She jammed her dress and the high-heeled sandals into the duffel bag on top of Wade's shirt, and picked up the pink scarf Wade had bought. She twisted her hair into a ponytail, and Indy immediately began flailing again.

"No, no," she said. "Stop." She pointed to her hair. "Body." She held the scarf out to him. "Clothes. Understand?"

Apparently not. She had to take him through the whole litany again, which took so long she was still tying her hair back when Wade opened the door.

He was carrying a bag of hamburgers, a molded cardboard tray of drinks, and a small plastic bag. "It's taken you all this time to get dressed?" he said, handing her the tray.

"Long story," she said, knotting the scarf, but he wasn't listening. He was looking at the open duffel bag.

"What were you doing in my bag?" he demanded.

"I was selling anti-abduction insurance to the Border Patrol, what do you think?" she snapped. "I was trying to explain the concept of clothes to Indy. When I tried to take my dress off, he freaked out. He thought my skin was peeling off or I was mutilating myself or something."

"Oh," he said. "Lyle, there goes your theory about aliens mutilating cows." He reached over her to zip up the duffel bag. "Your turn to go in. Lyle and I'll see what we can do with the license plate while you're gone."

"They had duct tape after all?"

"Nope, but they had masking tape and Magic Markers. You'd better hurry if you want to beat the geezers to the bathroom." He nodded at a couple of gray-haired women heading for the door.

She nodded, bent over to put on the moccasins Wade had bought, and saw Lyle staring open-mouthed at her tank top, or, rather, the lack of it. "You need to give me some money," she said to Wade.

"What for?"

"So I can buy a tank top that fits."

"We don't have time," Wade said, "and besides, that was the best of the bunch. The others all said 'Ride Me, Cowboy.'"

"I'll bet," she said, and held out her hand for the money.

He handed her a twenty. "Now go."

She went. "You look great, by the way," Wade called after her and then, "The restrooms are in the far corner of the building, past the cowboy boots. And no, we don't have time for you to take a shower."

In what? The bathroom sink? she wondered, hurrying across the hot pavement. And if she'd thought that Indy's panicked concern that she was hurt and that little detangling session meant Indy trusted her now, she was wrong. One of his unknotted tendrils whipped out and fastened itself around her wrist before she was halfway to the door.

But it was far less conspicuous than the getup she was wearing. When she held the door for the women with her non-tethered hand, they gave her disapproving looks, and she could have sworn she heard a whispered "Hussy!" amid their discussion of how they needed to hurry if they didn't want to miss the bus.

Not that they *did* hurry—they were *very* slow going through the door. *Come* **on**, Francie thought, looking longingly past them at the sign for the restrooms. Wade hadn't told her she would have to cross several acres of aisles filled with Navajo blankets, beaded belts, NRA bumper stickers, picture postcards, toy bow-and-arrow sets, Stetsons, strings of red chiles, agate bookends—not to mention rattlesnake ashtrays, rattlesnake-skin boots, rattlesnake travel mugs, and rattlesnake Christmas ornaments—but thankfully no people except a trio of seniors from the bus headed toward the restrooms.

She recognized one of them, the tiny woman with the dice-covered straw hat. She was carrying a tote bag with a sequined array of cards and the slogan LUCK BE A LADY TONIGHT on it, and she was talking to another woman in a T-shirt with LAS VEGAS OR BUST written across the chest, who was maneuvering her walker through the racks and racks of clothes between them and the door marked Restrooms.

There has to be something better than this tank top among all these clothes, Francie thought. But first things first. She made a bee-line for the restrooms, or as much of a beeline as possible considering Indy's tether. She didn't want to snag it on a Native American suncatcher or a longhorn belt buckle. Or a Roman candle. There were even more fireworks here than there were rattlesnake souvenirs.

But even though Indy's tentacle remained tightly around her wrist, the leash slackened as she turned corners and threaded be-

tween clothing racks, letting her move almost as if she wasn't tethered at all.

After what seemed like several miles, she made it to the restrooms. Next to the door marked Gals was one marked Showers,
which explained Wade's comment. In spite of what he'd said, she
stood there a moment, calculating whether she could get away with
a super-quick shower, just a quick soap-and-rinse.

No, better not risk it, she decided. The touch of water on Indy's
tentacle might freak him out like her undressing had. Or it might be
poison to him, like those movie aliens Lyle had talked about. And
besides, she wasn't sure that, wet, she'd be able to get back in these
shorts. Plus, she didn't have time to have a shower *and* buy a new
shirt. And some less indecent shorts.

After using the restroom, she hurried through the rattlesnake
area to the clothing racks and began flipping through the array of
T-shirts for something, anything that would cover more of her and
that was less garish than what she was currently wearing.

She owed Wade an apology—every shirt she found was either
gaudy or obscene, and often both. They were neon-colored,
rhinestone-studded, and emblazoned with Confederate flags, striking rattlesnakes, automatic rifles, and, of course, the RIDE ME, COW-
BOY! Wade had mentioned, as well as a HARLEY-DAVIDSON GALS DO
IT ON A MOTORCYCLE and SEXY BABE and MEN IN BLACK—WHEN IT
ABSOLUTELY HAS TO BE COVERED UP OVERNIGHT.

The Hawaiian shirts two racks over weren't any better: beer bot-
tles, naked women, Bowie knives, zombies, none of which Francie
wanted to have to explain to Indy. And the rack past that was all
black leather Harley-Davidson halter tops.

Surely there were other shirts somewhere. She looked up toward
the front of the store and saw two police officers standing just inside
the door, looking purposefully around. And these two weren't Border Patrol agents.

Francie grabbed a T-shirt and a cowboy hat at random and
headed toward the door marked Fitting Rooms. And ran straight
into the white-haired woman with the dice-covered straw hat.

"Do you mind if I ask your opinion?" she said, pulling Francie over to a counter full of cactus. "I don't know which to buy." She picked up two of them. "Which one do you think?"

"I don't know," Francie said. There was a tall rack of sunglasses between them and the police officers, and she was grateful for its concealing height. And for the cover the woman's talking to her was giving her. Who could suspect someone when they were with such a sweet, harmless-looking old lady?

Francie put her tethered hand casually behind her back and said, "They're both nice."

"I *know*," the woman said. "This one has a bloom, but *this* one's a prickly pear. I like its big round pads, just like a mouse's ears, except for the thorns. Which one do you think?"

"Mmm," Francie said noncommittally, sneaking a glance around the sunglasses rack. The officers were still standing by the door. One of them said something to the other, and they started resolutely in her direction.

"I'm terrible at making decisions," the woman was saying. "Everybody says so. 'Eula Mae,' they say, 'honestly, it takes you an hour to decide which slot machine to play,' and they're right! Could you hold them so I can compare them, dear?" she asked, and before Francie could think of an excuse, Eula Mae grabbed the T-shirt and cowboy hat out of her hands, dumped them next to the sunglasses rack, and thrust the two cacti at her.

Please don't let her notice Indy's tentacle, Francie prayed, taking the cacti from her, but the woman was totally focused on the plants.

"I like this pot better," the woman said, squinting at them, "but I like this color better."

"They're over here," one of the police officers said, and Francie's heart nearly stopped. She glanced at the side door, wondering if she should make a break for it, but her hands were full of cacti, Eula Mae was standing in her way, and if Indy's leash caught on the prickly pear's thorns—

"Jesus, they're miles away," the other officer said, and Francie's heart began to beat again. They were heading for the bathrooms, not her, and they passed her and Eula Mae without a glance.

Eula Mae was still talking. "And I tell them, I *like* to take my time deciding. Like at the casino. I go to casinos all the time, but I don't just walk in and sit down at the first slot machine I see. I like to make sure it's a lucky one. I wish I could do that with these cacti, but I don't have time. 'Be back on the bus in fifteen minutes or I'm leaving without you,' Jerry—that's our driver—says, and he means it. The driver we had before him, Raoul, always made sure everybody was back on, and if somebody was missing, he'd wait for them."

The officers had disappeared. *And I need to disappear, too, before they come back out,* Francie thought. "I think you should definitely buy the prickly pear," she said because the hand she was holding it in was the one without the tether, but Eula Mae was still talking. "Raoul knew some of us oldsters can't move very fast, and he took that into account, but not Jerry. Fifteen minutes, and he just shuts that door and goes."

The police officers would be out any minute. *I need to go before they spot me or Eula Mae spots my tether,* Francie thought, glancing down at her wrist—and realized to her horror that Indy's tentacle was no longer wrapped around it.

How long had it been gone? And what did it mean? Had something happened to Indy? Were there other officers outside? What if they'd seen Wade altering the license plate? Or worse, seen Indy?

"Mr. Dunn, he's one of our regulars, has prostate problems," Eula Mae was saying, "and it always takes him a long time in the bathroom, and last week Jerry just went off and *left* him! He had to take a taxi home. It cost him half his Social Security check and—"

"I have to go," Francie said, thrusting the cacti abruptly at Eula Mae, and shot across the miles of merchandise toward the side door. What if they'd tried to arrest Wade, and Indy'd thought they were hurting him and gone into his whirling dervish routine? What if they had guns and—

She pushed the door open and ran outside into the parking lot. There was no sign of the police.

Or of the car.

CHAPTER EIGHT

"You're gonna need a bigger boat."

—Jaws

For an endless minute, Francie simply stood there on the hot pavement and stared at the spot where the Navigator had been. It couldn't be gone. But it was.

They went off and left me, she thought. Sending her inside had been a setup, and all Wade's talk about not turning Indy over to the authorities and trying to help him get to where he was going had been a blind. And their stopping here hadn't been to disguise the license plate and get a change of clothes for her, but to get rid of her so he could take Indy to Roswell and exhibit him at the UFO Festival. And once she was safely inside and out of Indy's reach, he'd taken off in the Navigator.

But that couldn't be what had happened. She hadn't been out of Indy's reach, she'd been attached to him, and when he saw what Wade was doing, he'd have kept him from driving away.

Unless something had happened to him. Or to all of them. *The Border Patrol,* she thought, her heart beginning to pound, but their car was still parked where it had been, and the two Border Patrol officers were still inside the trading post. And the passengers were getting on the casino bus as if nothing had happened. If they'd seen an arrest, wouldn't they be standing around talking about it?

Maybe Wade had driven around to the other side of the building to keep the Border Patrol—or the police, or both—from spotting them.

She ran around to the front to see, and there, parked three spaces away from a Highway Patrol car, was the Navigator. What on earth did Wade think he was doing? The cops could come out of the building any minute.

We've got to get out of here, she thought, and flung the car door open. "You scared me to death," she said. "I thought—"

There was no one in the Navigator. The bag of food Wade had bought still sat on the back seat. The cardboard tray of cups had been knocked over, and coffee was spilled all over the seat.

Oh, no, she thought. There must have been more than one Highway Patrol car, and the cops had taken them into custody and driven off with them.

But how? Indy wouldn't have let himself be captured without a fight. He'd have grabbed the cops just like he had them. Unless they'd shot him.

But I'd have heard a shot, she told herself, trying to keep her panic at bay. *Or a siren.*

She leaned into the car, looking for clues to what had happened. The car keys weren't in the ignition. She checked the floor and under the front seats, but they weren't there, either. Which meant Wade had taken them with him.

But not his duffel bag, which lay on the floor of the back seat. It was halfway unzipped. Could Wade have hidden Indy in it when he saw they were going to be arrested? She pulled it out of the car, set it on the hood, and unzipped it the rest of the way. Wade's blue shirt was inside, though not her maid-of-honor dress and shoes, which meant the cops must have gone through the bag and Indy couldn't be inside, but she began to search through it anyway, pulling out Wade's shirt and the anti-abduction insurance policies to see if he was under—

"Miss? Miss?" a voice called from the corner of the building Francie had just come around, and Francie looked up, startled.

It was Eula Mae, the woman who'd wanted to know which cactus she should buy. She was carrying her LUCK BE A LADY TONIGHT tote bag and the T-shirt and cowboy hat she'd grabbed from Francie when she'd thrust the cacti at her. "You left these in the store," she called, and trotted over to the car.

"Oh, I'm so glad I caught you," she said, out of breath. "You forgot your purchases."

I didn't purchase them, Francie thought in a panic, hastily jamming Wade's shirt back in the duffel bag and zipping it up. *This is all I need, to be arrested for shoplifting.*

She looked anxiously past Eula Mae, expecting to see an irate clerk storming around the corner, no doubt with the cops for backup, but the only thing coming was an enormous black recreation vehicle, nearly the size of the casino bus, lumbering toward the gas pumps.

"Here," Eula Mae said, holding out the T-shirt and cowboy hat. "I felt so guilty. I was the one who made you set your things down, and I know how easy it is to forget things. One time at the Cities of Gold Casino I went off and left a stuffed toy I'd won at blackjack. It was a pink chihuahua, and it was the cutest little thing. It had a poker chip for an I.D. tag."

"Don't you need to be getting on your bus?" Francie said desperately. "I saw they were loading."

"Oh, I've got time," Eula Mae said carelessly. "So, anyway, I set the chihuahua on top of the slot machine while I got something out of my purse—"

I've got to get rid of her so I can find out what happened to Wade and Indy, Francie thought frantically. And the only way to do that was to accept the clothes even though she hadn't bought them.

"Thank you," she said, taking the hat and the T-shirt. "I really appreciate it." She laid them on the back seat and picked up the duffel bag, "but I'm kind of in a hurry—"

Eula Mae wasn't listening. "I forgot about it till I was halfway home on the bus," she prattled on, "and the next day as soon as I got to the casino, I asked about it— Oh, my!"

"What?" Francie said, alarmed.

"That RV," Eula Mae said, pointing at the black recreation vehicle, which had OUTLAW painted across its side in bright red letters and which was pulling into the gas station's island. "That's never going to make it under there." She pointed at the roof of the island. "It's too tall."

The driver of the RV seemed to have realized it, too. It slowed to a crawl, its side door opened, and two metal steps unfolded onto the pavement.

"Oh, good," Eula Mae said, "the driver's making somebody get out to check the height," and a swarm of tentacles lashed out from the open door.

It was exactly like the other times—Francie was grabbed and pulled into the RV without touching the steps, so fast she had no time to process what was happening. But this time Indy must have misjudged the distance or been thrown off by the RV's movement because Francie landed sprawled awkwardly on the floor in front of the RV's door on top of Wade's duffel bag, her face buried in rust-colored carpet.

Which is what I deserve for acting like a teenager, she thought silently, because her first thought at the sound of Wade's voice above her asking, "Are you okay?" had been pure joy. *He didn't go off and leave me,* she'd thought giddily. *He came back!* Even though that was patently ridiculous. Indy was the one who'd yanked her aboard. Wade hadn't had anything to do with it. It was idiotic to be so glad to see him.

"Are you okay?" Wade asked, squatting down beside her.

"No," she said, raising herself onto her elbows. "I came out and saw the car was gone and thought you'd gone off without me—"

"Never," he said, and she felt another ridiculous surge of happiness.

"I thought I'd better do what I could to make the car less recognizable, and I didn't think it was a good idea to do it with the Border Patrol likely to come out that door any minute, so I moved the car around, but—"

The RV gave another lurch as it backed up and then drove out of the parking lot, knocking Wade off-balance and sending Francie sprawling again. "But while I was getting out the masking tape to change the license plate," he said, fighting to keep his balance as the RV pulled onto the highway, "Indy apparently decided we'd be better off with another vehicle altogether."

"An *RV*?" Francie said incredulously. "With 'Outlaw' scrawled on its side? How exactly does that make us less conspicuous?"

"I guess Indy can't read," Wade said, and for the first time since Francie met him, he sounded rattled. He'd taken being abducted and then running out of gas completely in stride, but now he seemed apprehensive and unnerved.

He must think this is going to get us picked up by the Highway Patrol, she thought. *And we obviously can't outrun them in a lumbering RV.*

"Where is he?" Francie asked Wade.

"Up front." He extended his hand to help her up. "Unfortunately, he didn't give me—or Lyle—any advance warning of his little plan, which means everything we had, except your maid-of-honor dress and shoes, which for some reason he decided to bring along, is still in the car," he said, sounding genuinely upset, "including our lunch. And my duffel bag."

"Your duffel bag isn't in the car," she said. "It's right here." She took his offered hand. "I'm lying on it."

"You're kidding!" he said, pulling her to her feet. He snatched up the bag and hugged her—and it—to him. "This is great! I was afraid . . . You're wonderful!"

"Don't thank me, thank Indy," she said, rubbing her middle. "He grabbed me while I was talking to—" *Oh my gosh, Eula Mae!* She'd forgotten all about her.

"Wade," she said urgently, "we've got a problem. I was talking to somebody when Indy pulled me on board. If she saw that, she'll tell the police. There were two of them in the store. If she tells them—"

"She won't," he said and pointed behind Francie at the fringed buckskin couch on the other side of the RV. Eula Mae was sitting on it, clutching her tote bag to her like a shield. She looked wary, but not frightened.

Which means she didn't see Indy when he yanked her aboard, Francie thought, *and maybe we can tell her . . . something . . . and get her back to her casino bus with no harm done.*

"Eula Mae," she said, going over to her, "I am *so* sorry. This is all a big mistake. We'll get you back to your bus and—"

"Bus?" Wade cut in.

"Yes, she was on the Cities of Gold Casino bus."

"Jesus," he said. "They'll realize she's missing and call the police!"

"Shh, you're making it sound like we're kidnappers," Francie said, sitting down next to her. "Eula Mae, we're not criminals."

"Then who are you?" Eula Mae asked. "The Feds?"

"The *Feds*?" Francie said and looked up at Wade, who seemed as taken aback as she was.

"The Feds?" he repeated.

"Yes," Eula Mae said to him. "The Justice Department. The FBI. You obviously drugged me or tased me or—"

"No, he's not the FBI," Francie said. "Unfortunately. He's just someone who happened to be in the wrong place at the wrong time. Like you," she said, and realized too late that that sounded like Eula Mae had witnessed a crime and now they were going to rub her out or something.

"I mean, Indy picked you up by mistake," she said. "It was me he meant to take. Don't worry. Everything will be okay. I'll get him to take you back." She stood up. "You said he was up front?" she asked Wade.

"Yeah," he said. He jerked his head toward the front of the RV. "Telling the owner of this rig which way to go."

"The *owner*?" Francie said. "Oh, no, don't tell me he's abducted him, too?"

"'Fraid so. And I doubt if Indy intends to let either of them go."

"Where's Lyle?" Francie asked.

"He's up front with the driver, too."

Worse and worse. "He'll tell him all sorts of crazy things about Indy."

"It couldn't be helped. I had to make sure he didn't hurt you yanking you on board, and somebody had to stay with the driver and keep him from freaking out and driving us into the gas pumps. And anyway, we've got more pressing problems than Lyle and his conspiracy theories."

He pulled Francie into the RV's kitchen area, which had a refrigerator, a microwave, and a small pullout table with a Navajo-blanket-covered banquette curved around it like a booth in a diner, and dropped his voice to a whisper. "We need to find out how long we've got before somebody realizes your friend here is missing. If nobody saw you get snatched, that is. Did they?"

"I don't think so. I didn't see anybody, and there weren't any cars at the gas pumps."

"Or any windows in that part of the building," Wade said. "Good." He nodded toward Eula Mae, who was still sitting there, clutching her tote bag. "But even if nobody saw her get snatched, the bus driver will report that she's missing. We've got to get off the highway now." He started toward the front.

"No, wait," Francie whispered, grabbing his arm. "She told me the driver was a total stickler for them getting back on the bus on time, and if they weren't, he just went off and left them to their own devices. She said it's happened before." She told him about the man who'd been late getting back from the bathroom.

"You don't think the driver will go into the trading post and look for her?"

"No."

"Where was the bus? Could the driver or anybody else on the bus have seen what happened?"

"No, they were parked around the corner at the side of the building and all the way at the back."

"Did she have friends on the bus?"

"I don't know. She said she goes to the casino all the time, so probably."

"Well, try to find out. I'll go stow this and then try to convince Indy we need to get off the highway, just in case somebody saw what happened. And try to keep her from freaking out." He picked up the duffel bag and started toward the rear of the RV with it.

"But why do you have to stow—?" Francie began, but the RV lurched again, rolling from side to side, and she had to grab for the wall, and by the time she steadied herself, he'd disappeared.

She went over to Eula Mae, who was still sitting with the tote bag clutched to her. "Kidnapping is a federal offense, you know," Eula Mae said accusingly.

"I know," Francie said, "but this isn't exactly a kidnapping. Did you know anybody on the bus?"

Eula Mae didn't answer. She pursed her lips and stared straight ahead.

Francie tried again. "Were you sitting with someone? Someone who might realize you didn't get back on and would call the police?"

Eula Mae still didn't answer the question. Instead, she asked Francie, "Is Indy the one in charge?"

"Yes, only not the way you think. He's—"

"Holding you hostage," Eula Mae said. She leaned toward Francie. "I have some pepper spray in my purse," she whispered, "if you think that might help."

"No!" Francie said. "You mustn't—"

"Why not? Is he armed?"

Armed? Francie thought hysterically. *Oh, yes, he's definitely armed. He's got arms and arms and more arms.*

"Or are you in on whatever this is with them," Eula Mae whispered, "and that's why you're afraid the police might be after us? And why you want to know if there's anyone on my bus who will report me missing?"

"*Is* there?" Francie asked.

"Well, I'd hardly tell you that, would I, since you seem to be in league with this Indy person."

"He's not a person," Francie said. "He's—" There was no good way to do this. She sat down between Eula Mae and the door in case she tried to fling herself out of the moving RV when Francie told her. "He's an alien. From outer space. He abducted me and Wade and this other guy, Lyle, and now he's abducted you and the driver of this RV, too."

She'd expected Eula Mae to squeal, *A* **space** *alien?* but she didn't. She said, "I'd think if you'd been abducted by an alien, you'd hardly be trying to avoid the police. You'd *want* them to come rescue you."

"I know, and we did at first," Francie said, "but then we realized Indy—the alien—is trying to find something. We think it's his ship, that he's trying to get back to it. So we're trying to help him. If the authorities get hold of him, they'll—"

Eula Mae shook her head. "You sound just like Mr. Walters. He sometimes sits with me on the bus, and he claims he's in contact with aliens from another planet, too. He claims they talk to him through his TV. He has dementia."

"Look," Francie said. "I know you don't believe me, but I'm telling you the truth." She looked toward the back of the RV. Where was Wade? She needed him to back her up. But he was nowhere to be seen.

"I know this all sounds insane," she said, trying again, "but you have to trust me. It's really important that the Feds, as you call them, don't catch us, so you need to tell me if there was anyone on the bus with you who'd be likely to report you missing. Please."

Eula Mae wasn't looking at her. She was looking at Wade, who was coming back. "Thank goodness you're here," Francie said. "I told her about Indy, but she didn't believe me."

"I guess I wouldn't, either," he said cheerfully. "You have to admit it sounds pretty nuts."

Francie stared at Wade. His manner had completely changed. The apprehensiveness he'd shown before was completely gone, and his air of equanimity was back. What was in that duffel bag of his? Tranquilizers? Pot?

But he didn't seem stoned, just calm, as if he'd decided carjacking the *Outlaw,* abducting an old lady, and being followed by the police wasn't a problem after all. "You don't understand," Francie said. "She thinks we're criminals. You need to . . . where are you going *now*?"

"Up front," he said, walking toward the driver's compartment, "to tell them we need to take the next exit."

"But what about Eula Mae?"

"We'll take care of that after we get off the highway and to someplace out of sight."

"Out of sight?" Eula Mae echoed. "Take care of—?"

"He wasn't threatening you," Francie hastened to reassure her. "He—" The giant RV gave a lurch that nearly sent Wade into their laps.

Wade grabbed for the wall to brace himself, and then looked out the window in the door. "It looks like Indy beat me to it," he said. "We're already turning off."

Francie stood up and went over to the window. They were on a dirt road winding through an area of sandy hills dotted thickly with junipers and piñon pines.

The RV pulled off into a flat space surrounded by squat, dark junipers. "Are we out of sight of the highway?" she asked Wade.

"I don't know," he said, and went to look out a window in the back. "Yeah, and from the look of things, out of sight of that dirt road we were just on."

"Oh, good," she said and turned to look at Eula Mae, who was fumbling in her tote bag.

"Look out! She's got pepper spray!" Francie cried, grabbing for her hand.

Eula Mae was faster. She had the pepper spray out and the nozzle pointed at Wade.

But Indy was faster than either of them. A tentacle shot out from the front regions of the RV and snatched the pepper spray out of

Eula Mae's hand as a second one grabbed the latch of the door and opened it so the first tentacle could fling the pepper spray out into the junipers. It closed the door, and both tentacles snapped back like a measuring tape retracting.

"Oh, my!" Eula Mae said, pressing her hand to her chest. "What was that?"

"Indy," Francie said. "I'm so sorry. I should have warned you," but Eula Mae wasn't listening. She was watching Indy as he rolled toward them.

"Oh, my, you were telling the truth," Eula Mae said. "It *is* an alien."

"'Fraid so," Wade said. "Eula Mae, meet Indy, short for Indiana Jones," but she didn't seem to hear him.

She was looking at Indy speculatively. "He's so fast," she murmured. "I'd imagine he could—"

"He won't hurt you," Francie said.

"You don't know that," Lyle said, emerging from the front, followed by a tall, lanky gray-haired man with a handlebar mustache, wearing jeans and cowboy boots.

"Just because he hasn't killed us yet doesn't mean he won't," Lyle said.

"Shh," Francie said. "Indy, you can't keep abducting people like this," but he wasn't listening to her, either. He rolled over to the door, opened it, and tumbled out. "Indy!" she called after him as he rolled off through the junipers.

"Oh, my," Eula Mae said. "Where's he going?"

"To contact the mother ship and tell them he's collected more specimens," Lyle said. "And that he's abducted an RV to keep all of us in while he collects the rest."

"It's not an RV," the mustached man growled. "It's a Western trail wagon."

"And Indy's not going out to contact the mother ship," Francie said. "He's just checking his bearings."

"How do you know that?" Lyle said. "How do you know he's not saying, 'Dinner's ready! Come and get it! They're in the RV—'"

"I *told* you—" the mustached man began.

"It's not an RV, it's a Western trail wagon," Wade said smoothly, "and I can't tell you how grateful we all are for your hospitality. Joseph, I'd like you to meet the rest of our little band. This is Francie Driscoll and Mrs. . . . um, sorry, ma'am, I don't know your last name."

"Teasdale," Eula Mae said.

"And Mrs. Teasdale," Wade said.

"Miss," Eula Mae said.

"It's mighty nice to meet you, Francie," Joseph said, sweeping off his Stetson, "and you, Miss Teasdale, ma'am." He bowed to her.

"Oh, my," she fluttered. "There's no need to be so formal. Call me Eula Mae."

"It's right nice to—"

"This isn't a social occasion," Lyle said disgustedly. "We—"

"Lyle's right," Wade interrupted. "We've got serious matters to discuss." He looked around at their surroundings. "Is there somewhere we could all sit?"

"You're darned tootin' there is," Joseph said. "I've got a table I could set up outside."

"No," Wade said. "I think we'd better stay inside. In case we need to leave in a hurry. What about the table in the kitchen?"

"In the Chuckwagon, you mean?" Joseph said. "It's kinda puny, but I've got a leaf I could put in. It'll just take a minute."

"No, that's all right," Wade said. "We can all fit around it the way it is." He led the way up to the kitchen area.

"Would you ladies like some coffee?" Joseph asked. "I can cook you up some quicker than a jackrabbit."

"No, thank you," Eula Mae said primly. "You wouldn't have any tea, would you?"

"Afraid not."

Too bad. Tea would be appropriate, Francie thought. *After all, this is just like the Mad Hatter's tea party.*

"Or I could rustle up some grub."

Grub, thought Francie longingly, remembering she still hadn't had anything to eat. "That would be—"

"*Grub?*" Lyle exploded. "How can you be thinking of food at a time like this? You've been abducted by an alien, and he's taking us who knows where—"

"Which is what we need to talk about," Wade said, sitting down at the table. "Lyle, sit down. You, too, Joseph. I need to explain what's going on to our new friends."

They squeezed into the banquette, and Wade gave a quick summary of what had happened so far and why they'd decided to help Indy.

"He's obviously looking for something," he explained, "and he obviously has a deadline—"

"You keep sayin' 'obviously,'" Joseph said. "Don't you know?"

"No. We haven't been able to find a way to communicate directly with him—"

"But he understands what we say," Francie said.

"Actually, we're not even sure of that," Wade said. "We're going by his actions and his gestures."

"Sign language," Joseph said, nodding. "Just like the Native American sign language in *Six Gun Trail*. And *Winchester 73*."

"Yes," Wade said. "And we're afraid if the authorities catch up to us before we get him back to his ship, Indy'll try to grab them like he grabbed us and they'll shoot him before we can explain why he's here."

Joseph nodded. "Like in *The Sagebrush Trail,* where they find the son of the Chiricahua chief and are trying to get him back to his father before him being missin' causes a war. You gotta get Lash Larue here where he's goin' before the sheriff and his posse show up."

"Yes," Wade said. "Will you help us?"

"Hell, yeah!" Joseph said. "I been hopin' somethin' excitin' would happen."

Oh, no, Francie thought. *Another UFO nut. That's all we need.*

"I came on this here trip to see the Wild West," Joseph said, "but all I've seen up to now is Walmarts and strip malls. You folks are the first sign of somethin' excitin'."

"What about you, Eula Mae?" Wade asked.

"I suppose so," she said tartly, "though I don't like the idea of breaking the law—"

"We *ain't* breakin' it," Joseph said. "We're just bendin' it a little. Sometimes you got a duty to break the law so's you can help a harmless critter."

"Harmless!" Lyle exploded. "How do you know we won't be helping him take over the Earth and kill every human on it? He's an alien!"

"The Ringo Kid was an outlaw," Joseph shot back, "but that didn't mean he was a bad guy, and when push came to shove, he was what saved the passengers from—"

"What the hell are you talking about?" Lyle demanded.

"*Stagecoach,*" Joseph said.

Lyle looked blankly at him. "Stagecoach? What stagecoach?"

"Don't tell me you've never seen *Stagecoach*? John Wayne? John Ford? What about the rest of you?"

"I've seen it," Francie said.

Eula Mae shook her head.

"The rest of you've gotta see it," Joseph said. "One of the best Westerns ever made. I've got a DVD of it in the Opera House." He started to stand up.

Wade stopped him. "It's about a bunch of people stuck on a stagecoach together. On a trip to Lordsburg, right?"

"Yep, with the Comanches on their tail. There's a prim and proper Army wife"—he indicated Eula Mae—"and a saloon girl"—he pointed at Francie.

I have **got** *to find something else to wear,* Francie thought, glaring at Wade.

"And there's a cowardly whiskey salesman who's scared to death the whole time," Joseph went on, pointing at Lyle. "I figure myself for the grizzled old stage driver."

"And I'm the outlaw, right?" Wade asked. "The Ringo Kid?"

"Hell, no, your alien's the Ringo Kid, with that bullwhip of his. I figure he could twirl a rifle, too, with those tentacles, just like John Wayne."

"Then who do you see me as? The gambler with the heart of gold or the banker who's running off with the bank's money?"

"Neither one. I see you more as the sheriff who decides to ride along to protect the passengers."

"You *do*?" Wade said, and he didn't look happy. Francie thought he was going to ask Joseph why he saw him as the sheriff, but he didn't. "So you see this R . . . Western trail wagon as the stage-coach?" he asked instead.

"Yep, and the cops are the Comanches, and we gotta somehow outrun 'em."

Wade nodded. "And get the passengers to safety."

"So what do you say, Mrs. Mallory?" Joseph asked Eula Mae. "That was the Army wife's name. You on board?"

"She doesn't have any choice, does she?" Lyle said nastily. "None of us have any choice. We're all Indy's prisoners."

"You're right about that," Joseph said cheerfully. "He lassoed me neater than a six-month-old heifer, and I'll wager that whip of his is even faster than Lash Larue's. We don't have a chance in hell of getting away. It's just like in *The Searchers*," and at Lyle's blank look, he said incredulously, "Don't tell me you never seen *The Searchers*, neither?"

"No," Lyle said, "and I don't see what movies have to do with anything."

"The little girl got captured by the Comanches, and there wasn't any way for her to get away, either," Wade explained, and Joseph beamed at him.

"Speaking of getting away, do you know if anyone saw you at the trading post?" Wade asked.

"Nope. I'd just pulled in."

"Good. Then no one will be looking for your . . ." He stopped himself in time. "For the *Outlaw*."

"Plus, nobody in their right mind would use an RV as a getaway car," Lyle said. "We can't outrun anybody."

"She *ain't* an RV," Joseph growled. "She's a Western trail wagon, and I'll have you know this little filly is faster than she looks. She can do forty miles an hour if it ain't windy—"

"That's good to know," Wade said, "but I doubt if we'll have to outrun anybody. Nobody's looking for us, and New Mexico's a big state with a lot of miles for the Highway Patrol to cover. What about you, Joseph? Is anybody likely to report you missing if you don't show up tonight? The campground you were going to stay at or something?"

Joseph shook his head. "The *Outlaw* don't need a campground. I can park her anyplace, in the desert or in a canyon or out on the lone prairie. She's totally self-contained. Water, solar, electric system, sewage, the works. I swore when I set out on this trip I wasn't goin' to be tied down by a schedule. I spent my whole life dealin' with deadlines and schedules."

"So now you're retired?" Francie said.

"Nope. Just takin' a little time off. Finally. First vacation I ever took, and if my company had its way I wouldn't be takin' this one, but I was damned if I was goin' to die without ever seein' any of the places I'd always wanted to see. I've always been a big fan of Westerns, so I bought me the *Outlaw* here, and set out to go to all the places I'd seen in Westerns and see 'em for myself."

"I have a friend who sold his house and bought an RV, too," Eula Mae said.

"And there's nobody you're checking in regularly with?" Wade asked.

"Just my daughter. She makes me send her a postcard every week and tell her I'm okay, that I haven't fallen off a cliff or been captured by Apaches or something. She thinks I'm loco to be doin' this."

"When's the last time you sent her a postcard?" Wade persisted.

"Yesterday. And I've got enough stamps to send her a bunch more. I've been to Dodge City and Tombstone, and I was fixing to go to Sedona, where they filmed *Last Wagon* and *Broken Arrow*, when I got waylaid by you folks, and then on to Moab and Monument Valley. That's where John Ford filmed *Stagecoach* and *Fort Apache*."

"So she won't miss you for at least a week. Good. What about your job? Have you been keeping in regular touch with the company you work for?"

"Hell, no. They'd try to talk me into comin' back."

"And you're sure your boss or the head of your company won't try to get in touch with you and become alarmed when he can't?"

"Durned tootin' I'm sure," Joseph said, grinning as if Wade had said something funny, and Francie wondered if he was really on vacation or if he'd absconded with all the company's funds, like the banker in *Stagecoach*.

What she was thinking must have shown on her face because Joseph said, "You're lookin' mighty peaked, Miss Francie. You sure I can't boil you up some coffee? It's genuine cowboy coffee just like John Wayne drank in *True Grit*, coffee grounds and eggshells and all," he asked. "You look plumb hollow."

I am, she thought, but Wade was shaking his head at her. "No, I'm fine, thanks."

"What about you, Eula Mae?" Wade asked. "Is there anybody who's likely to notice you're missing and notify the police?"

"My neighbor Mrs. Ortega, but she's gone all this week to Truth or Consequences to visit her daughter."

"What about on the bus?"

She shook her head. "My friend Ida couldn't go this time. Her sciatica kicked up again, and it was too hard for her to sit all that way, and my other friend, Mildred, only goes on Triple Slot days."

"What about Mr. Walters?" Francie asked, and when Eula Mae looked at her blankly, she explained, "The one who said he was in contact with aliens."

"Oh! Mr. *Walters*," she said. "No, he only goes on Mondays and Wednesdays, and he wouldn't remember anyway. He has dementia."

"What about the bus driver?"

"Him?" Eula Mae sniffed derisively. "He wouldn't notice if the whole bus got abducted, and even if he did, I don't go to the same casino every day. I like to go to a lot of different ones," and at Wade's speculative look, she said, "Not to gamble, you understand. I go for the company. You meet such nice people. And for the buffets."

"Is there anybody at the casino who might come looking for you?" Wade asked.

"Oh, my, no, not at all," she said a little too vehemently, and Francie wondered if there was something she wasn't telling them.

"Do either of you have a cellphone?" Wade asked.

Joseph shook his head, and Eula Mae said, "My niece wanted to give me one, but I told her I wouldn't even know how to turn it on, let alone use it."

"This niece of yours," Wade was saying, "will she be worried if you don't come home tonight?"

Eula Mae shook her head. "She lives in Pennsylvania."

Wade turned to Joseph. "Does your R . . . Western trail wagon have a GPS system? OnStar or something?"

"Nope. Maps were good enough for Kit Carson and Buffalo Bill, and they're good enough for me."

"Do you have a computer on board?"

"Nope."

"What about the TV I saw back there? You're not streaming movies from the internet, are you?"

"Nope. I own 'em all on DVD. Pretty much every single Western ever made, starting with William S. Hart and goin' all the way up to the ones that came out this year."

"And I assume you've got food on board," Wade said, glancing at the refrigerator, and Francie thought, *Please, please say yes. I'm starving.*

"Yep," Joseph said. "I just went grocery shopping two days ago. And the *Outlaw*'s got a bathroom and a shower."

A shower, Francie thought, *and a bathroom,* frowning as she remembered the conversation she and Wade had had after they ran out of gas. She looked thoughtfully out the window at Indy, who was sitting on top of one of the sandy hills.

"We got everything we need right here. Beds, blankets, clothes if any of you need 'em," Joseph said, looking at Francie, "first aid kit—"

"First aid kit?" Wade said, worried. "You mentioned you had

high blood pressure. Do you take prescription drugs for that? How about you, Eula Mae?"

Francie hadn't thought of that, that they might have to stop at a drugstore to fill a prescription for her. That would lead the police straight to them.

"I filled a three-month prescription right before I left," Joseph said, and Eula Mae said, "I always carry my pills with me, just in case." She patted the tote bag.

"Good," Wade said, "so we won't have to stop for meds or food."

"And the *Outlaw* sleeps eight," Joseph said. "Ten in a pinch." He gestured toward the door. "Is Lash Larue apt to latch on to anybody else?"

"Not if we don't stop anywhere," Wade said, "and it sounds like we won't have to."

"Except to get gas," Joseph said. "That's what I was fixin' to do when Lash Larue there lassoed me."

"How much have you got?" Wade asked.

"Half a tank, but she goes through gasoline like a cowpoke fresh off the trail goes through whiskey. It's the only thing bad about her. She only gets four miles to the gallon."

"Not a problem," Wade said, grinning. "This is your lucky day."

"Unless Indy's trick only works on gasoline engines," Francie said. "Your trail wagon is diesel, isn't it?"

"Yes."

Wade's grin vanished. "Shit—sorry, Miss Teasdale, I didn't mean to swear—I hadn't thought about it being diesel."

"But cain't we just fill 'er up at the pump?" Joseph asked. "Indy could stay in the back where nobody could see him. And money's not a problem. I've got Visa—"

"No credit cards," Wade said sharply. "And no using ATMs, either. The authorities can use them to trace us. We'll have to use cash."

"Well, then, you better have a bunch of it," Joseph said. "It takes almost two hundred bucks to fill the *Outlaw* up."

"Then we'd better hope Indy's trick works on diesel," Wade said.

"And what if it doesn't?" Lyle asked.

"Then they'll get a fix on where we are the first time we stop for gas and come after us, and it'll be game over."

"Just like in *They Died with Their Boots On*," Joseph said happily.

"They died with—?" Eula Mae said nervously.

"It's a Western," Joseph said. "About Custer's Last Stand."

CHAPTER NINE

"If there's anything I don't like, it's driving a stagecoach through Apache country."

—*Stagecoach*

"If we don't want to end up like Custer, hadn't we oughta get movin'?" Joseph said, standing up from the table.

"We can't till Indy's ready."

"We have to wait till he finishes figuring out which way he wants us to go," Francie explained.

"Cain't you hurry him up?"

"No," Wade said, and Francie opened the door and looked out to see if Indy was showing any signs of coming back. He was still sitting there in the late afternoon sunshine, perfectly motionless.

"So what are we goin' to do in the meantime?" Joseph asked. "Just set here and wait?"

"No," Wade said. "You're going to show me how to drive the *Outlaw* so I can spell you when you get tired."

"That's a right good idea," Joseph said. "First, let me show you all where everything is. Up there's the Driver's Box"—he pointed toward the RV's cab—"and this part we're in is the Chuckwagon."

He led the way to the back, pointing out things as he went. "This here's the Bunkhouse. These couches make out into bunks. They sleep six, and back here are two more couches and another table that pulls out."

The RV was *huge,* much larger than Francie had expected, and every inch was decorated with Western memorabilia—a longhorn steer's skull above the door to the Driver's Box, a rifle over the side door, wagon wheels and branding irons and lariats and spurs.

He's obviously been shopping at Thunderbird Trading Post, Francie thought, but on second glance, these things weren't cheap. The fittings, the furniture, the paintings of wagon trains and cattle drives and buffalo stampedes, all looked expensive. One of them even looked like an authentic Remington. Joseph hadn't been kidding when he called it a Western trail wagon.

"My, it's all so . . . fancy," Eula Mae said, voicing what Francie was thinking.

"I got a really good deal on her," Joseph said. "Bathroom here, and shower's here. And in *here*"—he led the way through a door to a wide room in the back—"is what I call the Opera House, after them theaters they had in the old frontier towns." He made a broad gesture that included two Navajo-blanket-patterned Barcaloungers facing a giant flat-screen TV and walls lined with DVDs. "This here's my movie collection. I've got purt' near every Western ever made, goin' all the way back to the silents with Harry Carey and Tom Mix."

"Do you have *Cowboys and Aliens*?" Lyle asked. "It's about how the aliens are here to experiment on humans and then exterminate them."

Thank goodness Indy's outside, Francie thought. *I need to talk to Wade before Lyle says anything else.*

"Nope, I don't have *Cowboys and Aliens*," Joseph said, "but I got *Cowboy* with Glenn Ford and *The Cowboys* with John Wayne." He held them up. "And *The Singing Cowboy* with Gene Autry."

"Can you give me that driving lesson now?" Wade asked.

"Sure as shootin'," Joseph said and led Eula Mae and Lyle back up to the front, pointing out where bedrolls were stowed on the way. Wade started after them.

"Wait," Francie said, pulling him back into the Opera House, out of sight of the others. "I need to talk to you about something." She perched on the arm of one of the Navajo-blanket-covered chairs. "It's about the RV," she said, lowering her voice. "I've been thinking about why Indy stole it."

"It's not an RV," Wade corrected her, grinning. "You heard Joseph. It's a Western trail wagon. You wish Indy'd stolen something a little less Buffalo Bill–ish? You should be glad he didn't steal the Highway Patrol car. Or the casino bus."

"I am. That's not what I'm talking about. I'm talking about *why* he stole it. Remember that conversation we had where you said we're going to need a bigger boat, and I said preferably with a bathroom. And a shower?"

"Yeah. What about it?"

"I think Indy hijacked this R . . . Western trail wagon because it fit what I said I wanted, which means he *does* understand what we're saying and we need to be careful about what we say when he's around."

"You mean like me saying I wanted to throttle Lyle?"

"Yes. Indy might take you literally and do it."

"And that would be bad because—?"

"I'm *serious,* Wade. You need to talk to Lyle and get him to stop talking about probings and invasions and wiping out the human race. If Indy takes him seriously, who knows what picture he'll get of us? Plus, Lyle's scaring Eula Mae to death."

"Really?" Wade said. "I thought she seemed pretty calm and collected. As a matter of fact, she seemed a little *too* calm and collected."

"What does that mean?"

"Just that her response seemed a bit . . . understated for a little old lady who's just been abducted by an alien."

"You wanted her to scream and have hysterics like Lyle?"

"No, but she should at least have—"

"She *did* try to pepper spray you."

"But that was when she thought we were a gang of criminals and that the cops were after us, not when she saw Indy . . ."

"Maybe she's just an exceptionally brave old lady."

"Maybe," he said. "Or—"

"Or what?"

"Nothing. Never mind. We'd better get back up there so I can learn how to drive this boat."

"Western trail wagon," Francie said automatically. "But you promise you'll talk to Lyle?"

"Yeah," he said, going back up to the front, where Joseph was saying, "Help yourselves to what's in the fridge. The microwave's here.

"Oh, good," he said when he saw Wade. "Let's go."

Wade went up to the front area with the steering wheel, or, as Joseph called it, the Driver's Box. Joseph followed him, saying as he went, "If any of you want to take a shower, there are towels in the overhead cupboard. And the TV remote's on the table between the Barcaloungers."

"Wonderful," Lyle said sarcastically. "A remote should make a terrific weapon when the aliens arrive to exterminate us all," but he walked to the back, and a minute later Francie heard the TV going.

"Don't worry," Francie said to Eula Mae, who was looking nervously after Lyle, "the aliens aren't going to exterminate us. Indy's nice. He saved my life." She told her the story of the rattlesnake. "Don't listen to Lyle. He's watched too many science fiction movies."

Eula Mae didn't respond. She was fumbling in her tote bag.

"You're not looking for more pepper spray, are you?" Francie asked.

"No, my cards." She pulled out a deck of cards. "Playing solitaire helps settle my nerves," she said, and began laying the cards out on the table. "You go take your shower or whatever you need to do. I'll be fine."

What I need to do is tell Lyle he's got to stop talking about exter-
mination and invasions, she thought, heading toward the back.
"Lyle?" she called. "I need to talk to you."

No answer, just the drone of the television. *Oh, no,* she thought,
sliding the door to the Opera House open, *what if he crawled out*
the back window and has gone to alert the police? But he hadn't. He
was standing on the seat of one of the Barcaloungers, looking
through the cabinet above it.

"What are you doing?" Francie demanded.

"Looking for proof."

"Proof of what?"

"That Joseph's a Reptilian."

Oh, for—

"That mustache and those cowboy boots are just his disguise,"
Lyle said, "and his touring Western movie locations is a cover for his
traveling around the Southwest spying on us and preparing the invasion."

"Joseph is not a Reptilian," Francie said.

"Then how come he didn't freak out when Indy abducted him?"
Lyle asked, pulling pillows and blankets out of the cabinet. "He
acted like it was something that happened every day." He jammed
the bedding back in, banged the cabinet door shut, and opened the
one next to it. "And why did he agree to Wade's plan to help Indy
so fast?"

"You heard him. He likes adventure and he thinks our situation
is just like the movie *Stagecoach.*"

"You can't believe everything people tell you," Lyle said, going
through a pile of jeans. "And you can't go by appearances, either.
People aren't always what they seem. Sometimes they aren't even
people."

"I suppose that includes Eula Mae?" Francie said. "Is she a Reptilian, too?"

"The old lady? No, she's on the level. I saw her get off the casino
bus with the others. But Joseph's definitely a Reptilian. Look at his
eyes. If you look close, you can see the nictitating membranes. And
you can see them on your boyfriend, Wade, too."

"Wade is *not* my boyfriend," she said. "And he's not a Reptilian, either."

"Then where's his duffel bag?" Lyle said, starting in on a pile of cowboy shirts.

"I don't know. He said he was going to stow it someplace."

"Well, I've been through every cabinet and drawer, and it's not here, and you know how he's so protective of it. He won't let anybody touch it. That's because it's got his skin—"

"His *skin?*"

"Reptilians shed their human form every few days. It sloughs off like a rattlesnake's skin. He'd have to hide it somewhere, and he's probably got the device he uses to communicate with the mother ship in there, too, and the chips he's going to implant in us while we're asleep, and the probes—"

"There aren't any probes in Wade's duffel bag," she said.

But he does have something in there, she thought, remembering how upset he'd gotten when she'd opened it to get out his shirt to show Indy and explain "clothes" to him—and how overjoyed he'd been when she told him the duffel bag hadn't been left behind.

"Aha," Lyle said. "You think he's a Reptilian, too. I can see it in your face."

"Wade is not a Reptilian," she said firmly. "He got abducted just like you and I did."

"Did he? How do you know he didn't *arrange* to be out there when you came by and—?"

He stopped, listening. "They're coming back," he said. He crammed the shirts back in the cabinet, shut it, and jumped down off the Barcalounger. "If they find out we know what they are, they'll kill us. You can't say a word about this."

"Oh, trust me, I won't," Francie said. "And *you* shouldn't say anything about them taking over the world and exterminating us. Or about cattle mutilations or probing abductees or secret underground bases. If they *are* Reptilians, you don't want them to know that you know about their plans."

"That's true," he said, frowning, and Francie hoped he'd forgotten he'd said aliens could read minds.

He apparently had because he added, "Good idea," and led the way back up to the kitchen. He'd been wrong about Joseph and Wade coming. The only one in the kitchen was Eula Mae, laying out cards for a game of solitaire and looking at the ones still in her hand.

"Would you like me to make you something to eat?" she asked Francie. "A sandwich or something?"

Yes, Francie thought. *I am* **so** *hungry.* "That's okay, stay where you are," she said and opened the refrigerator. She found salami and cheese, made a sandwich, and cut it in half, only just managing not to gobble the entire package of salami down whole.

"Oh, now you're making *sandwiches?*" Lyle said. "What is wrong with everybody? We've been abducted by an alien from outer space, an alien who might be plotting the extinction of the entire human race at this very moment!"

And so much for my convincing him not to talk about extermination, Francie thought, but she was too hungry to try to stop him. She bit into the sandwich and opened the refrigerator, looking for milk.

"And *you* act like we're on a family vacation!" Lyle said to Eula Mae. "How can you just sit there and do *nothing?*"

"She's not doing 'nothing,'" Wade said, coming back from the front with Joseph in tow. "She's executing a time-honored survival strategy."

"Survival strategy?" Lyle said. "Playing *solitaire?*"

"You bet," Wade said, grabbing half of Francie's sandwich. "I'm surprised you've never heard of it. Say you're in the middle of nowhere, nobody for miles and no hope of rescue. You sit down and start playing solitaire and somebody will immediately come along and tell you to play the red eight on the black nine."

Francie and Joseph laughed.

"It's not funny!" Lyle said. "Besides, I thought you didn't *want* anybody to find us."

"I think Wade was joking, Lyle," Francie said.

"Yes, well, when the aliens lock us up and start experimenting on us, you won't think it's so funny. You'll be sorry you sat around doing nothing."

"We're not doing nothing," Wade said. "We came back to figure out where Indy might be taking us." He turned to Joseph. "You said you had a map?"

"Yep, all kinds of 'em. I bought a bunch before I started out on this trip. They're harder to find than a stray dogie in a blizzard. Nobody uses them anymore, what with all this GPS stuff. I had to get 'em from antique stores. What do you need?"

"A road map of New Mexico, for starters," Wade said, and Joseph went to the back.

Francie made some more sandwiches, found a bag of potato chips in the cupboard, and set them on the table. Lyle immediately grabbed a sandwich and took an enormous bite.

"You can play the two of diamonds on that ace," he told Eula Mae, and Francie suppressed a smile.

"Found it," Joseph said, returning with several folded maps. Eula Mae gathered up her cards, and everyone else picked up their plates so he could spread it out on the table.

He leaned over it. "Here's the Thunderbird Trading Post," he said, pointing, "and I figure this is where we are."

"And here's Storm Mesa Casino, one of the casinos I go to," Eula Mae put in.

"This is about where Indy grabbed me," Wade said, pointing, "and we picked up Lyle here." He put his finger on a spot just south of Vaughn. "And then we went north to here and then east to about here—that's where we ran out of gas—and then south and back west to the trading post, and from there he told you to go west to *here*, and then north. Lyle, what UFO sites are north of here?"

"Dulce," Lyle said promptly. "There's a secret lab under Archuleta Mesa." He scanned the map. "Here it is, right on the northern border with Colorado, near Pagosa Springs."

"That's a long way," Wade said. "There isn't anything closer?"

"Española's had some sightings in the last couple of years," Lyle said. "And Taos has had tons of them, always a bunch of glowing red orbs hovering just above the road followed by a blinding white light."

"Where's Roswell?" Joseph asked. "Isn't that where the UFO was supposed to have crashed back in the forties?"

"We've already been there," Wade said. "That's where Indy nabbed Francie."

"Oh, well, then, where's Area 51? Isn't it in New Mexico?"

"No. Nevada," Wade said.

"We need another map for that," Joseph said.

"No, Area 51's too far away," Wade protested, but Joseph was already unfolding a second map. "This one's of the whole Southwest," he said, spreading it out on top of the map of New Mexico. "Now, where did you say Area 51 was?"

"Here," Wade said, pointing to a spot north of Las Vegas. "If it existed. Which it doesn't. And even if it did, it's over seven hundred miles from Roswell. If Indy was going there, he'd have landed in Las Vegas or Reno."

"Not necessarily," Lyle said. "The aliens have machines that teleport them from one base to another instantaneously. There's one at Four Corners. He could be taking us there and then teleporting us to Area 51."

Wade shook his head. "If Indy had teleportation, he would have used it in the first place instead of kidnapping Francie to drive him there."

"Maybe he didn't have a machine on his ship," Lyle said. "Or maybe when his ship crashed, it was damaged."

"Like in *Riders of the Red Mesa*," Joseph said, "when Tex's horse goes lame and he has to steal the marshal's to get to Yuma in time to stop a hangin'."

"And Area 51's the logical place for him to go," Lyle said. "It's where the government took the UFO and the aliens after the Roswell crash, and where they take all the UFOs they capture."

"Is that true?" Eula Mae asked.

"No," Francie said. "And if he was taking us to Area 51, he'd be taking us west first, wouldn't he?" She traced a route leading west on I-40 to Arizona and then north on I-93.

"What about Monument Valley?" Lyle asked. "The Navajos

have been reporting UFO sightings for hundreds of years, strange white lights that shoot across the sky at impossibly high speeds. And those mysterious red orbs I told you about. Their name for Monument Valley is Rocks of the Sky." He leaned over the map. "Where *is* Monument Valley?"

"That depends," Joseph said.

"What do you mean, it depends?" Wade asked sharply.

"I mean, it's supposed to be here"—he pointed to a spot in northern Arizona—"but in the movies, it kinda moves all over the place."

"Moves?" Lyle said eagerly. "What do you mean, moves?"

"I mean, in *Stagecoach* it's between Tucson and Lordsburg." He pointed to the southern Arizona border. "In *How the West Was Won* it's in southwestern Arizona, in *The Searchers* it's in West Texas, and in the last *Back to the Future* it's smack in the middle of a drive-in theater."

"Yes, and as I recall, Thelma and Louise set out for the Mexican border from Missouri," Wade said, drawing a straight line connecting them, "and managed to end up all the way here at the Grand Canyon. All that means is that the movies couldn't care less about getting the geography right."

"*Or*," Lyle said darkly, "it means it *was* in different places. Maybe the aliens move it around."

"Right. They move ancient sandstone formations weighing hundreds of thousands of tons."

"They have forms of energy we don't even know about," Lyle said. "Look what they did to Francie's car, making it go without gas. And there was this guy I met last year at the UFO Festival who'd been levitated right through the wall and up to the aliens' spaceship. If they can do that, they can move Monument Valley."

"That doesn't necessarily follow—" Francie began, but Lyle wasn't listening.

"They could be doing it to throw off the people they abduct, so no one can find them after they let them go."

"Or to make their stories sound completely ridiculous," Wade said.

"Exactly," Lyle said, completely missing the irony. "There was a guy in Missouri who got abducted. He couldn't remember anything about what had happened or how he ended up on the road outside Socorro, but then he started having these dreams where he was on an operating table being probed by aliens and out the window of the UFO he could see this red desert with all these mesas and red sandstone spires. He said the aliens had taken him to their planet, but maybe it was Monument Valley."

"Or maybe he fell asleep watching *The Searchers* and imagined the whole thing," Wade said.

But Lyle wasn't listening. "Do you have a DVD of *The Searchers*?" he asked Joseph.

"Yes, but I was—"

"Where is it? In the back?" Lyle demanded, and when Joseph nodded he went back to find it.

"I didn't mean to get him all riled up like that," Joseph said. "The reason Monument Valley's in so many movies is John Ford liked the way it looked, and it had lots of Navajos and horses he could hire to be in his pictures. I didn't mean to put crazy ideas in his head."

"Don't worry, you didn't," Wade said. "They were all pretty much in there already."

And I'd rather have him talking about Monument Valley wandering around than about invasions and probing, Francie added silently. And Joseph had hundreds of movies. Looking through them for *The Searchers* should keep Lyle occupied for a while.

Now if Indy'll just come back so we can get going, she thought.

"Any sign of Indy finishing up?" Wade asked Francie.

She looked out the window. "No."

"Damn," he said. "I'd feel better if there were a few more miles between us and the Thunderbird Trading Post. If somebody *did* see what happened—"

Francie bit her lip, wondering if she should tell Wade about the unpaid-for cowboy hat and T-shirt. If the clerk had seen Eula Mae run out with them . . .

"Wade—" she said, and Indy suddenly roused himself and began to roll back down the hill.

"Indy's coming!" she called. Eula Mae began hastily putting away her cards as if she thought Indy would snatch them from her like he had the pepper spray, but Indy rolled straight past her toward the front of the RV.

Wade intercepted him. "Not so fast," he said. "We need you to do something first."

"Remember when my car ran out of gas, Indy?" Francie said. "Well, this"—she patted the wall of the RV—"will run out of gas, too, unless you fix it."

Indy sat there a moment and then rolled on up front.

"And there goes your theory that he understands what we're saying," Wade said.

"Not necessarily," she said. "Maybe he's going to get Joseph. He's the one who knows how to open the hood," and a moment later, Indy reappeared with Joseph in tow, a tentacle wrapped around his wrist and another around his waist.

"What's he figurin' on doin'?" Joseph asked.

"He's taking you to the mother ship to be operated on," Lyle said, appearing out of the back.

"No he isn't," Francie said. "He wants you to open the hood so he can fix the engine."

"You open it from the inside," Joseph said.

"Indy, let go of Joseph and let him go back up to the Driver's Box so he can open the hood," Francie said, and Indy unwound his tentacles. "Joseph, go open the hood for us. Indy, you come with me and Wade."

She led him out the door and up to the front of the RV, which stood half-open like a car door. *Please let him have understood what I said*, she thought. *And let whatever it is he did work on diesel engines, too.*

It did. He only messed with it for a minute or two, twining his tentacles around and through the massive engine before he rolled back inside and up to the front, followed by Wade. "I want to put as many miles between us and the Thunderbird Trading Post as I can," he told Francie, "even if it means driving all night."

Indy may not let us do that, she thought, looking out at the long shadows beginning to stretch across the hills. It would be dark in a couple of hours, and last night Indy had stopped for the whole night. What if he did that again?

"He's very nice-looking, isn't he?" Eula Mae said from the table. She'd gone back to playing solitaire on the end of it the map didn't occupy and was going through her hand one card at a time—queen of spades, six of diamonds, five of hearts.

"Who?" Francie said, looking out at the darkening sky. There was a line of pink clouds on the horizon. "Joseph?"

"No, Wade," Eula Mae said. "What did you say he did for a living?"

"He's a con man," Francie said.

"A con man? Really?" Eula Mae said, and Francie thought she sounded relieved. Lyle must have told her he was a Reptilian.

"Well, anyway, he's very nice-looking," Eula Mae said. "A good catch, as we used to say in my day." She paused, looking at the cards on the table, a five of spades in her hand. "Don't you agree?"

"You can play that five on the six of diamonds," Francie said, and went to check on Lyle.

He was watching a Western. "Look at this," he said excitedly, pointing at the TV screen where a cowboy was riding through Monument Valley's orange-red buttes and rock spires. "They've got it in Sedona, which is a well-known site for UFO sightings. Because of the ley lines. I'll bet that's where he's taking us," and went up to the Chuckwagon to look at the maps and tell Eula Mae she could play the nine of hearts on her ten.

In the time Francie'd been talking to Lyle, it had begun to get darker. The sky was a rapidly dimming lavender blue, and the clouds on the horizon had darkened to gray. She went up to the cab to see if Indy showed any signs of wanting to stop again, but he was sitting on the console between Joseph and Wade, his tentacle on the high dashboard, pointing steadily ahead.

Francie went back to the Chuckwagon, where Lyle was showing Eula Mae Area 51 on a map of Nevada. "See, there's the Extraterrestrial Highway, where the Black Mailbox is. That's where they saw all the sightings, and south of the highway is Dreamland."

"Dreamland?" Eula Mae said.

"Yes. Paradise Ranch. Area 51. Where the aliens from the Roswell crash are secretly working with the government."

Francie grabbed another sandwich and went back to take a shower while everyone was occupied. When she opened the cabinet to get a towel, Wade's duffel bag was inside, hidden behind a pile of bath towels. She stared at it, thinking about what Lyle had said—not the ridiculous Reptilian stuff, but Wade *had* snatched it away from her when she'd opened it to get a shirt to show Indy, and he *had* been disproportionately happy that it hadn't been left behind . . .

She took a quick look back toward the front and then grabbed it, took it in the bathroom, locked the door, and unzipped it.

There was nothing in it but some clothes, the anti-abduction insurance policies, a stack of 8x10 glossies of UFOs, a bright green baseball cap that said TRUST NO ONE, and a toothbrush, a razor, and a stick of deodorant.

And what did you expect to find? she thought. *A blaster? A discarded Reptilian skin? Monument Valley?*

She put the duffel bag back, piling all but one of the towels in front of it, and took her shower, which felt heavenly, even though the shower stall was almost too narrow to turn around in.

But it was still wonderful to be clean. *Thank you, Indy,* she thought, reaching for her clothes. She wished she had something else to put on. There was always her maid-of-honor dress, but if Joseph needed her to navigate at some point, she didn't want to light up the RV's cab and risk the Highway Patrol spotting her. If only she'd been holding that T-shirt Eula Mae had brought her when Indy yanked her aboard.

When she'd wriggled back into her saloon-girl shorts and tank top (no mean feat in that narrow space) and come out, it was nearly dark outside. Eula Mae was in the Opera House watching *Stage-*

coach and nodding off. Lyle was in the Chuckwagon, dishing himself up a bowl of stew.

Francie sidled past him and went up to the Driver's Box to see how Joseph and Wade were doing.

"I was just about to ask Wade here to take over," Joseph said. "I'm close to falling asleep."

Apparently Indy was, too. When Joseph stopped the RV, Indy's tentacle jerked like someone awakened from sleep, and wrapped itself around Joseph's wrist and ankle. "Whoa there, Lash!" Joseph said. "I'm just stoppin' so's we can change drivers."

"Let Joseph go, Indy," Francie said, and he did.

Joseph stood up. Wade took his place in the driver's seat and said, "How about staying and navigating for me, Francie? Or are you too tired?"

"No, I'm fine," she said and sat down in the seat next to him.

"Good," Wade said. "You can take over entertaining Indy."

"Entertaining him?"

"Yeah, by explaining the signs we pass."

"Why?"

"No clue. I guess he got the idea when we showed him those Thunderbird Trading Post signs, and now he jabs his tentacle at every single one."

"Could he be looking for the name of where he wants to go?"

"Maybe, but it's not just mileage signs, it's Do Not Cross Median and Wigwam Motel, and a billboard for the Georgia O'Keeffe Museum with one of her cloud paintings on it. I had a hell of a time explaining what a museum was."

"But isn't the Georgia O'Keeffe Museum in Santa Fe?" she asked, and when he nodded, she said, "Aren't we headed north?"

"Yes, but we were going west at the time. Indy's leading us all over the place."

Indy fastened a tentacle around Francie's wrist and, with another one, pointed out the side window at an upcoming sign. NEED A FLAT FIXED? TONY'S BIG O TIRES IN PERDIDO it read, and Francie spent the next hour trying valiantly to explain flat tires and soft-serve ice cream and authorized vehicles, interspersed by Indy's orders to turn onto assorted gravel and dirt and paved roads, keeping it up till it got too dark to see the signs, at which point he rolled up against Francie and went limp, except for his pointer tentacle, which he kept on the dashboard, pointing straight ahead.

"Is he asleep?" Wade asked.

"I think so."

"Good," he said, handing her a map and a penlight. "Can you figure out where we are? Indy's made so many turns, I'm completely lost. I think we're somewhere between Santa Rosa and Tucumcari going east. The last sign I saw said 'Perdido—thirty-eight miles.'"

Francie opened out the map, trying not to disturb Indy in the process. She shone the penlight on the map, looking for the town. "Are you sure we're going east?"

"No."

She looked some more, checking what few county road signs they passed, but to no avail. "I'm sorry," she said. "I don't have any idea where we are."

"Which hopefully means the authorities don't, either. The important thing is we're putting miles between us and the Thunderbird Trading Post. Although"—he turned to grin at her—"we don't know that. For all I can tell, we could be heading straight back there. Or straight to that mother ship Lyle keeps talking about."

"Did you talk to him about not mentioning . . ." She looked down at Indy. His pointer tentacle had fallen off the dashboard and lay trailing limply across the floor. He was definitely asleep, but she dropped her voice to a whisper anyway. ". . . about probes and cattle mutilations and aliens coming to Earth to wipe us out around Indy?"

"Yeah, and it went about as well as you'd expect. Short of telling Indy to tie him up again, he's not going to stop. Sorry."

"That's okay," she said. "I just wish he wouldn't scare Indy with all this talk of aliens going to a planet to wipe everybody out." She looked down at Indy again. "Speaking of which, I've been thinking about Indy's reason for coming here."

"And?"

"And we keep assuming it's some *big* reason—invasion or saving Earth or saving *his* planet, like in the movies—but what if we're wrong, and it's something smaller?"

"Smaller?"

"More personal," Francie said. "I mean, look at us. None of us came to New Mexico to blow it up or save it. You and Lyle came to go to the UFO Festival, Joseph came to visit Western movie shooting locations—"

"You came to be in a wedding."

Which I'm not going to make it to in time, Francie thought.

"Yes," she said, "we each had our own personal reasons for coming. Like the passengers in *Stagecoach.* They all had personal reasons for going to Lordsburg. The lieutenant's wife was going to see her husband, the banker was on the lam, the Ringo Kid—"

"Indy's here to get revenge for the guy who killed his brother?"

"No. Yes? I'm saying he might be here for a private reason, not on some big galactic mission."

"And that reason is?"

"I don't know."

"Great," he said. "You realize if it *is* personal, it doesn't make it easier to figure out. It makes it harder."

"I know," she said. "And it's worse than that. Things aren't always what they seem. I wasn't just here to go to a wedding. I was here to stop it."

She told him about Serena's weakness for nut jobs and her reliance on Francie to talk her out of marrying them.

"And Eula Mae doesn't just go to casinos to gamble," she said. "She's really going for the all-you-can-eat buffet."

"Maybe," he said. "Or not."

Francie ignored that. "So even if we're able to figure out what Indy's ostensibly here to do, that might not be the whole story. He might be here for another reason altogether. Like Eula Mae."

"You're right," he said. "And you're right about things not always being what they seem."

"You're thinking about Eula Mae?"

"Yes, and—" He stopped and stared silently at the darkening road ahead.

"And what?"

"Nothing. Never mind. We need to think of all the possible reasons Indy could have for coming here. There's the being on the lam thing we talked about, and the looking for a buddy who crashed theory, and the— Wait, I've got it. He's here on a scavenger hunt. He's got to collect a dress that lights up, a UFO nut, an anti-alien-abduction insurance policy, an RV, a mutilated cow, and an 'I Was Abducted by Aliens and All I Got Was This Lousy T-Shirt' shirt and bring them all back to the mother ship, and the one who does it first wins a prize."

"And the others?"

"Get probed."

But sitting there in the dark cab of the RV with Indy curled against her and Wade beside her, the only light the twin beams of the *Outlaw*'s headlights and the green dials of the dashboard, it was impossible to worry about that or anything else. She felt relaxed and safe for the first time since Indy had grabbed her, and she could feel herself nodding off. She yawned.

"It's okay," Wade said. "You can sleep if you want to. I'll wake you up if we run into any aliens."

"Or cops," she said, and sat up straighter. "I'm not sleepy," but she must have nodded off in spite of herself, because she woke to something touching her knee.

"Don't, Indy," she murmured drowsily, and tried to brush the tentacle away.

"Francie," Wade whispered, and she realized he was the one patting her knee.

"What is it?" she asked, blinking at him. It was still dark. "What's going on?" She tried to sit up.

"Shh, don't wake up Indy," Wade said, nodding his head at the alien, who was still tucked against her, his body curled into a tight ball and his pointing tentacle still trailing on the floor.

"What's happening?" she whispered.

"Look."

He pointed out the windshield. Far ahead of them on the two-lane road was a row of red lights. They looked like a car's tail-lights, only much larger. At least twenty of them stretched across the road in front of them like a fence—and fence-post-high.

As they got closer, some of them disappeared. And then came back on. "What are they?" she asked. "Aircraft warning lights?"

He shook his head. "They're too low. And there are too many of them."

"Did they just appear?" she asked, leaning forward to peer at them.

"Yeah. I mean, no. I came up over a rise, and there they were."

And they were the only things in sight. She couldn't see any lights along the horizon that might indicate a town, no scattered white lights that might indicate ranch houses. Just the round red lights, and as they drove toward them, even more of them appeared.

"What *are* they?" Francie whispered.

"I have no idea," Wade whispered back, and another dozen of the red lights materialized.

CHAPTER TEN

"Now, that's what I call a close encounter."

—Independence Day

The intermittently blinking lights weren't just lights. They were glowing red orbs. *Like Lyle said people saw over Monument Valley,* Francie thought.

Don't be ridiculous, she told herself. *There has to be a perfectly logical explanation.* "Could they be railroad signals?" she asked Wade.

He shook his head. "We crossed railroad tracks just a couple of miles ago. There wouldn't be another set of tracks this close. And besides, they're too high for railroad signals."

He was right. When she'd first seen them, the lights had seemed about fence-post-high, but as they grew closer, she saw they were higher than that—though it was impossible to tell exactly how high with nothing to compare them to in the darkness.

Or to tell how far away they were. She'd have guessed only a few hundred yards when she first saw them, but they'd driven a couple of miles since then, and the lights seemed no closer. "Do you know where we are?" she whispered, hoping that might provide a clue as to what the lights were, but Wade was shaking his head again.

"No. Not anywhere near a town, that's for sure. If we were, we'd be able to see its lights on the horizon," he said, and added almost to himself, "What would be in a line like that?"

"Telephone poles?" Francie suggested.

Wade shook his head. "They'd run parallel to the road, not at right angles to it, and so would power lines." And they were almost too tall. As they'd approached the lights, their apparent height had continued to grow till now they were far above the RV.

Some of the lights began to blink on and off, a few in rapid succession, others staying off for nearly a minute at a time. Francie watched them, trying to see a pattern, but there didn't seem to be one. Unless they were blinking out Morse code or something.

"Could they be airport landing lights?" she ventured.

"No, those would be blue and white, and they'd light up the runway. There's no way you could land by those."

"Maybe they're *alien* landing lights."

"That's occurred to me," Wade said grimly.

"Lyle said the sightings in Monument Valley took the form of glowing red orbs," she said, trying to keep her voice steady.

"Yeah, but we're nowhere near Monument Valley."

"I know, but Joseph said—"

"Monument Valley does *not* move."

"I *know*," she said, "but the aliens' ship could."

They'd been whispering the whole time so as not to disturb Indy, who was still sleeping next to her. "But if it *is* aliens," she said softly, "and they've come to rescue him, shouldn't we wake him up?"

"Yeah. *If* they've come to rescue him. What if he's running away from something, like you said, and this is it? We'd be handing him right over to them."

"But if they *are* after him, shouldn't we be turning around and making a run for it?" she said, and her voice shook in spite of herself.

"And give away the fact that he's here? If I keep driving, and he stays asleep, there's a chance they'll think we're just tourists and won't bother us."

"*Or* they'll beam us up to whatever those red lights are concealing and probe us like Lyle said."

"Yeah, which is why you're going to look for a side road we can turn off onto before we get there."

She immediately began trying to spot one, but there weren't any, not even a farm track. And they were getting steadily closer to the lights. They began to come even with them, and, as they did, several seemed to separate themselves from the line and come closer. "Look!" she said, unable to keep the fear out of her voice. "They're moving."

"No, they're not," Wade said, pointing. "We are," and she saw that what had looked like a single line of lights was actually a field full of them, row after row, but staggered, so that from a distance they looked like a single line.

One of the red lights went out, came back on, and then instantly went out again, for much longer this time, and a second one, off to the left, did the same thing. *The light isn't blinking,* she thought. *Something's moving in front of it.* Something huge. "Wade," she said, and reached for his arm.

"I know," he said, his hands clenched on the steering wheel. "Hang on. I'm going to speed up and try to get us out of—"

He stopped in mid-sentence. Another light, this one only a few yards away from them, disappeared, and this time Francie caught sight of something white and curved flashing past it. She braced herself for Wade to accelerate, her heart pounding, but Wade was slowing the RV.

"Go!" Francie urged. "Why aren't you trying to—?"

"Because I know what this is," Wade said. "It's a wind farm. Look." And as the light nearest to them cut off, she saw the curved white outline above them again, and this time, knowing what it was, she could clearly see the outline of the huge curved propeller blade as it swept in front of the light. And the ones that had gone dark for

long stretches hadn't blinked off; they'd been obscured by the massive pillars in front of them.

"So they *are* aircraft warning lights," Francie said, relieved.

"Yeah. Only they're on wind turbines," Wade said, and she could
hear the relief in his voice, too. "I should have thought of a wind
farm. There are lots of them out here."

But even though they were close enough now to make out not
only the turning blades but the tall white columns, her heart was
still pounding, only beginning to slow when they were fully past it.
When she turned to look back at them, the staggered ranks of lights
were frightening all over again, and a couple of minutes later when
she looked in the side mirror, they looked again like the ominous
single line of red orbs she'd first seen.

"Sorry I scared you over nothing," Wade said. "I should have
known there was a logical explanation."

"You didn't scare me," she said. "I scared myself. It's what I get
for listening to Lyle."

There was a silence, and then Wade said, "He's right, you know."

"*Lyle?*"

"Oh, not about invasions and aliens probing us and his other ridiculous theories. But he's right about our not taking this whole
thing seriously enough. Just because Indy acts like E.T. and doesn't
mean us any harm, it doesn't mean his people won't. And even if
they're friendly, too, they may have jumped to the conclusion that
we kidnapped Indy instead of the other way around and decide to
shoot first and ask questions later. Maybe we need to rethink this
whole thing. I mean, now we've got Joseph and Eula Mae to consider."

"So you want to turn Indy over to the *police*? Who are even more
likely to shoot first and ask questions later?"

He didn't say anything.

"Oh, I see," she said. "So you're back to your 'Send Francie into
the gas station and drive away fast' plan, only with Lyle and Eula
Mae and Joseph, too. It won't work. Even if Indy would let us go—
which he won't—Joseph wouldn't abandon his precious RV. Or his

Westerns. And I have no intention of abandoning Indy. He saved my life. I owe it to him to help him get wherever he needs to go."

"Then we're going to need to get him to tell us where that is before we run into some *real* aliens."

"You're right," she said, looking down at Indy. "In the meantime, why don't you show me how to drive this thing? That way I can take over if you start to get drowsy."

"That's not going to happen," he said, "not with the jolt of adrenaline I got back there. It'll keep me awake all night, and then some."

"I know just how you feel," she said. "My heart's still pounding."

"Yeah. Look, why don't you try to get some more sleep? I'll wake you up if there are any more wind farms—or aliens."

There was no way she was going to sleep, either. She had just as much leftover adrenaline coursing through her veins as he did. But she leaned back against the upholstered seat and closed her eyes, determined to at least get some rest so she'd have enough energy in the morning to tackle Indy and the communication problem . . .

"Francie," Wade said softly, and she jerked awake. She sat bolt upright.

"What is it?" she said, alarmed, looking automatically down at Indy. He was still asleep, one tendril twined loosely around her wrist and hand. "Is it more lights?"

"No," Wade said. "Sorry, I didn't mean to scare you." He pointed through the windshield at the sky in front of them. "I just thought you might like to see this."

"This" was a wide swath of feathery grayish-mauve clouds ahead of them in the pale predawn sky.

"Pretty, isn't it?" he said.

"Yes."

"Watch. It gets better," he said, and smiled as the clouds turned from grayish mauve to a pale seashell pink and then a flaming orange. "See? What did I tell you?"

"It's beautiful," she said, looking across at him as he leaned forward, peering at the clouds.

She couldn't figure him out. He was a con man, but he didn't act like one—or at least not the ones Serena tended to get herself mixed up with. They were unbearably slick and smarmy, presenting an aura (in the soul shaman's case, a literal one) of having all the answers and with a snake-oil-salesman charm that wouldn't have fooled anybody but Serena, and they'd all—the soul shaman, the ghosthunter, no doubt the Church of Galactic Truth priest—had only one goal: convincing their marks they were on the level so they could fleece them.

Wade talked about the UFOers who bought his anti-abduction policies like that, but it wasn't how he acted. He'd told her he was a con man almost as soon as he'd met her, and he seemed genuinely concerned about Indy—and about her when he thought she'd been bitten by the rattlesnake. And he certainly didn't act like he had all the answers. He freely admitted he didn't know where Indy was trying to take them or what he was doing here.

"See?" Wade said, nodding toward the windshield. "I told you it would get better."

It had. The clouds had deepened to rose, bathing the two of them and the cab of the RV in a rich pink light. "It's beautiful," Francie breathed.

"Yeah," he said musingly. "Most of the time the Southwest looks dry and barren, but there are times, like now, and in the early evening, when the shadows stretch across the landscape . . ." He turned and smiled at her. "You know how I told you before that Earth didn't have anything worth aliens' coming all this way to see? This might almost qualify."

"You're right," she said, gazing out at the clouds. The rose was transmuting to a burnished copper. "But then hadn't we better wake Indy up to see it?"

"It's too late," he said, and he was right; the coppery hue was already fading.

"Do those clouds mean we might run into rain?" Francie asked.

"Why? Are you worried Indy might melt, like Lyle says?"

"No, but I'm worried what Indy's response might be. You saw how he freaked out when I tried to change clothes."

"Another reason not to wake him up," Wade said. "And no, those clouds don't mean rain. They're not cumulus clouds. They're cirrus. They'll burn off in an hour or two."

Francie looked at him again, thinking about how he seemed to know all about clouds—and the history of UFO sightings and secret Air Force projects and why telepathy was impossible. He was obviously well educated, as witness his use of words like "sentient" and "nefarious" and "hydrophobic" and his references to Medusa and rare earth elements, plus his speaking French and German and Russian. Hardly what you'd expect from a con man.

So why—? she wondered, and as if he *were* telepathic, he said, "You're probably wondering how I know so much about meteorology. In between UFO festivals, I travel to county fairs in New Mexico and Arizona and convince people I can make it rain."

"And sell drought insurance, I suppose."

"Nope. Anti-tornado policies."

"There aren't any tornadoes in Arizona or New Mexico."

"See?" he said, grinning. "They work. Want to buy one?"

"Not if they work as well as your anti-abduction policies."

"Good point," he said, and after a minute, "Thanks."

"For what?"

"For not asking what a nice boy like me's doing conning people, and telling me I'm too good for a life of crime and should go into an honest line of work."

"I've decided to stop meddling in other people's lives," she said. "I tried to do that with Serena and look where it got me."

"Oh, come on, it's not as bad as all that, is it? I mean, this is pretty nice, isn't it? Being here together, watching a gorgeous desert sunrise?"

"Yes," she said, smiling at him. "It is."

"Francie, listen. I—" He stopped.

"What?"

"Nothing. Look, I know you're worried about your friend's wedding. It's tomorrow, right?"

"Yes."

"Well, you might still make it in time to stop it. Indy's dragged us

all over the place. Who knows? He might decide to take us back to
Roswell next."

"I wish," she said. "I just feel so bad. Serena was counting on me
to help her, and I've let her down. And don't tell me Russell's not a
nut job just because it turns out aliens are real—"

"No, he's a nut job, all right," Wade said.

"What do you mean?" Francie said. "You don't know Russell."

"No, but I know Lyle. If this Russell guy's anything like him, I
wouldn't want my worst enemy to marry him. But here's the thing.
You two are best friends. I can't see her getting married without you,
especially when you're missing and have possibly been kidnapped."

"True," Francie said. "But Russell was determined to get married
on the anniversary of the crash."

"You're forgetting there's been a new landing. He's probably too
busy trying to find the spaceship to get married."

*Or he'll insist on getting married right away so the two of them
can spend their honeymoon searching for it,* she thought, looking
out at the sunrise. The clouds had faded to a dull gray.

"Or maybe Indy will suddenly start talking," Wade said, "and
you can explain to him why he's got to take you back."

"I wish," she said, and tried to think of ways to get Indy to speak.
If he *could* speak. Joseph had mentioned something about sign language. If they could find an example in one of his Westerns and
show it to Indy . . .

The next thing she knew, the scene out the window was bathed
in sunlight, and she could smell bacon and the heavenly aroma of
Joseph's cowboy coffee. Wade had been right. The clouds had disappeared, and the sky was an unbroken blue. "What time is it?" she
asked, yawning.

"Early," Wade said. "You've only been asleep about an hour."

"I'm so sorry." She scrambled to unfold the map. "I was supposed to be navigating for you, and—"

"It's okay," he said. "I just saw a sign, and it looks like we're
somewhere in western New Mexico, between Grants and Gallup,
but, boy, Indy was all over the place. He woke up right after you fell

asleep again, pasted himself against the side window, and started giving orders—turn east here, turn south, take this ranch track and that cow path, and it's a good thing we don't have to worry about gas because we didn't pass a gas station all night, and if we'd run out of gas on some of those roads, nobody'd find our bleaching bones for years."

"Has he given any clue as to where he's trying to go?"

"No. If you want my honest opinion, I don't think he has any idea where he's going."

And as if to confirm Wade's opinion, Indy wrapped a tentacle around Wade's foot, moved it to the brake, and, as soon as the RV lurched to a stop, rolled back toward the door, obviously to try and get his bearings again.

"Wait, Indy," Francie called, leaping after him.

Joseph was standing at the stove, spatula in hand. "Good mornin'," he said. "How about some flapjacks and bacon, girlie?"

"In a minute," she said, squeezing between him and the opened-out table. The map of the Southwest still lay spread out on one end of it, and Lyle and Eula Mae were seated at the other. Lyle was eating bacon and eggs and Eula Mae was playing solitaire. "Indy, wait!"

Francie beat the alien to the door by inches and flattened herself against it. "I need to ask you something before you go outside."

"Does he understand what you say?" Eula Mae asked.

"Some of the time," she said. "I think. Indy, come here."

He rolled over to the table—past Wade, who'd followed her into the kitchen and was pouring himself a cup of coffee—and up onto the banquette.

"It sure as heck *looks* like he understands you," Joseph said, and Eula Mae nodded agreement.

"Let's hope so," Francie said, picking up a pencil. "Indy, this is a map. It shows where things are. This is Roswell, where you and I first met." She pointed at the town on the map with the pencil.

"Do you think he might be able to write with that tentacle of his?" Joseph asked.

"I don't know." She scrawled WRITE, on the margin of the map and then held the pencil out to Indy. "Write, Indy?"

His tentacle reached out tentatively, wrapped around the pencil, and handed it to Eula Mae.

"I'd say that's a 'no,' " Wade said.

Francie glared at him and pointed at Roswell again. "This is Roswell, and this is the road we took that first night." She drew her finger along the line of the highway. "These black lines are roads and these dots are towns. Can you show me on the map where you want to go?" she asked, pointing at his tentacle and then at her finger. "Can you point to it?"

His tentacle reached out and touched her finger with its tip. "Just like E.T. did," Lyle said. "He's reading your thoughts."

Francie ignored him. "No, Indy, not my finger. The map. Touch the map. Where are you trying to go? Is it Area 51?" she asked, pointing to Nevada. "Or Marfa?" She pointed at it. "Or Monument Valley? Show me where you want to go."

This time Indy's tentacle hovered over Tombstone and then came to rest squarely on Eula Mae's eight of spades.

"No, no," Francie said, "not on Eula Mae's cards. On the map." She pointed at the map and then at him. "Where do you want to go? Aztec? Four Corners? Devils Tower? Point to it."

He raised a tentacle, hovered over the map with it a moment, and then put the tip of it squarely down on the ace of spades and rolled off the banquette and out the door.

"Maybe he's telling us he wants to go to Deadwood," Joseph said, "where Wild Bill Hickok was shot."

"What does Wild Bill Hickok have to do with anything?" Francie asked.

"Dead man's hand," Eula Mae said. "Wild Bill Hickok was holding aces and eights when he was shot in the back," and when Wade looked curiously at her, she added, "I saw that in one of the movies we watched last night."

"Law of the Black Hills," Joseph said and went over to the door to look out at Indy. "So how long do you think he'll be out there this time?"

"I don't know," Francie said. "As long as it takes him to figure out which way we should go."

"Is that long enough for me to stir up some flapjacks for everybody?" Joseph asked, brandishing his spatula. "Lyle et all the bacon and eggs."

"At least," Wade said. "I figure Indy's got to get his bearings first, and that'll take a while. So, if nobody else needs the bathroom right now, I'm going to go take a shower." He started to the back, unbuttoning his shirt as he went.

Lyle got up from the table and pulled Francie aside. "See? That proves it. He's a Reptilian," he whispered to her.

"Because he wants to take a shower?" Francie said.

"Yes. They can only go so long without shedding their human skins," he whispered. "He's really in there washing his old skin down the drain and putting on a new one."

"I thought you said water was poisonous to aliens," Francie whispered back.

"You're going to be sorry you didn't listen to me," Lyle said, taking the plate of pancakes Joseph offered him and stomping off to the back. "If anything happens, I'll be in the Opera House watching a Western."

Or trying to get a sample of Wade's discarded skin as proof, Francie thought, taking a stack of pancakes from Joseph and pouring syrup on them, but she'd scarcely finished eating before Indy reappeared and rolled up to the front.

"Looks like you're gonna have to take over for me," Joseph said, handing Francie the spatula and starting for the back. "Tell Wade to come up and spell me as soon as he's finished his shower, and I'll get Lyle to come navigate till then," he said, striding past the bunks to the back.

"You'd better hurry," Francie said. "Indy doesn't like to be kept waiting."

"I won't be more'n two shakes of a dogie's tail," Joseph said, but though Francie could hear the sound of voices, neither he nor Lyle reappeared, and after she finished scooping up the pancakes and putting them on a plate, Francie went back to get Joseph.

He and Lyle were sitting in the recliners. Lyle was staring intently at the screen. On it, cavalry soldiers were saddling up their horses.

"Joseph," Francie said. "Indy—"

"I'm comin'," he said. "I just want to show Lyle this next part. This is *She Wore a Yellow Ribbon*. John Wayne and Harry Carey Jr. Directed by John Ford. The next scene's famous. They were filmin' the cavalry riding through Monument Valley—"

"Which is where?" Lyle asked.

"Well, they never say exactly, but it's right after Custer's Last Stand, so most likely it's supposed to be Montana. Anyhow, they were filmin' the cavalry riding across the Valley with the buttes and spires in the background, when a thunderstorm starts comin' toward 'em, and the cameramen want to pack up and go home, they say the equipment's liable to attract lightning—"

"Joseph, I really think you should come now . . ." Francie said, looking anxiously toward the front, expecting a tentacle to come whipping back any second to yank Joseph out of the recliner and up to the cab. "When Indy wants to go—"

"As soon as Lyle sees this," Joseph said, waving her off. "So they want to pack up, but Ford won't let 'em, he tells 'em to keep on filming and they got a great shot of this huge thunderstorm and a big rainbow. The cast and crew got drenched, but it was worth it. Won an Oscar for cinematography. Look, it's comin' up right now."

That's not all that's coming, Francie thought, moving so she was out of the line of fire of Indy's bullwhip—and saw Indy rolling back to get Joseph.

He rolled over to him and fastened a tentacle around Joseph's wrist. "Howdy, Lash," Joseph said. "I'll be right there—I just wanna show Lyle this next scene first." He pointed at the TV screen and Indy rolled toward it.

The cavalry was opening the gates of the fort and riding out, flags flying. Indy let go of Joseph's wrist, rolled over to the space between the two recliners, and settled himself on the floor.

"What's going on?" Wade said, appearing in the door, his hair wet, pulling on his shirt.

"*She Wore a Yellow Ribbon*," Joseph said, pointing at the screen, where the lieutenant at the front of the column was raising his arm to give the signal to ride out, and then a long shot of the cavalry riding across Monument Valley with the cinnamon-orange buttes and pinnacles behind them.

"What the—?" Joseph shouted suddenly, looking at Indy. The alien was quivering all over. His tentacles began flailing wildly.

"Oh my God, he's attacking!" Lyle shrieked, and reared back as if he'd been bitten. Indy's tentacles windmilled wildly.

"Indy, what is it?" Francie darted toward him. "What's wrong?"

He was too far gone to hear her. His tentacles lashed out, a whirling mass of whips, and she had to put up her hands to keep him from hitting her. Lyle and Joseph backed away.

He was acting just like he had in the car when she'd started to change clothes. "Indy, calm down!" she cried, and looked at Wade, who was still standing there half-dressed, his mouth agape. "Button your shirt!" she ordered him. "Indy doesn't understand the concept of clothes."

Wade fumbled with the front of his shirt, trying to button it up and tuck it into his jeans.

"Wade's not hurt! He's just changing clothes!" she said to Indy. "Remember how I explained 'clothes'? See?" She pointed at Wade, now dressed. "He's fine," but Indy continued to strike out wildly.

"I don't think I'm what caused this," Wade said, and he was right. Indy didn't even seem to be aware that he was there.

Then what had done it? They'd just been sitting there watching—

"Turn off the TV," she ordered.

Joseph made a tentative grab for the remote lying on the arm of the recliner and then stepped back out of range.

"Hurry!" Francie said, trying to grab for Indy's tentacles. "Before he totally ties himself into knots!" and Wade lunged forward, grabbed the remote, and pointed it at the TV and the cavalry still riding through Monument Valley.

The screen went blessedly black. "It's okay," Francie said soothingly. "You're safe, Indy. It's all gone," and Indy's tentacles slowly stopped flailing.

"Well," Wade said, "at least now we know where he *doesn't* want to go."

"You mean Monument Valley?" Joseph said, looking at the blank screen. "Is that what frightened him?"

"Of course it was," Lyle said. "I *told* you the aliens move it around. Indy probably thought they'd moved it here, right inside the RV."

"Western trail wagon," Joseph muttered.

"Go away," Francie said. "All of you. I need to calm Indy down," and the three men filed out, Lyle keeping a wide berth between himself and Indy, even though Indy's tentacles had gone from whipping around to waving feebly.

"Shh," Francie crooned, pulling Indy close to her. "Shh, you're okay," though he wasn't. He was a tangled mess. In his wild flailing, he'd managed to snarl his tentacles into knots far worse than at the trading post.

She sat down cross-legged on the Navajo rug and began to untangle them. "That's right, settle down, settle down. There's nothing to be afraid of. It was only a movie. It wasn't real. Hold still and let me untie your knots. Your tentacles are all braided and tangled up, just like Serena's hair that time she was dating the anime fan," she murmured, saying anything that came into her head, hoping the sound of her voice would soothe him. "I had to braid her hair into tiny little braids all over her head as part of her costume. You remember Serena? I told you about her. Remember I said I have to go to a wedding? Well, that's Serena's."

There was no sign he understood her or was even listening. He'd calmed down, but that could simply be because the image of whatever had frightened him was gone. And what had it been? Monument Valley like Lyle said, or the soldiers? Or their horses? Or something else altogether?

She couldn't ask him, for fear it would set him off again. If he actually understood what she said. *Maybe Wade's right, and I'm just imagining that we're communicating,* she thought. "I wish there was *some* way you could tell me what upset you. And where you want to go," and Indy laid the end of a tentacle gently over her hand.

"You wish it, too, don't you?" she said. "Oh, if only aliens were telepathic, like Lyle says! It would make things so much simpler!"

No response, and after a few more minutes of her working, Indy pushed himself away from her, even though there were still some tangles in his tentacles, and rolled back up to the front, Francie assumed to make Joseph start driving again. But when she reached the Chuckwagon, Indy was sitting on the banquette next to Eula Mae.

"Feeling better, Lash?" Joseph said. "Want some more flapjacks, Francie? Lyle ate up the first batch, but I can stir up some more."

She shook her head.

"Did you figure out what scared him?" Wade asked.

"No," she said. "Just that it was something on the TV screen."

"What all was in that scene?" Wade asked Joseph.

"Cavalry soldiers, horses, rifles, sabers, flags. The Stars and Stripes and the U.S. cavalry flag. They were flappin' in the breeze. Maybe they looked like tentacles flappin'—"

"Maybe," Wade said. "What else is in that scene? Mesas? Buttes? Monu—" He stopped, looking at Indy, and started again. "That place we were talking about's full of rock formations that look like mittens and sailing ships and cathedral spires. Maybe Indy thought one of them looked like a rocket ship."

"Not unless one of them's saucer-shaped," Lyle said. "It was definitely Monu—that place—that set him off. Before, when they were showing the fort, he was fine. It wasn't till the Monu—that scene, that he went nuts."

"There were lots of things in that scene, though," Wade said. "We need to find out exactly what it was that scared him. Joseph, can you find a scene with just a cavalry soldier in it? And one with just a horse and then one with just Mon—that place?"

"You bet your boots I can," Joseph said eagerly. "There'll be cavalry in *Rio Grande* and *The Hallelujah Trail* and a good shot of their flag in *Major Dundee*. Here." He handed the spatula to Lyle. "Flip those over." He started for the back. "Do you want the horse to be saddled or not?"

Wade didn't answer. He was watching Indy, who was tapping the table with the tip of his pointer-tentacle. "What's he doing now?"

"Maybe he wants me to teach him how to play solitaire," Eula Mae said.

"No, he doesn't," Francie said. "He wants to look at the map again. Eula Mae, pick up your cards. Lyle, move your plate."

She spread the map out on the table. "Indy, see this map? It's like a picture of where things are." She looked up at Wade. "Do you have any idea where we are right now?"

"Somewhere around here," he said, drawing a circle on the map with his finger.

"Indy, this is where we are," she said, pointing at the spot. "This is us." She grabbed a pencil and wrote *US* over the spot, saying "us" again as she did. "And this is where you rescued me from the rattlesnake," she said, writing *RATTLESNAKE* on the map. "And this is the Thunderbird Trading Post, where we stopped and picked up Joseph and Eula Mae." She pointed at each one of them as she said their names. "And this is Roswell, where you pulled me into the car, remember? Roswell." She drew her finger under the name on the map.

Unlike last time, this time Indy was paying close attention, following her every movement with his tentacle.

"Roswell," she said, drawing her finger under the name again and then printing it out. *ROSWELL.*

He'd been about to point at Roswell, but his tentacle froze in midair and stayed there.

"*Now* what's he doing?" Lyle said.

"Shh," Francie said.

Indy's tentacle remained frozen above Roswell, and after a moment it began to change color, turning to light green and then pale pink.

"He's having a seizure," Eula Mae said.

"No, he's not," Lyle said. "He's getting ready to attack!"

Indy's tentacles were beginning to quiver, just like they had before he'd started flailing while watching the television. *I shouldn't have mentioned the trading post,* she thought. *That's where he got so upset when he thought my skin was coming off.*

"Indy, it's okay, I'm not going to change my clothes," she began, but he'd stopped quivering and was pointing at the word *"ROSWELL"* again.

"That's right, Roswell," she said, and Indy thrust his tentacle sideways in front of Francie's face, its paler inside toward her. "What—?"

The letter *R* appeared on the tentacle in green, and then an *O* and an *S*.

"Oh my God!" Francie gasped.

W-E-L-L appeared on the pale flesh of his tentacle, and then *ROSWELL,* the letters moving down the length of his tentacle like words scrolling across the bottom of a television screen: *ROSWELL ROSWELL ROSWELL.*

CHAPTER ELEVEN

"You speak our tongue?"

—Geronimo, *Broken Arrow*

"Oh my gosh!" Francie said and clapped her hand to her mouth. "He can talk!"

"He can what?" Wade said.

"Talk," she said. "Well, not talk. Write. But he's communicating." She grabbed Indy's tentacle and held its inner side out in front of Wade. "Look!" She pointed at the letters spelling out *ROSWELL* down his tentacle.

"Jesus!" Wade said.

"Oh, my!" Eula Mae exclaimed, and Joseph came hurrying over to see what was going on.

"Well, I'll be hornswoggled!" he said, slapping his thigh. "Will you look at that!"

"Wonderful," Lyle muttered. "An alien who can text. He's probably sending our location to the mother ship right now, and they'll be here to destroy us any minute."

"He's not texting anybody," Francie said. "He's *talking* to us."

"But why didn't he do that before?" Wade asked.

"Because he hadn't made the connection between spoken and written words," Francie said. "He must not have vocal cords and his species communicates exclusively by writing, and since all we did was talk, he couldn't figure out a way to communicate with us till now."

"That must have been what he was doing when he was pointing at the road signs," Wade said. "Trying to make that connection. But why didn't he scroll 'MOTEL' or 'MUSEUM,' then?"

"Because we were talking about the signs, not reading them, and besides, he wouldn't know which word was which. He had to hear and see the word at the same time. Like Roswell," she said.

"ROSWELL," Indy scrolled.

"That's right, Indy," she said, pointing to Roswell on the map. "That's where you abducted me." She wrote *ABDUCTED* on the map. "Where you made me get in the car."

"ABDUCTED," Indy scrolled, and pointed at the Thunderbird Trading Post on the map. "THUNDERBIRD TRADING POST."

Francie nodded. "That's right. And I am Francie." *FRANCIE,* she wrote.

He pointed at the place on the highway she'd shown him before. "US," he scrolled.

"Yes!"

"By George, I think he's got it," Wade said.

"Oh, my, it's just like that movie!" Eula Mae said, clasping her hands together. "You know, the one where Annie Sullivan teaches Helen Keller to talk!"

"Where do you want us to take you, Indy?" Wade asked. "Indy? Can you spell it out?"

Indy ignored him. He was busy pointing at Albuquerque and Santa Rosa and Truth or Consequences and having Francie read them to him.

He pointed at Socorro. "Socorro," Wade said. "Is that where you want to go?" but Indy was already pointing at Lordsburg.

"Lordsburg," she said, and did the same thing for Las Cruces and Wagon Mound.

"Are you sure he's really communicating?" Wade asked after he'd pointed to nearly every town in New Mexico and was starting in on Arizona.

"Yeah," Joseph said. "All he's doing is repeating what you say. That doesn't prove he knows what the words mean."

Eula Mae added, "Maybe he thinks you're playin' some kind of game."

"I don't think so," Francie said, but it was obvious she was going to have to prove it. "Does anybody have a piece of paper?" she asked.

"I have a little scratch pad," Eula Mae said, fumbling in her tote bag, "to keep track of how much I've won and lost. So I won't go over my limit," she added, still digging. "Here it is."

She brought up a tiny pad of paper. The top sheet was covered with sequences of letters and numbers. She hastily tore it off and handed the pad to Francie.

"Indy," Francie said, pointing at him and then writing *INDY* on the scratch pad.

"INDY INDY INDY," he scrolled.

"That's right," Francie said, and pointed at her own chest.

"I wouldn't do that if I were you," Lyle said. "What if he thinks you're inviting him to stick his tentacle down your chest, like in *Alien?*"

"Shut up, Lyle," she said, and pointed at her sternum again. "Indy, who am I?"

"FRANCIE," he scrolled.

"Where did you abduct me?"

"ROSWELL."

"There, you see?" she said. "It's not a game. He understands the words stand for something."

"You're right," Wade said. "Indy, where do you want us to take you?"

No answer.

"That means it isn't any of those places we've named," Francie said and started pointing to Tombstone and Yuma and Apache Junction, but Indy wasn't interested. He was pointing at Wade's chest.

"Wade," Francie said, and wrote it on the pad.

"WADE," Indy scrolled, and pointed at Eula Mae and then at Joseph and Lyle, followed by Eula Mae's hat, the sequined dice on it, Eula Mae's deck of cards, her tote bag, Joseph's Stetson, Lyle's T-shirt, the table, the window, the door, the wall, the floor, the hanging lantern, the light switch, and the curtains.

The scratch pad gave out, precipitating a search for something else to write on. Joseph came up with a stack of napkins, and when Francie'd filled those up, Wade went back and got some of his anti-abduction insurance policies. "This side's blank," he said.

"You can't use those," Lyle said. "What if he asks you to read him the words on the policy? You're the one always saying we shouldn't give him ideas."

"You mean he might try and abduct us?" Wade said dryly, and handed the policies to Francie.

The vocabulary lesson resumed, with Indy leading her through the RV, asking her to name things. He pointed at her tank top and shorts. "Clothes," she said, opening Joseph's closet and showing Indy Joseph's cowboy shirts to make sure he got the message.

"CLOTHES," Indy scrolled.

"That's right, clothes," she said, and he pulled out a denim shirt.

"CLO," he scrolled.

Clo? she thought, and then realized he must think that was the singular for "clothes." Which meant he understood plurals.

Which meant he wasn't just learning words. He was learning the language.

"Yes," she said, but he'd already moved on to the bunks, the longhorn steer's skull on the wall, the rifle, the spurs, the wagon wheel, the bison in the painting.

"Which is great if Indy's trying to take us to a buffalo stampede," Wade said, "but doesn't help at all in finding out where he wants to take us."

"Building a base vocabulary's the first step in learning a language," Francie said defensively. "Then he can extrapolate from that," but she took him outside and taught him everything within

sight, hoping he might be able to describe where he wanted to go:
"gravel," "sagebrush," "rocks," "sky."

It was a bright, unbroken azure and she wondered if she should
try to teach him "blue," but decided that was too abstract. She
needed to stick to names: "yucca" and "dirt" and "stones" and
"RV."

"Western trail wagon," Wade said.

"Shut up," she said amiably, and pointed to the road. "Road."

"ROAD," Indy scrolled.

"Where do you want us to go on the road?" Wade asked, and
Indy's tentacle went blank.

"He doesn't know the word 'go,'" Francie said, and took Indy
back into the RV and up front to the Driver's Box, with Wade right
behind her. She sat down in the driver's seat and draped her arm
over the dashboard the way Indy always did, her forefinger pointing
ahead like the tip of his tentacle did. "Go," she said, and printed it
on the scratch pad: GO.

"GO GO GO," Indy scrolled, and pointed at the windshield.

"Yes, go," Francie said.

"*Where* do you want us to go?" Wade asked. "You have to tell
us where you want us to take you," Wade said. "Do you want us to
take you to Roswell?"

"He can't answer you," Francie said. "He doesn't know the word
'where.' Or 'yes.' Or 'no.'"

"Well, then, we need to teach them to him," Wade said.

"I'm not sure that's a good idea."

It wasn't. After half an hour teaching him "yes" and "no" and
then leading him through every word on the map of New Mexico
except for Monument Valley and having him answer "no" to each
one, Francie said, "Indy, we need to stop for a few minutes now so
I can rest," and he promptly scrolled, "NO NO NO NO NO NO
NO NO NO!"

"But at least now when we ask the right question, he'll know how
to tell us 'yes,'" Wade said cheerfully, and she wanted to smack him.

"Indy, is the place you want to go on this map?" Wade asked,
writing the question down as he said it.

No answer.

"Would you like us to take you to someone who could help you tell us where you want to go?" Francie asked.

"What are you—?" Wade began.

Francie waved him off. "Our government—the FBI—has all kinds of translators and experts in different languages. They could help figure out what you're trying to tell us."

Mistake. Indy's tentacles began to flail as he scrolled an entire armful of "NO NO NO NO NO NO NO NO NO NO."

"I'm sorry," Francie said. "We won't bring anyone from the government here, Indy."

"That's right, buddy," Wade said. "No FBI. I promise," but it took fifteen minutes to get Indy fully calmed down.

When he was finally quiet, they started naming things again, but after a few minutes at it, Wade stood up and began pacing back and forth. "We don't have time for this. Basic vocabularies are all very well, but we need words that he can use to tell us where he wants to go. Place words, like 'mountain' and 'canyon' and 'valley,' and we can't do that without pictures. Joseph, do you have any books about the West with you?" he asked. "Preferably with pictures."

"No, just *150 Famous Western Movie Locations*," Joseph said, "but it doesn't have any pictures in it."

"What about your movies?" Eula Mae suggested. "They'd have mountains in them, wouldn't they?"

"You bet," Joseph said, and immediately headed back to the Opera House. "What do you need?"

"The Rockies, for starters," Wade said. "And then desert mountains, like the ones around Albuquerque."

"ALBUQUERQUE ALBUQUERQUE ALBUQUERQUE," Indy scrolled.

"And *then*," Wade repeated, "what's the countryside around Socorro like, Lyle?"

"Desert, rock formations, hills," Lyle said. "It's along the Rio Grande."

"We'll start with *How the West Was Won*," Joseph said happily, pulling a movie out.

"No!" Francie said. "I thought you said that had"—she went over to Joseph and whispered in his ear—"Monument Valley in it."

"It does," he said, "but not till the very end. Don't worry, I won't show him that part. Just the parts we need."

Francie went and got Indy. "Sit in the chair," she said, and Indy rolled up onto the recliner.

"Are you sure this is going to work?" Wade said, standing behind the recliners, his arms folded.

"No," Francie said.

"Don't worry," Joseph said. "If *How the West Was Won* doesn't work, I've got plenty of other movies," and cued up Jimmy Stewart riding a horse along a river.

It went about as well as Francie had expected. Indy wasn't nearly as interested in the river that Francie pointed out as in everything else in the scene—the cottonwood trees along the river, Jimmy Stewart's horse, saddle, blanket, reins, rifle, and beaver pelts. And after she'd said "canteen" and written the word out, he continued to tap the image of the canteen impatiently.

"What is it?" she asked him. "You want me to show you what a canteen is? Show?"

"SHO," he scrolled.

Of course, if "clo" is the singular of "clothes," then "sho" is the logical spelling of "show," she thought. "No. Show." She wrote the word out for him.

"It means to demonstrate something or to explain. Is that what you want, for me to explain 'canteen'?"

"YES YES YES SHOW."

Another mistake. He demanded "SHOW" for nearly every word she taught him from then on.

"I've created a monster," she told Wade after he'd demanded she "SHOW OUTLAW" and then wanted her to explain why the RV was called *Outlaw,* too. "Do you suppose Annie Sullivan was ever sorry she'd taught Helen Keller to talk?"

"Probably," he said. "The worst part is we still don't know where Indy wants to go, and he seems to have completely forgotten about going there."

It was true. He didn't once drag Wade or Joseph up to the Driver's Box and point demandingly at the windshield, or roll outside and over to the nearest high spot to get his bearings. All he cared about was learning new words and getting Francie to explain them.

"Maybe that's the reason he came here," Eula Mae suggested, "to learn our language, and now that we're teaching him, he doesn't need to go anywhere else."

"Yeah," Lyle snorted, "he came to learn the language so his people could pretend to be human and infiltrate our planet."

"How could they pretend to be human?" Joseph, who was fixing lunch, asked. "They look like tumbleweeds."

"They're shape-shifters," Lyle said. "They can disguise themselves to look like anything. They've been doing it for years, making themselves look exactly like us and walking among us. They've infiltrated the military, the government, the FBI. It's all part of their invasion plan."

"SHOW INVASION PLAN," Indy scrolled.

"Now see what you've done, Lyle?" Francie said.

"What do you mean, now see what *I've* done? Those are the words you should be teaching him—'secret underground base' and 'invasion command center' and 'cattle mutilation,' not 'fort' and 'saloon' and 'livery stable.'"

"SHOW CATTLE MU—" Indy began.

"Indy," Eula Mae interrupted, "why don't you come over and sit by me, and I'll teach you the names of all the cards."

Indy obligingly rolled up onto the seat of the banquette, and scrolled, "JACK QUEEN KING ACE" as Eula Mae showed him the cards and wrote out the words, followed by the names of different games that could be played with them: "SOLITAIRE FIVE CARD STUD DRAW TEXAS HOLD EM."

"Now, *that's* really likely to help," Wade said, but Francie was grateful for the break, and for Eula Mae offering to teach Indy how to play solitaire so she could eat lunch.

But the moment she'd finished the bowl of chili Joseph had handed her, Indy was right back at her elbow, demanding that she explain "deck," "discard," "shuffling," and "spades."

Wade was just as bad. He spent all afternoon making Joseph find examples in his Westerns of bridges, ghost towns, streams, dry washes, buttes *not* in Monument Valley, mesas (ditto), gorges, ravines, and (apparently remembering their conversation about *Close Encounters*) Devils Tower, and when none of those evoked a response from Indy he decided the problem was that Indy didn't know the words for directions and demanded that Francie help him act out "north," "south," "east," "west," "near," "far away," and "where?" When Wade asked Indy for the umpteenth time, "This place you want us to go to? Is it north of here?" Indy's tentacles remained maddeningly blank.

"West?"

Nothing, and nothing for "east," "south," and "thataway."

"Maybe we were wrong," Francie said. "Maybe he *doesn't* understand what we're saying," at which point Indy rolled over to where Eula Mae was playing solitaire, and pointed at two of the cards in turn.

"TEN," he scrolled. "JACK."

"What does he mean?" Eula Mae asked.

"He's telling you to play your ten of hearts on the jack of clubs," Wade said, and grinned. "I *told* you solitaire was a great survival strategy. It works every time."

"Except it's not going to get us out of the wilderness," Francie said.

"No, but it proves he understands what we're saying. And what *he's* saying." He thought for several moments. "What if this place he wants us to take him to *isn't* a place?"

"What does *that* mean?"

"What if it's a thing?"

"You mean like a lost gold mine or something?" Joseph said. "That's what they were searching for in *The Treasure of the Sierra Madre*—a lost gold mine."

"Exactly," Wade said, and went tearing off to find Joseph's DVD of it.

"Thanks a lot," Francie said to Joseph, and sank down at the table. "I don't know how much longer I can keep doing this. Indy's like a living ticker tape." She put her head down on her folded arms. "I am *so* tired."

Joseph nodded. "You look like you been rode hard and put away wet. How about I fix you some of my genuine cowboy coffee?"

"I don't need coffee," she said, looking longingly back at the Bunkhouse. "I need a nap."

Indy nudged her, shoving one of the insurance policies toward her, and pushing the pencil into her hand with his tentacle.

"Here, let me do that for you," Joseph said, taking the pencil and the policy from her.

"*Thank* you," Francie said. "But it doesn't solve the problem. If only there were some other way to teach him words and phrases without pointing and writing them down one at a time. If I still had my phone, we might be able to use a language program, like Babbel or Rosetta Stone or something, but . . ."

Joseph nodded. "Yeah, it's too bad I threw out the trash right before he hijacked me. I had some old newspapers we could have read to him—"

He stopped abruptly. "Now, why didn't I think of that before? Yippie-ki-yay!" he crowed. "I got just the thing!" and raced off to the back.

"What's going on?" Wade said. "Did Indy tell you what he's looking for?"

"No," Francie said. "Joseph—"

"Wade, did you find *The Treasure of the Sierra Madre*?" Joseph demanded.

"No, I was—"

"It doesn't matter. Any of 'em 'll do." He grabbed a movie, yanked it out of its case, and stuck it in the DVD player.

"*Paint Your Wagon*?" Francie said, looking at the title on the case.

"Yep," Joseph said, grabbing the remote and pointing it at the TV.

"But we already showed him the mining town in this movie,"

Francie said. "Did you think of some other geographical formation in it?"

"Nope." Joseph was fiddling with the settings. He pushed a button on the remote and fast-forwarded past the logo, the credits, a wagon accident, and a funeral.

Joseph hit Play, and a bearded Lee Marvin stomped his foot on a man's hand and said, "I claim this gold mine in the name of me and my pardner."

"I don't see—" Francie began.

"Look," Joseph said, and pointed to the words on the bottom of the screen: "I CLAIM THIS GOLD MINE IN THE NAME OF ME AND MY PARDNER."

"Closed captioning," Francie said.

"Yep," Joseph said proudly. "Now you won't have to write out every word. You can just set him in front of the TV."

"And he'll be learning whole sentences," Wade said, "which, if your theory about learning language is right, will get him to the point where he can extrapolate sooner."

"But what about . . ." She leaned forward and whispered in his ear, "Monument Valley?"

"Don't worry," Joseph said. "I won't show him any of those."

"But all these Westerns are full of violence—gunfights, range wars, Custer's Last Stand. He'll get the idea humans are horrible."

"Or it'll give *him* ideas," Lyle said, coming in. "Like massacring us. And mutilating cows."

"Westerns don't have cattle mutilations in them," Wade pointed out.

"What about hog-tying steers? And branding? What if he decides to truss us up again and put his brand on us? Or massacre us, like they massacred the buffalo?"

"He's not going to massacre us," Francie said.

"Don't worry, Francie," Joseph said. "I'll see to it he doesn't watch anything violent." He hit Eject, took out *Paint Your Wagon*, put in *Support Your Local Sheriff*, and Indy rolled up into one of the recliners and began to watch: "Is there really any gold in this town?" James Garner said.

"IS THERE REALLY ANY GOLD IN THIS TOWN," Indy scrolled.

"See?" Joseph said. "The movies can take over his teachin' while you go get some shut-eye. Now you go on. Git."

But it seemed like she'd no sooner curled up on the bunk, pulled a blanket over her, and dozed off, than Indy poked her and scrolled, "SHOW YOU LAZY BASTARD."

What's that doing in **Support Your Local Sheriff**? she thought drowsily.

Indy poked her again. "SHOW YOU DAMN SON OF A BITCH."

That **definitely** *isn't in* **Support Your Local Sheriff**, she thought. She must have been asleep longer than she realized. She followed Indy to the Opera House, where she found Joseph asleep, a bloody gunfight in progress on the TV screen, and an open DVD case on the floor.

She picked it up. "Joseph!" she said. "Wake up! What's Indy doing watching *The Wild Bunch*?"

"Sorry," Joseph said, yawning. "He must have figured out how to work the DVD player himself."

"That's it," Francie said. "No more Westerns."

But that was easier said than done. Indy loved watching the closed captioning, and when they unhooked the DVD and hid the connecting cable, he made it work anyway, and they eventually compromised by hiding *Once Upon a Time in the West, The Quick and the Dead, Django Unchained, The Good, the Bad, and the Ugly,* and all the movies with Monument Valley in them and hoping for the best.

He watched movies for the rest of the afternoon. On the bright side, he didn't seem all that interested in what he was seeing on the screen, only in the words he was seeing and hearing, as evidenced by the fact that he fast-forwarded through the action sequences to get to the dialogue. And it kept him occupied so Francie could snatch some sleep in between the stretches when Indy was asking her to explain "stampede," "whiskey," "hitching post," and "war paint."

"At least it's better than explaining Lyle's 'probe' and 'exterminating humans,'" Wade said.

"SHOW EXTERMINATING," Indy scrolled.

"I have a better idea," Francie said. "Let's go watch *Cat Ballou*," and she led Indy to the back, which succeeded in diverting him, though Francie had forgotten it had a train robbery, several shootings, and a public hanging in it, all of which she had to "show," along with "sheriff," "gunfighter," "drunk as a skunk," and "Hole-in-the-Wall."

"It's a place where outlaws go when they're being chased," she explained.

"CAT BALLOU GOTHES."

"Gothes?" Francie said, bewildered.

"NO NO NO GOTHES," he scrolled. "CAT BALLOU GOTHES HOLE IN THE WALL HIDE POSSE."

Oh, *goes*. He thought the plural of "go" was "gothes," which made perfect sense if the singular of "clothes" was "clo," and he'd never seen "goes" written out.

I need to write them out for him so he knows how they're really spelled, she thought, but Indy wanted her to explain "posse" first, and then "payroll" and "Tintoretto" and "Hallelujah, Brother!" and then Joseph came in to watch *The Virginian*.

Francie left Indy in his care and went up to the Bunkhouse, hoping to get another nap, but Wade was asleep in there, and Eula Mae was in the kitchen, playing solitaire as usual. *And I suppose Lyle's in the Driver's Box,* she thought, but no, Eula Mae said he was outside watching for spaceships.

Good, Francie thought, and went up to the driver's compartment, leaned the passenger seat all the way back, and closed her eyes. *Another half an hour,* she thought, *that's all I ask.*

She didn't get it. She'd only just closed her eyes when she heard a crash, followed by a shriek from Eula Mae, a number of thrashing sounds, and a muffled shout from Joseph.

"What the hell—?" she heard him yell before his words were abruptly cut off.

Francie scrambled out of the leaned-back seat and ran toward the rear and nearly into Wade.

"What's going on?" he asked, alarmed.

"I don't know," she said, squeezing past him and on to the Opera House.

Eula Mae was standing in the doorway, her back to the wall and her tote bag clutched to her chest like a shield. Joseph was trying to get to the remote, and saying, "Now, whoa there, Pilgrim! Settle down!" Indy was flailing wildly around again, completely out of control.

"What happened?" Francie demanded. "What were you doing?"

"N-nothing," Eula Mae said. "We were watching *The Virginian*. Joseph dozed off, and they were going to string up a cattle rustler, and you said no violence, so I took it out and put in *The Harvey Girls*."

Francie glanced at the screen, but it didn't show anything but Judy Garland in an old-fashioned, high-necked dress leaning against the door of a train's caboose, singing, according to the closed captioning: IN THE VALLEY WHERE THE SUN GOES DOWN . . .

"I tried to calm him down," Eula Mae said, "to explain to him that it was just a movie set, but—"

"It's my fault," Joseph said. "I forgot *The Harvey Girls* had—"

"Had what?" Francie asked, but she already knew the answer.

"Did you write it down for him," she asked Eula Mae, "the thing you were explaining?" but she already knew the answer to that, too.

Indy's tentacles were lashing out in all directions, and every one of them was scrolling, "MONUMENTVALLEYMONUMENT VALLEYMONUMENTVALLEYMONUMENTVALLEY" in vivid, slashing red.

CHAPTER TWELVE

Ben: They call him Rotten Luck Willie. You couldn't beat him with five aces.

Pardner: Oh, I don't gamble.

Ben: Neither does he.

—*Paint Your Wagon*

"'m sure sorry," Joseph said. "I forgot I even had *The Harvey Girls*. It ain't really a Western, it's one a' them musicals, but it's got cowboys and dance hall girls, so I—"

"It's all right," Francie said tightly. "Just turn it off."

"I'm tryin'," he said, dropping to his knees, shielding his head from Indy's lashing-out tentacles. "Indy knocked the remote out of Eula Mae's hand." He reached under the recliner.

"Indy . . ." Francie inched toward him, trying to avoid his writhing tentacles, which were slashing out everywhere, hitting her and Joseph and Eula Mae and one another. "Indy, it's okay. I'm here. It's okay," but the words on his tentacles scrolled brighter and faster, "MONUMENTVALLEYMONUMENTVALLEYMONUMENT VALLEY," though the scene had changed to a Western town and a train station.

"What's going on?" Wade said, appearing in the door. "Oh." He pointed at the television. "Shouldn't you turn that off?"

"We're trying," she said. "Is there a way to turn it off manually or unplug it or something?"

"No," Joseph said from under the recliner, "it . . . Found it!"

He reemerged, waving the remote, and pointed it at the TV. The screen went black. "I'm really sorry about that," he said. "I—"

"It's okay," she said, though turning off the TV had had no appreciable effect on Indy's frantic flailing. "Everybody out so I can get him calmed down."

Joseph and Eula Mae filed out, apologizing as they went.

Wade lingered in the doorway. "Well, at least now we know for sure it was Monument Valley that scares him," he said. "But why?"

"I'll try to find out," Francie said, "*after* I get him calmed down. You, too. Out."

"But—"

"Out," she said, and slid the door shut on him.

She turned back to Indy. "Shh, Indy, it's okay. Monument Valley's all gone." She tapped the TV screen. "All gone."

"ALL GONE?" Indy scrolled.

"Yes," she said firmly, and the writhing slowed a little, though it was another ten minutes before she could calm him down to the point where she could coax him onto her lap to untangle his knotted-up tentacles and then another five before she dared broach the subject of what had frightened him.

"What happened at Monument Valley?" she asked, watching his tentacles closely in case he started to lash out again. "Is that where your ship landed?"

"NO NO NO," he scrolled.

"Is it where you want us to go?" she asked, and every tentacle scrolled, "NO NO NO NO NO!" in bright orange and began to flail again.

"We won't take you there, I promise," she said hastily. "We won't go anywhere near it. You don't have to be afraid. It's a long way from here—"

"NO NO NO NO NO!" he scrolled.

What did that mean? That it wasn't far from here in terms of how fast a UFO could fly? Or in terms of galactic distances?

She had no idea how to ask that. "Is there someone at Monument Valley you're afraid of?" she asked instead.

"YES YES YES POSSE."

Posse? "Someone's after you? They're chasing you?"

"YES YES YES."

"And Monument Valley's where *they* landed?"

"NO NO NO."

"They're *going* to Monument Valley?"

"NO NO NO *POSSE*." The word "posse" was brighter than the others, as if it were underlined.

"So the posse's after you, and you're afraid they'll catch you?"

"YES."

"And you've been trying to get away from them. That's why you've had us drive where we did. You want us to take you somewhere they can't find you."

"NO NO NO."

"Then where *do* you want us to take you?"

Dead end. His tentacles went blank.

I give up, Francie thought. *If he isn't running from them, what's he—?* "Indy," she said at a venture, "are you trying to get somewhere and do something before the posse catches you?"

"YES YES YES YES YES!" he scrolled, his relief palpable in the bright green of the words.

Of course. That explained his desperation and why he'd had to kidnap her to drive him. He didn't have much time. "Can you tell me what it is you need to do?"

"HELP."

"Help who?" she asked. "Help us?"

"NO NO NO."

"Are you trying to go somewhere to get help?"

"NO NO NO."

"Are you trying to go somewhere to help someone?"

"YES YES YES."

"Help who?"

The tentacles went completely blank again.

Wonderful. She was right back where she'd started. Still, she'd found out something, and after she got him settled watching *Shane,* which Joseph assured her didn't have any Monument Valley scenes in it, she shared the information with the others, who were gathered around the table, drinking coffee. Lyle was eating a sandwich.

"Indy's here to help someone—he couldn't tell me who," Francie said, "but that isn't all. Someone's chasing him. Indy said a posse."

"A *posse?*"

"Yes, and he's trying to get to whoever it is he's trying to help before they catch him."

"The other aliens," Lyle said, getting up to get a package of cookies, "because he betrayed their presence to Earth by abducting us."

"I thought you told us he was taking us back to the mother ship to be probed," Eula Mae said.

"Right," Lyle said.

Which makes as much sense as Indy's responses about Monument Valley, Francie thought. "Indy said he was trying to help someone. Or some thing," she told them.

"But he didn't say who or what," Wade said to Francie. "Why not? Is it a secret he can't tell us or is it just that he doesn't know the word for it?"

"I don't know."

"And you say it's all somehow connected with Monument Valley?" Wade asked thoughtfully.

"Yes," Francie said, "but when I told him not to worry because Monument Valley was a long way from here, he kept scrolling 'No.'"

"I *knew* it," Lyle said. "It *does* move, just like you said, Joseph."

"I was just joshin'—" Joseph began, but Lyle cut him off.

"Aliens have all kinds of mysterious powers," he said. "They can beam people up to their spaceships and manipulate time and read people's thoughts. Why couldn't they move it?"

"Why would they move Monument Valley?" Wade said, exasperated.

"To make abductees sound like they're crazy, for one thing, and to—"

"It was a rhetorical question," Wade said, and to Francie, "Probably it's just a language miscommunication and when he learns to talk better it'll all make sense. Just like this stuff about a posse. How do we know what he means by that? You have to keep talking to him and trying to find out who it is he needs to help. In the meantime, Joseph and I'll go through his Westerns and find some posses we can show Indy and check that that's what he really means and not rustlers or bandits or something. You've got some movies with posses in them, don't you, Joseph?"

"Are you kiddin'?" Joseph said eagerly. "Purt' near every two-reeler made in the 1930s and *Butch Cassidy and the Sundance Kid* and *The Long Riders,* but—"

"They've got Monument Valley in them?" Francie asked.

"No, that's not the problem." He looked around the table. "The problem is, we can't stay here."

Wade nodded. "You're worried the longer we're in one place, the more likely somebody is to come along and ask us if we're having car trouble, and Indy'll snatch them, too," Wade said.

"It ain't that," Joseph said. "We're runnin' out of grub."

Everyone looked up. "But I thought you said you'd just stocked up before you picked us up," Francie said.

"I had, but that was for one person, not five, and *some* of us"— he looked pointedly at Lyle, who was munching cookies—"have been eatin' from sunup to sundown. We're runnin' low on bread, milk, lunch meat, just about everything."

"Okay, then, I guess we'll have to find a grocery store," Wade said.

"But, Wade, I thought you said we shouldn't stop anywhere," Francie said.

"We'll park out back, send one person in, and use cash," he said. "How much does everybody have? Francie?"

"None. I didn't take my purse when I went to Serena's car to get the twinkle lights for her, and the twenty you gave me at the trading post got lost when Indy yanked me on board."

"What about you, Lyle? How much have you got?"

"I *had* fifty bucks in my phone case," he said, glaring at Indy, "which he threw out in the bushes, and another ten to pay for the chips and Coke I was buying—which I dropped when he grabbed me. So all I've got is a Visa and a debit card."

"No cards," Wade said.

"Then that leaves me out, too," Joseph said, "unless we can stop at an ATM."

"No ATMs. Eula Mae?"

"A roll of quarters and one of nickels," she said, fishing in her sequined tote bag. "That's twelve dollars. And I had four dollars for the lobster buffet." She laid them on the table.

"Four dollars for *lobster*?" Lyle said.

"I had a coupon." She looked apologetically at Lyle. "Most of the slots don't take cash anymore. Just credit cards."

Wade fished in his jeans pocket, brought up several crumpled bills and some change, and put them on the table. "I've got five dollars and eighteen cents."

"What about all those ten-dollar anti-abduction insurance policies?" Francie asked.

"I was on my way *to* Roswell, remember? Not coming from there."

"Well," Francie said, "assuming Indy didn't bring any money with him, either, we've got a grand total of twenty-one dollars and sixteen cents, which won't even buy us breakfast tomorrow, let alone lunch."

"It'll have to," Wade said grimly.

"Not necessarily," Eula Mae said, and everyone turned to look at her.

"What do you mean?" Wade said. "Have you got some money tucked away you didn't tell us about?"

"No, but . . . the thing is I . . . I can always tell if I'm going to have a lucky streak, and I just feel like I'll have one tonight. And if we're where you said we are, there's a casino real near here . . ."

"A *casino*?" Lyle said. "So you can gamble away what little money we have? At least with what we've got, we can buy peanut butter and bread."

"I have to go along with Lyle," Joseph said, though it looked like it pained him to say it. "I don't think we should risk it. I say we stop at a Walmart and buy as much peanut butter and bread as we can with what we've got."

"And Cokes," Lyle said. "You're almost out. And you're out of Doritos, too."

"I wonder why," Joseph said dryly.

"Eula Mae, I know you want to help," Francie said, "but if you lose—"

"I won't lose," she said, looking not at Francie but at Wade.

"You can guarantee it?" he said.

"Yes."

"Okay," Wade said, and Francie stared at him in amazement. "Where's this casino of yours?" he asked.

"Here," Eula Mae said, pointing to it on the map. "Apache Buttes is about twenty miles away." She showed him the route.

"Are you sure it'll be open?" Joseph asked. "It's gettin' kinda late."

"Casinos are *always* open," Eula Mae said confidently.

"Great," Wade said. He scooped up the rolls of coins and the heap of crumpled cash and handed them to Eula Mae. "Apache Buttes it is."

"What? Are you crazy?" Joseph and Lyle said, but Eula Mae had already put the money in her bag, and Wade was already heading for the Driver's Box.

"Keep teaching Indy words, Francie," he called back to them as he went. "And the rest of you see if you can come up with some more money. Check the couch cushions."

"Wait, you can't just—" Francie said, starting after him, but Lyle had opened the refrigerator door, blocking her way.

The RV lurched to a start, making her grab for the table to keep her balance, and pulled onto the road. She glanced instinctively toward the back, expecting to see Indy's tentacle shooting forward to stop Wade, but it didn't, and when she went back to the TV room, steadying herself on the counters and the bunks, Indy was curled up in a recliner, watching *Rio Bravo.*

Traitor, she thought, and went back up front, past Lyle, who was drinking the last of the remaining Cokes, and telling Eula Mae, "You can play the black three on the red four," and Joseph, who said, "I found another thirty-five cents."

"Wonderful," she said, sidling into the Driver's Box to confront Wade.

"What do you think you're doing?" she demanded, plopping down next to him. "You know what the odds are of her losing every cent we've got."

He didn't say anything.

"Look, if your idea of having her go into this casino is to give her a chance to get away, I'm with you a hundred percent. She's an innocent bystander in all this, and I'd love to see her safely out of it. She's not like Joseph. He can take care of himself, but she's just a sweet little old lady."

She paused, but he still didn't say anything. His eyes stayed steadily on the road.

"But this isn't the way to do it. In the first place, it won't work. You saw what happened at the gas station and at the trading post. If she makes the slightest move toward escaping, Indy will snatch her back in front of who knows how many people, all of whom are going to alert the authorities."

"Indy won't be worried about her escaping. We'll tether him to her wrist so he can keep an eye on her like he did on us at the trading post. Nobody'll see him."

"All right," Francie conceded, "but that still doesn't change the fact that she's going to lose all our food money."

"She guaranteed she'd win."

"And you *believed* her?" She looked at him, frowning. "You know something I don't know," she said. "What are you up to?"

"Me? Nothing."

"Look, if you're planning to send Indy in there with her to pick pockets, that's not going to work, either. There are security cameras everywhere. Using one of Joseph's credit cards at a grocery store would be a lot less dangerous. The police obviously haven't figured out he's been abducted yet, and it'll look like he's just stocking up for the rest of his trip."

"Nope, we're going to the casino. Just trust me, okay?"

"Okay," she said reluctantly. "Do you want me to stay up here and navigate?"

"No, I think I know where we're going, and I need you working with Indy. Try to get him to tell you what this 'posse' he's running from is and why he's so scared of Monument Valley. And tell Lyle to come up here and bring the map."

"I thought you said you knew where you were going."

"I do, but don't tell him that. I don't want him eating up the last of the food, just in case Eula Mae does lose." He grinned at her. "Tell him I need him to navigate for me. And tell Eula Mae to move that red king over."

She did (the former, not the latter), but when she reached the Opera House, she didn't ask Indy about posses. Or Monument Valley. Knowing someone was chasing him and that he needed to help someone still didn't tell them where he needed to go, and they could show him places and landforms for days without hitting on the right one. She needed to think of some other way to get him to tell them.

"Indy," she said, turning off the TV and taking him into the Bunkhouse, "I need to ask you some questions." She sat him down on one of the bunks. "What's your name?"

"INDY," he scrolled, and pointed out the window at a roadside sign. "READ."

" 'Gas—Phillips 66,' " she read. "No, not the name we call you. What's your *real* name?" she asked, but they'd turned onto the highway, and it was lined with billboards, all of which Indy insisted she read: WALL DRUG—933 MILES, APACHE BUTTES CASINO—LOOSEST SLOTS IN THE SOUTHWEST, and CASCABEL MOTEL. AIR-CONDITIONED ROOMS.

"What's your name back home?" she asked when there was finally a break in the signs. "What do people call you back on your own planet?"

"SHOW CASCABEL," Indy scrolled.

"It's Spanish for 'rattlesnake,'" she said, wondering why on earth a motel would name itself that and reminding herself *never* to stay there.

"FRANCIE SAVE INDY RATTLESNAKE."

"Yes, and Indy saved Francie from the rattlesnake. We both saved each other. What is your name in—?"

"SHOW SPANISH."

"Spanish is another Earth language. We speak different languages," she said, trying to think of an example, "like Pedro in *Riders of the West*. He speaks Spanish. I speak English. And you speak your language. Understand?"

He didn't answer. He was already pointing at another sign, this one advertising Las Vegas with a picture of a pyramid, the Eiffel Tower, a gondola, and a pirate ship. "'Visit Fabulous Fun Fantastic Las Vegas!'" Francie read. "'We've Got Everything!'"

"SHOW LAS VEGAS," Indy scrolled.

I can't, she thought. *There's no explaining it.*

"*Las Vegas* is Spanish for 'meadows,'" she said.

"PEDRO," he scrolled.

"Yes, like Pedro. He speaks Spanish. What language do you speak on your planet?"

"SHOW SLOTS."

"They're a machine that . . . Eula Mae will have to explain 'slots' to you."

Mistake. Indy immediately started to roll off the bunk. "No, stay here," Francie said. "You can ask Eula Mae about slots later," and the RV started to slow down.

"We're here," Eula Mae called from the front.

Francie looked out the window. They were pulling into a huge parking lot, in the center of which stood an equally huge neon-lit pink adobe casino. In spite of (or maybe because of) the late hour, the parking lot was nearly full.

Wade pulled into the least well-lit corner of the lot and stopped, and Indy immediately rolled up to the front of the RV. Francie went after him and found Eula Mae patting at her gray hair and adjusting her hat.

Indy rolled up to her and scrolled, "SHOW SLOTS."

"We've been reading highway signs," Francie explained.

"Oh," Eula Mae said. "They're gambling machines you put money in and spin the wheel, and you can win a jackpot."

"EXPLAIN JACKPOT," Indy scrolled.

"It's what Eula Mae's about as likely to win as a calf is to get itself out of quicksand," Joseph said.

"EXPLAIN QUICK—" Indy began, and Wade appeared, asking Eula Mae, "All set?"

"Yes." She stood up and grabbed her tote bag.

"I still think this is a mighty bad idea," Joseph said. "Ain't the odds always with the house?" and Lyle said, "How do we know she'll come back? I think one of us should go with her."

"Don't worry, one of us will," Wade said.

"No!" Eula Mae said sharply.

"See, I told you!" Lyle said. "She's going to duck out on us. With *our* money!"

"You didn't have any money, remember?" Wade said, and to Eula Mae, "You're not going to do that, are you?"

"No," she said, "but luck might not work with someone else there distracting me."

"He won't distract you," Wade said. "You won't even notice he's there. Will she, Indy?"

"The *alien's* going with me?" she said.

"Nobody'll see him," Wade assured her, and Francie explained, "His tentacle was wrapped around my wrist the whole time I was talking to you in the Thunderbird Trading Post."

Well, almost the whole time, she thought, but this seemed like the wrong moment to bring that up. "I wasn't even aware of it."

Or aware of the fact he'd let go, she added silently.

Wade opened the side door and jumped out to lower the steps for Eula Mae and help her out, and Indy rolled down the steps after her and onto the pavement.

"GO GO GO," Indy scrolled.

"No, Indy, you can't go," Wade said, looking anxiously around to see if anyone in the parking lot was looking their way.

"YES YES YES GO," Indy scrolled. "SLOTS."

"And you're certainly not going to play the slot machines," Francie said. "Look, Indy, you can't go. People might see you."

"NO NO NO," Indy scrolled and wound himself into a sphere the size of a ball of yarn.

Wade looked at Francie. "Did you know he could do that?"

"No. But, Indy, you still can't go. You have to stay here with Wade and me."

She expected an argument, but Indy resumed his normal size, and fastened a fishing-line-thin tentacle around Eula Mae's wrist.

Wade turned to Eula Mae. "If we need you to come back, we'll have Indy yank on your tether. And if *you* get in trouble, tell Indy to tell us. On your other tentacles, Indy. No scrolling inside the casino. Understood?"

"YES YES YES," Indy scrolled.

"Okay," Wade said, and to Eula Mae, "Off you go."

She started off across the parking lot, and Wade and Indy came back inside. "So now what?" Lyle said.

"Now we wait till she comes back." He sat down at the table, picked up Eula Mae's cards, and began finishing the hand of solitaire she'd laid out.

"Are you sure Indy's tentacle will stretch that far?" Joseph asked, looking out the window.

"Ask Lyle," Wade said.

"Very funny," Lyle said, and started to open the refrigerator door.

"Nope," Joseph said, coming over and shutting it. "The Chuckwagon's off-limits till Eula Mae gets back and I know whether we have to ration the grub we've got left."

"*If* she comes back. She's probably in there right now calling the FBI," Lyle said. "And they'll tell the aliens where we are, and the next thing you know, we'll all be vaporized," and he stomped off to the Driver's Box, presumably to look for the arriving warships.

Francie had assumed Indy would insist on staying by the door to monitor Eula Mae, but instead he rolled up onto the banquette by Wade and began telling him which cards to play, so she took him back to the Bunkhouse to try to continue talking to him. But Indy refused to cooperate. He planted himself next to the window and made Francie read the words on the buses in the parking lot (GOLDEN YEARS NITETIME BUS, THE BLACKJACK EXPRESS, WEE HOURS ADVENTURE TOURS) and then the giant, brightly lit sign towering over the casino.

It was one of those video signs that changed every couple of minutes, and it kept Francie reading and "showing" the shifting images—BLACKJACK-O-RAMA AUGUST 14 and TRIPLE JACKPOTS and SENIORS EAT FREE FRIDAYS.

It was a good ten minutes before the images began to repeat, at which point she had to "show" why that was happening. *Eula Mae will be back before I have a chance to talk to him,* she thought, but there was no sign of her.

She pulled the curtains shut and tried again. "You know how I said Spanish was another Earth language? Different languages have different words for things. In Spanish the word for 'rattlesnake' is *cascabel* and for 'meadows' is *vegas*. The word for 'go' is *vamos* and the word for 'place' is *el lugar*. Can you tell me the word for the place you want to go in your lang— What?" she exploded as the door slid open again.

It was Lyle.

Oh, not now, Francie thought.

"Is Indy still attached to Eula Mae?" he asked.

Francie glanced quickly at Indy. The tentacle he'd tied around Eula Mae's wrist was still stretched taut. "Yes."

"Then why isn't she back yet? It's been half an hour."

He sat down next to her on the bunk. "What if they're *both* Reptilians," he whispered, "and this whole casino thing is just a cover so they can hook up with their contact and get their orders for the next phase?"

"The next phase of what?"

"The invasion! The complete destruction of Earth!"

"In that case, hadn't you better go back up front and keep an eye on Wade, in case he starts to shed his skin?" Francie said. "Or shoot lasers out of his nictitating membranes?"

"It's *not* funny," Lyle said. "When he reveals his true self, you'll be sorry," and he stomped back to the front.

"SHOW COMPLETE DESTRUCTION," Indy scrolled.

"It's what I'd like to do to Lyle," she said and then realized he might take her seriously. "I didn't mean that," she said hastily. "It's just a metaphor, a figure of speech," and then had to spend forever explaining what *that* was.

It was fifteen minutes before she was able to work the conversation back to Spanish and translations. "Remember when we watched *Fort Comanche* and Captain Gatewood was talking to the Comanche chief?"

"GREAT HAWK."

"Yes. That was what Captain Gatewood called him, but it wasn't his real name. His real name was Itza-Chu. Great Hawk was a translation of his Comanche name. Can you tell me what your name is in *your* language?"

His tentacle remained blank for a long moment, and then he began scrolling, but it wasn't letters. It was symbols she'd never seen before, a cross between Chinese characters and Egyptian hieroglyphics, but far too complicated for her to write them down, let alone translate. She'd have to try something else.

"Itza-Chu wasn't Great Hawk's name, either, because Comanche writing uses different lett— *What?*" she exploded as the door slid open again.

"Sorry to interrupt your pow-wow," Joseph said. He had his Stetson in his hands. "I was just wonderin'—"

"I'm sorry. I thought you were Lyle," Francie apologized. "What did you want to talk to me about?"

"It's been over an hour, and Eula Mae's still not back. Wade says not to worry, but I'm afeard she's lost our stake and she's just settin' in there afraid to come out and tell us. I've been in those casinos before and there's no way in hell a little old lady like that can win at them slots. And I was just wonderin' if mebbe one of us should go in there and get her, pore little thing."

"What does Wade say?"

"He says it'll all work out and we just need to give her a little more time . . ."

"Then I think that's what we should do," she said. "I'm sure Eula Mae will be back soon," even though she was sure of no such thing.

"You're the boss lady," he said, and slid the door shut, and Francie turned back to Indy.

"Itza-Chu wasn't Great Hawk's name, either, because Comanche writing uses different letters—different symbols—from English writing. Itza-Chu was his Comanche name written with English letters."

That wasn't true, the Comanches hadn't had a written language, and she and Indy were speaking, not writing, but it was the best she could do. "Can you do what the Comanche chief did?" she asked. "Can you tell me where you want to go in your language but with English letters?"

"Here she comes," Joseph shouted, and Indy rolled off the bunk and up to the kitchen, with Francie right behind him.

Joseph and Lyle were glued to the window. Wade was still playing solitaire. Francie pushed past him and looked out. Eula Mae was coming across the parking lot carrying her tote bag in one hand and a large white plastic bag in the other.

It was impossible to tell from this distance and with just the lights of the parking lot whether she was discouraged or elated. She was walking slowly, but that might be due to her age rather than dejection. Or to the weight of the white bag, which looked full of something.

"It better be full of money," Lyle said darkly.

"Shouldn't one of us go meet her and carry that for her?" Joseph said.

"No," Wade said, placidly turning over cards. "She'll be fine."

"But an old lady like that," Joseph said. "I know you don't want us to be seen—"

"Wait, where's she going?" Lyle said, and Joseph and Francie both pushed forward to see.

Eula Mae had stopped heading toward them and was heading toward the buses.

Lyle said, "She's gonna—"

"Shh," Francie said, stopping him before he could finish saying, "She's gonna try to get away," and looked at Indy, but neither he nor Wade seemed at all concerned. Indy's tethering tentacle wasn't even taut. It was draped loosely on the table next to the king of hearts.

Eula Mae had disappeared out of sight behind one of the buses. If she could make it onto the bus and persuade the driver to shut the door . . .

But the rest of the bus's passengers were still inside the casino, and the bus wouldn't leave till they were all on board. Surely by then Indy would have noticed what she was doing. Especially with Lyle shouting, "Look!" like he was.

Francie looked. Eula Mae had reappeared, walking toward a bus parked facing north, with its door on their side, and as soon as it was between her and the casino, she altered course and came straight toward them, walking faster.

She wanted it to look to any casino surveillance cameras like she was getting on that bus, Francie thought, impressed.

Wade finally put down the deck of cards and went over to the door to open it for Eula Mae.

She climbed up the steps and got in the RV, puffing. "Oh, my, but it's a long way across that parking lot," she said, and Joseph glared reproachfully at Wade, who didn't look at all contrite.

"Well?" Lyle said impatiently. "Did you win?"

"I'm sorry I'm so late," she said, setting her burdens on the table and opening the plastic bag. "Today was the Hawaiian Luau Buffet"—she pulled a white Styrofoam box out of the bag and handed it to Lyle—"and this nice older gentleman gave me a coupon for it, which meant it was only three dollars, so I thought I should take advantage of it. They don't usually let you take food home since it's all-you-can-eat, but I told them it was for my little dog who I had to leave on the bus. This is pork chow mein"—she handed Lyle another box and then a third—"and that's pineapple and ham pizza, and this one's egg rolls."

"Well, at least she got some food out of the deal even if she didn't win," Lyle said, handing the boxes to Joseph to put in the refrigerator, "but this is hardly going to feed us for—"

"Oh, but I *did* win," Eula Mae said, digging in her tote. "I told you I felt like this was my lucky day, and it was." She pulled out several dinner rolls wrapped in a paper napkin and then a large ziplock bag full of quarters. "It was amazing! I just kept hitting jackpots!"

She handed the baggie to Wade. "I'm sorry it's in quarters, but I was afraid if I took all of them to the cashier's cage to be changed for bills they might get suspicious, and I figured whoever goes into the grocery store could use one of those Coinstar machines."

"How much is in that bag?" Lyle asked.

"Around forty dollars, I think."

"But that's barely more than we sent you in with. I hardly call that winning."

"Oh, but that isn't all of it," she said and, after rummaging around in the tote some more, brought out a thick wad of twenties, fives, and ones.

"Jumpin' Jehoshaphat!" Joseph exclaimed. "How much have you got there?" and Lyle made a grab for the bills.

"By my count, it's $386.00," Eula Mae said, scooping the money out of Lyle's way and handing it to Wade. "And the $40.00 in quarters makes it . . . oh, dear, I'm so bad at math . . ."

"$426.00," Wade said, handing it to Joseph.

"I hope that's enough," Eula Mae said.

"Enough?" Joseph said. "It'll keep us in beans and coffee for a month."

"And Cokes," Lyle reminded him.

"And Cokes," Joseph said. "I can't believe you were so lucky!"

Neither can I, Francie thought, looking at Wade.

"I think Indy was my lucky charm," Eula Mae was saying. "I used to have a little charm bracelet that my friend Bernice gave me, and every time I wore it to the casino, I had good luck! And today having Indy wrapped around my wrist felt just like that bracelet."

"But I still don't see how—" Lyle began.

"I hate to break this up," Wade said, "but we need to be getting out of here before somebody spots us. Joseph, how about you take this shift? And Lyle, you ride shotgun."

"Okay," Joseph said, stuffing the bills in his jeans pocket. "Where are we heading?"

"I don't know," Wade said. "Indy?" and looked at the alien, but he was messing with the bag of quarters. "For now, why don't you head for a town with a grocery store?"

"I doubt if we can find one open this time of night."

"Oh, that's right. Okay, find us someplace safe to spend the night, and we'll hit the grocery store first thing tomorrow morning."

Joseph nodded and went up front. Lyle followed, stopping to grab a fork and the container of chow mein, and Eula Mae sat down at the table and began calmly laying out a game of solitaire.

"How are you coming with Indy?" Wade asked Francie as they pulled out onto the highway and started west. "Any luck getting him to tell you where he needs to go?"

"No."

"How about letting me try? Come on," he said to Indy, who was sitting by the window pointing at the passing signs, and Indy followed him back to the Opera House.

So did Francie.

"You didn't have to come," Wade said. "You've had him for hours, and I can 'show' a movie the same as you can." He indicated Indy, who'd rolled up into one of the recliners with the remote and was watching *Maverick*. "Go get a slice of pineapple and ham pizza or something."

She folded her arms militantly across her chest. "Not until you tell me what's going on."

"Going on?" he said, turning wide, innocent eyes on her. "What do you mean?"

"I mean, there's no way that an old lady could walk into that casino and win over four hundred dollars playing a slot machine."

"You saw the sign—they have the loosest slots in the Southwest," Wade said.

"Yes, well, they're not that loose. And don't give me any garbage about Indy being her lucky charm bracelet, either. I want to know the truth."

"Okay." He walked past her and slid the door to the rest of the RV shut. "You remember how Lyle said that you can't judge people by appearance, that underneath they may be Reptilians?"

"You're telling me Eula Mae is an *alien*?"

"No," he said. "I'm just telling you Lyle's right that people aren't always what they seem. Eula's not a sweet old lady who goes to casinos for the all-you-can-eat buffet. She's a professional gambler and card sharp."

"But—" Francie said, and then thought of the $426.00. "How did you figure it out?" she asked.

"For starters, the whole 'sweet little old lady' bit was a little *too* good. And her reactions when Indy grabbed her were all wrong. She'd just been abducted by an alien, but the only thing that scared her was the thought that the cops might show up. So I—"

He stopped as if he'd just thought of something, and then said, "Have you watched her shuffle the deck when she's playing solitaire and then lay out the cards? That's no amateur."

And now that Francie thought of it, she remembered that Eula Mae had known exactly where the nearest casino was.

"And when she was explaining card games to Indy," Wade was saying, "she knew every rule of stud poker and craps and blackjack. Which I suspect is her game of choice and that, in spite of her pretending to be bad at math, she's a card counter. But she couldn't do that today. Winning that much that fast would have aroused suspicions, and card counting's specifically illegal, so she had to stick with the slots."

"But how could she have done that? I thought the slot machines were designed to prevent cheating."

"They are, but there are devices for hacking the source codes and light wands that can trigger the switch for the coin hopper. My guess is she's got one of those in that cute sequined tote bag of hers."

"But how could you be sure she was a professional card sharp and not just someone who spends a lot of time in casinos?"

"Intuition," he said, and grinned disarmingly at her. "It takes one con man to spot another."

Or you had a look in that tote bag, she thought. Was that what he'd started to say when he'd begun, "So I—" and then stopped? But even if he had, how had he known what a slot machine light wand looked like? Unless he was a professional gambler himself.

But if he was, why hadn't *he* gone into the casino? And why would he waste his time selling anti-abduction insurance policies at UFO festivals?

She must have shown what she was thinking because Wade took a deep breath and said, "Speaking of the truth—"

"Yes?" Francie said, and Indy wrapped a tentacle around her wrist and laid a second one on her arm. "What is it, Indy?" she asked. "Is something wrong?"

"NO NO NO GREAT HAWK."

"Great Hawk?" Wade said. "Who's that?"

"A Comanche chief in a movie we were watching," Francie said.

"ITZA CHU," Indy scrolled.

"That's right," Francie said. "You've been thinking about what we were discussing? About writing Comanche words with English letters?"

"YES YES YES."

"What—?" Wade began.

"Shh, Wade," Francie said. "Where do you need us to take you, Indy?"

"TSURRISPOINIS."

CHAPTER THIRTEEN

"Never draw to an inside straight."

—Maverick

"There," Francie said happily, "I told you he knew where he wanted to go."

"Yeah, but there's just one problem."

"What?"

"We don't know what this *tsurrispoinis* is. Or where it is."

"But it's a start. And now that we know the word for it, we can ask him what it means."

"Fine," Wade said. "Indy, what's a *tsurrispoinis*?"

No answer. His tentacles remained blank.

"Is it a place?"

Still blank.

"A thing?"

No response.

"Which way is *tsurrispoinis*?"

No response.

"Are you sure *tsurrispoinis* isn't just some other Apache word he heard in the movie?" Wade asked.

"Yes," Francie said, though she wasn't. "Indy, is the *tsurrispoinis* where you want us to take you?"

"YES YES YES HURRY."

"Yes, well, we could hurry a lot faster if you'd tell us where it is," Wade said. "It's too bad cowboys were the strong, silent type. If they'd talked more, Indy would've heard the word by now."

"You're not helping," Francie said. "Go help Joseph find someplace to stop for the night, and I'll talk to Indy," and as soon as he was gone, she asked, "Indy, do you know where the *tsurrispoinis* is?"

No response.

"Do you know *what* it is?"

"YES YES YES INDY NOTHES."

He means "knows," she thought, and asked, "Can you show me what it is?"

Nothing.

"Is that because we haven't showed you one yet?"

"YES YES YES."

So it wasn't a town, a mountain, a butte, a sagebrush, a billboard, a deck of cards, a casino, a canteen, Monument Valley, or a rattlesnake. Or any of the dozens of other things they'd shown him. But that still left thousands of things it could be. That meant Joseph would have to keep showing him Westerns. And she'd have to think of some other way to approach this.

"Do you remember when Captain Gatewood talked to the chief in *Fort Comanche*?" she asked. "And sometimes he called him Itza-Chu and sometimes Great Hawk?"

"YES YES YES."

"Itza-Chu was how the chief's Apache name sounded in English and Great Hawk was what his Apache name *meant* in English. Can you tell me what *tsurrispoinis* means in English?"

His tentacles went—and stayed—blank.

I hope that means he's thinking about it, she thought, *like before, when I asked him to tell me how his name would sound, and he'll suddenly scroll it at some point.*

In the meantime, she tried another tack. "Can you tell me *why* you need to go to *tsurrispoinis?*"

There was a long pause, and then he scrolled, "HELP SREN-NOM."

Great. Another word she didn't know.

"Is *srennom* the thing you need to do at *tsurrispoinis?*"

"NO NO NO."

"Is *srennom* a place?"

"NO NO NO."

"Is *srennom* a thing, like an apple or a deck of cards or a car?"

"NO NO NO," and this time there was a tinge of red to the letters that could have meant he was insulted by the very idea. "SREN-NOM FRANCIE WADE JOSEPH INDY."

"Srennom's a person?"

"NO NO NO SRENNOM INDY."

"Srennom's someone like you."

"YES YES YES."

So he was an alien, and Srennom was his name. "Is Srennom a relative?"

"SHOW RELATIVE."

"Someone who's part of your family. A brother or a nephew or a . . ." She stammered to a stop. What sort of relatives would Indy have? She had no idea. Maybe they didn't even have the concept of a family. And Indy hadn't met any families here on Earth. "A family is a group of people or aliens or creatures who are related . . ."

"SHOW RELATED."

"It means . . . um . . ." She stopped, flummoxed.

"MARIAN JOEY JOE," Indy scrolled, and when she looked blank, "SHANE."

Shane? "Oh. Yes. Marian and Joe and Joey in *Shane* were a family. They were relatives. Is that what Srennom is? A relative of yours?"

"NO NO NO."

Okay. One down. And this time she knew how to approach this. "Is Srennom your mate? Like Clay Boone and Cat Ballou? Or—"

"FRANCIE WADE."

"No!" Francie said, more violently than she intended. "Wade and I are just friends."

"SHOW FRIENDS."

"Shane and Marian," she started to say and then decided that was a bad example. Marian had obviously been in love with Shane. She'd better use Shane and the little boy. "Shane was Joey's—"

There was a knock on the door, and Wade leaned in. "We found a good place to stop," he said. "I've told everybody to get some sleep. How's it coming?"

She told him what she'd found out.

"So Srennom isn't his sister or his girlfriend—"

"Or boyfriend," Francie said. "Which means he or she must be his friend."

"Or teacher or guardian or parole officer. Or something we don't have the equivalent of here on Earth. So what are you going to do?"

"Keep questioning him," she said. "If we can figure out what relationship he has to Srennom, it might go a long way to telling us what the *tsurrispoinis* is."

Wade nodded. "We should probably keep showing him movies, too. I'll go ask Joseph what he's got with things in it we haven't shown Indy so far." He looked at her. "Unless you want to try and get some sleep."

"No, that's okay. Maybe later. I'd really like to find out what Srennom and Indy are to each other first."

He nodded. "I'll go talk to Joseph," he said, and as soon as he slid the door shut, she picked up where she'd left off.

"Shane was Joey's friend. He—"

"KILLS BAD GUYS."

Oh, dear, she thought, *I need a less violent example of friends.* "Remember when I told you about Serena?" she said. "Serena's my friend."

"SERENA WORRIED SICK," he scrolled.

I said that that first night, she thought. *Which means he* **did** *understand what we were saying, even though he couldn't talk. I need to tell Wade that—*

"FRIEND WORRY SICK?"

Only when her friend has been abducted by an alien, Francie thought. *Or when her friend's about to marry a nut job and you're not there to stop it.*

Serena's wedding's tomorrow, and I am hundreds of miles away from Roswell, with no hope of making it there on time. And no chance of talking Indy into taking her back, not when he kept talking about a posse being after him and scrolling, "HURRY HURRY HURRY." Her only chance was finding out where the *tsurrispoinis* was and getting Indy to it in the next few hours.

"Yes," she said. "Friends worry about each other, and do things with each other, and go places together."

"FRANCIE WADE EULA MAE JOSEPH LYLE."

They go places willingly, she thought, and then decided the important thing was to put across the idea of friendship. "Yes," she said, "Wade and Eula Mae and Joseph and Lyle are my friends."

"INDY FRANCIE."

"Yes, you and I are friends."

"GO PLACES TOGETHER."

"Yes." *If you'll just tell me where it is you want to go.*

"KILL BAD GUYS."

No! she thought, and was grateful when Joseph interrupted with a list of movies for Indy to watch.

She spent the rest of the night watching *The Big Country, Dodge City,* and *The Magnificent Seven,* or rather, trying to stay awake while Indy watched them.

She didn't succeed. When Joseph knocked on the door, she was slumped in the recliner, sound asleep.

"Sorry," Joseph said, "but we're coming up on Holbrook, and I wondered if there was anything you needed from the grocery store."

She sat up, yawning. "What time is it?"

"Seven thirty," he said, "and already hotter'n hell. It's gonna be a real scorcher. So, anything I can get you from the store?"

"No, thanks," she said, and turned to Indy to start quizzing him again, but he was already rolling off toward the front, where he sat down next to Eula Mae and demanded she read him every sign they passed till they pulled into the Safeway parking lot.

Indy wanted to go into the grocery store with Joseph, but Eula Mae persuaded him to stay in the RV (with a tethering tentacle attached to Joseph) by promising to read him all the signs in Safeway's windows.

Lyle proved harder to dissuade. "I can help carry the groceries," he argued. "And it'd be faster with two people."

"And twice as likely that one of you would be recognized," Francie said.

"You're not going anywhere," Wade said. "I can't afford you screaming, 'Aliens from outer space!' the minute you get inside and scaring the good people of Holbrook."

"I wasn't going to—"

"Or making a break for it."

"I definitely wasn't going to do that. I learned my lesson last time. Indy would just snatch me back—"

"And you'd have blown our cover in the process. No. You're not going."

"But—"

"Besides, I need you. If you're not here, who'll come up with cockeyed ideas about where Indy's taking us? Don't worry. Joseph'll get you your Cokes."

"Get at least two twelve-packs," Lyle said. "And some Doritos. And a couple packages of Oreos."

"I'll get you *one* six-pack," Joseph said. "If we can afford it."

He apparently thought they could. He brought back two six-packs of Coke and a bag of Cheetos, handing them to Lyle with a flourish, and then reached into the bag again. "For you, Indy," he said, and handed him a bag of Reese's Pieces.

"SHOW REESES PIECES," Indy scrolled.

"It's a joke," Wade said.

"SHOW JOKE."

"Thanks a lot, you guys," Francie said. "Now I'll have to explain *that* to him."

"Sorry," Joseph muttered.

"Where to next, Indy?" Wade said.

"Don't ask him that," Francie said. "He doesn't know where the *tsurrispoinis* is, remember?" but Indy had set down the bag of Reese's Pieces and headed for the door.

Francie and Wade both dived to get in front of him. "Whoa!" Wade said. "Not here. We need to get out of town first," and went up front to start the RV and drive out of town while Francie took Indy to the back and grilled him about the *tsurrispoinis*.

"You know where the *tsurrispoinis* is?" she asked, but all Indy would scroll was "SHOW REESES PIECES JOKE," and by the time she'd finished telling him about *E.T.*, Wade had pulled off the highway and onto a rutted track leading north and parked next to a dry wash bordered with mesquite bushes.

There wasn't a hill or even a bump in the landscape, but Indy rolled out the door, went a few yards into the mustard-colored, rock-strewn desert, and sat down.

Francie got out, too, grateful for the chance to get some fresh air and to get away from everyone else and the cramped quarters of the RV.

She was immediately sorry. The heat hit her in the face like a blowtorch after the air-conditioned RV. It had to be a hundred and ten out here, without a cloud in sight to protect her from the blazing sun, only a few wispy, crisscrossing vapor trails high up in the stratosphere.

"Those aren't vapor trails," Lyle said, coming out to stand next to her as she looked up at them.

"I know," she said resignedly. "They're chemtrails dropping hallucinogenic drugs to keep us from being aware of the aliens' presence."

"No," he said. "These aren't. These are a coded alien map. They're here to guide Indy to the mother ship. Look how they converge at a single point," he said, pointing off to the east. "That's where the mother ship is. They're guiding Indy straight to it."

"Well, they're not doing a very good job," Francie said after Indy had rolled back inside, had them turn west on a county road, and then, after only a few minutes, had them stop again so he could repeat his getting-his-bearings thing and point them back east and then southwest, at which point, he lost interest and rolled back to sit next to Lyle and try to get him to read road signs to him.

"I'm eating breakfast," Lyle said, pointing to an enormous plate of scrambled eggs and sausage, "and I'm not about to reveal any information about our planet. Ask Eula Mae," and Eula Mae immediately set aside her plate and began reading: VISIT AMAZING METEOR CRATER and LEFT LANE CLOSED AHEAD and LAS VEGAS HAS IT ALL! SLOTS! WEDDING CHAPELS! SHOWS! LAP DAN—

"Come on," Francie said. "Let Eula Mae eat her breakfast. Let's go watch a movie," and when she got him back to the Opera House, resumed questioning him.

"Remember how we were talking about friends?"

"YES YES YES SHANE JOEY FRIENDS MAGNIFICENT SEVEN FRIENDS."

"Right, the Magnificent Seven *were* friends."

"KILL BAD GUYS."

No, no, no, Francie thought. "Friends don't *like* killing bad guys. The Magnificent Seven had to kill the bad guys to protect Joey and Marian and Joe, and the Magnificent Seven had to kill the bad guys to protect the townspeople, but they didn't want to kill anyone. Friends—"

"SHOW PROTECT."

"It means making sure your friend doesn't get hurt and keeping them from making stupid mistakes and rescuing them if they get in trouble. Remember when we saw the rattlesnake, and you kept it from biting me? You *protected* me."

"NO NO NO FRANCIE PROTECT INDY."

"We both protected each other. If you're friends with someone you have a duty to protect each other."

Indy's tentacles were blank for a moment, and then he scrolled, "BEN."

Ben?

"WHERE AM I GOIN I DONT KNOW."

Oh, no, Wade was right. Indy didn't know where he was going.

"WHERE AM I HEADED I AINT CERTAIN GOT A DREAM BOYS GOT A SONG PAINT—"

"Oh, the movie *Paint Your Wagon*," Francie said, suddenly enlightened. "Ben Rumson and Pardner."

"YES YES YES I GAMBLE AND CHEAT AT CARDS BUT THERES ONE THING I DO NOT DO I AINT NEVER GULLED A PARDNER THE ONE SACRED THING EVEN TO A LOW SCUFF LIKE ME IS A MANS PARDNER."

"Yes!" Francie said. "That's exactly it. When you're friends—or partners—you have a duty to take care of each other and try to help them do what they need to do." *Or help them talk themselves out of getting* **married,** she thought, and realized with a pang the wedding was today. "A duty," she repeated, and expected him to scroll, "SHOW DUTY," which was going to be almost impossible to explain, but instead he spelled out, "CODE OF THE WEST."

Code of the West? Was that a Western he'd watched or something Joseph had talked to him about?

"BE THERE FOR A FRIEND WHO NEEDS YOU," Indy scrolled.

"Yes!" Francie said. "Is that what you're trying to do for Srennom? Be there for your friend?"

"YES YES YES."

"And you have to find him?"

"YES YES YES HURRY MONUMENT VALLEY."

Monument *Valley*? "The *turrispoinis* is at Monument Valley?"

"NO NO NO."

"You want us to go to Monument Valley instead of the *tsurrispoinis*?"

"NO NO NO."

"You want us to go to the *tsurrispoinis* and *then* Monument Valley?"

"NO NO NO POSSE!"

Posse. "The people who are chasing you are in Monument Valley?"

"NO NO NO!" he scrolled, practically apoplectic. But it still didn't help her understand what he was saying.

She switched back to asking about Srennom. "You're trying to find Srennom so you can help him?"

"YES YES YES."

"Because he's your friend?"

"YES NO YES NO YES."

"What are you trying to help him do?"

His tentacles went blank.

She was getting nowhere. And questioning him was exhausting. It was a relief when Joseph interrupted again to tell her Wade wanted to talk to her.

"I'll be right there. Can you watch Indy for me while I talk to him?" she asked Joseph.

"Sure enough," he said, and started toward Indy.

"Just a minute," she said, and pulled him into the Bunkhouse. "Indy said something about the Code of the West. Was that a movie?"

"Yep. In 1947. James Warren and Steve Brodie, but the Code's in almost every Western. I told him about it when we was watchin' *The Man Who Shot Liberty Valance.*"

"And what did you say?"

"I told him it's the code cowboys live by. Never shoot first. Be hospitable to strangers. Be loyal to your partner. When you make a promise, keep it."

Oh, good, Francie thought. *At least it doesn't say anything about killing bad guys,* and went up front to the driver's compartment.

"Any luck at finding out what this *tsurrispoinis* is or where it's at?" Wade asked her as she flopped wearily down in the passenger seat.

"Not yet," she said. "Sometimes it takes him a while to process what I've asked him." She told him everything Indy'd said.

"Monument *Valley?*" he said. "I thought he was scared to death of it."

"He is. He doesn't want to go there and he says neither the *tsurrispoinis* nor whoever's after him are there, but it obviously has something to do with it."

"Did you *ask* him what it had to do with it?"

"*Yes,*" she said angrily. "You don't understand how hard it is to talk to him. It's like playing twenty questions in a minefield, and every time I ask him something, he makes me explain it. 'Show Reese's Pieces,' 'Show protect,' 'Show duty.' It's like pulling teeth!"

"Hey, hey," Wade said, "don't get mad. I'm sorry. I know you're trying. It's just that we're running out of time here, and he obviously doesn't have any idea which way to go. He's leading us in circles. I've had to turn around twice because the road he sent me on dead-ended. And half the time he's not even up here telling us which way to go. Maybe you need to stop asking questions and try the map again."

She sighed. "All right." She started to stand up, and then paused. "Why did you say that we're running out of time?"

"What?" he said, startled. "Oh. Nothing. It's just that Indy keeps saying, 'Hurry, hurry, hurry!' and talking about people chasing him, and they're bound to catch up with us pretty soon. He's already been on the run three and a half days."

"Oh. Which state do you want me to start with?"

"Arizona, since we seem to be headed southwest. For the moment."

"Okay," she said and stood up to leave, but she wasn't even all the way out of the passenger seat before Indy's index tentacle came shooting toward them and hit the windshield, pointing firmly ahead.

"It looks like he knows where he's going now," she said.

"If he doesn't turn around and take us in the opposite direction five minutes later."

But he didn't, and when they came to I-40 a few minutes later, he unhesitatingly indicated for them to head west again.

"You're right," Wade said. "Maybe he *does* know where his *tsurrispoinis* is. So what changed?"

"I don't know," Francie said. "Joseph was watching him. I'll go see what I can find out."

She went back to the kitchen. Joseph was washing the breakfast dishes and Lyle was lounging at the table, drinking a Coke and eating Oreos by the handful. Indy wasn't there.

"Eula Mae's watching him," Joseph said when she asked, jerking his thumb at the back.

"Are they watching a Western?" she asked, thinking, as she went, *Maybe he finally saw the* **tsurrispoinis** *in one of the movies.*

But the two of them were in the Bunkhouse, rolling dice on one of the beds. "I was trying to teach him stud poker," she said brightly, "but I couldn't make him understand he shouldn't scroll what cards he was holding, so I decided to teach him how to shoot craps instead."

Which wasn't likely to be the thing that had triggered it. "What did you two talk about while I was up front?" she asked. "Did you show him anything on the map?"

"No. Lyle tried to, but Indy wasn't interested. He wanted me to read him the signs along the highway."

"What did they say?"

"Say? Oh, my, let me think," she said, setting down the dice, which Indy immediately grabbed and took back to the kitchen. "There were several for the Grand Canyon and Las Vegas and Wall Drug and one for an A&W Root Beer Drive In, and, let's see, what were the others? Oh, there was one for a bank. It said, 'Bank with Wells Fargo, Flagstaff, twenty miles ahead,' and then underneath, it had a picture of a stagecoach, and Indy started to get upset like before and I had to reassure him it wasn't the stagecoach he saw in the movie *Stagecoach* and that Flagstaff wasn't in Monument Valley and that we weren't going anywhere near there. Then he asked me about Jason and Prudy."

"Jason and Prudy?"

"In *Support Your Local Sheriff*. Jason was the sheriff and Prudy was the mayor's daughter. I watched it with him when he was doing the closed captioning thing. Such a nice movie. Not so full of shooting as most Westerns. Just a nice, sweet love story."

"What did Indy ask you about Jason and Prudy?"

"He wanted to know whether they were friends, and I said they were mates—at the end of the movie they're getting married—and then he wanted to know what mating was."

Oh, dear. "And what did you say?"

"I tried to explain 'falling in love,' but I don't think I did a very good job of it. He kept asking me to explain things—'getting married' and 'rescued'—Jason rescues Prudy from a bunch of rowdy cowboys—and 'kissing.'" She pursed her lips primly. "I wasn't about to get into the whole sex thing."

Very wise, Francie thought. God only knew what questions he'd ask about that. "You didn't talk about anything else?"

"No, except for Meteor Crater."

"Meteor *Crater*?" Francie had read him a sign for Meteor Crater earlier this morning.

"Yes," Eula Mae said. "Lyle showed it to him on the map."

"And what did you tell him about Meteor Crater?"

"That it was a meteor crater," she said. "That was the only thing I knew about it."

"What did Lyle tell him?"

"I don't know," she said. "That was when I was in the back, using the little girl's room. You'll have to ask him."

Francie did.

"Why?" Lyle asked, immediately interested. "Did he tell you that was where he wants to go?"

"No, but he's apparently figured out where he wants to go, and Wade wants to know whether there's anything he might have heard or seen in the last few minutes that might have triggered it. What exactly did you tell him about Meteor Crater?"

"That a blinding green light passed over Meteor Crater in 1948, and that the Hopis believe it's the site where the Blue Star prophecy will be fulfilled and the world will come to an end."

"I thought you said the light was green, not blue."

Lyle glared at her. "The *point* is that Meteor Crater's had dozens of sightings over the years—1955, 1971, 2012. Some people think it wasn't a meteor that caused it, that it was an enormous crashed flying saucer, and the aliens are trying to salvage pieces of it, but I think it's an extraterrestrial transfer point, and the place where aliens go if they're stranded on Earth and need a ride home."

"It's the place where aliens go if they're stranded on Earth in a movie called *Starman,*" Wade said when Francie told him. "Plus, we already passed Meteor Crater a ways back."

"Maybe he's taking some other route to it," Francie said. "West and then south and—"

Wade shook his head. "He's taking us north. Indy just had me turn onto Highway 93. Go check the map and see where that takes us."

She didn't have to. When she asked the others to move the lunch dishes so she could spread out the map and find Highway 93, Eula Mae said, "He's taking us to Las Vegas!"

"No, he's not," Lyle said. "He's taking us to Area 51."

"He is *not* taking us to Area 51," Wade said when Francie reported back. "It doesn't exist. Ask him if there've been any UFO sightings between here and Las Vegas."

"I did. He said there'd been mysterious lights north of Kingman and over Lake Mohave, Nelson, and Panaca, and there are secret underground bases at Dry Lake and Caliente. Or, if Indy turns east again, there've been sightings at St. George, Kanab, and the north rim of the Grand Canyon."

But Indy didn't turn east. He kept Wade and then Joseph driving northwest on Highway 93 for the rest of the morning while Lyle regaled them with his theories of where they were going. "It has to be Area 51."

"Area 51 doesn't exist," Wade said patiently.

"Of course it does," Lyle said. "The government even admitted it did."

"They admitted there was an Air Force installation there. It's a top-secret air base for testing experimental aircraft," Wade said.

"And they're still secretly testing advanced nuclear weapons there," Lyle said.

Wade ignored him. "They tested the U-2 plane there," he explained to Francie, "and then the X-15 and the Stealth Bomber. The talk about UFOs started because of the Stealth Bomber."

"And how do you think they came up with the technology for it?" Lyle asked. "They reverse-engineered it from the flying saucer they captured."

"Why do they have to reverse-engineer it if they're working with the aliens? Wouldn't the aliens just explain it to them?"

Lyle ignored that and said to Francie, "They've been keeping the Roswell flying saucer and the aliens who were in it at Area 51 since the crash, and Indy's come to break them out."

"If that's the case, he's a little late, isn't he?" Wade asked Indy. "The crash happened over seventy years ago."

"Time operates differently for aliens," Lyle said glibly. "Indy's going to rescue them. That's what he meant when he scrolled 'HELP SRENNOM.' *Srennom* obviously means 'Roswell aliens.' Don't you see? *Srennom*'s an anagram for 'Roswell.'"

"Except for the *m* and the two *n*'s," Francie said.

"They probably don't have those letters in their language."

"Yeah, well, *Srennom* might also be the alien word for 'moron,' except for the *s* and the *e*," Wade said.

Lyle ignored that. "You watch, Indy's going to take us straight through Las Vegas"—he traced the route on the map with his finger—"and then north on 93 to the Extraterrestrial Highway."

"Extraterrestrial Highway?" Francie said.

"State Route 375," Wade explained. "The governor named it as a publicity stunt."

Lyle shook his head violently. "He *named* it that because it's the road to Area 51 and Groom Lake and the Black Mailbox."

"The Black Mailbox?" Francie asked.

"Yes. Halfway between Alamo and Rachel is a black mailbox

that marks the spot where the UFOs from Area 51 fly over. Alien-hunters camp there to try and get pictures of them and leave messages for the aliens in the mailbox. Maybe that's why Indy's taking us there, so he can leave a message telling the invasion fleet where he is."

"He's not taking us to the Black Mailbox."

"Then he *has* to be taking us to Area 51. It's the only other place up there. That has to be it. Unless he's taking us to Ely. A UFO crashed on the railroad tracks there," Lyle said. "Or to Mount Rainier."

"Mount *Rainier*?" Wade exploded. "In Washington? Why the hell would he take us to Mount Rainier?"

"Because that's where the first UFO sighting was."

"I thought it was in Roswell," Francie said.

"No, that was the second UFO incident. The Mount Rainier sighting was June twenty-fourth, two weeks before Roswell's. A pilot looking for the wreckage of a crashed plane saw a bright flash of light and then nine flying saucers going two thousand miles an hour."

"He is *not* taking us to Mount Rainier," Wade said.

"Lyle, there *has* to be someplace closer than Washington," Francie said.

Lyle thought about it a minute. "I suppose he might be taking us to Area 52."

"Area 52?" Francie said. "How many of these top-secret areas are there?"

"Three that we know of. Wright-Patterson Air Force Base, Area 51, and Area 52," Lyle said. "It's seventy miles northwest of Area 51, under Paiute Mesa. There's a huge underground chamber there, big enough to hold twenty-five thousand troops. They made it by detonating a nuclear bomb, and—"

"Wait," Francie said. "They detonated an A-bomb? What about the radiation?"

"There wasn't any," Lyle said. "It was a clean nuclear bomb. They got the technology for it from the aliens."

Of course, Francie thought.

"Some UFOlogists think Area 51's just a cover for Area 52, which is where they've actually got the aliens and the Roswell flying saucer."

"Those people being Bugs Bunny and Daffy Duck," Wade said. "In the classic film *Looney Tunes: Back in Action.*"

"No," Lyle said huffily. "A cement-truck driver who helped build the underground hangars testified that they were there. And after he told what he saw, he mysteriously disappeared."

"I'm not surprised," Wade said, getting an apple out of the refrigerator, and sitting down next to Francie. "Any progress with Indy?"

"No," she said. "All he's interested in is shooting craps with Eula Mae."

"You don't suppose she put him up to going to Las Vegas, do you? So she could play the Venetian's slots? Or the Golden Nugget's?"

"Why? You think Las Vegas is where he's taking us?"

"It seems that way. Unless he suddenly decides to turn off to Searchlight."

But there wasn't so much as a flicker from Indy's pointer tentacle when they passed the sign for Searchlight in midafternoon, nor when Joseph stopped in Boulder City to change places with Wade as driver, though shortly after they started up again, Indy abandoned his craps game and came to get Francie so she could read him the billboards that crowded both sides of the road now that they were approaching Las Vegas: LAS VEGAS! WHERE THE SKY'S THE LIMIT! and GET READY FOR FUN! LAS VEGAS: 22 MILES AHEAD and YOU'RE ALMOST THERE! KENO! BLACKJACK! SLOTS! SHOWS—

"Oh my gosh," Francie said, handing Indy over to Eula Mae and racing up to the cab to talk to Wade. "I just thought of something. That sign for Las Vegas we just passed said 'Shows,' and Eula Mae read another one that said 'Shows!' earlier this morning."

"And?"

"And he thinks 'show' means 'explain,' and I asked him if he could show me what *tsurrispoinis* meant, and he said no."

"I still don't—"

"The sign also said 'Las Vegas Has It All.' What if he thinks that includes explanations? Show!" and when Wade still didn't get it, Francie continued, "What if he's confused 'show' with '*show*'?"

"I think he's more likely to think if Las Vegas has it all, that that includes a *tsurrispoinis*," he said. "Besides, he didn't see whatever it was that decided him till we were nearly to Needles."

"Sometimes it takes him a while to process what he's heard or seen—"

"Not that long. Don't worry. If he's taking us to Vegas, it's more likely to be because Eula Mae put him up to it. But I don't think he is. And I don't think he's taking us to Area 51, either. It's a government base, and you saw how Indy acted when we suggested calling the authorities. He doesn't want to go anywhere *near* them."

"Then where *does* he want to go?"

"I don't know. Hoover Dam?"

"Or Las Vegas itself," Francie said. "You said we didn't have anything unique enough for aliens to come all this way out to the middle of nowhere, but you have to admit Las Vegas is unique."

"Yeah, that's not the word I'd use," Wade said. "But wherever it is he's going, our job is to get him there before this posse from Monument Valley catches up to us. Look." He pointed ahead. "We're coming into Las Vegas. Check the map. Is there any way we can get through Vegas without going straight through the middle of town?"

She wrestled with the map, trying to find the inset for Las Vegas. "Yes," she said. "There's a highway that goes around it. I-215. It's a ring road that'll take us around the edges."

"Good. I want to get through here and on to wherever Indy's taking us as soon as possible."

"Why? Are you afraid of letting Eula Mae anywhere near the Strip?"

"Yes, and of having to explain the Blue Man Group to Indy."

"Let alone what the Statue of Liberty's doing here, or the Eiffel Tower. Or that," she said, waving at the endless line of signs touting shows, casinos, all-you-can-eat buffets, and nude dancing.

"Especially the nude dancing," Wade said.

"Yes. Do not, repeat, *do not* explain that. Or *that*—" She pointed to a sign that read TOPLESS! BOTTOMLESS! ALL MAJOR CREDIT CARDS ACCEPTED, and a second announcing BEST LAP DANCES IN VEGAS. "Or anything else connected with sex to him."

"Why not? You afraid he'll scroll 'SHOW'?" Wade asked, grinning, and Indy rolled into Francie's lap.

"What are you doing up here?" Francie said. "I thought you were with Eula Mae."

"EULA MAE SAID GO ASK FRANCIE READ SIGNS," he scrolled.

"I'll bet she did," Francie said. "Come on, let's go find Joseph. He wants to show you a movie."

"NO NO NO MOVIE SIGNS." He rolled over to the side window and plastered two tentacles against the window and then half a dozen. But he didn't say anything.

Maybe he's got information overload from the array of words and images, Francie thought, looking at a larger-than-life photo of a showgirl wearing a G-string and nothing else. *Let's hope so.*

"SHOW LAP DANCING," Indy scrolled.

"Not now, Indy," Wade said. "Francie's busy," and to her, "I need you to help me find the signs for—what was it? I-215?"

"Yes," she said, peering through the forest of signs. "There it is." She pointed. "Just ahead. Get in the right lane. There's the exit."

Wade clicked on the turn signal, glanced in his mirrors, and started to move into the right lane, then jerked the RV back to the left and went on past the exit.

"What are you doing?" Francie asked.

"What am *I* doing?" he said, pointing down at his hand and his right foot, both wrapped in one of Indy's tentacles.

"Oh," Francie said, snatching up the map. She checked it and then leaned forward to peer at the signs. "You're still okay. You can take I-15. It's just before Las Vegas Boulevard—that's the Strip—and it'll take you north through town."

But Indy was apparently not going to let him do that, either. The only thing he'd allow was turning onto the Strip. Along with every-one else. They were immediately in a barely moving traffic jam.

"Apparently Indy wants to see the Strip," Francie said.

"Apparently," Wade said. "Get Eula Mae up here."

"What about the map? Don't you need me to read it to you?"

"Why? We're not going anywhere."

He was right. The traffic had come to a halt as tourists in shorts and KNOW WHEN TO HOLD 'EM, KNOW WHEN TO FOLD 'EM T-shirts and tank tops, sporting fanny packs and carrying mai tais in pink plastic glasses, streamed past them.

A cluster of young women wearing feather boas and pink T-shirts proclaiming BRIDESMAID went past, chattering, followed by a bald man using a walker with VEGAS OR BUST! taped to the front of it. They surged past the stopped cars, threading their way between them, stopping in front of them to take pictures, and making any forward movement impossible.

Francie clambered out of the passenger seat and went to get Eula Mae, who was sitting at the window pointing things out to Lyle and Joseph. "Look, there's the Four Seasons. And Mandalay Bay."

"Wade wants to talk to you," Francie said to Eula Mae, and all three of them stood up and hurried forward to the front.

The *Outlaw* had moved forward maybe half a block. "We're going to be here all day," Wade said, exasperated. "Did you put Indy up to this, Eula Mae?"

"Up to what?"

"Taking the Strip through Vegas."

"No, though now that we're here, I'd be happy to get us some more food money. The Luxor would be the best place to stop," she said, pointing at its Egyptian pyramid. "They've still got manual slots."

"We are *not* stopping at the Luxor."

"But they've got bottomless margaritas," Eula Mae said, "and I could easily get them to comp us a suite there or at New York New York—"

"We are not stopping *anywhere*," Wade said, even though the

RV was sitting there motionless. "Lyle, have there been any UFO sightings in Las Vegas?"

"Yeah, over the Mirage and Planet Hollywood and around the Sky Beam."

"The Sky Beam?" Francie asked.

"Yeah, the beam of lights that shoots straight up from the Luxor's pyramid. You can't see it during the daytime, only at night. It's supposed to be a beacon to guide tourists to the Luxor, but it's really a signal to alien ships."

"It is *not* a signal to alien ships," Wade said.

"Yeah, well, why else would it be bright enough that it can be seen from space? They—"

"Where else?" Wade said.

"Hovering over the Vegas Vic sign downtown—you know, the neon cowboy who waves and says 'Howdy! Welcome to Las Vegas'?—and in the casinos."

"The casinos?"

"Yeah, there've been hundreds of reports of aliens being sighted inside mingling with the gamblers and the tourists. They can disguise themselves to look exactly like humans."

"Then how do they get sighted?" Francie asked.

"By their nictitating membranes."

"*Which* casinos?" Wade said.

"Just casinos in general. Why?"

"Because Indy's obviously looking for something here on the Strip or he wouldn't have made us come this way. Eula Mae," he said, inching along past the Luxor and the Excalibur's turreted castle, "what exactly did you tell him about the Strip?"

"*Nothing.* Except what was on the signs he asked me to read him on our way here."

"Which was?"

"I don't remember exactly. 'Stay at the Beautiful Bellagio!' and 'Now Appearing at the Flamingo—Wayne Newton!' "

"And 'Hot Babes Direct to You!' " Lyle said.

"Shut up, Lyle," Wade said. "I need to know what Indy read or saw about the Strip that made him—"

Indy flung a tentacle in front of Wade's eyes. "STOP," he scrolled, and pointed off to the right.

"What's he pointing at, Francie?" Wade asked.

"I don't know," she said. "The Tropicana's over there, and the MGM Grand, but—"

"GO TROPICANA," Indy scrolled.

CHAPTER FOURTEEN

Jack: Do you know what a straight flush is? It's
like . . . unbeatable.

Betsy: "Like unbeatable" is not unbeatable.

Jack: Hey, I know that now, okay?

—*Honeymoon in Vegas*

"Did you read him a Tropicana sign, Eula Mae?" Wade demanded.

"Yes, but I certainly didn't try to talk him into going there. The pickings are a lot better at Bally's. Or downtown, like at the Golden Nugget."

"Yes, well, we're not going to stop there, either. We're not stopping anywhere. Indy, we've got to go find your *tsurrispoinis*."

"Maybe it's here," Lyle said. "I told you, aliens frequent the casinos in disguise."

"And Tropicana *does* sound a mite like *tsurrispoinis*," Joseph said.

"Indy," Francie asked him, "is your *tsurrispoinis* at the Tropicana?"

"NO NO NO," Indy scrolled, and stuck the tentacle inches from Wade's eyes. "STOP STOP STOP."

"Tell him I can't drive with that tentacle in front of my face," Wade said to Francie. "And that I can't just stop in the middle of the street."

"There's a parking lot," Lyle said helpfully.

Wade glared at him. "The *Outlaw* won't fit in it," he said. "Francie, explain to Indy that we can't stop, that there's no place to park."

"TURN TURN TURN," Indy scrolled, at the same time wrapping two tentacles around the steering wheel, and there was nothing for Wade to do but pull in.

The huge lot was full of tourists streaming past the entrance, gawking at the Tropicana's tall white hotel and palm trees and video signs and taking photos and selfies with their phones.

"Tell Indy you can't park for all the people," Francie said, but Wade was looking at the tourists. As soon as there was a break in the flow, he nosed into an empty spot and parked.

"What are you *doing*?" Francie said. "I thought you said you wanted to get through Vegas as soon as possible."

"Indy wants to go to the Tropicana," Wade said. "So we're going to the Tropicana."

"YES YES YES," Indy scrolled, and rolled off.

"Wait, Indy," Francie cried, leaping past everyone to get between him and the door, "you can't go in there by yourself," but he was rolling toward the rear of the RV.

"You can't take Indy in there. It's too crowded," she told Wade, who'd followed her back to the Chuckwagon. "What if someone sees him? We don't exactly have room for an entire casino full of people in the *Outlaw*."

"They won't see him," he said. "We'll hide him."

"In your duffel bag?" Lyle said, watching Wade narrowly.

"No, it's too big," Wade said. "What about your 'Luck Be a Lady Tonight' tote bag, Eula Mae?" he asked, and she brought over her bag, with its array of sequined cards on it.

"But don't they check bags at the entrance?" Francie said.

"It'll be fine," Eula Mae said, pulling things out of the bag and sticking them in her pockets. "It has a false bottom."

"Come on, Indy," Wade called, and Indy appeared out of the back, dragging Francie's maid-of-honor dress behind him.

"What—?" Francie said, and Indy pushed it against her.

"WEAR TROPICANA," he scrolled.

"I can't," she said. It would be even more conspicuous than her tank top and short shorts. She started to explain that to Indy, and he thrust it against her again.

"WEAR TROPICANA."

"Sorry, pal," Wade said, taking the dress from him. "They don't allow dresses inside casinos. Now come on, curl yourself up like you did at the Apache Buttes Casino and get in."

"NO NO NO," Indy scrolled, lashing out with his tentacle to grab the dress back.

"Fine," Wade said, stuffing it in the tote bag, "you can take it with you," and Indy curled himself into a sphere the size of a golf ball and scuttled in after it. "Now, you have to promise to stay in there," Wade said. "And no tethering yourself to any of us except the one carrying you."

"Do you mean we're *all* going in?" Francie said. He hadn't even let Lyle go into the grocery store with Joseph. What on earth was he thinking?

"Yes, we're all going," he said.

"But aren't there surveillance cameras everywhere inside? And security guards?"

"It'll be fine," Wade said. "We won't be in there that long. Besides, what happens in Vegas stays in Vegas." He grinned and turned to Eula Mae. "Eula Mae?"

She put the false bottom back in place and held the bag open for them to see. It looked empty.

"Now, listen up," Wade said. "We're going in for one reason and one reason only, and that's to find whatever Indy thinks is in there. As soon as we do, we come straight back out."

"Can't we even get something to eat?" Lyle said, pointing at one of the signs. "It says they have a surf-and-turf buffet."

"No," Wade said and handed the tote bag to Francie. "Okay, everybody out."

Joseph and Lyle scrambled down the steps, followed by Eula Mae, who'd gone back for her straw hat. Francie slung the tote bag over her arm, and Indy reached out a tentacle and wrapped it around her wrist. She went over to the door and then looked back at Wade, who was just standing there. "Aren't you coming?"

"In a sec," he said. "I need to make sure the AC's shut down. Go on without me. I'll catch up."

She nodded and went down the steps and over to the others.

"Where's Wade?" Joseph said.

"Shutting off the AC," Francie told him, and started across the parking lot toward the casino. "He said he'd catch up with us."

"I already shut it off," Joseph said. "I told him—"

"I still don't see why we can't eat here since we're stopped anyway," Lyle cut in. "I'm starving. And these casinos have really cheap buffets."

"Not cheap enough for us," Joseph said. "We need to save what we've got left for groceries."

"Not a problem," Eula Mae said. "I can—"

"No," Wade said, catching up with them, slightly out of breath. "No gambling. No eating. And no wandering around. Stick close to Francie and Indy. We may have to leave in a hurry. And don't do anything to get us noticed. The key word is 'inconspicuous.'"

"That would be a lot easier to achieve if I didn't have a rhinestone UFO across my chest, a pink tote bag covered with sequined playing cards, and an extraterrestrial bracelet that might start scrolling at any minute," Francie hissed.

"Are you kidding? You'll fit right in," Wade said, nodding at the other people trekking across the parking lot toward the casino, including a large man in a chartreuse-and-orange Hawaiian shirt and purple plaid shorts and a blonde in a yellow bikini top and hot pink shorts with FEELING LUCKY? written across her rear end.

"Nobody'll notice us," Eula Mae said. "Everybody'll be too busy looking at their cards or watching the reels spin on their slot machines."

"Or looking at their phones," Wade said, nodding at the blonde, who was busily texting.

"Not in the casino, they won't be," Eula Mae said. "There's no coverage."

Wade stopped walking. "Phones don't work inside the casino?"

"No," Eula Mae said. "It's so people can't use them to count cards. Why?"

"No reason," he said. "Actually, that's a good thing. I was worrying about Indy suddenly lashing out and flinging somebody's halfway across the casino. Francie, keep a tight hold on him. And all of you, keep a low profile."

That was easier said than done. To get into the casino, they had to not only go through a metal detector but edge past a platform outside on top of which was a shiny red convertible, a giant roulette wheel, and a shimmering sequined sign saying SHOWGIRL SPIN.

A middle-aged man in a gold lamé suit stood next to the car, shouting, "Enter our Showgirl Spin! It's absolutely free. Spin the wheel and win a car! Or a delicious steak dinner!"

"Did you hear that?" Lyle said. "We could win a free steak dinner!"

"No, you couldn't," Eula Mae said. "And you can't win a car, either. The only thing anybody ever wins is a ticket to the *real* Showgirl Spin inside. It's a come-on to get you into the casino and make you sit in the bar buying drinks while you wait for the Spin, which only happens once every two hours."

"But—" Lyle began.

"No," Wade said and pushed him and Eula Mae past the convertible and into the casino, followed by Joseph.

Francie started after them, but a gaggle of women wearing tiaras and neon-orange feather boas pushed in front of her, chattering. *A bachelorette party,* she thought, thinking bleakly of Serena. Today was her wedding, and Francie wasn't there to do anything about it.

"You there in the short shorts!" the man called, and she turned to see him pointing at her. "With the sequined tote bag! Wouldn't you like to win a car? Or a pair of tickets to the Tropicana's brand-new, world-famous Fabulous Follies?"

Not with an alien in my tote bag, she thought. "No, thanks," she murmured, and started past the platform.

"Come on, don't be shy! What's your name?"

She smiled and shook her head.

"Oh, I get it. You don't want your boyfriend to know you're in Vegas. Well, we won't tell, will we?" he asked the crowd, and they shouted "No!" and held up their phones to take her picture.

"That's right! What happens in Vegas stays in Vegas! Come on up and take a spin!" He extended a hand to help her up onto the platform. "Every number wins a prize. There's no way you can lose!"

That's what you think, Francie thought, backing away.

"Come on, let's give her a little encouragement, folks!" the man said, and the audience clapped and whistled and more people gathered to see what was going on. "Come on, everybody wants to see you spin the wheel. Don't you, folks?"

More cheers and whistles. "If it's your bag you're worried about, I'll hold it for you while you spin the wheel."

No! Francie thought.

He extended a hand. "Come on up. What do you wanna see her win, folks? Tickets to the Follies? A hundred dollars in chips?"

"A showgirl!" a man called from the middle of the crowd, and she turned to see Wade pushing forward to the platform. "You said it was called the Showgirl Spin, so that means you can win a showgirl, right?"

The crowd laughed.

"Afraid not," the man said. "But you *can* win two tickets to the Showgirl Spin inside the casino, presided over by one of our very own real-life Follies showgirls! How about that?"

Wade shook his head. "I had my heart set on winning a real live showgirl. It says *right there*"—he pointed at the sign—"Showgirl Spin," and Francie realized every eye in the crowd was now fixed on him. She took the opportunity to scuttle inside.

Into a cacophony of light and sounds. Pop music blasted from loudspeakers, interrupted by a constant chorus of bells, whistles, siren whoops, and clanking coins, and the enormous room stretching before her was like a visual manifestation of the noise: mirrors everywhere and row upon row of red- and blue- and gold-lit slot machines, each with its own sound effects and flashing LEDs and moving tracer lights and animated screens—wheels of fortune, pots of gold, treasure chests, timber wolves, unicorns, dragons, locomotives, starbursts of scarlet and purple and orange and green.

The tourists were almost as colorful: middle-aged men in light-up sunglasses and T-shirts reading PAR-TEE! and WHAT HAPPENS HERE STAYS HERE; young women in halter tops and shorts even shorter than Francie's; middle-aged women in flowered capri pants. And *lots* of women in the dresses they'd told Indy weren't allowed—sundresses and sarongs and caftans. Even a redhead in a long white wedding dress, holding a bouquet in one hand while she worked a slot machine with the other.

I'll bet Serena's marrying Russell right about now, Francie thought. *I am* **so** *sorry I let you down,* and then, *I'd better not let Indy see that bride. He'll demand that I put on my maid of honor dress.*

But Indy didn't seem to notice the bride in all the chaos. And neither did anybody else, even though the bride was wearing a veil and had a JUST MARRIED sign pinned to her back.

Eula Mae was right. Nobody looked at anything but the slot machines in front of them, which stretched as far as the eye could see, their images doubled in the mirrors. People of all ages sat in front of them, pushing buttons, and the carpeted aisles were crammed with people shuffling along, carrying umbrella-adorned cocktails, searching for a vacant machine.

She couldn't see Eula Mae or Joseph or Lyle anywhere in the throng. She stood indecisively in the middle of the aisle, scanning the room and wondering how to go about finding them.

"GO GO GO," Indy scrolled, and pointed toward a row of garish slot machines.

I **knew** *Eula Mae was behind this,* Francie thought. *Next he'll demand to play.*

"We have to find the others first," she whispered. "Do you know where they are?"

"HERE," Indy scrolled, and Francie turned to find Wade at her elbow.

He said, "Where is everybody? I told you to all stick together," and handed her a small piece of cardboard.

"What are these?" she asked.

"A chit good for two tickets to the Showgirl Spin over at the bar. I had to spin the wheel just to get out of there." He looked down at Indy's tentacle wrapped around her wrist. "Lyle was right," he said. "There *are* aliens in the casinos."

"Very funny," she said.

"Sorry. Any indication of what Indy's looking for?"

"No," she said, "and no sign of the others." And just then she saw them, standing in front of a slot machine.

Eula Mae was apparently explaining how it worked to Lyle. "They don't have an arm you pull down anymore," she said. "You push a button instead."

"How can they be one-armed bandits if they don't have an arm?" Lyle said.

"Trust me, Pilgrim, they're still bandits," Joseph said. "The only difference is that this way's faster at separating you from your money. And so's this," he said, indicating a slot on the side. "You don't have to feed in coins. You just insert your credit card. It tallies the cost automatically."

And keeps you from having any idea how much you're losing, Francie thought.

"Where have you been?" Eula Mae asked Wade. "I thought you wanted us to stick together."

"I do," he said. "I'm going to go check out the exit situation in case we need to leave in a hurry."

"There's only one exit. They want to make leaving as difficult as possible," Eula Mae said, but Wade had already vanished into the crowd.

"So what do we do now?" Joseph asked.

"Wait till he comes back," Francie said. "And try not to look suspicious."

"Then we need to be playing the slots," Eula Mae said. "There's nothing more suspicious in a casino than just standing around." She nodded toward one of the guards, who was headed their way.

Francie shook her head. "Wade said no gambling."

"It's not gambling the way Eula Mae does it," Joseph remarked, and Eula Mae said, "If you'll give me a couple of minutes, I can get us a credit card."

"And get us all arrested? No," Francie said firmly.

"Fine," Eula Mae muttered grudgingly, and pulled a roll of quarters out of her pocket.

"Where'd that come from?" Joseph demanded. "You were supposed to turn over your winnings so I could buy groceries."

"I did—except for these. I thought I'd better hold back some for a stake."

"I thought you said the machines didn't take money," Lyle said.

"These don't. We need the cheap slots. Or better yet, a video poker machine," Eula Mae said, and, before Francie could stop her, she'd headed down the aisle to the banks of machines against the far wall.

The guard was headed straight for Francie. She put her Indy-wrapped-hand at her side and hurried down the aisle to the first opening, went over an aisle and down it to a vacant slot machine, and pretended to fumble in the tote bag.

The guard came up to her. "Need change?" he asked.

"No, I've got Visa," Francie said.

The guard nodded and passed on. Francie looked around for the others. They were nowhere to be seen. She stood on tiptoe to see down the aisle they'd been in and then looked back toward the front. There was a huge crowd at the entrance—the Showgirl Spin was obviously still going—and at the edge of it she thought she saw Wade.

No, it couldn't be, because the guy was making a phone call, and before she could move to get a better look, Indy tightened himself around her wrist and scrolled, "GO," and pointed toward the rear of the casino.

"What are you looking for?" Francie asked him. "Why did you want to come here?"

"BBHBINIITS," Indy scrolled. He stuck a second tentacle out of the tote bag and pointed toward the rear of the casino. "GO GO GO."

"All right," she said and started down the main aisle and then down a cross aisle, following Indy's pointing and trying to figure out what he was looking for.

Not a particular slot machine, even though many of them displayed aliens and flying saucers—Star Battles, Alien Attack, Martian Invasion, UFO Wars. He didn't spare them a glance, even when a woman in a flowered caftan won a jackpot, and a whoop-whooping red siren began flashing while coins jangled noisily into the tray. And when they reached the craps tables, and beyond them, the Keno parlor and the restaurant Lyle had talked about, Indy was equally uninterested. His tentacle continued to point in one direction, then another, leading her on a zigzag circuit of the entire casino—the blackjack tables, the cashiers' cage where chips could be cashed in, the sports betting area, the bar.

Looking for what? Lyle had said aliens had been spotted in casinos, disguised as humans. Was that what he was looking for? A slightly off person? If so, there were dozens to choose from: a stout fortyish woman with bleached blond hair, wearing crocheted lace shorts and high-heeled sandals, who wobbled awkwardly when she walked—no, she was only drunk; a blond man wearing a Star Trek jersey, swim shorts, and hiking boots; an emaciated-looking woman in a peacock-blue sari and a necklace made of blinking dice; a gray-haired woman in a prim navy-blue dress, white gloves, and a hat with a small veil, carrying a coffee can full of quarters.

But none of them had nictitating membranes that Francie could see, and Indy didn't show any interest in them or in the tote bags slung over their arms and shoulders where an alien like him might be hiding.

Indy tapped suddenly at her wrist. "GO."

"Go?" she whispered. "Go where?"

He pointed back across the casino at the entrance they'd come in through.

Oh, no, she thought. *Don't tell me it was the Showgirl Spin he wanted to come here for.* "Do you mean go back outside to the big wheel and the red car?"

"NO NO NO GO," he scrolled urgently. "OUTLAW."

"You want to leave the casino?"

"YES YES YES GO."

"Why? Isn't the *tsurrispoinis* here?"

He didn't answer that. He just kept scrolling, "GO."

"Why do we have to go?" she said, and was going to ask him, *Are the Monument Valley people chasing you?* but she couldn't afford to have him freak out in the middle of the casino.

She scanned the crowd, looking for aliens—or Men in Black—but no one was showing them the slightest interest. Nevertheless, Indy was determined to leave. "GO GO GO," he scrolled, the letters now bright orange. "GO GO GO GO GO!"

"All right," she whispered, "but we've got to find the others first."

She scanned the room, looking for Eula Mae's straw hat and Joseph's Stetson, but she couldn't see them anywhere, and it was impossible to hear anything over the constant ka-ching and chime of the slot machines.

I suppose I should follow the sound of the jackpots, she thought. *That's where Eula Mae probably is,* and started for them, looking down every aisle as she went.

Wade appeared suddenly at her elbow. "Where have you been?" he hissed.

"Where have I— Where have *you* been?"

"I told you. I was checking out the exits. Look," he said urgently, "we need to go. Do you think you can convince Indy to go back to the RV?"

"I don't have to. He wants to leave."

"Oh, good," he said, taking her arm and steering her toward the front door.

"Why do we need to go?" Francie asked. "Did somebody spot Indy? Or Eula Mae?"

"No," he said, and seemed to notice for the first time that the others were missing. "Where are they?" he demanded. "I told you to stick together," and, before she could defend herself, said, "Go to the front door. I'll round them up," and he took off toward the blackjack tables.

"GO," Indy scrolled. "NOW."

"We're going. Put your tentacle back in the tote," she ordered, and as soon as he did, she zipped it all the way shut and headed for the front, keeping an eye out for Eula Mae.

She was at a video poker machine at the far end of the aisle, scooping quarters out of the tray and stuffing them in her pockets. "Oh, my stars, this is so exciting," she was saying to the woman next to her as quarters poured out of the machine. "I can't believe it! I've never won anything in my life!"

Francie took her by the elbow. "We need to go," she said. "Where are—?"

Eula Mae cut her off. "This is my granddaughter, Susan," she told the woman. "She never wants me to have any fun. Susan, you remember how you told me I should never draw to an inside straight? Well, I did, and just look!" She held out a double handful of quarters. "Can you put some of these in your tote bag?"

"Absolutely not," Francie said. "Where's Joseph?"

Eula Mae shrugged. "He and Lyle said something about wanting to check out the buffet. Joseph and Lyle are my in-home care providers," she confided to the woman. "They're no fun, either."

"We need to find them and go," Francie said. "Now."

"I can't leave without my winnings," Eula Mae said, grabbing the tote bag and scooping quarters into it.

Francie grabbed it back. "Yes, you can. Come *on*."

"Oh, all right," Eula Mae said. "Here." She scooped up the rest of the coins and dumped them in the woman's tray. "That's for being my lucky charm," she said, and let Francie drag her away.

"What did you do that for?" she asked as soon as they were out of earshot of the woman. "I was having a lucky streak."

"Is *that* how you managed to win that jackpot?" Francie said dryly, dragging her along the aisle toward the door. "Wade told you no gambling."

"I was just trying to be inconspicuous," Eula Mae said, trotting to keep up with Francie. "Do you know how suspicious you look being in a casino and not gambling? And leaving your winnings behind? I was only trying to blend in."

"Sure," Francie said, looking over at the door where, thankfully, Wade had Joseph and Lyle in tow. Joseph was sipping a drink with an umbrella in it, Lyle was chewing on a lobster claw, and Wade was motioning insistently to her and Eula Mae.

"Come on," Francie said, and hurried Eula Mae over to them. "We're all here."

"Including Indy?" Wade said.

"Yes, of course," Francie said, and opened the zipper an inch.

Indy promptly fastened a tentacle around her wrist and scrolled, "GO."

"Excellent idea," Wade said, and hustled them out the door, past the Showgirl Spin, where luckily the emcee had the bachelorette party up onstage and was cracking wedding jokes, and out to the parking lot.

Once there, Wade left them, ran ahead to start the *Outlaw,* and drove to meet them before they'd crossed half the distance. They piled in, and Wade drove quickly back the way they'd come, out a side entrance of the parking lot and down two blocks before circling back to the Strip and the still-inching-along traffic. Francie handed Indy and the tote bag to Lyle, said, "Let him out," and went up to the driver's compartment. "Is something wrong?" she asked Wade. "Did something happen at the casino?"

"No," he said, his eyes on the traffic. "I just thought we'd better go, that's all. Did Indy tell you what he was looking for?"

"No, just that he wanted to go."

"Well, let's hope that doesn't mean he thinks it's in some other casino, because there are hundreds of them here," at which point Indy rolled up onto the console between them, plopped a tentacle on the dashboard, and began moving it from side to side as the RV inched forward, pointing at billboards, marquees, signs, obviously looking for something, and Francie watched nervously as they passed the Venetian and then Caesar's Palace, afraid Indy would demand to stop again.

Wade must have been thinking the same thing because he said, "We need to get off the Strip if we can. Go tell Joseph I need him up here and to bring the map of Nevada with him."

She hurried back to fetch him.

Lyle came with him. Wade said, "Joseph, see if you can find Nellis Air Force Base on the map. It should be north and east of Vegas."

"Nellis?" Lyle said excitedly. "That's the old Nevada test site! It's Dreamland. I knew it! He *is* taking us to Area 51!"

"Ignore him," Wade said, glancing in the rearview mirror. "Find Nellis Air Force Test Range. Or Rachel."

"Rachel?"

"It's a town."

"Rachel . . ." Joseph murmured. "Here it is. It's on State Route 375."

"The Extraterrestrial Highway," Lyle said. "I knew it! Indy's going to bust out the Roswell aliens."

"Did you find a route, Joseph?" Wade asked, and Francie noticed him glancing in the rearview mirror again.

"You take 93 north toward Hiko and then 375 northwest."

"Is there another way to get there?" Wade asked.

"Um, let me see," Joseph said, wrestling with the map. "You can take 95 northwest to Tonopah and then go back east on U.S. 6 to 375 south, but it's a lot farther."

"And how do we get to 95? Besides staying on the Strip?"

"It's the Men in Black, isn't it?" Lyle said. "That's why you want to get off the Strip. Because they're following us."

"I want to get off the Strip because we're going nowhere fast," Wade said, gesturing at the bumper-to-bumper traffic, "and it's getting late. If Indy's taking us somewhere north of here, I'd like to get there while it's still daylight. Joseph, have you found another route we can take?"

"Yeah, it looks like you can take Eastern or Maryland Boulevard," Joseph said. "They're both east of here," and Wade promptly turned right.

Francie had expected Indy would object to their getting off the Strip, but he didn't. His tentacle continued to rove unceasingly across the windshield and the side windows, searching.

Wade drove a block and turned north again. There was no traffic on this street, and he drove three blocks in the time it would have taken him to go ten feet on the Strip. *Good,* Francie thought. *We'll be through Vegas in no time,* and Indy's tentacle shot suddenly in front of Wade's nose, scrolling, "STOP STOP STOP."

"Stop?" Wade said, looking around in bewilderment. They were on a block with a bar, a wedding chapel, and another bar—this one proclaiming LAP DANCES!—on one side and a bowling alley and a casino on the other.

"STOP STOP STOP," Indy scrolled, and for good measure wrapped a tentacle around the gearshift and yanked hard on it. The RV lurched to a halt, throwing Lyle into Joseph and the map.

"Hey!" Joseph said, fighting the folds of paper. "You'll strip the gears!"

"Why are we stopping?" Eula Mae said, coming up from the back with a deck of cards in her hand.

"I have no idea," Wade said. "Indy, we don't have time to stop at another casino."

"NO CASINO NO," Indy scrolled.

"Then *what*?" Wade asked. "You want to go *bowling*?"

"NO NO NO," Indy scrolled, "WEDDING," and pointed out the window of the RV at the wedding chapel. It had a white steeple and a neon sign that read THE CHURCH IN THE DESERT, LAS VEGAS'S OLDEST WEDDING CHAPEL, OPEN 24 HOURS DAILY.

"You want to go to a *wedding chapel*?" Wade said.

"YES YES YES," he scrolled. "FRANCIE," and Wade turned to her.

"Did you tell him you wanted to go to a wedding chapel?" he demanded.

"No."

"Then who did?" He glared accusingly at the others.

"Why would we tell him we wanted to go to a wedding chapel?" Joseph said.

"I think maybe I'm the one responsible," Eula Mae said defensively. "There was a billboard back on I-40 that said 'Casino—Wedding Chapel—All You Can Eat Buffet,' and after I read it to him, he asked me what a wedding chapel was, and I said it was a place where they had weddings, but I never said anything about going to one—"

"NO EULA MAE WEDDING," Indy scrolled. "FRANCIE WEDDING NEED GO."

"Oh, dear," Francie said, watching the words scrolling by. "I think this is my fault. When Indy first abducted me, I told him he couldn't keep me captive, that he had to take me back because I had a wedding I needed to go to. I told him I had to be there. He must have misunderstood and thought a wedding was a place, not a thing."

"That must be why we stopped at the Tropicana," Eula Mae said.

"What?"

"There was another billboard, just as we came into town, for the Tropicana, that said 'Say "I Do" at the Tropicana Wedding Chapel: The Perfect Place for a Wedding.' That must be why Indy insisted we go there."

"And why he kept looking around the casino," Francie said. "He was trying to find it. And maybe that was why he seemed so uncertain about which way to go just now."

"Jesus," Wade said. "Are you telling me this whole time what he's been trying to find was Serena's wedding?"

"No," Francie said. "That can't be it. I didn't tell him that till after he'd kidnapped me, and he clearly knew where he wanted to go when he first grabbed me." She turned to Indy. "Is a *tsurrispoinis* a wedding?"

"NO NO NO," Indy scrolled promptly.

"Well, at least that's something," Wade said. "Indy, listen, we don't have time to go to the wedding now. We need to go find the *tsurrispoinis* first."

"NO NO NO," Indy scrolled.

"Look, after we find your *tsurrispoinis,* we'll come right back here and go to the wedding, I promise. *Tsurrispoinis* first," he said, reverting to pidgin. "Then wedding."

"NO NO NO," Indy scrolled. "WEDDING," and slung a tentacle into the back of the RV with a sharp, short movement like a fisherman casting his fishing line into the river, narrowly missing Joseph's map and the deck of cards Eula Mae was holding.

"WEDDING," he scrolled, "FRANCIE," and reeled the tentacle back in with Francie's maid-of-honor dress clutched tightly in the end of it. He deposited it in her lap with a flourish.

"What's he doing now?" Wade asked, exasperated.

"I told him the dress was for wearing to a wedding," Francie said.

Indy pointed at the dress and then out the window at the wedding chapel. "WEDDING."

"Francie, tell him we don't have time for this," Wade said, exasperated. "Can't you explain a wedding isn't a place, that it's a thing?"

"And have him make us turn around and take me back to Roswell?" she whispered. "To say nothing of trying to explain to him once we get there that the wedding will already be over? It'll be easier—and faster—to let him think this is the place I needed to go. I can give him a tour of the chapel and then we can leave."

"All right," Wade said, "but make it quick."

"I will," Francie said. "Eula Mae, give me your tote again." Eula Mae dumped out the quarters and handed it to Francie.

"Indy, get in," Francie said, holding it open. "Just like you did at the casino."

"NO NO NO," Indy scrolled, snatching up the maid-of-honor dress and holding it up against her like he had in the car back at the Thunderbird Trading Post.

"He wants you to put it on," Joseph said helpfully.

"Oh, for God's sake!" Wade exploded.

"He thinks I need it for the wedding," Francie explained.

"But we don't have *time*," Wade said. "Indy, she doesn't need that for the wedding," but Indy continued to press it against Francie, as if he could make it stick to her by brute force.

"Okay, I'll put it on," she said, and to Wade, "I'll be quick."

She grabbed the dress and ran to the back, not even taking the time to go into the bathroom. She stripped off her clothes, stepped into the dress, zipped it as far up as she could, and hurried back up to the others. "Okay, I'm ready," she said, backing up to Wade and holding up her hair so he could zip her up the rest of the way. "Indy, get in the tote, and I'll take you to the wedding."

"NO NO NO," he scrolled, "ALL GO," and began pushing Lyle and Eula Mae and Joseph toward the door.

"Oh, for God's sake!" Wade said. "That'll take forever! You can't all go."

"It's all right," Francie said hastily. "We'll show him around the chapel and come right back. Come on, everybody," which wasn't necessary. Indy was already herding them out the door and down the steps to the street.

"Indy, get in," Francie ordered him, holding the tote open, and the alien obligingly rolled into the bag.

"Be as fast as you can," Wade said. "We—"

"Need to get going," she said. "I know." She turned to face him. "Are you sure there's nothing wrong? Did a policeman spot us at the Tropicana?"

"What?" he said. "No, of course not. I just want to get Indy out of Vegas before he decides we should stop somewhere else. Vegas is a minefield."

"You're right. We'll be back as soon as we can," she said, and started out the door.

Indy shot a tentacle across the door to stop her and another one over to Wade to fasten around his waist. "NO NO NO WADE GO."

"Oh, for—" Wade said. "I can't go. I have to stay here and watch the RV."

"WADE GO," Indy scrolled stubbornly.

"I'm afraid you're going to have to park and come in," Francie said. "Can't you pull over to the curb and—?"

"*No*," he said, and when Francie looked at him in surprise, he explained, "I don't know if it's legal to park here, and the last thing we need is to come out and find the RV's been towed. I'll go park it around the corner and catch up with you," and apparently Indy understood what he'd said because he immediately tightened the tentacle around his wrist.

"Ow," Wade said. "Francie, make him understand that I can't park the car here."

"Indy, the *Outlaw*'s too big to park here on the street. Wade's going to go put it in the parking lot, like at the Tropicana, remember?"

"NO NO NO GO WEDDING," Indy scrolled, and wrapped yet another tentacle around Wade's wrist.

"Wade will be right back."

"I promise," Wade said, and Indy let go of his wrist.

"WADE PARK OUTLAW GO WEDDING," Indy scrolled.

"That's right," Francie said, and got off the RV before Indy could make any more demands. "Wade—"

But Wade had already shut the door. He pulled out from the curb, drove the lumbering *Outlaw* down the street, and disappeared around the corner.

CHAPTER FIFTEEN

Clay Boone: I'll even marry ya.

Cat Ballou: *Marry me?*

Clay Boone: Well, that's what I said. I mean, if that's what I gotta do to save you, why, I'll do it.

—*Cat Ballou*

Francie stood looking anxiously after Wade and the RV till Indy wrapped himself around her wrist and scrolled, "GO WEDDING."

"Yes, yes, wedding," she said. "Now get into the tote and stay in there till I say it's okay. This is just like the casino. You can't let anybody see you. Do you understand?"

"YES YES YES," he scrolled, and wrapped a tentacle around her wrist like he had at the Tropicana.

"You can't let anybody but us see you scroll, either," she admonished him. "You can't let anybody else know you can talk. Understand?"

"YES YES YES."

"No matter what happens, you mustn't scroll anything to anybody you don't know, and you mustn't start scrolling if there's *any-body* around except us."

"YES GO GO GO."

"All right." She zipped the tote nearly all the way shut, leaving only a half inch for his tentacle, and crossed the street to where the others were standing in front of the steepled building.

"Okay, we're just going to take a quick tour," she told them, putting her hand on the white wooden door. "Everybody quiet in case a wedding's in progress."

If one was, that would be perfect. They could sneak in the back, watch it and tell Indy they'd "gone to a wedding," and it needn't take more than a few minutes. Las Vegas wedding ceremonies were notoriously short. "Shh," she said, putting her finger to her lips, and opened the door.

It didn't open onto a chapel but onto a small, pine-paneled reception area that looked just like the office of a seedy motel, and beyond the area there was a hall with several doors labeled Garden of Love, Candlelight, and Cupid's Chapel.

They crowded into the office and went over to the counter, which contained a cash register, an old-fashioned bellman's bell, a bouquet of artificial flowers, and a pink plastic binder labeled Weddings.

The wall behind the counter was covered with snapshots of what Francie presumed were weddings the chapel had performed, and the other walls and the long hallway beyond it were lined with framed photographs of Las Vegas in the 1950s: the marquee of the Sands Hotel, the neon sign of cowboy Vegas Vic towering above the downtown casinos, an advertising poster with pictures of a roulette wheel, a swimming pool, and a showgirl in front of a giant mushroom cloud, with the slogan COME TO VEGAS! IT'S A BLAST!

Next to the counter stood a slot machine, which Eula Mae made a beeline for. "No playing the slots," Francie said. "We don't have time," and looked down the hall, trying to see if she could spot anyone, but there was no one there. They must be in the middle of a wedding.

"Do you want me to hit the bell?" Joseph asked, his hand poised above it.

"No," she said, hoping she could sneak in the back of whichever chapel was in use, let Indy see a bit of the ceremony, and convince him that was the wedding. She started down the hall, straining to hear a sound that would tell her which chapel was occupied.

"Hey, come here!" Lyle shouted from the counter.

"Shh," Francie said, hurrying back. "What is it? Is Wade coming?"

"No," he said. "You gotta look at this." He had the pink binder open and was leafing through its plastic-covered pages. "You wouldn't believe all the kinds of weddings you can have here. Vampires, Zombies, Beach Party Bingo, Outlaw Gang . . ."

That's appropriate, Francie thought, wondering how on earth she and Wade were going to explain any of this to Indy. And *where* was Wade? He'd said he was just going to park around the corner.

"Roaring Twenties," Lyle said, continuing to flip through the pages, "Liberace—"

There was a sudden clatter of coins from the slot machine.

"Sorry," Eula Mae whispered, scooping up the quarters spilling out. "I accidentally bumped into it, and it paid off."

"A likely story," Joseph said, and went over to help her gather the quarters up.

"They've got *Star Trek* and *Star Wars* weddings, too," Lyle said, still leafing through the book. "And something called the Atomic Wedding. Listen to this," he said, and began to read from the description. " 'A retro wedding from the days of Nevada's A-bomb tests. Complete with anti-radiation coveralls, goggles, and Geiger counters. It's a real blast!' "

"Shh," Francie said. The last thing she needed was to have to explain "atomic bombs" to Indy.

"And look at this," Lyle said. "Lord of the Rings Wedding: wizards, hobbits, matching bride-and-groom traveling cloaks and rings of Sauron."

"SHOW RINGSOFSAURON," Indy scrolled.

"Shh," Francie said, "someone's coming," and a harried-looking man hurried into the office carrying a black leather jacket and a pair of motorcycle handlebars.

"I'm so sorry," he said, putting them down on the counter. "I didn't hear you come in. Today's been a madhouse. We've already had three weddings this morning and two this afternoon, plus two scheduled for this evening, one at six and one at seven thirty, and I don't know if I'm coming or going. I hope you haven't been waiting too long."

"No," Francie said. "We—"

"Welcome to the Church in the Desert, Las Vegas's Oldest Wedding Chapel, established in 1952, the same year the Sands opened and the first A-bomb was tested just a few miles north of here. I like to say we opened with a bang," he said, and laughed. "I'm Reverend Murray, owner and fully licensed wedding officiant in the state of Nevada."

"I'm Francie Driscoll," Francie said. "We came to—"

"Get married. Of course, and the Church in the Desert is just the place to do that. You must be the blushing bride," he said, pointing at Francie's maid-of-honor dress, ignoring its wrinkled and smudged state, and then turning to Joseph. "And I presume you're the groom."

"No," Francie said, and Reverend Murray turned inquiringly toward Lyle, who was still leafing through the pink binder. "Then you must be—"

God, no! Francie thought, and Joseph said smoothly, "He's not here yet. He had to go find a place to park."

"He'll be here any minute," Eula Mae said.

"So there are five in your wedding party?" Reverend Murray asked.

Six, Francie thought, glancing involuntarily at the tentacle around her wrist. "Yes. Five. But—"

"Oh, good," Reverend Murray said. "Our large chapels are booked this evening, but Cupid's Chapel is available, and it's perfect for a wedding of your size. Do you know what kind of wedding you want?"

"Do you have one with a UFO theme?" Lyle asked.

Francie shot him a murderous look, but Reverend Murray was taking it in stride.

"I'm afraid not," he said. "We really should. So many people ask for that. We *do* have a *Star Trek* wedding"—he went over to the counter to show Lyle the page—"and two different *Star Wars* weddings—Original and Reboot."

"Actually," Francie said, "we—"

"You want to wait till the groom gets here," he said. "I completely understand. In the meantime, you might want to look through the binder," and picked up the handlebars and the leather jacket. "I'll just take these in to the Harley-Davidson wedding—it's at seven thirty—and you ring when the groom gets here."

"Harley-Davidson?" Eula Mae asked.

"Yes, it's one of our most popular weddings. The bride and groom wear biker helmets and black leather jackets. Were you interested in something like that?"

"No," Francie said firmly. "Actually, we were wondering if you could give us a tour of your chapel."

"NO NO NO," Indy scrolled, and she had to hastily slap her hand over her wrist to hide it from Murray. "To see what you have to offer?"

"Comparison shopping, eh?" Reverend Murray said. "I can assure you, you won't find any finer or less expensive weddings in all of Vegas. We've been here since 1952, and we have a reputation for—"

He launched into a promotional speech, but Francie didn't hear it. She was too distracted worrying about what was keeping Wade—and by Indy, who had her wrist in a death grip. "NO TOUR," he scrolled. "WEDDING," and then "FRANCIE BBHBINIITS."

"We received a five-star rating from the Las Vegas Association of Wedding Chapels and a commendation from the Las Vegas Wedding Chamber of Commerce," Reverend Murray said. "You don't need to take my word for it. It's all on our website, churchinthe—" Wade burst through the door, breathing hard.

"Sorry, I had to park miles away," he said, pointing vaguely off the way they'd come. "What did I miss?"

"We were discussing your wedding," Reverend Murray said.

"Our *wedding*?" Wade said, and a middle-aged woman with a

bouffant hairdo came in, carrying a motorcycle helmet in one hand and a phone in the other. "Sorry to interrupt," she said, "but the Harley-Davidson wedding wants to know if they can ride in on their own motorcycle instead of ours, and I can't find the Dracula's castle backdrop for our six o'clock."

"This is my assistant, Miss Cheree," Reverend Murray said. "I need to take care of this, but I'll be right back. In the meantime, you can look at our wedding selection and decide which one's right for you." He went off down the hall with Miss Cheree, asking, "Did you look in the Candlelight Chapel, behind the deck of the *Enterprise*?"

"What's this about a wedding selection?" Wade whispered, and Francie showed him her wrist.

"Indy refuses to settle for a tour. He insists on a wedding."

"So why can't we just watch the Dracula wedding?"

"Because it doesn't start till six o'clock, and you said we were in a hurry. And anyway, I don't think Indy will settle for that." She held up her wrist, where Indy was scrolling, "WEDDING FRAN-CIE WADE."

"He's cutting off my circulation," she said. "I'm afraid if he doesn't get a wedding, he'll kidnap Reverend Murray and the entire Dracula wedding party."

"Geez," Wade said. "Talk about your shotgun wedding. Did he say why 'WEDDING FRANCIE WADE'?"

"BBHBINIITS," Indy scrolled.

"*Bbhbiniits?*" Wade said. "That means this wedding must have something to do with the *tsurrispoinis*. You don't suppose that's why he kidnapped you, do you? *Because* you were dressed for a wedding, and not because he needed someone to drive him some-where?"

That had never occurred to her. "But why would he need a *wedding*?" she asked.

"I don't know, but he apparently does. Which means we've got to give him one."

"So we stay and go to the six o'clock wedding?"

"No. We can't afford to wait that long."

"Then what—?"

"We get married," he said, and Reverend Murray reappeared.

"Have you two had a chance to look at our wedding selection?" he asked.

"No," Wade said. "Look, we just want something simple. And fast. We're on kind of a tight schedule."

Reverend Murray looked thoughtful. "Our Elvis weddings are very nice," he said, going over to the counter for the pink binder. "Three Elvis songs, an Elvis impersonator officiant—"

"No, I meant just a basic, straightforward wedding," Wade said. "You know, flowers, candles—"

"I have just the thing. Our Old-Fashioned Garden Wedding. It comes with scented candles, a rose-covered trellis, and a video sunset, but it'll take several hours to set up—"

"Elvis is fine," Wade said.

"Excellent. Now, we have several packages to choose from: the Blue Hawaii, the GI Elvis, the Jailhouse—"

"Whichever's the quickest."

"That would be the Viva Las Vegas. Our last Cupid's Chapel couple chose it, so it's ready to go right now."

"Fine," Wade said. "We'll take it."

"Excellent. Now if you'll just come this way, we'll fill out the necessary paperwork," Reverend Murray said and hurried down the hall.

Wade started after him.

Francie grabbed his arm. "What are you *doing*?" she whispered. "We can't get married."

"We're not . . ." He glanced at the tentacle around her wrist and lowered his voice. "We're not getting married. We're staging a wedding for Indy's benefit."

"But—"

"It won't be real. We'll give fake names."

"But I already told Reverend Murray my name."

"Then *I'll* give him a fake name."

"But isn't that against the law?"

"We've got more crucial things than legality to worry about," he said. "Look, it's obvious Indy's not going to let us leave till he gets a wedding, and we need to get going. So we give him one. Unless you have a better idea?"

She looked down at her wrist, where Indy was scrolling, "WEDDING FRANCIE WADE ELVIS."

"No," she said.

"Then come on," he said and grabbed her arm. "Stay here," he ordered the others.

"And no more slots," Francie added, and went down the hall with Wade.

Reverend Murray was waiting in a small office covered with photos of wedding couples in Star Trek uniforms, zombie costumes, and Hawaiian shirts and leis. He was seated behind a desk with a thick sheaf of papers in front of him.

He motioned them to sit down. "You said the Viva Las Vegas Wedding," he said, filling in the topmost blank of a long form. "Now, for the processional, you have a choice of 'Love Me Tender' or 'Can't Help Falling in Love.'"

"'It's Now or Never'?" Wade asked, and Francie kicked him under the table.

"'Can't Help Falling in Love,'" she said, and Murray filled that in.

"Now, for the wedding officiant, would you prefer the traditional White Jumpsuit Elvis or Gold Lamé Tuxedo Elvis?"

"Traditional," Francie said.

"And for the wedding solo? We have 'I Want You, I Need You, I Love You,' 'Always on My Mind,' or—"

"We don't want a solo. Just a nice, basic ceremony," Wade said.

"Of course. Now, Miss Driscoll, as to your bouquet, real flowers or one of our lovely premade silk bouquets?"

Premade sounded faster. "Silk," she said.

"Excellent," Murray said, and reached for another binder. "We have several choices of bouquet—roses, daisies, carnations—"

"Roses," she said, and to move things along, "pink," but it didn't do any good.

"Long or short veil?" he asked, and when she said "short," Murray inquired, "Tiara, circlet of flowers, or headband?"

"Look," Wade said impatiently, "we don't want any extras—"

"Oh, but they're not extras," Murray said. "They're all part of the Viva Las Vegas Wedding package, along with a wedding ring, a champagne toast, and a photo session."

"No photo session," Wade exploded. "No champagne toast. Just the ceremony. A *short* ceremony."

"You understand I'll still have to charge you—"

"Yes," Wade said tightly. "Fine. Can we just—?"

"Of course," Murray said. "Now, I just need to see your marriage license—"

"Marriage license?" Wade said blankly.

"I thought *you* gave us that," Francie said to Murray.

"No, no, wedding chapels are only authorized to perform the ceremony, not issue the marriage license. For that you'll have to go to the Marriage License Bureau on Clark Avenue."

"How long will that take?" Wade said.

"Oh, usually only an hour or two."

We don't have an hour or two, Francie thought. "And we can't just fill out the forms online or something?"

"No, Nevada state law requires you to get it in person. You'll need the certificate and a driver's license or other legal ID."

Which I don't have, Francie thought. *And there goes Wade's idea of using a false name.*

"I can't perform your wedding without it," he said. "The penalties for wedding chapels breaking the law are very stiff. Perhaps you'd rather schedule your wedding for tomorrow— What is it, Miss Cheree?" he said as she poked her head in the door.

"I can't find the vampire bats," she said.

"Did you look in the . . . oh, never mind, I'll go find them. And you two decide what you want to do." He handed Wade the form and hurried off with Miss Cheree.

"Listen, Indy," Francie said as soon as they were gone. "I'm not sure we're going to be able to have a wedding. We don't have the right paperwork. You need to have a marriage license, and we don't have one. We may have to go to your *tsurrispoinis* first and then have the wedding."

"NO NO NO WEDDING TSURRISPOINIS."

"Why?" Wade asked.

"BBHBINIITS," he scrolled.

"Which means we're not going to be able to talk him out of this," Francie said. "So what now? Do we wait and go to the Dracula wedding after all?"

"NO NO NO WEDDING DRACULA," Indy scrolled. "WEDDING FRANCIE WADE."

"But we *can't*," Francie began.

"We'll have to," Wade said. "Look, you go find Miss Cheree and tell her she needs to get your veil, and I'll take care of the rest."

"What does *that* mean? You're not going to have Indy tie Reverend Murray up and *force* him to marry us, are you?"

"No, of course not," he said, but just to make sure, Francie took the tote bag with her.

She found Miss Cheree in the Garden of Love hanging vampire bats and wooden stakes and told her Reverend Murray had given the wedding the go-ahead and that she needed her veil.

"Of course," Miss Cheree said, and showed her to a dressing room, returning in a moment with a bouquet and a veil. "I'd stay and help you," she said apologetically, "but I've *got* to finish setting up the Dracula wedding—"

"I totally understand," Francie said. "Go on. I'll be fine."

"*Thank* you," Miss Cheree said. "Cupid's Chapel is the last door on the right."

She went out, and Indy immediately pushed his way out of the tote bag, scrolling, "GO WEDDING FRANCIE WADE."

"Yes, we're going to the wedding," she said. *I hope.* She wondered what Wade intended to do. Was he going to try to bribe Reverend Murray with Eula Mae's slot machine winnings? But if Reverend Murray refused to be bribed, or, worse, called the police . . .

"GO WEDDING GO WEDDING," Indy scrolled, pushing the veil at her.

"Yes," she whispered, then put it on and dabbed at the smudges on her dress with a wet tissue. "But when we go into the chapel, you have to stay in the tote bag and keep *totally* quiet. No scrolling at all. I'll tell Eula Mae to hold the bag up so you can see—"

"NO SEE BAG GO FRANCIE WEDDING."

"You *can't* go with me. The minister'd see you. I'll tell Joseph to sit in front of you so you can extend—"

"NO NO NO," Indy scrolled, rolled over to the bouquet, and before she could see how he did it, he inserted himself into the middle of it, twining his tentacles between the roses and the baby's breath and altering his tentacles to the size and color of a vine's tendrils, and then spoiling the effect by scrolling, "SEE WEDDING YES" in bright orange.

"All right," she said. "But no scrolling till I put you back in the tote bag. And you can't move *at all*." She could only imagine the effect a suddenly writhing bouquet would have on Reverend Murray as he officiated.

If we get that far, Francie thought. But when she opened the door of the chapel (after another whispered warning), Miss Cheree was pinning a carnation to Wade's denim shirt. "Oh, my, what a lovely bride you make!" she said. "I'll just go get the rest of your wedding party and let Reverend Murray know you're ready."

"What happened?" Francie said as soon as she was gone.

"I convinced him to let us do the wedding now and get our marriage license afterward."

"I thought that wasn't legal."

"It is. Reverend Murray just doesn't like to do them unless there are extenuating circumstances. They call it a commitment ceremony. It's just like a wedding ceremony, but it only becomes legal when you get the marriage license—"

"What extenuating circumstances did you tell Reverend Murray there were?"

"I'll tell you later. The important thing is that this means this won't be a—"

Francie cut him off before he could say "real wedding." She didn't want Indy to hear that. "Listen, Indy refused to—"

"Here we are," Miss Cheree said, leading in Joseph and Lyle. And Eula Mae, who'd apparently ignored her orders in regard to the slot machine in the office. The pockets of her dress were bulging suspiciously. "Oh, my," she said, looking around at the chapel. "Isn't this nice?"

"Nice" wasn't the word Francie would have chosen. A large photo of the Strip at night with VIVA LAS VEGAS in gold-sequined lettering across it hung at the front of the chapel, flanked by two guitar-shaped candelabras with gold candles.

"Are you sure this here's a good idea?" Joseph whispered to Francie. "In every dang Western I ever seen, people who pretend to get married end up really gettin' hitched by the last reel."

"Do you have a best man?" Miss Cheree was asking Wade. "We'll need a second witness to sign the marriage certificate."

Anybody but Lyle, Francie said silently, and Wade must have been thinking the same thing. "Joseph, would you mind?" he asked.

Joseph nodded.

"Now, if you'll just stand here . . ." Miss Cheree said, positioning them, and Francie took the opportunity to hand Eula Mae her tote bag, which she'd partially zipped, leaving it open an inch so it would look like Indy was still inside. *And please don't let her look to make sure,* Francie prayed.

She didn't. Eula Mae took the tote, nodding knowingly at Francie, and sat down primly in the second row of gilt chairs, placing the tote on the seat next to her and directing Lyle to take the seat in front of it so the bag couldn't be seen from the altar.

"Now, you need to go to the back so you can walk up the aisle," Miss Cheree told Francie, leading her back down the aisle to the door. "Oh, good, it looks like they're ready."

Francie looked toward where Wade and Joseph and now Reverend Murray, barely recognizable in a white rhinestone-studded jumpsuit and black pompadour, stood.

"I'll go start the processional," Miss Cheree said.

"Couldn't we just skip that part?" Francie said, looking anxiously at Eula Mae, afraid that at any minute she might realize Indy wasn't in the bag and scream, "He's gone! He's escaped!"

"Oh, no, the processional's part of the package," Miss Cheree said, and ducked out of the chapel.

Francie looked over at Eula Mae and then down at her bouquet. It was motionless and silent—for the moment, but the second the strains of "Can't Help Falling in Love," began, she galloped down the aisle before Lyle or Eula Mae had a chance to stand up.

Miss Cheree reappeared and took up a position next to her, and Reverend Murray said (unnecessarily), "You may be seated," and then launched into the ceremony.

"Hey, Little Mama!" he said in an exaggerated Elvis drawl, "and Daddio, and all you Little Mamas and Daddios out there, we're gathered here to get these two hitched. If any of y'all are agin this marriage, let 'em speak now or forever hold their peace."

Even though this whole thing had been Indy's idea, Francie automatically looked down at her bouquet, which was still, thankfully, silent.

"All right, then," Reverend Murray said, "if nobody objects, let's get this show on the road. Do you have the ring?"

"No," Wade said, looking startled. "We . . ." and Miss Cheree leaned forward to whisper, "It's part of the package," and handed a gold band to Joseph. Joseph passed it to Wade, and Miss Cheree reached to take Francie's bouquet.

"No—" Francie said, grabbing for it, but it was too late. Miss Cheree had already taken it and stepped to the side.

"Don't worry, darlin'," Reverend Murray said, laughing. "She'll give it back to you. Now repeat after me: I, Francie Driscoll, do solemnly promise . . ."

She repeated the vows, scarcely listening to him, scarcely hearing her own responses or Wade's when Reverend Murray said, "Do you, Wade, take Francie?," barely noticing when the ring was slipped on her finger, her attention entirely on not giving in to the overwhelming urge to turn around and look at Miss Cheree.

Her whole body was tensed, waiting for Miss Cheree's scream, and her mind was so focused on willing Indy to stay still that Reverend Murray's "I now pronounce you daddio and wife" caught her by surprise.

He must have been listening when Wade told him to keep it short, she thought, and then, *We did it. Now if we can just get out of here before Miss Cheree sees Indy,* and she turned to take the bouquet from her.

"Hold on there, darlin'," Reverend Murray said. "Ain't you forgettin' somethin'?" He turned to Wade. "You may kiss the bride."

"Oh," she said. "Sorry," and leaned forward.

And Wade kissed her.

CHAPTER SIXTEEN

Trust no one.

—*The X-Files*

ade's kiss caught Francie completely off-guard. He'd been in such a hurry through this whole wedding thing, she'd expected a quick distracted peck on the lips, but he kissed her as if he had all the time in the world. And nothing else at all on his mind.

And for a lovely, lost, time-stands-still moment she forgot everything, too—Indy and this ridiculous farce of a wedding ceremony and the need to hurry—everything except wanting to kiss Wade back. And wanting it to go on forever.

"Whoa, there, you two," Reverend Murray said from a long way away, "let's save some for the honeymoon," and Wade let go of her, looking as dazed as she felt.

Miss Cheree and Joseph and Lyle burst into applause, and Eula Mae dabbed at her eyes with a handkerchief. "Oh, my, what a lovely wedding! It was perfect!"

It was, Francie thought, and then, *Let's hope Indy thinks so, too*— And then, *Oh my God, Indy!* and grabbed the bouquet back from Miss Cheree.

It was thankfully still motionless—and silent, but who knew how long that would last. She needed to get Indy safely back in the tote bag before he did anything. "Thank you," she said, grabbed Wade's hand, and started down the aisle at a trot, snatching the bag from Eula Mae as she went.

"Now, hang on there, you two," Reverend Murray said, still in his Elvis voice, "I know you're itchin' to get started on that honeymoon, but you aren't done yet. You've got a certificate to sign."

"I know," Francie said. "I'll be right back. I just need to . . ." and took off for the dressing room.

And just in time. The moment she shut the door, Indy's tentacles exploded out of the bouquet, writhing wildly and scrolling ecstatically, "WEDDING WEDDING WEDDING FRANCIE WADE," and "GO TSURRISPOINIS."

Thank goodness. Whatever he'd needed from the wedding, he'd apparently gotten it, and now they could go. "We'll go to the *tsurrispoinis,*" she promised, taking off her veil and picking up the tote bag, "but we have to sign the marriage license first, which means you have to get in here and keep very, very quiet."

She was afraid he'd object, but he immediately disentangled himself from the roses and baby's breath and clambered into the tote bag. "No moving," she said, zipping it up. "And *no* scrolling."

She'd intended to zip it all the way shut, but Indy had already wrapped his tentacle around her wrist, and Miss Cheree was outside, asking, "Ready?"

"Yes," she said, and opened the door. She handed Miss Cheree the veil and the bouquet.

"Oh, no, dear, the bouquet is yours to keep. It's part of the package," she said, and led Francie to Reverend Murray's office, where Wade was already bent over the certificate.

He looked up when she came in, and her breath caught, but he seemed completely composed—and all business. "Where do I sign?"

he asked, and when Reverend Murray pointed to the line, he nodded and signed.

"Now if you'll just sign here," Reverend Murray said to Francie, indicating the correct line and then whisking the certificate away from her so that Miss Cheree and then Joseph could witness it. He took the certificate back as soon as they were done so that he could sign it himself and notarize it.

"You understand this is just a wedding certificate," he said, folding it and handing it to Wade, and Francie held her breath, afraid he was going to say, "Your wedding isn't legal till you get a marriage license," and Indy would insist on going to the license bureau, but all he said was "You've got ten days to apply for a license before the certificate becomes invalid."

Wade nodded, took the folded certificate, stuck it in the pocket of his shirt, and motioned to Joseph to follow Miss Cheree out of the office.

"Where—?" Wade began, but Reverend Murray was extending his hand. "It's been a pleasure doing business with you," he said, abandoning the Elvis drawl. "I hope you'll tell any of your friends who are planning to get married about us." He stood up. "Now, if you'll excuse me, I'm sorry to rush off, but I need to change for my six o'clock. You know the way out, right?" and he hurried off to put on a Dracula cape and a Bela Lugosi accent and whatever else the next wedding entailed.

"Okay," Wade said, "I'll go—"

Miss Cheree was back, carrying a bottle of champagne and two glasses. "You're sure you won't change your mind about the champagne toast? It's part of the—"

"Cheree," Reverend Murray called from down the hall. "Where did you put my fangs?"

"I'm coming," she said, and smiled at them. "I just *know* you two will have a long and happy marriage!" and scurried off.

It's not a marriage, Francie thought glumly, watching Wade as he watched Miss Cheree leave.

"Good, they're both in the Garden of Love Chapel," he said.

"That means you'll all be able to wait for me in the office. I'll go get the *Outlaw* and bring it around to the front door, and while I'm gone, you see if you can find out from Indy what the connection between weddings and the *tsurrispoinis* is."

"I'll try," she promised.

He took off at a run, and she walked back down the hall to the lobby, where Lyle and Joseph and Eula Mae all stood with small pink-beribboned packages. "Wade left so fast we didn't even have a chance to do our surprise," Eula Mae said disapprovingly.

"What surprise?" Francie said, looking suspiciously at the packages. "What is that? Rice?"

"No, they're bubbles!" Eula Mae said, opening the package to reveal a tiny bottle.

"It was part of the wedding package," Joseph explained, and Eula Mae blew a tiny, multicolored globe at Francie.

"You call that a bubble?" Lyle said, blowing a larger one. Joseph joined in, and Francie took advantage of the distraction to carry the tote bag into the hallway and open the zipper several inches so she could talk to Indy. "Tell me why we needed to go to the wedding before the *tsurrispoinis*," she said.

"BBHBINIITS," he scrolled.

"You have to tell me what *bbhbiniits* means," she said, but he wasn't listening. He'd extended a tentacle to the framed picture in front of them, a vintage photograph of the Sands' marquee, which read APPEARING NOW. FRANK SINATRA. SAMMY DAVIS JR.

"SHOW," Indy scrolled.

"It's a sign for the Sands Ca—" She stopped. She didn't want to say "casino" and give him any ideas. "The Sands Hotel," she said instead, and he moved his tentacle to the next photo, the one of Vegas Vic. Was he going to take her through every photo in the hall?

"Indy, we don't have time—" she began, but he tapped insistently at the photo, which showed the neon cowboy wearing a Stetson, a checked shirt, and a red bandanna, smoking a cigarette and greeting visitors with the words "Howdy Pardner."

"That's Vegas Vic," she said. "It's a sign welcoming people to Las Vegas."

Indy tapped the photo. "TSURRISPOINIS."

"Vegas Vic is the *tsurrispoinis*?"

"NO NO NO."

What was it they called downtown Las Vegas? "Glitter Gulch is the *tsurrispoinis*?"

"NO NO NO," he scrolled, tapping the center of the photo.

There was nothing there except blue sky and a single puffy cloud. "The sky?" she said, and stopped, peering at the cloud. It was an odd ballooning shape, with a white column underneath that made it look like—

Oh my God. That wasn't a cloud. It was the mushroom cloud from an atomic bomb.

A shiver of dread went through her. *Lyle was right,* she thought, *Indy* **is** *trying to get hold of a nuclear weapon and use it against us.* Wade had said the old Nevada test site was part of Area 51, and Lyle had said advanced nuclear weapons were still secretly being tested there. Was Indy planning to steal them? Or worse?

I don't believe it, Francie thought. *Not Indy. There must be some other explanation. Maybe he's pointing at something else. Or it's not a mushroom cloud,* and she bent to look at the caption under the photo. It read *Atomic bomb test visible from Las Vegas, 1955.*

She had to face it. *Tsurrispoinis* meant "atomic bomb." But if that was what Indy was after, why would he have landed in Roswell and driven them all over New Mexico?

He was looking for Los Alamos, she thought. *Or the Trinity site.*

But that was west of Roswell, and he had made her drive due north. She remembered when he'd stopped at the intersection just north of Roswell the night he'd captured her, looking all around, as if for some indication of which way to go, and then making her drive north. He couldn't possibly have seen a mushroom cloud then. Could he have mistaken the thunderstorm that had been off to the northeast for one? She'd mistaken the mushroom cloud in the photograph for a regular cloud. Maybe he'd—

She stopped, staring blindly as a dozen images racketed through her mind: the lightning from the thunderstorm as it had moved off to the east that night and the line of clouds on the horizon the next morning, the crisscrossing contrails, the cloudless day when Wade had complained they were going in circles, the billboard for the Georgia O'Keeffe Museum with its rows of puffy white clouds, Indy's suddenly insisting they turn east after the gas station. Toward a scattering of clouds off in the distance.

A **tsurrispoinis** *isn't an atomic bomb,* she thought. *It's a thunderstorm!*

No wonder he hadn't been able to find the *tsurrispoinis* on a map. And no wonder he hadn't been able to figure out where he wanted to go—it had changed every time he spotted a cloud. And when there hadn't been any, or they'd seemed to point in all directions, like the contrails, he'd taken them first in one direction and then another, trying to find it.

But after he'd learned how to communicate with them, why hadn't he just pointed at a cloud and scrolled "TSURRISPOINIS"?

Because there weren't any, she thought. The sky had been perfectly clear after that.

No, that wasn't true. There'd been those pink clouds Wade had woken her up to show her and the thunderstorm in the Monument Valley scene in *She Wore a Yellow Ribbon.* But Indy had been too freaked out by the sight of Monument Valley to notice it.

He wasn't freaked out that morning Wade showed me the pink clouds, she thought. Why hadn't he seen those and scrolled "TSURRISPOINIS"?

Because he was asleep, she thought, remembering his limp, trailing tentacles as he curled against her.

We should have woken him up, she thought. *If we had, we'd have known what a* **tsurrispoinis** *was yesterday morning.* He must have seen a cloud off to the north just before they got to Highway 93, and that was why he'd insisted they head north—not Las Vegas, not Area 51.

She wondered why he needed to go to a thunderstorm. *It doesn't matter,* she thought. *What matters is that now we know what a* **tsurrispoinis** *is.*

If I'm right, she thought. *If I haven't just fastened on the idea of a thunderstorm because I can't bear the thought of its being a mush-room cloud.* "Come here, Indy," she said. "I need to show you something," and carried him in his tote bag quickly down to the end of the hallway to the photo of the "Come to Vegas! It's a Blast!" poster.

She pointed at the mushroom cloud. "Tsurrispoinis?"

"NO NO NO," Indy scrolled, and she felt a weight lift off her.

But she had to be sure. She started back down the row of photographs, looking for clouds and praying the Dracula wedding party wouldn't arrive and make her have to shut Indy up in the bag.

There weren't any clouds in the background of the Sands marquee photo or the ones of the Sputnik Bar and Lounge or the El Morocco. *The sky in the Southwest is entirely too clear,* she thought, continuing down the line of photographs: Bugsy Siegel and a bunch of fellow mobsters standing in front of the Flamingo, a line of Follies showgirls, the Church in the Desert, emblazoned with a Now Open sign, standing in a vacant lot filled with prickly pears and Joshua trees.

Here was what she was looking for. A swimming pool lined with palm trees and women in one-piece swimsuits and bathing caps, and above it, rising into the Kodachrome blue sky, a towering thunderhead.

She didn't even have to ask Indy. He was already pointing at it, tapping the glass and scrolling out, "TSURRISPOINIS TSUR-RISPOINIS TSURRISPOINIS."

I've got to tell Wade, Francie thought. "Indy, I need you to get back in the bag," she said, "now," and as soon as he'd pulled his tentacle in, she zipped the tote bag all the way shut.

She ran into the office, where Eula Mae was laying bets on who could blow the biggest bubble. "Here," Francie said, thrusting the bag into the arms of Lyle, who was closest. "I have to go tell Wade something."

"But he said to stay here," Eula Mae protested. "And you haven't even thrown your bouquet yet."

"Here." Francie tossed it at her, and ran over to the door.

"But you don't know where he parked," Joseph said.

"I'll find him." She opened the door.

"He said he'd be right back," Joseph said. "Can't—?"

"No." She ran outside and out to the sidewalk. Straight into the arms of a man in a black suit and tie and sunglasses.

He clapped a hand over her mouth before she had a chance to cry out and warn the others, or even to quite realize what was happening, and, with his other hand, pulled her hands behind her back, handcuffed her, and manhandled her, struggling, out to the black van waiting at the curb.

The rear door was open, and two more men, both in black suits and sunglasses, too, stood next to it. They didn't have badges, and there was no lettering on the van, but Francie knew exactly who they were, and it wasn't Lyle's mysterious Men in Black. It was the FBI, and they were after Indy.

That was why Wade had been in such a hurry to leave the casino, and why he'd asked Joseph if there was some other way out of town. He must have spotted them at the Tropicana. And then when Indy'd demanded they stop at the wedding chapel . . .

The men by the van stepped forward to take her from the man who'd grabbed her, thrust her bodily into the back of the van, and slammed the door shut.

It was dark inside. "Let me out of here!" she shouted and flung her shoulder against the back door.

It didn't give. There was no handle on the inside, and she couldn't pound on it with her hands behind her back. She flung her shoulder against it again, shouting, "Lyle! Joseph! Eula Mae! Run! It's the FBI!"

Silence. No sounds of struggle, no cut-off yelps, nothing. *Maybe they heard me,* she thought, *and were able to run out the back and get away.* Or the FBI had grabbed them one by one as they came through the door before they'd had a chance to cry out, just like they had with her.

If only I'd handed Indy to Joseph instead of Lyle, she thought. He'd have had the presence of mind to stow the tote bag out of sight behind the counter when they burst in—or to unzip it and let Indy out. Even an inch would have been enough to allow Indy to do his bullwhip thing, shackling their hands and ankles, knocking their guns out of their hands.

Not before they shot him, she thought, and pressed her ear against the door, listening for gunshots, but she still couldn't hear anything, and the door didn't open for them to shove Lyle and the others in with her. And she hadn't heard any other car doors open and slam shut.

Maybe they didn't wait for them to come out, she thought. Maybe they'd stormed inside and grabbed them in the office—and were waiting there now to ambush Wade when he came back with the RV. *And he'll walk straight into the trap.*

I have to warn him, she thought. But if she tried, it would alert them to the fact that he existed, and they might not know about him. And if they didn't, he might still have a chance to avoid capture.

A car door slammed, and a muffled voice said, "Is the alien in custody?"

"Yes, sir."

Her heart sank.

"And the three others?"

"Yes, sir."

Three others. That meant they didn't know about Wade. Which meant he hadn't come back, he'd seen the van and the agents and realized what was happening, and all was not lost. He'd find a way to rescue them.

Another car door slammed, and she heard the same voice she'd heard before ask, "Is Agent Hastings here yet?" and a reply she couldn't hear.

Hastings. That was the name of the FBI guy she'd tried to call that first night. He must have gotten her message after all, and they'd been chasing her ever since. *Oh, why did he have to catch up with us now, right when we were about to take Indy to his* **tsurrispoinis**? *We'll never get him there in time now.*

But Hastings knew Serena—and Russell—so maybe he'd be willing to listen to her if she explained that they had to get Indy there. If she ever got the chance to talk to him.

"Let me out!" she shouted, flinging her shoulder against the door again. "I want to talk to Agent Hastings!"

No response, but a couple of minutes later a different voice said, "We're all set to go. Is Agent Hastings back yet?"

"No, he went to show Wakamura where the RV they hijacked is parked."

Oh, no, she thought. *They know about the RV. Does that mean they got Wade?*

"Did Hastings say how they ended up with an RV?"

"No, sir. We haven't had a chance to debrief him yet on the time he spent undercover with them."

The time he spent undercover?

"Well, when you do, I want to know what the hell they were doing here and why he—what name was he using again?"

"Wade," the first voice said. "Wade Pierce."

CHAPTER SEVENTEEN

"They got him locked up over in the jail."
—*Support Your Local Sheriff*

Francie spent the next two days? three days? being shuttled from place to place. She was driven somewhere in the van for several hours and then left in a locked room with a table, a chair, and a cot overnight, then put on a plane and flown and then driven somewhere else and put in another locked room.

Where? Wright-Patterson Air Force Base? Quantico? Abu Ghraib?

She had no way of knowing. The SUV had had blacked-out windows and a barricade between her and the driver, and they'd blindfolded her and put headphones on her each time they moved her.

But even if they hadn't, she was too numb to care where they were taking her. She felt concussed, as if someone had hit her over the head with a shovel, and sick at heart. Wade—correction, Agent Henry Hastings—had betrayed her.

He betrayed all of us, she thought. Especially Eula Mae, who was probably wanted in a dozen states and now he'd handed her over to the law she'd been dodging for years. And Indy, who'd trusted Wade to get him to his *tsurrispoinis.*

We all trusted him, Francie thought bitterly. *And he lied to all of us.* All that talk about not using credit cards and not calling anyone so the government couldn't track them—and the whole time he'd secretly been in contact with them, telling them where they were and what they'd learned from Indy and when to close in. *Lyle was right,* she thought bitterly. *Wade* **is** *a Reptilian.*

She wondered how he'd communicated with them. With some fancy technological FBI gadget? Or some sort of sonic-detection equipment, like the Roswell-crash weather balloon?

No, she thought. *He didn't need anything like that.* Because he'd had a phone. In that duffel bag of his. That was why he'd been so defensive when she'd opened it, so grateful when he found out she'd salvaged it from the car.

He **hugged** *me when I told him I had it,* she thought furiously. *I should have known then there was something fishy about it. I should have looked inside it right then and there.*

Lyle had gone through it once they were in the *Outlaw,* but Wade had obviously retrieved the phone by then. And then stowed it somewhere in the RV, because she remembered him telling her he'd catch up to them at the Tropicana and then staying behind for a minute. *So he could get it out of its hiding place,* she thought, *and then once we were inside Eula Mae told him there was no coverage inside the casino.*

So he went outside to call, not to check out the exits, she thought, and it *was* him she'd seen standing out by the Showgirl Spin making a call. *To tell the Feds where we were so they could move in.*

But then why had he hustled them out of the casino and asked Joseph for alternate routes out of Las Vegas? And argued with Indy over stopping at the wedding chapel?

It was all part of the act, she thought. Wade wouldn't have wanted his men to arrest them at the Tropicana, where there were so many people around. He'd have wanted them to do it where they were less likely to be seen.

But then why choose a wedding chapel where they could have run straight into the Dracula wedding party? Why hadn't they waited till they were back out in the desert and on their way to Area 51, where there'd have been no one at all around? And nowhere for them to run?

Maybe that had been the plan, and Wade had been ordered to leave the Tropicana and drive out of town as quickly and inconspicuously as possible, and then Indy had screwed it up by insisting they stop at the wedding chapel. In which case maybe Indy and the others had gotten away. On the way here, wherever "here" was, she'd seen no sign of any of them.

Maybe Eula Mae, ever on the lookout for the police, had realized something was wrong and herded everybody into the Candlelight Chapel and out the fire exit. And the "three" the agents had said they'd taken into custody were actually Reverend Murray and the bride and groom from the Dracula wedding, and—

She was forgetting about Wade—correction, Agent Hastings. He knew who they were supposed to take into custody and what Indy could do. And even if Lyle had somehow managed to let Indy out, Indy wouldn't have attacked Wade. He trusted him.

Like I did, she thought bleakly. She'd stupidly trusted Wade, and, as a result, they were all here, being held in featureless rooms like this one while the Feds did who knew what to Indy.

She tried to tell herself that they wouldn't hurt him, that they needed to find out why he'd come here and if there were others of his kind on the way. And they needed to know how he managed to make cars run without gas.

If he was talking. Before they'd gone into the wedding chapel, she'd drilled it into him not to scroll when there were other people around. If he'd just remain silent—

She kept forgetting about Wade. He'd have told them Indy could talk and how he did it. Worse, he'd have told Indy it was okay to talk to the other agents.

At least they didn't know what the *tsurrispoinis* was. She hadn't told Indy the English word for it was "thunderstorm." She'd been too eager to tell Wade. *You sprang your trap too soon,* she thought. *If you'd just waited five minutes, I'd have blabbed the whole thing to Agent Hastings.* Thank God she hadn't—and that she'd been in too much of a hurry to tell the others.

But they didn't have to know that she'd figured out what the *tsurrispoinis* was. All Joseph or Lyle or Eula Mae had to say to put them on the scent was that she'd suddenly gone racing off to find Wade.

And if they knew she knew, she had no doubt they'd be able to get the information out of her—with Sodium Pentothal or "enhanced interrogation" or something—and once they knew, she could only imagine what they'd do with the information.

They'd never believe *tsurrispoinis* meant "thunderstorm." They'd latch onto the mushroom cloud Indy had pointed at and conclude the aliens intended to get their hands on the nuclear arsenal and use it against Earth and had to be killed before they succeeded.

Which meant she had to get out of here, wherever here was, before they questioned her.

But unlike the resourceful cowgirls in those Westerns Joseph loved, she didn't know the first thing about escaping from the bad guys. She knew nothing about decrypting door codes or jimmying locks.

The ceiling was solid, not made of those removable panels they always had in movies, and, anyway, it was too high for her to reach, even standing on the one folding chair she had. And the air-conditioning vent was too small to squeeze a hand into, let alone her whole body.

She didn't have any pillows or blankets to make a dummy out of—they'd come and taken them and the cot away when they'd brought her breakfast—and no rope or duct tape or Swiss Army knife. She didn't even have a hairpin. The circlet of artificial flowers attached to her wedding chapel veil might have had some wires holding the flowers in place, but the Feds had confiscated it at the first place they'd taken her to and showed no signs of giving it back.

Which left her maid-of-honor dress. But while she was trying to figure out how to tear the skirt into strips and braid it into a glow-in-the-dark bullwhip, the door opened.

It wasn't an agent, come to question her. Or Wade, thank goodness. It was only the guard, bringing her lunch? dinner? on a tray.

"I want to make a phone call," Francie said.

He set the tray down.

"I know my Miranda rights," Francie said. "I'm allowed one phone call. I insist you let me call my lawyer."

He shook his head. "No phone calls."

"How long are you going to keep me here?" she demanded. "At least I have a right to know that."

He didn't answer. He went out and shut the door behind him.

She banged on it for a while, shouting, "I'll sue you for kidnapping and unlawful arrest!" and then went over to the tray to see if it had anything on it she could use as a weapon.

It didn't. There was a sandwich, potato chips, an apple, a container of yogurt with a flat wooden spoon, and a bottle of water. The tray was cardboard, which ruled out standing behind the door and bashing the guard over the head with it the next time he came in.

She supposed she could throw the apple at him, but that would probably only make him mad, so she ate it and the sandwich and potato chips and tried to figure out what day it was.

Tuesday, she decided. Which meant Serena was already on her honeymoon, and Francie had let her down completely.

She'd let Indy down, too. She'd promised to help him get to his *tsurrispoinis* and she'd failed. The chances of his reaching it before whoever or whatever was chasing him did were getting slimmer by the minute, and there was nothing she could do about it. She couldn't even untangle the knots he was probably tying himself in from fear right now.

And the worst part was that this was all her fault. *I was the one who called the FBI and left that message for Agent Hastings*, she thought. *I was the one who sicced him—and them—on you. I am so sorry, Indy.*

Why couldn't you have yanked that phone out of my hand before I made that call? she thought, but it wasn't his fault. It was hers.

She had been so stupid. The clues that Wade wasn't just a hitch-hiker had all been right there. He hadn't acted nearly shocked enough when he realized he'd been abducted by an alien. And instead of demanding to know what was going on and talking about how to get away, he'd immediately begun asking questions about where Indy was taking her and whether he could talk and did he understand what she was saying—questions that had been entirely too intelligent and pointed for a scam artist who made a living out of tricking UFO nuts into buying anti-abduction insurance.

*Except that he **was** a scam artist,* she thought. *And he was very good at it.*

It was perfectly clear now exactly what the scam had been—he'd intended to leave her at the gas station and take Indy in to interrogate him, but Indy had thwarted that plan and then, before he could try again at the trading post, Wade—correction, Agent Hastings—had realized she was able to communicate with Indy and had decided she might be useful and made up that story about hiding Indy from the authorities and helping him find the *tsurrispoinis.*

And as soon as they'd succeeded in getting Indy to speak and taught him enough vocabulary for the FBI to be able to communicate with him, he'd called in his storm troopers to take over. And they were holding her and the others here to keep them from talking, to keep the public from finding out an alien had landed, till they got what they wanted out of Indy. Which meant she wouldn't be questioned after all.

But she'd no sooner had the thought than the guard came in and took her upstairs to be questioned.

He ushered her into a windowless room with two chairs facing each other across a metal table and motioned for her to sit down in one of the chairs.

"I want to call my lawyer," Francie said.

"You'll have to take that up with Agent Sanchez," he said and, in spite of herself, she felt a massive relief at the news Wade wouldn't be the one questioning her.

Of course he wouldn't be. He wouldn't want to face her after what he'd done. But despite the fact that he'd betrayed her, her heart had quailed at the thought of seeing him again, as if she was the one who'd done something wrong.

I did, she thought. *I trusted him. I liked him. And when he kissed me, I—*

The door opened, and Agent Sanchez came in. She was extraordinarily pretty, with long black hair and huge brown eyes. She was carrying a laptop and several files, which she set down on the table. "Hello, Ms. Driscoll," she said, extending her hand. "I'm Agent Sanchez."

And next she'll tell me she's Agent Hastings's fiancée, Francie thought bitterly.

Agent Sanchez sat down in the chair opposite her and opened the laptop. "I have some questions I'd like to ask you. I know you've been through a frightening experience—"

"I want to call my lawyer," Francie said.

"I'm afraid phone calls aren't allowed. This is a highly classified situation."

"I'm allowed one phone call," Francie said. "It's the law."

"That only applies if you're under arrest. You're not under arrest. You were abducted—"

"By you."

"—by an extraterrestrial," Agent Sanchez went on imperturbably, "which has to have been terrifying. I understand you were abducted in Roswell. Can you tell me exactly what happened?"

"Not until you tell me why *you* abducted me," Francie said. "And why you're holding me if I'm not under arrest."

"You're under quarantine," Agent Sanchez said. "You may have been exposed to an extraterrestrial disease. I need to know—"

"If I'm not under arrest, then why can't I make a phone call? My friends are probably frantic about me."

"No outside contacts are allowed, due to the classified nature of the situation," Agent Sanchez said. "I understand the extraterrestrial abducted you when you went to get something out of your friend's car."

"Can I at least send a message to them telling them I'm all right?"

"Did the extraterrestrial force you to get in the car?" Agent Sanchez said, and Francie knew she'd better answer the questions if she didn't want Sanchez to break out the truth serum. And at least this was one she *could* answer without giving away anything about the *tsurrispoinis*. Or the fact that Indy had kept talking about Monument Valley. If they knew that, they might take him there, and his panic at the prospect might kill him.

"Yes," she said.

"What did the alien do then?" Agent Sanchez asked.

Francie told her what had happened that night, being careful not to mention the thunderstorm or the clouds on the horizon the next morning.

"Did you see any indication that it was setting up a landing site?" Agent Sanchez asked. "Or a signaling station?"

Lyle has to have told them that, she thought. "No. He didn't do anything. He just sat there."

"You say it told you where to drive by pointing its tentacles in that direction?"

"Yes. No. One tentacle."

Agent Sanchez wrote that down. "Did it employ any other means of communication besides pointing?"

What?

Agent Sanchez must have taken Francie's surprised expression for a "no" because she asked, "Did it do anything at all that might have been an *attempt* at communicating? Sounds? Squawks? Gestures?"

"No," Francie said, thinking, *They don't know about Indy's scrolling.* He must have kept quiet like she'd told him to. Or else he'd been so traumatized he *couldn't* scroll.

"And you're sure it didn't make any grunts or hisses or clicks that might have been talking?"

"I'm sure," Francie said honestly. "He didn't make any sounds at all."

"What about telepathy?"

"*Telepathy?*"

"Yes," Agent Sanchez said, "we have reason to believe extraterrestrials may have developed the ability to communicate directly from mind to mind."

Lyle definitely has to have told them that, Francie thought.

"You didn't receive any telepathic messages from the extraterrestrial," Agent Sanchez persisted, "or notice anything that made you think it was reading your mind?" and when Francie shook her head, Sanchez continued, "It's critical that we find a way to communicate with the alien. During the time you were captured, did you see or hear *anything* that might have been an attempt at communication?"

They don't know Indy can talk! she thought. *Wade didn't tell them,* and felt a stab of hope so strong it was painful. Maybe Wade hadn't betrayed them after all, in spite of how it looked.

She remembered his sudden urgency about leaving the casino, his anxiety about the wedding chapel delay, and his saying "Francie, listen, I—" That morning when they were watching the sunrise. Had he been trying to tell her who he was? Maybe—

"Ms. Driscoll?" Agent Sanchez was saying. "I asked you if during your abduction you made any attempts to communicate with the extraterrestrial."

"I asked him why he'd kidnapped me and where he was taking me. And I asked him to take me home."

"And did it give any indication it understood what you were saying?"

Francie hesitated, trying to decide what to say. If she said no, they might conclude Indy wasn't sentient, but if she said yes . . .

"Let me put it another way," Agent Sanchez said. "How much of what you said to it do you think it understood?"

"I don't know," Francie said, and that was the truth. She *didn't* know how much of what she said he understood or how he interpreted it.

Agent Sanchez questioned her for another half hour or so and then had the guard take Francie back down to her cell, saying as

Francie left, "If you think of anything, anything at all, that might give us a clue to communicating with the extraterrestrial, just tell the guard you want to talk to me."

"I will," Francie lied, and when she was once again behind a locked door, sat down on the folding chair to think about what she'd just found out.

The fact that they didn't know about Indy's scrolling could mean only one thing—Wade hadn't told them. *He isn't in it with them,* she thought, *despite his working for them.*

Or was that what they wanted her to think? Had Agent Sanchez asked her all those questions about not being able to communicate with Indy so she'd believe she'd misjudged Wade and he was still on her side, so that when *he* came to talk to her, she'd tell him everything she knew? Including about the *tsurrispoinis*?

If so, he'll be the next one through that door, she thought, and moments later she heard it being unlocked.

Please don't let it be Wade who comes through it, she prayed. *Please let it be Agent Sanchez. Or the guard bringing me some more food. Please let it be the guard.*

It was. He opened the door an inch and said, "She's in here, Agent Hastings," and then pulled the door all the way open to reveal Wade standing there.

CHAPTER EIGHTEEN

"Hold on to Fred, son. Here comes the cavalry."
—*Smokey and the Bandit*

For one ecstatic, heart-shaking moment, in spite of the fact that he was wearing a suit and an ID badge and looking down at some kind of official form, Francie thought, *He didn't betray us. He's here to rescue me.*

And then he glanced up at her, and the look he gave her was the same as Agent Sanchez's, businesslike and impersonal—and irritated, as if she were a minor annoyance that had to be dealt with.

She felt furious all over again. "Well, if it isn't *Agent Hastings*," she said. "I suppose they sent *you* because Agent Sanchez couldn't get anything out of me. Well, forget it. I'm not telling you anything. I know whose side you're on. That fact became painfully clear the minute your goons pushed me into that FBI van. The way you set that up was really clever, by the way, having us grabbed while you were off getting the RV so we wouldn't realize you were in on it. I actually hoped you'd figured out what was happening and managed to get away. Can you believe that? I didn't realize you didn't *have* to figure it out because it was your idea in the first place, you Benedict Arnold."

If she'd expected him to deny it, to try to defend himself, she was sorely mistaken. He didn't even have the grace to look guilty. "I'm not here to interrogate you," he said coolly. "I'm here to take you to your transport. You're being transferred."

Transferred? she thought with a stab of fear. If they took her to some other facility, she'd have *no* chance of rescuing Indy. "Transferred where?" she asked belligerently. "To Guantánamo for a little waterboarding?"

"I don't have time for this," he said and took hold of her arm.

She pulled away from him. "I'm not going anywhere. You can't make me."

"That's what you think," he said, and produced a pair of handcuffs, grabbed her arm again, and snapped one of the bracelets onto her wrist.

"I should have run over you that first day when you stepped out in front of my car," she said as he reached for her other wrist. "You're a snake, you know that?"

"No talking," he said, and handcuffed her hands in front of her, took hold of her arm, and started toward the door.

She resisted, pulling back against him. "A rattlesnake."

"Do that again, and I'll shackle your ankles, too," he said grimly, and yanked her toward the door.

"You were in touch with them all along, weren't you?" she said. "Telling them where we were and what we were doing, how we were teach—"

He gripped her arm painfully. "I said no talking. No. Talking. I mean it," and knocked on the door to be let out.

The guard opened the door. Wade—correction, Agent Hastings—showed him the form. The guard read it, nodded, and handed it back to Wade, and he led her down the hall and through a door, into a stairwell. He motioned for her to start down.

She grabbed hold of the railing. "I'm not going anywhere," she said, gripping it tightly. "Not till you tell me where Indy is."

"Oh, for—" he said, and tried to pry her fingers free. "Let go."

"No," she said, hanging on for grim death. "Not until you've told me what you've done with him. If you've hurt him—"

"*Hurt* him?" he said, and let go of her fingers. He sounded genuinely shocked and wounded by the accusation. But then he'd sounded just as convincing when he told her he wanted to help Indy. And when he'd repeated his marriage vows.

"I'd never hurt him," he insisted. "I'm trying to *help* him. And you."

"Oh, really? How? By handing us over to the Feds?"

"No, by getting you out of here," he said.

"You're—?"

"Trying to bust you out," he said. "This is an escape attempt, you moron. I'm trying to rescue you and Indy so we can get him to his *tsurrispoinis*. So come on. And keep quiet."

She let go of the railing, and Wade hustled her swiftly down the stairs and out into a hall lined with offices, after taking another cautious look for guards. But it was empty. And so was the second stairwell he led her into. Suspiciously so.

As he led her down the stairs, she grabbed for the railing again. "How do I know this isn't just another setup?" she said. "Like you just happening to be hitchhiking that day. 'Howdy, ma'am, I'm workin' my way to Roswell to scam the rubes.' And your pretending to be running from the FBI when you were actually one of them? How do I know this isn't just another trick to get me to tell—?" she started, and then stopped abruptly when she realized she'd almost said, "to tell you about the *tsurrispoinis*." Francie amended hastily, "To get me to talk? How do I know this isn't just another one of your scams, like anti-abduction insurance?"

"You'll know in about five minutes when they catch us," he muttered. "Look, you'll just have to take my word for it."

"Take your *word* for it? That's rich. I'm not going anywhere until you tell me why there are conveniently no guards around and why it's so easy to 'bust out' of a place like this, if that's what you're really doing."

"I don't have *time* for this," he said, exasperated. "I'll tell you the whole story, but *not now.*" He grabbed her hand and tried to pry it from the railing. "Come on, let go."

She clung tighter. "Not till you tell me why I should trust anything you say."

"Because I've got Indy."

"You've—?"

"Yep," he said, loosening his tie and unbuttoning his shirt to reveal Indy clinging to his chest, his tentacles wrapped around it, crisscrossed like a web of bandages, scrolling, "FRANCIE FRANCIE FRANCIE."

"Indy, no," Wade said. "Remember what I told you? No scrolling till I say so," and Indy's tentacles went instantly blank, but he unfastened one of them from Wade's chest and wrapped it around Francie's wrist.

She put her hand tenderly over it. "Indy! I'm so glad to see you! Are you all right?" She looked up at Wade. "How did you get him out?"

"I'll tell you later. Right now, *we've* got to get out of here. Indy, back inside."

The tentacle withdrew and wrapped itself back around Wade's chest. Wade buttoned his shirt back up and tightened his tie. "Come on," he said, and hurried her down the rest of the stairs.

"What about Eula Mae and Joseph and Lyle?" she asked as they crossed the landing. "Are you trying to get them out, too?"

"There isn't time," he said. "Besides, they're creating a diversion."

"A diversion?" she said. "What kind of diversion?"

"Suffice it to say Eula Mae and Joseph are trying to give us enough time to get out of the building."

"And then what?"

"Then we've got to figure out where Indy wants to go, and go there. But first we've got to find some transportation."

She stopped short. "You mean you planned an escape without finding us a getaway car first?"

"No, of course not," he said, pulling a ring of keys out of his shirt pocket and jangling them at her.

"Then why do you need—?"

"*Shh,*" he said, and opened the door a crack to look out. "Wait here," he whispered, slipping through and shutting the door behind him.

And what now? She looked nervously up the stairs, listening for any sound of someone coming, but all she heard was a cut-off yelp from the hallway. *Indy,* she thought, expecting to find a trussed-up guard when Wade opened the door and motioned her out of the stairwell, but the hallway was empty.

"Come on," Wade whispered, heading for a door at the end that said Exit. He took a firm grip on her arm. "Now, remember, you're my prisoner," he admonished, and led her swiftly to the door and opened it.

She blinked at the sudden bright sunlight and the buildings around them. Off to their right was a busy street with a green-and-purple banner hanging across it proclaiming THE TRUTH IS RIGHT HERE! WELCOME TO THE UFO FESTIVAL!

"We're in Roswell!" Francie said, astonished.

"Yeah," Wade said, "which is a good thing. I could never have gotten you out of where we were."

"Which was where?"

"Shh. You're supposed to be my prisoner, remember?"

He walked her quickly across the parking lot to a line of black vans, clicked the remote at the one at the end, handed her into the passenger seat, and shut the door.

He went around to the driver's seat, got in, and pulled the door nearly to. "Luckily, the Head wanted us to be as close to the landing sites as possible," he said, and began to unbutton his shirt again.

"Wait," Francie said. "What landing sites?"

"Later," he said, unbuttoning another button. He looked down at his chest. "Okay, Indy, you can let them go now," and a half-dozen nearly invisible filaments she hadn't noticed before came flashing back at blinding speed from the door they'd just emerged from. Which explained the yelp she'd heard from the hall before—and the absence of guards.

The filaments snapped back around Wade's chest. "Oof!" he said, and then recovered, shut the door, and began quickly rebuttoning his shirt.

"Aren't you going to let Indy out? And un-handcuff me?" she asked, holding out her shackled hands.

He shook his head. "We've got to get out of here first," he said, but instead of starting the car, he unhooked the van's remote from the keychain and stuck it in his jacket pocket. He put the key in the ignition, started the car, pulled out of the parking lot, and headed north on Main Street.

"Where are we going?" Francie asked.

He didn't answer. He surveyed the oncoming traffic, rolled down his window, and as a pickup truck passed them going the other way, tossed the remote into the back of it. Then he sped up to another pickup, this one going their way, and pulled into the left-hand lane beside it.

The light changed to red. Wade fumbled in his pants pocket, pulled out a phone, and put it in Francie's handcuffed hands. "When the light changes, and he starts to pull away," he said, pointing at the pickup, "throw it in the back."

She did. "Good," Wade said. "That should keep them from figuring out where we're going at least for a little while."

"Where *are* we going?" Francie asked. "And what's this about wanting to be close to the landing sites? Do you mean of the aliens who are after Indy?"

"Or the aliens who are after them," Wade said, his eyes on the road. "Or possibly an invasion force. We won't know till they land."

"But I thought they'd already landed?"

"Yeah, well, that's the problem." He turned left and started down a residential street. "We don't know if they have or not. There have been definite indications that several ships have landed—multiple video sightings, high-frequency radio transmissions, motion and in-frared sensor readings, plus the fact that Indy's been getting more scared by the minute and keeps scrolling 'Monument Valley'—"

He broke off, grabbing at his chest. "Ow!" he cried. "Stop, Indy, you're squeezing me to death! We're not going to Monument Valley. I was just telling Francie what you said. We're not going there, I promise," and then, soothingly, "I know, buddy. It's okay, it's okay. I won't let them get you."

And Indy apparently loosened his grip because Wade said, "Thanks, Indy," and looked at Francie. "Jesus, he's like a python. Where was I?"

"You said he keeps scrolling about . . . you know," she said, looking anxiously at Wade's chest.

"Oh, yeah. Ever since I got him out, he's been scrolling the MV word and then 'HERE GO GO GO.' Whoever they are, they're def-initely here. We just don't know where."

"How can you not know where they are?"

"We don't know that, either. Maybe they have cloaking devices, like Lyle said. Or look like tumbleweeds, like Indy. Or sagebrush. Or billboards."

"Could Lyle have been right," Francie said, "and they *do* have underground bases?"

"I don't know." He turned north again. "All I know is we've got to figure out where the *tsurrispoinis* is and get Indy there *soon*." He glanced in the rearview mirror. "Is there anybody following us?"

She looked in her side mirror and then turned around and looked out the back window to make sure. "No."

And why wasn't there? The moment Indy released the guards he'd trussed up, they'd have sounded the alarm that Indy was loose.

As if she'd spoken aloud, Wade said, "None of the guards except yours saw me, so they'll be looking for Indy, not us, and they know he can't drive, so hopefully they'll be looking for him in the building and the surrounding area."

"What about the agents who were guarding Indy? Didn't they see you when you got him out?"

"I *didn't* get him out. He did that himself. Escaped from the laser-beam-security cage they were keeping him in, slid under the locked door, and came and found me."

Which sounded plausible. But so was the possibility that they hadn't escaped at all, that this was just another setup to get her to tell Wade what a *tsurrispoinis* was.

But he doesn't know I know, she thought.

Indy could have told him I do, she argued, *and he's arranged the whole rescue thing to make me trust him enough to tell him,* and some of her skepticism must have shown in her face because Wade said, "You still don't trust me. I suppose I don't blame you, after everything that's happened." He paused. "Look, I was operating undercover. I *couldn't* tell you who I was. Anybody behind us now?" he asked.

She looked. "No," she said, and he turned down an alley.

"What are you doing?" Francie asked.

He didn't answer. He drove halfway down the alley and stopped. "Give me your hands."

"So you can look deep in my eyes and swear you're telling the truth?" she said bitterly.

"No, so I can take off your handcuffs." He grabbed her wrists. "If they *are* following us, I want to give you half a chance of getting away." He unlocked the bracelets and handed them and their key to her. "*Or* to handcuff me to the steering wheel and grab Indy and split, since you seem to think this is all some kind of setup—"

"And why wouldn't I?" she said. "After you tricked me—us—into believing you were trying to help Indy, and then, when we'd figured out how to communicate with him and you didn't need us anymore, you handed us over to the FBI."

"Is that what you think I did? Jesus."

He looked in the rearview mirror, glanced ahead to the street beyond the alley's opening, and then drove forward to where a driveway backed up to a garage.

He pulled into the driveway far enough to keep anyone looking down the alley from seeing the van, stopped the van, and said, "I *didn't* hand you over to the FBI. And I *was* trying to help Indy. I could see he needed to find his *tsurrispoinis,* whatever the hell it is, and that if I followed regs, he'd never get to it in time. I convinced the Head to let me try it my way, that we were making progress in figuring out how to communicate with him, and he said okay, but then when they started getting indications of another, larger landing, they got nervous and told me they couldn't wait any longer, that I had to bring him in immediately.

"I tried to tell them that would ruin everything, that we were getting close, and all I needed was a few more hours—that's what I was off doing at the Tropicana, trying to talk them into waiting—and when they said no—"

"You tried to make a run for it," she said, thinking, *That's why he was in such a hurry for us to leave, why he'd asked Joseph if there were any alternate routes out of town.*

"Yeah, I tried to get us out of Vegas," he said, "and we would have made it. I'd told them we were at the Bellagio, and as we left the Tropicana I dropped my phone in the purse of a tourist who I overheard saying she was headed to Treasure Island. And then Indy screwed it up by insisting we stop at that damned wedding chapel."

That's why Wade had told them to go inside immediately—and why he'd parked the RV so far away—because they were being followed.

"I should have refused to stop, but—hang on," he said, got out of the car, crept cautiously to the alley to look both ways down it, and then got back in, backed out of the driveway, and drove to the next street.

"I should have refused to stop," he went on when they were safely back on the street, "but I figured we'd be safe there, that it was the last place they'd think to look for us. And that even if they did figure out where we were and put up roadblocks, I'd have time to explain the situation to you. But I was wrong on both counts, and by the time I got back, it was too late to do anything except keep Indy from scrolling, and keep them from finding out he *could* scroll till I could figure out a way to get him out."

"And me," she said.

"No, that was Indy's idea. I'd intended to just take him—it was a lot faster to get the two of us out, and it was obvious that either his deadline, whatever it is, is almost here or whoever's after him is. Or both. If I hadn't managed to convince him to conceal himself by wrapping himself around me, he'd be a mass of tangles right now. But he absolutely refused to go without you. He kept scrolling 'FRANCIE NOTHES,' whatever the hell that means." He looked at her. "You don't happen to know, do you?"

Yes, she thought. *It means "Francie knows."*

"And I don't suppose you know what the wedding chapel has to do with all this?" Wade asked. "He kept scrolling that, too. Any ideas?"

Yes, she said silently. *He was trying to say, "I told Francie at the wedding chapel."*

I need to tell him, she thought. *But how do I know I can trust him? He—*

"Hang on," Wade said, sped up, and then turned abruptly onto another street and drove along it at a crawl.

"What are you doing?" Francie asked.

"I told you, we've got to find some transportation. This car's a walking, talking 'Here we are! Come and get us!' sign. GPS monitors, real-time tracking devices, locational sensors, geo-fencing, you name it. We wouldn't make it five miles out of town before they caught up with us."

"Unless the Feds are letting us escape," she said. "Maybe Indy didn't escape from his cage—maybe they let him out so he'd lead them to the aliens. They know they're after him. Maybe they're using him as bait. They let him go so the aliens would follow him. And they can follow us and find the aliens."

Wade considered that. "It's possible," he said. "In which case we definitely need a car they can't trace."

"You're not going to have Indy commandeer another car, are you?"

"No, the last thing we need is to drag yet another innocent by-stander into this. I'm talking about *stealing* a car. And since I doubt if we can find one with the keys still in it, it'll have to be one I—or Indy—can hot-wire," he said, looking carefully at each of the parked cars they were passing. "Which means it needs to be an older model, and hopefully one the owner won't miss immediately."

"I have a car," Francie said.

"What do you mean, you have a car? The Navigator's still at Thunderbird Trading Post."

"No, that was Serena's car, remember? I rented a car to drive to Roswell in. If it hasn't been towed or something, it should still be where I parked it."

"I *love* you," he said. "So where is it? In front of the UFO museum?"

"No. Because of the UFO Festival, there wasn't any place to park, so I had to park on a side street."

"Please tell me you remember which one."

She nodded. "Pennsylvania Street. Four blocks south of the UFO museum," she said, and he immediately made a U-turn and started toward downtown.

"I don't suppose you left the keys in it?" he said.

"No," she said. "And I locked it."

"Don't worry about that. Indy can slip a tentacle in and unlock the door," he said. "It's starting it that might be a problem. Where are the keys? I assume you left them behind when you went to get Serena's Navigator."

"No. I put them on the keychain with the keys Serena gave me. Which means they're probably still in the ignition of the Navigator at the trading post."

"No, they're not," he said, and pulled them triumphantly from his jeans pocket. "The agents confiscated the keys to the RV but they didn't take mine. This is Pennsylvania Street. What does your car look like?"

"It's a Jeep Wrangler," she said, looking down the street, praying it was still there.

It was. "There," she said, pointing at it, but he didn't stop. He drove right past it and on to the next block.

"What are you doing?" she asked.

"I don't want them to be able to draw any connection between this car and yours, so I'm going to drive around the block and drop you off and then you come pick us up." He pointed down the street toward a strip mall. "I'll be in that parking lot."

He turned up the next street and drove back to where the Jeep was parked and past it to the church, which now had a sign saying SUNDAY'S SERMON: THE GOOD SAMARITAN, and when she looked questioningly at him, he said, "In case you've forgotten, you're wearing a bridesmaid dress."

"Maid of honor."

"Whatever. This at least gives you some cover."

She nodded, took the keys he handed her, got out of the car, and then hesitated. If they got separated, he wouldn't know what the *tsurrispoinis* is. "I need to tell you something first, about—"

"Tell me later," he said. "Go. Now, before somebody comes." He pulled the door shut, and then rolled down the window. "Oh, and if we get caught, I want you to calmly drive off, go back to the main drag, and get the hell out of town."

She walked purposefully up to the church's front door and then stopped as if she'd forgotten something, and walked quickly across the street to the Jeep, unlocked it, and slid into the driver's seat.

The windshield was dirty from the car's having sat there for days, and there was a folded piece of paper stuck under the windshield wiper. *Leave it there,* she told herself, but she was afraid it was a parking ticket, which would mean the police would have the Jeep's make and model and license plate number, making this car just as easy to track as the FBI van.

She glanced in the mirrors to make sure no one was coming and then slid out, snatched the piece of paper, and leaped back in just as a car turned onto the street behind her. Hopefully whoever was in it was still too far away to have seen her dress.

She wasn't going to wait to see. She stuck the keys in the ignition and pulled out hastily, while the car was still half a block away, and drove off, going several blocks to make sure the car wasn't following her.

It turned off after two blocks, and, after another block, she turned up an alley, stopped the Jeep, and unfolded the paper.

It wasn't a parking ticket. It was a flyer for the UFO Festival. "Come have your very own close encounter," it read.

I've had one, thank you, she thought, and started back toward the strip mall.

And let's hope I can find it, she thought. *And that Wade's still there.*

He wasn't, and the van was nowhere to be seen. *Oh, no,* she thought, driving around the corner to see if it was there.

It wasn't. *They caught him,* she thought, driving back through the strip mall's parking lot, *and it's my fault. If I'd come straight here*—and before she could finish the thought, Wade popped out from behind a bush and jumped in the passenger's side.

"Where the hell have you been?" he demanded. "I thought you'd gone off without me."

"Now you know how it feels," she said. "Do you want to drive?"

He shook his head. "We don't have time to switch. Go."

She pulled out of the strip mall and drove north. "Where's the van?"

"In the landing bay behind a liquor store, and I put a bunch of boxes in front of it and disabled as many of the trackers as I could find." He took off his jacket, threw it in the back seat, and rolled up his shirtsleeves. "I doubt if I got them all, but at least my hiding it there should keep the local police from spotting it. We've already got enough people—and aliens—on our tail. Turn left."

"Where are we going?"

"Wherever Indy tells us to. *If* he tells us. I'm hoping once we get out of town and it's safe to let him out, you can get him to tell you what this *tsurrispoinis* of his is and where it's located. He trusts you."

"Wade—"

"I know. We're running short on time, but this is Roswell, re-member? Home of the alien sighting. We can't risk somebody seeing him and reporting what kind of car he was in. Go two blocks and then turn left again. Our first order of business is to get out of town, and I don't want to use the main road if we can help it. Hopefully we can find a street that connects up with Highway 380 east of the junction."

"I've got a map," she said. "In the glove compartment."

"You're kidding!" he said, leaning forward to open it. "A map, a car. You've got everything!" He grabbed it and unfolded it. "Roswell . . . Roswell . . . okay, it looks like North Atkinson Road will get us to Highway 105. Keep heading east."

"This next street is Main Street," she said, and he looked up.

"We've got to cross it sometime," he said. "See if you can find an intersection without a traffic light. That way we won't have to stop there like a pair of sitting ducks waiting for the light to change."

She nodded, went up two blocks, pulled up to the intersection, waited for what seemed like an eternity while a car and two semis went past, and then shot across, past the still-present signs for the UFO Festival and the alien-headed lampposts and into an area of warehouses and industrial buildings.

"Go east," Wade said, looking at the map. "We need to find a through street that'll take us to North Atkinson Road and then the highway and hope this *tsurrispoinis* of Indy's is someplace east of town so we don't have to cross the junction with 285. Turn here," he ordered, pointing.

She turned onto the road and headed east, past a large squat silo and several low buildings, toward the edge of town.

Wade was still poring over the map. "If the *tsurrispoinis* turns out to be a place that's west of here, we can go south on Highway 2 to 13 and then take that south to 82."

I need to tell him what the **tsurrispoinis** *is,* she thought. *Now, before the FBI or the aliens—or both—catch up to us.*

She looked over at Wade. He was still intent on the map.

One of Indy's tentacles had unbuttoned one of his shirt buttons, freed itself from Wade's chest, and was tapping him on the arm. "COMING! HURRY HURRY HURRY!" it scrolled feverishly, the letters bright red.

"We're trying," Wade said. "You've gotta tell us where it is."

"FRANCIE NOTHES."

"Yeah, but see, we don't know what 'nothes' means."

"I do," Francie said. "It means 'knows.'"

"What?" Wade said blankly.

"'Knows,'" she repeated. "He's trying to tell you 'Francie knows.'"

"Knows what?" he said, still lost.

"What a *tsurrispoinis* is."

"*What?*" He stared at her. "How long have you known?"

"Since two minutes before I got grabbed by your thugs."

"Oh my God!" he said. "You didn't tell them, did you?"

"No, of course not."

"What about Lyle and Eula Mae and Joseph? Did you tell them?"

"No. I handed Indy and the tote bag to Lyle and told him I had to go talk to you, but I didn't say about what, and none of them were close enough to see what we were doing."

"Which was what?"

"You remember those photographs of Las Vegas in the hallway? One of them was a picture of downtown Vegas in the fifties, with the Vegas Vic sign in the foreground and a mushroom cloud in the distance. Indy tapped the cloud and scrolled 'TSURRISPOINIS.'"

"A mushroom—? Jesus!"

"No, no," she said, and explained how she'd realized he'd thought what he was pointing at was a cloud and how she'd confirmed it with the other photos. "A *tsurrispoinis* is definitely a thunderstorm. That first night when he abducted me there was one north of Roswell. He was trying to get to it, though I didn't realize it at the time." She explained about the clouds the morning they'd picked him up, the airplane vapor trails, the sign for the Georgia O'Keeffe Museum.

"That explains why he acted so confused that day," Wade said, "because the clouds were pointing in all directions. And why he kept changing directions, and we couldn't figure out where he was going," Wade said. "He was just following whichever cloud he happened to see. But wait, what about that morning I woke you up to see that sunrise? He didn't try to follow those clouds."

"He was asleep, remember? He didn't wake up till later, and by then they were behind us, and by the time he took his bearings again, they'd disappeared. And the next clouds he saw were off to the north."

"In the direction of Las Vegas," Wade said. "Wow, a thunderstorm. And he couldn't tell us because he didn't know the word for it." He frowned. "Hang on. Wasn't there a thunderstorm in that movie he threw a fit over? The one set in Monu—"

"Shh," Francie said, jabbing a warning finger at his chest.

"—that movie with the cavalry," he finished. "Maybe that's what he saw, and the reason he freaked out was because he was trying to tell us and we didn't understand. Did he tell you what he wants with this thunderstorm?"

"No. All I know is that a *tsurrispoinis* is a thunderstorm, and that that's what he's trying to get to."

"But now where are we going to find one? Shit, I wish I hadn't dumped my phone. We need to find somewhere with a TV so we can check the Weather Channel and find out which way to go."

"No, we don't," Francie said, pointing to the east. They'd passed the last of the storage buildings and sheds that marked the edge of Roswell, and there, along the horizon, like a gift from heaven, stood a fully formed thunderhead.

CHAPTER NINETEEN

Butch Cassidy: How many are following us?

Sundance Kid: All of 'em.
                    —*Butch Cassidy and the Sundance Kid*

The thunderstorm was already a long way east of them, so far away that they could see it in its entirety, the sculpted mounds of white cloud thousands of feet high, the signature flat anvil top and equally flat bottom, with a dark blue-gray curtain of rain under it obscuring the countryside beyond.

"A fully formed cumulonimbus," Wade said. "Just what we need."

"If we can catch up to it," Francie said. "It's moving away from us."

"Yeah," Wade said. "To the southwest, I think."

"How fast do thunderstorms move?"

"I don't know. Twenty miles an hour? Thirty?"

"Good. Then we should be able to catch it," she said, and sped up. "At least we're not in Joseph's RV."

"Western trail wagon," Wade said automatically. "But we've still got a problem. How do we know this is the thunderstorm Srennom's at?"

"We don't, but I haven't seen a single thunderstorm since the night Indy abducted me, and the weather forecast said there wasn't supposed to be any rain for the next ten days, so let's hope it's the only one Srennom's been able to find, too."

"And let's hope a mother ship doesn't suddenly emerge out of it like in *Close Encounters*."

"You watch too many movies," Francie said.

Wade grinned at her. He'd been unbuttoning his shirt to let Indy out as she spoke. Indy unwound his tentacles from Wade's chest, shook himself out into his normal tumbleweed shape, stuck his index tentacle up on the dashboard, and exploded into words. "TSURRISPOINIS TSURRISPOINIS," he scrolled in bright orange and red and glowing violet. "SRENNOM GO."

"I'm going," Francie said, and put her foot down hard on the gas pedal.

"Watch it," Wade said. "The speed limit's sixty-five, and we can't afford to be stopped by the Highway Patrol."

"What do you mean?" she asked, glancing in the rearview mirror. There was no one behind her, and no other car anywhere. The road behind them—and ahead—stretched emptily for miles. There was nothing but sagebrush and browning grass, and nothing, not a tree or a road sign, a patrol car could hide behind. "What happened to, 'It's a big state, with thousands of miles of road for the Highway Patrol to cover'?"

"Yeah, well, about that. That wasn't exactly true. As soon as you picked me up that first day, and I assessed the situation, I called HQ and told them to cancel the APBs and call off the cops, that you were okay and I had you and the alien in custody and the situation under control, and not to interfere and to see to it we had safe passage."

Of course, she thought. That was why nobody had stopped them, even after they'd picked up Lyle and his car had to have been found abandoned. *I should have known.*

"You were in touch with the FBI the whole time," she said.

"Yes. No. We're not exactly FBI agents, though we're technically part of the Bureau."

"So what are you?"

"I can't tell you," he said sheepishly. "It's classified."

She stared at him openmouthed. "Oh my God, you're that ultra-secret government agency Lyle kept talking about. You're one of the Men in Black."

"Yes, except we don't have dead aliens in storage at Hangar 18 and we're not secretly working with them on alien technology at Area 51. Which is where they took all of you, by the way, when they first picked you up."

"So Lyle was right. Area 51 *does* exist. I suppose there are secret underground bases, too."

"No," he said, "and the government isn't secretly in cahoots with aliens. We'd never seen one till Indy, and we didn't even know for sure that they were real till three months ago, when we started picking up anomalous signals from SETI, followed by several sightings of UFO landings and then the phone message from you that you'd been abducted."

"So you were already tracking Indy, and when you got my message, all you had to do was change into your con man outfit and print up some anti-abduction insurance policies," Francie said.

"Actually, they were already printed. I was in Roswell for a week two months ago, gathering data on some sightings they were having and talking to the local UFO community."

"Including Serena's fiancé."

"Yeah. We were pretty sure the sightings weren't anything, but just in case, the plan was for me to go back out to the UFO Festival, this time undercover as an anti-abduction insurance salesman, and see what I could pick up on them. But then your roommate's fiancé invited me to their wedding, which was even better. I thought there'd be lots of UFO people at the reception."

"You figured right," Francie said, thinking guiltily of the now-long-since-over wedding and how she hadn't been able to do a thing to stop it.

"But I still don't understand—how did you get out here so fast? Serena said you'd had to change your flight to a red-eye. What did you do? Change it back after you got my message?"

"No, I didn't have to. I was already out here. I'd come back to investigate the sighting west of Roswell on Monday."

"So your calling and telling Serena you were delayed, that you were going to have to take a later flight, was a lie, too?"

" 'Fraid so," he said. "I was actually out at the site of that crash west of Roswell that everybody was claiming they'd seen when you called. All I had to do was find out where the alien had taken you, grab the insurance policies, and get my partner to take me out to where he could intercept you."

"They coptered you in," she said, remembering the helicopter she'd heard that morning.

"No, we located you by the GPS on your phone."

"But I didn't have the phone. Indy threw it—"

"And then the copter got a visual on you and told me which way you were headed, and Cooper, the agent I was working with, drove me out to a few miles north of where you were and dumped me by the side of the road."

"So you could waylay me and tell me a pack of lies."

"Look, my orders were to assess the situation," he said, "and try to find out if the alien was dangerous—or contagious—and what he was doing here, whether he'd accidentally crash-landed here or gotten lost, à la E.T., or was an advance scout for an invasion. And to get any civilians to safety before I did anything else—"

"I *knew* it," she interrupted. "You *did* try to dump me at that gas station."

"Of course I did. I didn't have any idea what Indy was capable of, especially after his little bullwhip stunt, and I thought the best thing to do was get you out of harm's way—"

"So you could assess the situation," she said dryly.

"Yes, but Indy wasn't having it, and after he snatched Lyle, the King of Conspiracy Theories, I obviously couldn't break my cover. There was no telling what he'd do if he found out I was an agent.

And no telling what Indy would do. He *clearly* didn't want me to call the authorities, and I was afraid if I did, he'd lash out at them the way he had with us, and they'd shoot him. And even if they didn't, they'd lock him up and question him and he wouldn't be able to make it to his *tsurrispoinis* on time."

"So you decided continuing to lie to all of us about everything was the best plan."

"I didn't lie about everything. I only—"

"Lied about what was going on and who you were and what you were doing on that road and who you worked for and—"

"Okay, okay, I get your point. But—"

"And about what your name is," she finished. "So what am I supposed to call you now? Agent Hastings? Henry? Lowdown, Dirty, Lyin' Sidewinder?"

"I think you'd better stick with Wade," he said. "Anything else will only confuse Indy."

"I'd just like to know, was anything you said that whole time the truth?"

"Yes," he said. "One, that I wanted to help Indy. And two—"

"NO TALK," Indy scrolled, pushing his tentacle right in front of her face and blocking her view of the road. "GO TSURRISPOI-NIS!"

"Indy, I can't see to drive," she said. "Wade!"

"It's okay, pal," Wade said, lowering Indy's tentacle out of Francie's line of vision. "We'll get you to your *tsurrispoinis*."

"HURRY HURRY HURRY!"

"We're hurrying," Francie said, and, in spite of what Wade had said about the Highway Patrol, she sped up to seventy.

"Why do you need us to hurry, Indy?" Wade asked the alien. "Why do you need to go to the *tsurrispoinis*? What's Srennom doing there?"

Indy responded with several tentacles full of letters.

"What did he say?" Francie said, glancing over.

"Beats me," Wade said. "I didn't recognize a single word."

"Lyle said the aliens come here for things they don't have on their planet," Francie said thoughtfully. "Maybe they don't have thunderstorms."

"You mean you think Srennom's a *stormchaser*?"

"He might be. Serena was engaged to one, you know."

"Of course she was."

"And *he* said that people traveled from all over to see tornadoes—Australia and South Africa and Japan. Maybe they come here from other planets, too."

"Jesus, that's all we need, a stormchaser taking us straight into a tornado."

Francie shook her head. "It's the wrong season for tornadoes. But maybe there's some other reason for them to be looking for a thunderstorm. Maybe it has something they need."

"Like what? Raindrops? Hailstones? Flying cows?"

"No—"

A sudden flicker of lightning lit the clouds from within, outlining their piled-up shapes. "Maybe it's the lightning Srennom's after," Francie said. "It's a source of energy. Maybe they need it to power their ships."

Wade shook his head. "If they're advanced enough to have come here, they're advanced enough to have harnessed electricity. Indy'd hardly need to get power from a thunderstorm."

"But maybe his electricity-generating thingie got damaged in the crash, and he needs to get electricity from somewhere else. Or maybe he needs it to power himself somehow."

"Then why didn't he hook himself up to your car battery?"

"Maybe it takes a special *kind* of electricity that only thunderstorms have."

"Electricity doesn't *have* kinds. And where does Srennom fit into all this?"

"I don't know. Maybe—" She stopped, staring blindly at the thunderstorm ahead. "I just thought of something. I saw a thunderstorm on my way down to Roswell the day Indy abducted me. It was west of Highway 285, near Vaughn."

"When was this?" Wade asked.

"About four o'clock, three hours before Indy abducted me. What if the reason Indy's looking for a thunderstorm is because he saw Srennom land in that thunderstorm, or try to? They're notorious for having crosswinds and downdrafts. What if he saw Srennom crash and abducted me to try to go find the crash site? And that's why he wanted me to go north toward the thunderstorm."

"Oh, Jesus," Wade said. "You realize what that means, don't you? It means he didn't realize thunderstorms move. Or dissipate. That they're temporary phenomena. He thought it was a stationary object, like a mountain or a river, and when he couldn't find it, he thought he'd gone the wrong way. That's why he hauled us all over the place. He was convinced it, and Srennom, had to be somewhere. But if Srennom *did* crash, he and his ship are where *that* thunderstorm was, not at this one."

"And we're going the wrong way," Francie said.

"NO NO NO NO NO," Indy, who'd been seemingly ignoring their conversation, suddenly scrolled. "RIGHT WAY SRENNOM TSURRISPOINIS."

Francie shot a look at Wade. "Indy, did you see Srennom land in a *tsurrispoinis*, a thunderstorm?"

"NO."

"He didn't crash?"

"NO NO NO SRENNOM HERE INDY COME."

"We know you're coming," Wade said impatiently. "How do you know Srennom's here?"

"That's not what he means," she said. "Indy, you came because Srennom was here?"

"YES YES YES SRENNOM TSURRISPOINIS INDY COME FIND."

"*Why* did you come to find him?" Francie asked.

"SRENNOM TSNIBITAI INDY HELP WARN CLAY WARN CAT."

"Well, that's as clear as mud," Wade said.

"Shh," Francie said to Wade, and she asked Indy, "You came to find Srennom and warn him, just like Clay Boone did in *Cat Ballou*

308

when he came to tell Cat that the sheriff and his posse were coming?"

"YES YES YES," he scrolled, and then, after a minute, "MONUMENT VALLEY."

Monument Valley? Francie thought. "What do you mean, Indy?" but he didn't respond. He just kept scrolling, "TSURRISPOINIS HURRY SRENNOM HURRY."

"My guess is he thinks of Monument Valley and thunderstorms as the same thing," Wade said, "since that's where it was in the movie."

But it can't be, Francie thought, because he didn't want to go there—he freaked out at the sight of it—and he *wants* to go to the thunderstorm. "Indy, what—" she began, and the alien thrust his tentacle in front of her face, scrolling, "HURRY HURRY HURRY."

"I am hurrying," Francie said, and looked over at Wade. "Do you think I dare go faster?"

"Yeah. Gun it."

"Are you sure? What about the Highway Patrol?"

"If they stop us, we've got Indy," he said, and she put her foot down hard on the pedal.

"Don't worry, pal," Wade said. "We'll get you there."

Maybe, Francie thought, watching the storm, still far ahead of them. In spite of her speeding up, they didn't seem to be gaining on it at all.

She glanced at the gas gauge. It read a little over three-eighths of a tank, but the storm was still a long way away. "Maybe we should stop and have Indy switch the car to his no-gas-needed mode."

"No, there's no time," Wade said, and glanced behind them again. "Thank *God* we're not in Joseph's RV."

"Western trail wagon," she said automatically. "Speaking of Joseph, you said he and Eula Mae were creating a diversion to help us get away. What kind of diversion?"

"Eula Mae's showing the agents how she managed to hack the slot machines at the Tropicana. And Joseph's unleashing his corporate lawyers on them, threatening to sue for false imprisonment, unlawful confiscation of property, assault, and everything else under the sun. He—"

"Wait, where did Joseph get corporate lawyers?"

"They work for him. It turns out Cowboy Joe isn't just any old retiree. He's J. P. Pangborn."

"J.P.—the head of StudioPanorama?"

"Yep. And number four on *Forbes'* list of gazillionaires."

"But he said he had to sell his house to buy his RV—"

"Western trail wagon," Wade corrected automatically. "And he never said that. Eula Mae just assumed it. According to Agent Sanchez, he's got mansions in Beverly Hills, the Hamptons, Tuscany, Hong Kong, and the Caymans. And a team of lawyers that would terrify even Lyle's Reptilians. They're in there promising lawsuits and Senate investigations and threatening heads will roll, which means the agents are focused on keeping their jobs and not on Indy, at least for the moment."

"And all three of you were lying about who you were," Francie said. "What about Lyle? I suppose he's not what he seems, either. What is he? A famous UFO debunker?"

"I wish," Wade said. "Unfortunately, he's exactly what he seems to be—a raving UFO lunatic who's been spilling his guts ever since we picked him up."

"Oh, no! Couldn't you—?"

"Stop him? You're kidding, right? He's waited *years* to tell the government his theories."

"But I thought you said he was creating a diversion."

"He is. He just doesn't know it. Don't worry. He'd already told Sanchez about the aliens' invasion plans and the ley line transfer zones and was starting in on their secret underground bases when I left. And when they were bringing you in, I told Lyle, whatever happened, *not* to tell them about the Reptilians." He grinned. "Or the Grays at Area 51."

So even if he does tell them about Indy's scrolling and the **tsurrispoinis,** *they won't believe him,* Francie thought.

"With luck, he'll keep Sanchez busy for hours."

"We may need it," Francie said. "We're still not gaining on this storm."

"MONUMENT VALLEY HURRY HURRY HURRY," Indy scrolled.

"I'm already going eighty," Francie muttered and took the Jeep up to ninety, and gradually they began to catch up to the storm. Its clouds towered above them, blindingly white in the sunlight, and so tall they could no longer see the top, and the wind picked up, blowing dust across the road.

"The storm's moving to the south of us," Wade said, peering through the windshield. "We're going to have to turn off," and pointed at a dirt road off to the right and half a mile ahead.

"Do you think that's a good idea?" Francie asked. "In rain, it'll be muddy."

"GO GO GO!" Indy scrolled, pointing at it.

"You're the boss," Francie said, and turned onto the road, and before she'd gone a mile, the sky had turned overcast, and the temperature began to drop precipitously. Francie turned on the Jeep's lights.

A few miles later, she started to smell the sharp, clean scent of wet sagebrush, and rain began to spatter the windshield. "Okay, we're at the storm," she said. "Now where am I supposed to go?"

"SRENNOM," Indy scrolled, his tentacle pointing ahead. She kept going, and the drops turned into a steady rainfall and then a downpour, and a lightning strike flashed ahead of them, lighting the underside of the clouds and a huge expanse of rain-flattened grass.

Wade leaned forward, scanning the desert ahead.

"Did you see anything?" Francie asked him.

"No. Indy, where's Srennom supposed to be?"

"TSURRISPOINIS," Indy scrolled.

"*This* is the *tsurrispoinis*," Wade said. "Which part of it is Srennom in?"

"TSURRISPOINIS."

"What does *that* mean?" Francie asked, struggling to deal with the muddy road and the wind that was battering them and to see through the increasing downpour. And to be heard over the increasing din of rain hammering on the car roof.

"It means he doesn't know," Wade shouted.

"Then what should I do?"

"Aim for the storm's center."

"Which is where?"

"I don't know. Where the rainfall's heaviest, I guess," Wade said, and when a zigzag of lightning slashed through the rain directly in front of them, followed almost immediately by a crash of thunder, "and where there's the most lightning."

She spared a moment of keeping her eyes on the road to look incredulously at him. "You're kidding, right?"

"No. Don't worry. We're completely safe in here. The car acts like a Faraday cage. It conducts the electrical current around the outside so anything inside is safe. Trust me. Just drive toward where the lightning strikes and the rain are the heaviest."

"That would be here," Francie said, looking out at the driving rain. She could no longer see the road. Wade swiped at the inside of the windshield with his hand, as if to clear it, but after a few more yards, the rain began to sluice across the windshield in sheets.

"I can't see a thing," Francie shouted over the din. "I'm going to have to pull over."

"NO NO NO NO NO!" Indy scrolled, his tentacles flailing.

There was a blinding flash, and then, right on top of it a deafening crash of thunder that shook the car. "I'm sorry, Indy," Francie shouted over it. She pulled over to what she hoped was the side of the road. "We'll have to wait till it lets up a little."

Indy wasn't listening, even if he could have heard her through the banging and crashing all around. "SRENNOM!" he scrolled, grabbing at Wade's hands and pushing them toward hers as if to make him force her to start the car. "GO GO GO GO GO!"

"We *can't*," Francie said, "we—" and Indy abruptly let go and pointed out the driver's window, through which nothing could be seen except rain.

"THERE THERE THERE," he scrolled hysterically.

"Where?"

"THERE!" and he rolled himself out the door and across the field.

"Indy!" Francie cried, leaping out into the pelting rain after him, but she couldn't see which way he'd gone, couldn't see anything at all through the blinding, all-encompassing rain. "Indy!" she called, trying to wipe her wet hair out of her eyes. "Where are you? Come back!"

"Francie!" Wade shouted, suddenly beside her. He was soaked, his drenched shirt plastered to his arms and chest, his hair and face dripping. "Get back in the car. We can't stay out here in this!"

"I have to get Indy!" she shouted back. "He doesn't know what lightning is. He doesn't know it can kill him!"

"It can kill us, too!" Wade yelled, grabbing her arm and pulling her back toward the car, which she couldn't see, either. "Do you know how much voltage there is in those lightning bolts? We have to—"

"No!" she said, yanking herself free. "I've got to find Indy," and suddenly saw him, or, rather, the words on his tentacles, bright orange against the gray of the rain, as bright as a neon sign. "Look!" she shouted, pointing at the red-orange letters.

"Indy!" Wade shouted, splashing toward him. "Get back in the car!"

"You have to wait till the storm lets up, Indy!" Francie called. "The lightning's dangerous!" and Indy stopped long enough for her to read on one tentacle, "SRENNOM" in red, and on another, in neon orange, "FIND!" and then he rolled off again, his tentacles a revolving blur of orange-red.

"No!" Francie shouted, splashing through the now-muddy grass. "The lightning can *kill* you! Like the rattlesnake, only faster. And faster than you!"

"A hell of a lot faster than you!" Wade echoed right behind her and, as if to demonstrate, a bolt of lightning zigzagged down within yards of them, so close Francie could see it sizzle and smell the sharp acridness of ozone and then see the purple afterimage of it.

"See?" Wade shouted, and was drowned out by the eardrum-shattering clap of thunder that followed almost instantly. "The next one's going to come down right on top of us," he warned, and Francie looked up fearfully.

"Oh my God!" she murmured.

CHAPTER TWENTY

"Watch the skies!"

—*The Thing from Another World*

Francie clapped her hand to her mouth. Suspended in the foggy air far above her in the pouring rain was a tumbleweed. It was flailing wildly, its tentacles lashing out in all directions.

"Indy!" she cried, and looked down at where she'd seen him rolling off into the rain, afraid he'd somehow been swept up like a kite by the wind, but he was on the ground, far ahead, and still scrolling.

She looked up at the suspended tumbleweed again. She'd been wrong. The tentacles weren't flailing blindly like Indy's had been when he was panicked. They were moving with a quick sureness, like someone weaving or typing, and she caught the glitter of something shiny gripped in the curled ends of its tentacles.

"Indy!" she called to him, pointing up at the tumbleweed, but he'd already seen it and was rolling back to her side.

He stopped a few feet from her, and his still-scrolling tentacles shot up into the sky and wrapped around one of the tumbleweed's appendages, and her comparison had been apt. He pulled it down exactly like a child yanking on the string of a kite.

Srennom—it had to be Srennom—resisted, scrolling something in bright green that Francie couldn't make out but that looked furious, and then, when he realized who was tugging on him, let himself be pulled down to Earth with a muddy splash.

Indy grabbed him, Srennom grabbed back, and they embraced each other, their tentacles twining and entangling like a French braid that had gotten out of control, both of them scrolling too fast for Francie to make out any of it, especially through the rain, which was coming down harder than ever, but they were obviously saying the alien equivalent of "What are you doing here?" and "I've been looking for you everywhere!" and "Come on, we've got to go before the posse gets here!" but this time it was Srennom resisting, arguing, explaining, saying he wasn't finished.

"We're all going to be finished if we don't get in out of this storm!" Wade shouted at Indy. "The lightning—"

"NO NO NO," Indy scrolled and went back to talking to Srennom, this time apparently telling Srennom who Wade and Francie were and what they were doing here.

"You can explain all that later," Francie said, looking nervously at the lightning flashing everywhere. "We need to go."

"NO NO NO," Indy scrolled. "SRENNOM HAS TO DONE."

"He can do it after the storm," Francie said.

"NO NO NO," Indy scrolled. "SRENNOM TSINIBITAI BBH-BINIITS."

"Don't stand here arguing with him," Wade shouted. "Every minute we're out here, we increase the chances of getting killed."

"NO NO NO," Indy scrolled.

"Yes yes yes," Wade said. "You don't understand, lightning's dangerous! It—"

He didn't have a chance to finish the sentence. A blue-white flash, so bright it hurt, exploded around them, sending Francie sprawling.

This is it, she thought, *we've been struck by lightning,* and braced herself against the killing shock, the searing pain, that had to be coming.

It didn't come, and when the thunder did, a nanosecond later, it sounded like a faraway rumble. "What—?" she said, wondering if the thunder had made her deaf, and realized she was no longer out in the rain.

She looked up. She was under some sort of transparent shelter that was protecting her from the rain. And the thunder. No, not an umbrella, a tent. The see-through material extended all around her. She could see the wet mud and grass underneath her hands and feet, but what they were touching was completely dry, and as she scrambled to her feet, she saw she was completely enclosed in a sort of transparent bubble.

And alone. Where were the others? "Indy! Wade!" she called, peering through the side of the bubble, trying to see them, but the glow from the lightning had faded, and all she could see was rain, sluicing down its sides like it had over the windshield.

And I don't have windshield wipers, she thought, and heard Wade distantly calling, "Francie! Where are you?"

"Here," she called back. "I'm in some kind of—"

"Giant soap bubble?" he said, his voice muffled, and, tracking the sound of his voice, she could just barely make him out in a second bubble of his own ten feet or so away from hers. "I was wrong, Indy was faster."

She could barely hear him. "What?" she said, cupping her hand to her ear.

"I said Indy was faster," he shouted. "Than the lightning." Wade pointed at the bubble. "I think this is a giant-size repeat of Indy's rattler trick."

"You mean we're inside one of his tentacles?"

"Either that, or we've landed in Oz, and we're in one of those things Glinda floated around in," he said, trying awkwardly to move his bubble closer to hers and nearly falling in the process. "Though frankly I don't see what she saw in them."

He patted the walls exploringly and looked up at the ceiling. "At least it also appears to be a Faraday cage, which is good. Otherwise, we'd be toast. Literally."

"But if this is a repeat of Indy's rattler trick, as you call it," she said, remembering how Indy had expanded a part of his tentacle to enclose the snake, "then he was still out in the rain when the lightning struck."

"Which apparently isn't a problem," Wade said.

"What do you mean, it isn't a problem? Lightning—"

"I mean they don't seem particularly bothered by it," he said, shuffling clumsily closer to her bubble and pointing past Francie.

She turned around. Through the rain, she could see Indy and Srennom sitting next to each other a few feet from Francie's bubble, having an animated discussion, Indy scrolling in bright red and Srennom in neon green.

A bolt of lightning slashed down on them.

"Oh, no!" Francie gasped, clapping her hand to her mouth, but they went right on talking, oblivious to the electricity bouncing off their tentacles and sizzling along the edges. And to the deafening crash of thunder that followed.

They were speaking Indy's language, but occasionally an English word flashed along one of Indy's tentacles: "GO" and "NOW NOW NOW" and "HURRY."

"Indy's trying to talk Srennom into leaving," Francie told Wade, "but he won't go."

"Why not?"

"I don't know. Indy!" she called through the din. "Why won't Srennom come with us?"

"NO DID," he scrolled.

"You mean he hasn't finished what he came to do yet?"

"YES YES YES."

"What is it he's doing?" Wade asked, and Indy scrolled an incomprehensible string of symbols like a cross between cave drawings and Egyptian hieroglyphics, which was no help at all.

"How long will it take him?" Francie asked.

"TWO," he scrolled.

"Two *hours?*" Wade said.

"NO NO NO," Indy scrolled. "TWO LONG STORM GOTHES," which Francie assumed meant it would take Srennom too long to do whatever it was he was doing because the storm was moving on, though she couldn't see any sign of that. The rain was coming down as hard as ever, and the number of lightning strikes was, if anything, increasing.

But Srennom presumably knew. "Can you help him do whatever it is he's doing?" she asked Indy.

"YES NO YES NO."

"What the hell does that mean?" Wade shouted.

"Shh," Francie hushed Wade. "You can help him, but it isn't enough?" she asked Indy, and when he started to scroll a series of "YES"s, she eagerly asked him, "What about us? Can we help, too?"

"YES," Indy scrolled in a bright pink Francie'd never seen before. "YES YES YES YES YES THANK THANK THANK!"

"That's okay," Francie said. "Just tell us what to do."

Indy turned to Srennom, hieroglyphics scrolling excitedly up and down his tentacles, and then back to Francie, holding bunches of what looked like Christmas tinsel in two of his tentacles. That must have been what Francie had seen glittering in Srennom's tentacles before, when Srennom had been suspended in midair.

"How's he going to get that to us without removing the bubble?" Wade asked, looking uneasily up at the sky, but Indy simply touched the wall of Wade's bubble, and it thickened slightly on either side, leaving a narrow opening. He passed one tentacle's tinsel through, handed it to Wade, and did the same thing with Francie.

"What do we do with these?" she asked.

"LASSO," Indy scrolled, which was as clear as mud.

"You mean like this?" Francie said, and whirled the strip above her head like a rope.

"NO NO NO," Indy scrolled. He reached through the opening, took a strip of tinsel from her, held it by its end so that the rest of the strip hung down limply against the wall of the bubble, and then handed it back to her, scrolling, "SEE?"

She didn't quite, but she nodded, and Indy withdrew his tentacle, went back over to Srennom, got two dozen tentacles-full of the tinsel, and scrolled, "READY."

"Yes," Francie said.

"I don't see how we're going to be that much help," Wade said. "These things are so cumbersome to move. We—" and he suddenly shot straight up in the air.

"Where—?" Francie began, and her bubble shot skyward, too. She lurched against the wall of the bubble, off-balance, and then tried to stand up, bracing her hands against opposite sides, and it steadied.

She'd dropped the tinsel when she fell. She stooped and gathered it up from the curved bottom surface, and then slowly straightened and shuffled over to the bubble's wall, pulled a single ribbon of tinsel out, and placed the end gingerly against it, and the tinsel lashed out like one of Indy's tentacles, impossibly long, impossibly fast, and shot through the side of the bubble and out into the storm.

In her surprise, Francie let go of it, but she was able to grab the end with her other hand as it shot out and just before it retracted and curled itself into a tight spiral.

She stuck it in her pocket and held another one up to the wall, wrapping that one around her hand to keep from dropping it when it shot out, and then did another. And another.

The bubble, impossibly bulky and cumbersome on the ground, was graceful in the air. It seemed to adjust to her movements, keeping her upright as the wind wafted it this way and that through the slashing rain and the blinding lightning strikes.

Amazingly, it wasn't frightening. It was almost fun, floating through the mist and fog of the storm's interior, occasionally catching sight of the aliens as they floated past, swimming as gracefully as octopuses in an ocean, moving first this way and then that with their glittering silver ribbons, which they shot out into the storm every few seconds.

When Wade's bubble drifted by, she called out, "What are we doing?"

"I have no idea," he called back. "Collecting samples of rain-drops? Or ozone?"

"Why would they need those?" she asked.

"I don't know. But I figured out how to control this thing. Put your hand flat against the side in the direction you want to go, or on top if you want to go up."

"What about if I want to go down? Do I put my hand on the bottom of the bubble?" she asked, but his bubble had already wafted away from hers.

She leaned down to place her hand on the floor of the bubble, and gasped at how high above the ground she was. "Wade!" she cried, grabbing for the ungraspable sides of the bubble against the sudden vertigo she felt.

Indy immediately appeared beside her, his tentacles full of tinsel. "I'm afraid I'll fall!" she told him. "Let me down!"

"NO NO NO HURRY HURRY HURRY," he scrolled back. "HANG ON COWPOKE DON'T LET 'ER THROW YOU!" which she assumed was supposed to be encouraging, and even if it wasn't, it was apparent he wasn't going to take her down until she'd finished with her tinsel. She held the silvery strips to the edge of the bubble one after the other as quickly as she could, trying not to panic as her bubble soared up into the heart of the storm and then suddenly dipped down again like a roller coaster.

As soon as she'd done all her strips, she called to Indy, "I'm out of—" But before she could finish, he'd handed her another bundle, scrolling, "HURRY HURRY HURRY TSURRISPOINIS GO."

And this time she saw what he meant. In this part of the storm, the rain was letting up a little, and she could see a narrow opening in the clouds to the west. The main part of the storm must be moving on.

Indy and Srennom picked up the pace, shooting strips one after the other out into the storm like a barrage of silver arrows, and Francie tried to do the same, though she wasn't nearly as fast.

"Here," Wade said, bringing his bubble next to hers. "Give me some of yours."

"How?" she said, and he thrust his hand through the surface of the bubble.

"I didn't know you could do that," she said, handing him half of her strips.

"I didn't, either," he said, withdrawing his hand and pushing his bubble off from hers like a swimmer pushing off from the edge of a pool. The force of the push carried him nearly into the bank of clouds surrounding them before Indy brought it back to the center, where lightning had just struck.

They're definitely collecting ozone samples, Francie thought, *or taking measurements of the electricity in the lightning strikes,* and maneuvered her own bubble toward another flash, but Indy pulled her back over to where she'd been before, whipping his own tentacles out high above her.

The western edge of the storm was really starting to break up now. The rent in the clouds was larger, a long, ragged tear, and there were smaller tears on either side of it. Through them, she could glimpse bright blue sky and piles of heaped white cloud, though inside the storm everything was still gray and blurred, and rain was still falling.

She was out of tinsel again. "Indy—" she called, looking around for him. She couldn't see him or Srennom.

"Wade!" she called, and his bubble appeared beside her. "Where are they?"

"On the ground," he said, pointing below them. "I think they're out of tinsel."

"Oh, good," she said. "Then we can go down?"

"In a minute," Wade said, and thrust his arm through the wall of his bubble and then Francie's, grabbed her by the arm, and pulled her through into his bubble with him.

"Come on," he said and pressed his free hand hard on the ceiling of the bubble. It shot straight up into the storm, so fast she'd have fallen if he hadn't put his arm protectively around her.

Up here the clouds were breaking up rapidly. Sunlight shone through the break between them, washing the mist with pastels, pink and peach and lilac, and staining their bubble's surface with an opalescent sheen just like Glinda's had had. "Pretty nice, huh?" Wade said, waving his free hand at the scene.

"Is that what you brought me up here for, to show me that?"

"No," he said. "I brought you up here to tell you what the other thing was."

"The other thing?"

"The other thing that was true," he said. "You asked me if anything I'd said to you was true, and I said yes, that one of them was that I wanted to help Indy, and then we got interrupted before I could tell you what the other one was," and Francie's heart began to pound.

The torn clouds gave way, and sunlight poured in, refracting the still-falling raindrops, turning them into a million glittering prisms, flashing with colors as vivid as Indy's scrollings—crimson and orange and gold, emerald and sapphire and amethyst and indigo, filling the air itself with rainbows.

"What was it?" Francie breathed. "The other thing that you said that was true?"

"This," Wade said, bending toward her, and the bubble suddenly dropped out from under them like a plunging elevator, knocking them both to the floor in a heap as it plummeted.

Francie yelped as it came to a stop inches from the ground, and Wade bellowed, "What the hell?"

"GO GO GO," Indy, standing next to them, scrolled, and Srennom started rolling toward the Jeep, his tentacles full of tinsel curls. "TROUBLE POSSE."

"I *know*," Wade said. "If you'll just give me one minute, I have something I need to tell Francie." He put his palm against the roof of the bubble.

It collapsed around them and shrank back into the shape of a tentacle, sending them sprawling again and leaving them out in the still-falling rain. "NEED GO HURRY."

"Thanks a lot, Indy," Wade said, helping Francie to her feet. "Sorry. I guess I'll have to give you a rain check." He glanced up at the falling rain. "Literally. Right now we've got to get Indy and Srennom back to their ship and safely off-planet before whoever's chasing him catches up with us."

"YES YES YES," Indy scrolled, grabbing hold of Francie's wrist.

"Who is it, Indy?" she asked. "Who's chasing you?"

"POSSE."

"I know. Who are they?"

"MONUMENT VALLEY."

And so much for the theory that when he said "Monument Valley" he was referring to the thunderstorm. "They're in Monument Valley?" she asked.

"NO NO NO."

"They *landed* in Monument Valley?"

"*NO NO NO!*" he scrolled, so vividly she was clearly on the wrong track.

"Did *you* land there?"

"NO."

"Did *Srennom* land there?"

"NO NO NO MONUMENT VALLEY GO GO GO!" he scrolled in giant red letters, and dragged Francie toward the Jeep, where Srennom waited with a heap of tinsel in front of him. He was tucking them into the spaces of his tumbleweed body.

By the time they reached him, the curls had all disappeared, and Francie wondered if he'd eaten them and Wade had been right—the thunderstorm had provided some sort of nutrition—but Indy scrolled some hieroglyphics that apparently meant "Where did you put them?" because Srennom reached inside his own middle with a tentacle and pulled out one to show Indy, and then stowed it away again.

Indy opened the back door. Srennom rolled in. Now that she'd gotten a good look at him, Francie could see that Srennom was slightly different from Indy. He was larger, and his tentacles were pale green, with curling offshoots along them, like the tendrils on a sweet pea vine.

Indy motioned Francie and Wade to get in the front, and he rolled into the back with Srennom. He extended his pointer tentacle between the seats and stuck it in Wade's face. "GO!"

"Where?" Wade asked, sticking the key in the ignition and starting the car.

"WEST," Indy scrolled.

"Are you sure that's a good idea?" Wade asked. "We're likely to run right into the arms of whoever's chasing us."

"WEST," Indy scrolled in an even brighter pink, "MONUMENT VALLEY," and he pointed out Wade's window. "TURN TURN TURN."

"He wants you to turn around and go back the way we came," Francie said. "And from the color of those words, he wants you to step on it."

That was putting it mildly. When Wade didn't respond fast enough, Indy wrapped a tendril around his foot and ankle and pushed down hard.

The Jeep's wheels spun in the wet mud, throwing up sheets of water. "Hey!" Wade said. "I'm the one driving here. You'll have us off the road." He glanced at Francie. "Tell him I get the message—he wants to go fast—but I need to do the driving."

Indy loosened the tentacle but didn't remove it.

"I mean it," Wade said, and Indy instantly retracted it, only to unfurl it again in front of Francie's face. "HURRY HURRY HURRY," it said, and now the letters were bright red.

"He's hurrying," Francie said to Indy.

Wade drove the Jeep back to the dirt road they'd come in on, now a mass of puddles, and along it toward the highway they'd pulled off of. "See if you can get Indy to tell you something more specific than 'west,'" he instructed Francie.

She nodded. "Indy, where do you want us to take you?" she asked. "To your ship? To Srennom's ship?"

"NO NO NO MONUMENT VALLEY HURRY."

"You want us to take you to Monument Valley?"

"NO NO NO," and, as if it explained everything, "MONUMENT VALLEY!"

"I don't understand. What do you mean? What's Monument Valley?" she asked, and she could practically see the frustration in his scrolling: "TROUBLE HURRY GO GO GO!" But even though she continued to probe, asking the question different ways, she couldn't get any more out of him.

They reached the highway. "WEST," Indy scrolled, pointing left out Wade's window.

"Isn't there another road we can take?" Francie asked. "The FBI—" but before she could finish her sentence, Indy directed them north onto a narrow paved road.

Francie looked out her window at the thunderhead, now off to the east of them. It had turned from white to a pale pink, and as she watched, it deepened to rose and then salmon against the evening sky.

"WEST," Indy scrolled. "TURN."

"Onto what?" Wade asked. "The lone prairie?"

But there turned out to be a road, and, even better, it was a two-lane highway, and straight as an arrow. And without a car in sight. Wade put his foot on the accelerator.

It was getting dark. When Francie turned to look behind them for any cars that might be following, she couldn't see any lights at all. The thunderhead had faded from rose to periwinkle, and the sky above and around it had darkened to the purple-blue of twilight. Francie could see a couple of stars, but no lights that might have been a spaceship.

But the best indication that they weren't being followed was Indy. He wasn't scrolling "HURRY HURRY HURRY," or pointing urgently at the windshield. He was calmly scrolling to Srennom, apparently catching him up on what had transpired since they last saw each other.

Good, she thought, and turned back around in her seat. "There's nobody behind us," she told Wade. She peered ahead at the darkening landscape. "Shouldn't you turn on your lights?"

"Yeah, I guess I'm going to have to," he said, and did.

And she'd been wrong about Indy's having forgotten about their being chased. One of his tentacles lashed out to turn off the lights while a second thrust itself in Wade's face, scrolling, "NO NO NO."

Wade jammed on the brakes and jerked the car to a stop. "Look," he said, turning to face Indy. "I can either drive without lights or I can hurry. Not both. Which'll it be?"

There was a pause, and then Indy wrapped a tentacle around the turn signal lever and switched the lights back on.

"Good," Wade said. "I'll get you there, I promise, but you have to tell me where your ship is. Is it west of Roswell, where they reported seeing a crash?"

Indy didn't answer. He scrolled, "WEST HURRY GO!"

"I'm going," Wade said and stepped on the gas.

"Do you know where the UFO crash was?" Francie asked.

"Yes and no," Wade said. "I know where our people reported seeing it come down. But we didn't find anything there or in the immediate vicinity, and our calculations of where it came down didn't turn up anything, either." He glanced in the rearview mirror. "You don't see anybody behind us, do you?"

She glanced in her side mirror. "No. Why?"

He jerked a thumb toward the back seat. "Because they seem to think we're being followed."

He was right. Srennom and Indy's tentacles were both glued to the back window, and Srennom's tentacles were flailing wildly. "What is it, Indy?" Francie asked, straining to see out the back through their writhing tentacles. All she could see was darkness, no distant line of lights that would mean a town, no scattered ranch lights, nothing.

No, wait, there was a flicker of light far behind them, where the thunderstorm had been, and Srennom jerked as if he'd been shot and began flailing more wildly.

"It's only lightning," Francie said to him, "like we saw inside the storm. Lightning. Tell him that's all it is, Indy."

Indy scrolled some hieroglyphics at Srennom, and he finally calmed down, at least to the point where she could see past him out the window. There was nothing behind them back there but darkness, not even another flicker.

"It was definitely lightning," Francie told Wade. "Or if it wasn't, we lost whoever it was," she added in a whisper, and as if in answer, Indy thrust another instruction in front of her, directing Wade to turn again. And hurry.

He repeated the action every few minutes, instructing Wade to turn onto a narrow, paved road or an even narrower gravel or dirt one, jogging sometimes north and sometimes south, occasionally even backtracking to the east for a few miles before heading back west again. It was impossible to tell if he was leading them somewhere or taking evasive maneuvers.

If it was the latter, he was doing a good job of it. After another half hour of zigging and zagging, Francie'd completely lost track of which direction they were headed in.

"Do you have any idea where we are?" she asked Wade finally. "Or where Indy's taking us?"

"No," he said. "But it may not matter. Look behind us." She glanced in the side mirror. Far back on the road behind them was a red light.

"Is it a police car?" Wade asked.

"I don't know. I can't see the light flashing. Oh, wait, yes it is," she said, as she made out the familiar flicker of white and blue mixed with the red. "It's definitely a police car. Or the FBI," she said. "Or whoever it is you are. What color flashing lights do they have on their cars?"

"None," he said. "They must have sent out an APB to the Highway Patrol. Is there more than one?"

Francie turned around in the seat to look—and was smacked in the face by one of Indy's tentacles. It grabbed her around the neck, and he thrust a second tentacle in front of her eyes. It scrolled frantically, "GO GO GO!"

"Indy, let go!" she cried, pulling at the tentacle around her neck. "I'm trying to see!"

It was impossible. The back seat was a mass of writhing tentacles, totally blocking the view out the back window, and when she tried to look in the side mirror, Indy thrust a tentacle in her face— "HURRY HURRY HURRY!"—and another in Wade's.

He brushed it impatiently aside. "I *am* hurrying," he said, flooring it, and then, "Shit!"

"What?" she asked, her heart pounding.

"Up ahead. There's another one." He pointed at a red light ahead of them to the left.

"That's not a police car," Francie said. "It's too high up. It's probably a cellphone tower or a radio tower."

"Then why isn't it blinking?" Wade asked. "Is the patrol car still there?"

She looked in the side mirror. There was no light behind them. "No," she told Wade. "Maybe you outran it."

"I don't think so," he said, and jerked a thumb toward the back seat. "Look."

Srennom was having hysterics again, waving his tentacles around and scrolling bright green hieroglyphics, and Indy's were racing with "GO"s and "HURRY"s, though she couldn't see any lights at all behind them.

The one ahead was still there. "Maybe it's a railroad signal. Or an aircraft warning light on a windmill, like the ones we saw on that wind farm we went through."

"Yeah, only I don't remember seeing any railroad tracks *or* wind farms on our way out, and if that's what it is, why are they going nuts?" he asked, inclining his head toward the aliens.

Now Indy and Srennom were both plastered against a side window, flailing as wildly as Indy had over Monument Valley, their tentacles tangling and knotting uncontrollably in their panic. "It's all right, Indy," Francie said, vainly trying to reassure him. "It's just a railroad signal."

"I don't think so," Wade said, pointing off to the left, and she turned to see another red light in that direction, and another one ahead, close enough that if it was a patrol car they'd definitely have been able to see its flashing blue and white. But it remained a solid, unblinking red.

"It *is* a wind farm," she said in relief, and was grabbed around the neck by Indy.

"TURN!" the tentacle he thrust at her said in frantic glowing purple letters. "RUN!"

Indy was practically choking her. "He wants you to go back!" she gasped to Wade, who was, inexplicably, slowing down.

"I don't think that'll do any good," he said with a nod toward the rear.

"Why not? Indy, let go!" Francie shouted, and freed herself to look out the back window, which was still a blur of flailing tentacles. "Srennom, calm down!"

She pushed the aliens off to one side. And saw the round red lights, rank on rank behind and around them, stretching into the distance as far as she could see.

CHAPTER TWENTY-ONE

"You take the trees, I'll take the bushes."
—Butch Cassidy and the Sundance Kid

"I don't suppose it could be the police, could it?" Francie said dismally. "Or your people?"

"No," Wade said. "In fact, this would be a good time for them to show up."

"So what do we do now?"

"I have no idea."

"Indy, what should we do?" she asked the alien, but Srennom's tentacles were flailing so wildly Francie could hardly see Indy, and when she managed to part them, Indy had tangled himself up so thoroughly she couldn't read what was written on his.

"Can you turn around?" she asked Wade.

"No," he said, glancing in the rearview mirror. "They're still behind us, too." He looked out his side window. "We're pretty much surrounded."

She looked ahead at the now nearly touching row of red lights.

"Do you think if you gunned the engine, you could break through them, whatever they are?"

"I doubt it," Wade said, but he put his foot on the accelerator anyway.

The car moved forward a scant yard, sputtered, and died. "Did they do that?" Francie asked.

"Either that, or the Jeep's out of gas," Wade said, looking at the line of lights, which seemed to be moving toward the car.

"They're coming this way," Francie whispered.

"I know," he whispered back. "Indy, who are these . . . ?" He gestured at the lights. "Why are they after you?"

"TSIJJDI," Francie was able to make out as he crawled into her lap and wrapped his hopelessly tangled tentacles around her waist. "AOOGLOSBAI TSILLAO TROUBLE," he scrolled, squeezing her tightly.

"He says we're in trouble," she told Wade.

"Yeah, I figured that out," he said, peering out at the lights, his open hand to his forehead, shading his eyes. "Can you see what—or who—is out there?"

"No," she said, squinting to see what lay beyond the lights. If anything. She remembered Lyle's theory that the glowing orbs people saw *were* the aliens.

As she squinted at them, half a dozen of the round red lights separated themselves from the main line and began moving toward them. Indy squeezed more tightly.

"It's all right," she murmured to Indy, even though it obviously wasn't, and tried to untie the knots in his tentacles.

The lights continued to advance. "Lock your door," Wade ordered Francie, but in his panic, Indy had climbed up her chest and was clasping his tentacles around her arms and her neck, keeping her from doing anything. And anyway, locking her door would do exactly nothing.

The red lights moved steadily, noiselessly, toward the car, like something out of a nightmare, where you couldn't move, couldn't scream.

"Listen," Wade whispered, "if we get separated, don't panic."

"Separated?" she said. "What do you mean? What are you going to do?"

"If they try to ask you questions, don't try to be a hero," he said, ignoring her question. "Just tell them the truth about what you did and answer whatever questions they ask you. Our only hope is in trying to establish communications."

The lights continued to come silently toward them. "If they get any closer," Francie said, "they'll be in the car."

"I know," Wade said, "stay here," and with a sudden movement he opened his door, got out of the car, and flashed his badge. "I represent the United States government," he said to the lights. "Agent Hastings, FBI."

No response.

"Welcome to Earth," he said. "And to New Mexico. I'm authorized by my government to negotiate with you. What is it you want?"

Still nothing. If she could just see them—or if they'd make some kind of sound—it wouldn't be nearly so terrifying, no matter how awful they looked. But she couldn't see anything except the lights. And meanwhile they were moving toward Wade, surrounding him. In another minute, they'd swallow him up.

"Indy, let go of me," she said. "I need to get out of the car."

"NO NO NO NO NO NO!" he scrolled.

"I have to. Let *go*," she said, and, when he relaxed his grip, she opened her door and got out. The lights instantly stopped closing in on Wade and turned toward her.

"Francie, get back in the car," Wade shouted.

"No," she said, and slammed the door closed behind her.

But not in time. Indy had launched himself into her arms before it shut, wrapping himself around her, scrolling, "NO NO NO!"

The lights converged on Indy. "No! You can't have him," she said, clutching him tightly to her. "I won't let you!"

"Neither will I!" Wade shouted, and put himself between her and the lights.

And this is the moment we all get obliterated, she thought.

But there was still no response, except that some of the lights turned to an intense white like a klieg light. Or the blinding glare in *Close Encounters.* She'd always thought they'd used that super-bright, diffuse light to keep from having to spend money on special effects, but now she saw they had it right. You couldn't see anything beyond it. Wade had put both hands up to shade his eyes from its brightness, and Francie had to fight the impulse to let go of Indy and do the same thing. She squinted, trying to see what whatever-they-were were doing, which was opening the car door.

They had it half-open when Indy suddenly released his strangle-hold on Francie and launched himself at the car, inside which Srennom was screaming, if the brightness of his scrolling was any indication.

Indy flattened himself across the doors, holding them shut and scrolling, "NO NO NO NO NO!" and a stream of purple-red hieroglyphics interspersed with words. "SRENNOM AOODINIIH TSINIBITAI," he scrolled, followed by hieroglyphics that probably meant no more to the whatever-they-weres than they did to her and Wade.

Francie looked back toward the lights again, squinting against the glare. And saw something moving out of the light toward the car.

"Indy!" she cried. "Watch out!" and she moved to put herself between him and it, but she wasn't fast enough. Indy had seen it and, inexplicably, let go of the car, extended a no-longer-scrolling tentacle to the door handle, and opened it. Srennom rolled out and over to Indy.

"What are they doing?" Francie whispered to Wade.

"I don't know," Wade said. "Obeying the cops' order to get out of the car, maybe, and putting their hands over their heads?"

Indy's tentacles writhed and fluttered and threatened to tangle into knots, and Srennom was scrolling hysterically, the hieroglyphics coming so fast they overwrote each other till they became indecipherable.

"NO NO NO SRENNOM SHH," Indy scrolled. "ITS ALL RIGHT NOBODYS GOING TO HURT YOU SHH," and Francie recognized the words she'd used to quiet him in the car when she'd tried to take off her dress. "SHH ITS OKAY," but Srennom reared away from him and from the blinding light, out of the glare of which was sliding a large vine-like tentacle.

In spite of the fact that it was huge, as big around as a boa constrictor, and coming straight toward them, Francie felt less frightened. Wade was right—what you could see was never as frightening as what you could imagine. And these were the same species as Indy, not Reptilians or, God forbid, the Monument Valley aliens.

"These are Indy's people," she whispered to Wade.

"Yeah," he said, "but they don't look very glad to see him. Or Srennom."

"Or us," she breathed.

The tentacle rose up, reminding Francie of nothing so much as a beanstalk, with curling tendrils twisting out from it, and was pointing down at their heads. It scrolled a single dark green hieroglyph.

"FRANCIE," Indy scrolled. "WADE TSINIBITAI."

Another single hieroglyph, and this one obviously meant "Explain," because Indy began scrolling out a stream of bright red hieroglyphics.

"What's he saying now?" Francie whispered.

"God only knows," and the beanstalk-like tentacle shot out and wrapped around Indy's tentacle, cutting his scrolling short, and then displayed a single character.

Indy scrolled a long string of hieroglyphics and then, "WHATS HE SAYING NOW?" then more characters followed by, "GOD ONLY KNOWS."

"He's translating to them what we just said," Francie reasoned.

"Thank God," Wade replied. He took a step forward and repeated what he'd said before: "Welcome. My name is Agent Hastings, and I'm authorized by my government to welcome you to our planet," but the tentacle wasn't paying any attention to him.

It printed out a short burst of hieroglyphics, and Indy began scrolling with two tentacles side by side, one with the alien hieroglyphics and one in English: "OH MY GOD YOURE AN ALIEN I

CANT DRIVE YOU NO KEYS YOU HAVE TO HAVE KEYS TO START THE CAR."

"That's what I said that first night when he kidnapped me," Francie said. "He must be telling them what happened."

A second tentacle emerged from the haze, this one looking like Indy's, scrolling more orders, and Indy upped the number of his scrolling tentacles to four and then eight, going so fast Francie could only catch glimpses of phrases as they flew past.

"I HAVE TO BE IN A WEDDING IM CALLING FROM BEHIND THE CAR YOUVE GOT TO CALL THE AUTHORITIES."

"That's from the phone call I tried to make to you that first night," she whispered to Wade. "Which means he understood what we said even before he figured out how to communicate with us."

"Yeah. It also means his hearing is a lot better than we thought it was," Wade said, pointing at the words: "HAS HE TRIED TO COMMUNICATE WITH YOU? SIGN LANGUAGE WOOKIEE MUSICAL NOTES CLOSE ENCOUNTERS?"

Oh, no, Francie thought. *What else did he hear us saying?*

"KILL US ALL INVASION OH MY GOD HES GOING TO PROBE ME," Indy scrolled, and then a slew of words going by too fast for her to decipher and then, in bright red, "INDY WATCH OUT POISONOUS THEY HAVE FANGS DID THE RATTLESNAKE BITE YOU THANK YOU FOR SAVING MY LIFE YOU SAVED HIS."

Another order from the beanstalk, and Indy's scrolling became too fast to catch more than an occasional word or phrase: "THUNDERBIRD . . . MARFA LIGHTS . . . ACES HIGH . . . FOUR CORNERS . . . COFFEE FIVE CENTS . . . OUTLAW . . . CHILI . . . WHOA THERE TAKE IT EASY PILGRIM . . . EXTRATERRESTRIAL HIGHWAY . . . TROPICANA . . . WEATHER BALLOONS."

God only knew what Indy's people were making of it. It was a mishmash of blackjack rules and Lyle's conspiracy theories and dialogue from the Westerns Indy had watched. She caught fragments of the wedding ceremony and what the Showgirl Spin guy had said and the billboards she'd read aloud to Indy. To say nothing of Lyle's crazy UFO theories. She caught "CHEMTRAILS . . . MUTILATE . . . MIND CONTROL . . . ALIEN HUMAN HYBRID . . . SECRET UNDERGROUND BASE . . . PROBE . . . REPTILIANS" as they raced by. And "ICE CREAM TEN CENTS . . . PARDNER . . . CLOSE ENCOUNTERS . . . ELVIS . . . HE CAN TALK . . . GO PARK THE VAN . . . GRAYS . . . WITH THIS RING . . . RIGHT BACK . . . ABSOLUTELY QUIET . . . DO NOT TALK UNTIL I TELL YOU YOU CAN . . . WHAT ARE YOU . . . LET ME GO."

"You don't think this is a trial, do you?" Francie whispered to Wade.

"And Indy's testifying against us, you mean?" he whispered back. He watched the scrolling for a minute. "No, I don't think so. I think what they're doing is using what Indy said to us to learn our language. In which case we may be able to communicate with them, and we might just get out of this alive."

Indy continued to scroll—"REESES PIECES . . . ARE YOU HERE TO INTERROGATE ME . . . TROPICANA . . . PAINT YOUR WAGON . . . SHOWGIRL SPIN . . . ESCAPE . . . CAR . . . THUNDERSTORM . . . GUN IT . . . I THINK WE LOST THEM."

Suddenly, halfway through a word, the beanstalk-tentacle reached out and grabbed one of Indy's tentacles, stopping his scrolling abruptly, and the creature it belonged to slid out of the blinding light with a movement exactly like a snake's, and it took all of Francie's courage not to turn and run.

It stopped in front of Wade and Francie and straightened, and she saw she'd been right the first time. It was a beanstalk, with the same thick stalk and twining tendrils.

It extended the tentacle it had been using to scroll toward Wade and turned it sideways in front of him so he could see what was written there. "FRANCIE?" it scrolled.

"You want to know our names?" Wade said. "I'm Agent Hast—" But the beanstalk had already slid its tentacle over to Francie and asked again, "FRANCIE?"

"Yes," she said, willing her voice not to shake. "My name is Francie."

"YOHWATAAH," the beanstalk scrolled, pointing his tentacle toward himself.

"Yohwataah," Francie repeated. "That's *your* name."

"NO NO NO," he scrolled. He touched another alien's tentacle, and it rolled forward. It looked like Indy, except larger and leafier, like an enormous mesquite bush.

The beanstalk pointed to it and then to himself. "YOHWATAAH."

"Oh, that's the name of your people," Francie said. "We're . . ." She hesitated, looking at Wade.

"Earth humans," Wade said.

"Yes," she said, pointing at him and then herself. "Earth humans."

"REPTILIANS?" the beanstalk scrolled.

"No no no," Wade said, shaking his head vigorously. "We're not Reptilians."

"GRAYS?"

"No, we're not Grays, either," Wade said. "There aren't any Grays or Reptilians. Lyle just made them up."

"LYLE LYING SIDEWINDER?"

"Yes," Wade said.

What about the aliens Indy's so afraid of? Monument Valley? Francie wondered, but the beanstalk was talking to Wade again.

"Earth humans," he said, pointing at his chest. "People." He pointed at the aliens. "Yohwataah."

"YOHWATAAH FRANCIE ABDUCT INDY TROUBLE," the beanstalk scrolled, and then, in a green so dark it was almost black, "CRIME."

"Wh-what?" she stammered, thinking, *They misunderstood what Indy told them. Wade was wrong—they haven't learned the language.* "No, no, I didn't abduct Indy. He abducted me."

"YES YES YES," he scrolled. "CRIME."

She looked helplessly at Wade. "Does he mean I committed a crime by letting Indy abduct me?"

"I don't know," he said. "Yohwataah," he asked, "who has committed this crime of abducting Francie?"

The beanstalk pointed at Indy. "TROUBLE YOHWATAAH SORRY SORRY SORRY."

"They're not accusing you," Wade said. "They're apologizing."

"Oh, thank goodness," she said, and to the aliens she offered, "That's okay," and to make sure they understood her added, "I accept your apology." .

"YOHWATAAH MIGHTY GRATEFUL MA'AM," the beanstalk scrolled, and the mesquite bush rolled over in front of Wade.

"AGENT HASTINGS?" it scrolled.

"Yes," Wade said.

"SORRY SORRY SORRY."

"I accept your apology, too," Wade said solemnly. "And so does the U.S. Government."

"MIGHTY GRATEFUL MAAM," the mesquite bush scrolled, and it rolled back in front of Francie. "WADE?"

"This is Wade," Francie said, pointing at him.

"NO NO NO AGENT HASTINGS."

"He's both," Francie said. "Wade *and* Agent Hastings."

The mesquite bush scrolled "SORRY SORRY SORRY," to Wade and turned back to Francie. "JOSEPH?"

"He's not here," Francie said.

"LYLE?"

"He's not here, either," Wade said. "He and Eula Mae and Joseph are in Roswell."

There was a long, silent moment, during which the beanstalk and the mesquite bush conferred, scrolling back and forth, and then the bush scrolled "SORRY AFTER" to Wade. It turned to Francie and scrolled, "WANT WATCH THEM STRING EM UP?"

"What?" Francie said, taking a step back. "Lyle and Eula Mae?"

"NO NO NO NO NO," the alien scrolled, "INDY," and it pointed at Indy and then at Srennom. "SRENNOM WANT SEE THEM STRING EM UP?"

"What do you mean, 'string them up'?" Wade asked.

"NECKTIE PARTY LYNCH HANGING EXECUTE."

"Executed? *No,*" Francie said. "Of course I don't want them executed!"

The mesquite bush lashed out and grabbed one each of Indy's and Srennom's tentacles and began to lead them off behind the glare of the lights, out of sight.

"No, no, no," Francie cried, "I didn't mean I don't want to watch them being executed. I meant I don't want them executed at *all*! You can't hang them! They haven't committed any crimes!"

"UNLAWFUL ENTRY PROSCRIBED CONTACT RUSTLING."

Rustling? Francie thought.

"ROUGH EM UP PRIVATE PROPERTY."

"I think it means your phone," Wade whispered.

"But Indy was just trying to keep me from contacting anyone because he needed me to help him find Srennom and he didn't know what our laws were! You can't punish him when he didn't—"

The mesquite bush laid a thick tendril across her wrist like it had across Indy's, clearly ordering her to stop talking, but she brushed it off. "You can't 'string up' Indy—or Srennom! I won't let you!"

The bush thrust another tentacle in front of Francie's face. "NO TALK," it scrolled, and rolled itself in front of Wade's face before scrolling, "TALK US MARSHAL."

"Us marshal?" Wade said blankly.

"It means 'leader,'" Francie said. "It's using terms from the Westerns Indy watched. U.S. Marshal."

"US MARSHAL," the bush scrolled. "SHERIFF HEAD HONCHO AROUND HERE."

"*I'm* the head honcho," Wade said, "and I will not allow you to hurt the alien we call Indy."

"Or Srennom," Francie said.

"Or Srennom."

"INDY SRENNOM TRESPASS EARTHHUMANS," the bush scrolled. "CLOSE ENCOUNTERS CRIME YOHWATAAH REQUIRE ATONE PUNISH OUTLAWS."

"They're not outlaws!" Francie burst out. "Indy was just trying to help Srennom." She went over to where the mesquite bush was holding Indy. "Indy, tell them what you were trying to do."

"FIND SRENNOM," Indy scrolled. "TSURRISPOINIS."

The mesquite bush shoved its tentacle between Francie and Indy and scrolled a stream of hieroglyphics and the words "NO TALK."

"But—" she began.

"NO TALK," it scrolled, in glowing green this time, and it was clearly a threat.

Wade stepped between them. "Whether Indy and Srennom are outlaws or not," he said, "executing them isn't the way to atone."

"YOHWATAAH LAW—"

"Yes, well, I don't care what Yohwataah law requires, the laws of this planet say you can't do that. It's a crime to execute people who've just been trying to help someone. As head honcho around here, I forbid—" The dark horizon was suddenly pierced by flashing red, blue, and white lights and wailing sirens.

"Oh, shit," Wade breathed.

"WHO?" the beanstalk scrolled, pointing at the lights.

"Is it your people?" Francie asked.

"It looks like it," Wade said. "Plus the FBI, and it looks like the Highway Patrol and the Army are right behind them. And they couldn't have picked a worse possible moment."

"Maybe if we go talk to them and explain—?" Francie started to ask.

Wade shook his head. "They'd arrest us and throw us in the back of a van before we could say anything."

"Maybe not," Francie said. "I mean, we have got backup." She gestured at the aliens.

"So have they," Wade said. "And the next thing you know, we've got *War of the Worlds*."

The wailing squad cars were closing in, encircling the ring of alien lights. She could hear the whump-whump of a helicopter overhead, and the beanstalk and the mesquite bush were scrolling to each other so fast she couldn't tell what language they were speaking.

"What do you think they're saying?" Francie asked Wade.

"They're probably discussing what to do if they're attacked," Wade said. "Which is going to happen any second! Damn, if I just had my phone so I could talk to the Head and tell him to call off his people! Maybe if *I* go—" Before he could take a step, the beanstalk lashed out with a tentacle and grabbed him around the waist.

A searchlight shone blindingly from the direction of the flashing lights, and a voice on a bullhorn shouted, "You're under arrest. Come out with your hands up!"

"Shit shit shit," Wade muttered, and raised his hands in a gesture of surrender. "Don't shoot!"

"Indy!" Francie shouted. "Do you remember the rattlesnake? Can you do the same thing to them?" She pointed at the squad cars. "Not the throwing-into-the-field part, just the enclosing part. I don't want you to hurt them."

"NO NO NO CLOSE ENCOUNTERS TROUBLE," Indy scrolled.

"I know, but if you don't, something bad might happen to the Yohwataah and Srennom. And to me."

"SAVE LIFE FRANCIE?"

"This is your last chance," the bullhorn voice shouted.

"Yes," she said. "Save life Francie."

"We're coming in!" the bullhorn blared. "Come out immed—"

The voice on the bullhorn abruptly cut off, and so did the whump-whump of the helicopter. But not the lights. She could still see them flashing red and white and blue through the clear bubbles Indy had encased them in.

She looked up. The helicopter was encased, too, and was being gently lowered, its rotors still turning, to the ground between the bubbles. Indy'd encased each of the squad cars and vans, and each of the groups of people—the very bewildered groups of people—in their own separate bubbles.

She looked at Indy. Every one of his tentacles was fully extended. He didn't have a single one left to defend himself with against the beanstalk and the mesquite bush, who'd surrounded him and were scrolling furiously at him. In a second they'd lash out and stop him, and they'd be right back where they started.

"Don't!" Francie said, moving between them. "I told him to do this. Those people out there are the head honcho's friends," she said, talking as fast as they were scrolling. "They've come to meet you and learn of you, and we want them to do that. But they have come too soon. Before they are allowed to make contact—to have a close encounter—with you, we must learn your language and your laws, and you must learn ours."

"And we must communicate these things to my people," Wade interjected, "so that they will be ready to meet you."

"Once these things are done," Francie said, "you can decide whether you will contact—close encounter—them or not. But we must do these things with you in private. They cannot be done with the others involved." She gestured back toward the flashing lights. "So the head honcho around here and I asked Indy to provide privacy for us."

The beanstalk scrolled something to Indy, and he scrolled back in their language and in English: "HAD TO FRANCIE BBHBINIITS."

"NO NO NO NO," the beanstalk scrolled.

Oh, no, he wasn't buying it.

"STOP," he scrolled, and Indy instantly retracted his tentacles, removing the bubbles.

The sirens' wail started up again, and there was a roar as the police started their engines.

"They'll—" Francie began, and one of the mesquite bush's tentacles lashed past her with a crack like a sonic boom. The sirens cut off, and Francie saw that the cars and people were now encased in one giant bubble.

"They'll try to fight their way out of there," Wade said.

"NO NO NO NO NO LOOK," the beanstalk scrolled, and Francie saw that their weapons had been encased in their own separate bubbles. The soldiers were trying frantically to get to them.

"I still need to talk to them," Wade said, "to explain what we're doing. Is there a way I can do that?"

"YES YES YES," the beanstalk scrolled, and motioned Wade toward the bubble, whose membrane thinned as he approached it till Francie could hear the sirens again, though more faintly.

Wade walked right up to it and shouted, "I need to talk to Agent Sanchez."

She came over. "What's going on?" she asked, pointing at the blinding glare behind him.

"We've found the aliens," he said. "Is the Head here?"

"No, but we're in phone contact. If phones still work in here."

"They seem to," another agent confirmed.

"Good," Wade said. "I need you to tell him that we've located the extraterrestrials and we're communicating with them, and we need him to get out here ASAP to talk to them. And in the meantime, you need to make sure nobody interrupts us or screws up negotiations. Turn off your sirens, and no firing on them or calling for backup or drones or air cover. You've seen what they can do." He tapped the membrane. "Trust me, it's just the tip of the iceberg."

"I've got the Head on the phone," the agent called out.

"Good. Put the phone on speaker. Evans? You need to get out here. It's first contact time. And call off the Army and the Highway Patrol. They haven't seen the aliens yet, and we might be able to keep this under wraps if you act fast."

"Are you saying this under duress?"

"No. The aliens seem to be friendly. In fact, they seem to be apologizing for violating our planetary space and are offering to make amends. Or at least I think that's what they're saying."

"You're *talking* to them?"

"Yes, but we still have a ways to go on the whole language thing. Which is why I need you to call off the dogs and give us some time. And get some linguists out here as fast as you can."

Francie couldn't hear Evans's answer because a patrol car's siren started up just then and then cut off, but Wade turned back to her and said, "The Head's coming. And I think I bought us some time."

He walked back over to the Yohwataah. "Thank you for providing privacy so we can talk."

They scrolled at him for several minutes, and then he came back and said, "They want to talk to us separately. They need to talk to me about 'atonement,' whatever that is, and they want to talk to you about you and Indy, but apparently there's some kind of deadline, and they think it'll be faster if they split us up. Metaphorically, not literally. I made sure before I agreed to ask you. So, what do you think?"

"How do we know it's not a trick to get us away from Indy and Srennom so they can string them up? Or us?"

"They've promised they won't take any action against Indy and Srennom till after they're done questioning us." He paused. "They said they'd be 'mighty grateful, ma'am,' if you'd agree."

"All right."

"Good. I have no idea what they'll ask you, but if you could steer clear of talking about humans' penchant for violence and chemical warfare and nuclear bombs in your answers, that'd be good. Especially nuclear bombs. Whatever you do, don't mention that photo of the nuclear test cloud at the wedding chapel. But don't lie. We don't know what all Indy's already told them or whether they can tell when we're lying."

"Great," Francie said.

"I know. Just do the best you can," he said, and went back over to the aliens. "Francie agrees to meet separately with you," he said, and she should have remembered these were Indy's people they were talking to because one of the beanstalk's tentacles lashed out toward her, and she suddenly found herself in a windowless cabin with curved walls and stainless-steel fittings. *I should have made them specify* **where** *this questioning was going to take place,* she thought, hoping it wasn't on their home planet. Or out in space somewhere.

There was no way to tell. There were no windows—or portholes—in the walls, and nowhere to sit. There was no furniture at all. Did the Yohwataah use furniture? And if they did, what would it look like?

And where were they? Wade had said they wanted to question her, but there was no sign of anyone. *This is just like Area 51, waiting in an empty room for someone to come question me.* Except there, she'd had something to sit on. And the worst thing that might come through the door there was an FBI agent, not a giant beanstalk.

I hope I get the mesquite bush instead, she thought, and was debating whether to sit down on the floor when a door opened in the wall behind her and three aliens rolled in. They didn't look like either of the aliens she'd seen so far, or like Indy. One of them resembled a yucca plant, the second looked like a ball of twine, and the third like a head of cabbage.

The yucca poked at a spot on the wall with one of its spear-like leaves and two blocks of stainless steel with concave tops rose from the floor. The ball of twine and the cabbage rolled up into them.

The yucca poked its spear at the wall again, and a narrow stainless-steel slab emerged from the wall at waist height and extended into the middle of the room. It looked exactly like the operating table Lyle had described in his wild stories about abduction, the operating table the aliens used for probing abductees.

CHAPTER TWENTY-TWO

"The time has come," the Walrus said,
"To talk of many things,
Of shoes—and ships—and sealing wax,
Of cabbages—and kings . . ."

—Lewis Carroll

There is no way I am getting up on that operating table, Francie
thought, but she didn't have any choice in the matter. The head
of cabbage had already lifted her up to sit on it, using a splayed
tentacle that looked like a floppy cabbage leaf but was as strong as
the beanstalk's.

All right, she thought, *but I'm **not** lying down.* "If you think
you're going to get me to submit to being—" she began.

But he was looking at her dangling legs. "SORRY SORRY
SORRY," he scrolled, and lashed across to touch the opposite wall.
Another metal block rose out of the floor next to the head of cabbage, and he pushed it over to her and motioned for her to put her
feet on it.

"Thank you," she said.

He didn't respond. He rolled over to the ball of twine, touched the wall again, and sat down in a bowl-shaped seat that rose out of the floor.

"Where have you brought me to?" she said. "What is this place? Are we in space?"

"NO NO NO NO NO," the head of cabbage said, and touched another part of the wall. It slid up, and she could see the red lights and the glare of the klieg lights outside, though not the police cars' flashing lights. And beyond the lights, she could make out the tall dark outlines of what had to be wind turbines. Thank goodness. They were still on the ground. And the red lights, or at least some of them, had been a wind farm.

"FRANCIE WANT GO SPACE?" the yucca scrolled, and the ball of twine wrote, "IF FRANCIE WANT GO SPACE TAKE MIGHTY GRATEFUL MA'AM SAVED LIFE," and then a string of hieroglyphics that had to be Indy's name in their language.

"He saved my life, too," she said. "And he helped me escape from the F—" She couldn't say that, not with them on their way out here to negotiate with the aliens. "He helped me escape," she said instead. "And if you're really mighty grateful ma'am, you need to release Indy."

"SHOW RELEASE," the yucca scrolled.

"SHOW F," the ball of twine scrolled.

"NO NO NO," the cabbage scrolled, and he was clearly the one in charge because the others immediately deleted their words. "BEGIN CLOSE ENCOUNTER."

I hope that doesn't mean they intend to start probing me, she thought.

"BEGIN CLOSE ENCOUNTER FRANCIE."

Oh, *her* close encounter. And they wanted her to begin at the beginning. She hoped.

"I'd come out to Roswell to be the maid of honor in my friend Serena's wedding," she said, "and Serena sent me to get some lights for the wedding. She'd left them in the car."

"SHOW LIGHTS," the cabbage scrolled.

She looked up at the ceiling to see if there was some sort of light

fixture she could point to, but there wasn't. The light seemed to
come from all around. "They're decorations. To make the wedding
look nice," and hoped he wouldn't ask her to explain "decorations."

He didn't. He scrolled, "SHOW ROSWELL."

"Roswell's a town in New Mexico," she said. "A ship of yours
was supposed to have crashed there."

"NO NO NO NO," the head of cabbage scrolled.

Take that, Lyle, Francie thought. *We told you aliens didn't land
in Roswell.*

"SHOW MEXICO," the yucca scrolled.

"SHOW COME OUT," the ball of twine scrolled.

At this rate it's going to take years to tell them what happened,
she thought, and decided to just ignore their questions. "Serena sent
me to get the lights," she said, "and when I got to the car, Indy was
in it," and all three of them immediately scrolled, "SHOW INDY."

"Indy, the alien you were looking for," she said, suddenly at a
loss for how to explain. "Not Srennom, the other one, the one who
abducted me. We called him Indy because he was as fast as a whip,
like Indiana Jones." And now they were going to ask who Indiana
Jones was, and how was she going to explain that? Luckily, she
didn't have to. The head of cabbage came to her aid, scrolling,
"INDY HUMAN NAME KLIIHAI," followed by the string of blue-
green hieroglyphics that she recognized from before as Indy's name
in Yohwataah, and the ball of twine scrolled, "KLIIHAI SERENA
CAR," which she assumed meant he wanted her to tell them what
happened next.

"I opened the door of the car and was looking for the decorations," she said, "and then I saw that Indy—Kliihai—was in the
front seat, and he grabbed me and pulled me into the car."

They all began frantically scrolling to one another, and, after a
minute, the head of cabbage scrolled "SORRY SORRY SORRY" at
her in bright red letters.

"But he didn't hurt me," she said hastily. "He was just trying to
get me to take him to find Srennom, and he didn't know how to
communicate that to me," she added, and the string of "SORRY"s
immediately got longer and brighter.

Oh, no, I'm making things worse, she thought, and decided she'd better not mention his yanking the phone out of her hand or leaving her tied up in the driver's seat overnight. But even though she downplayed Wade's abduction—"Wade *made* us stop. He was hitchhiking."—and told them Indy had saved her life when he kept her from being bitten by the rattlesnake, their questions indicated they were horrified by the fact that Indy had abducted them and made them accompany him, which was somehow a separate crime, as was preventing her from being at Serena's wedding.

"But he *tried* to get me to the wedding," she said. "He just didn't understand what it was. He thought it was something *I* needed to do. That's why he took me to the wedding chapel," and got bogged down completely trying to explain Indy's thinking that her saying she needed to be in a wedding meant she wanted to marry Wade.

"FRANCIE WANT MARRY WADE?" the yucca asked.

Yes, she thought, but she wasn't about to try explaining that to them. "No," she said, and the way they started scrolling again clearly meant they were adding that to his list of crimes.

"Indy—Kliihai—was only trying to help me do what I'd told him," she said. "He just didn't understand our language very well."

"SHOW WEDDING CHAPEL," they said, and when she did her best to explain what it was, they demanded, "SHOW ELVIS PRESLEY SHOW VEIL SHOW MARRIAGE LICENSE."

She did the best she could, explaining concept after concept, word after word, though sometimes she got the sense they weren't interested in the substance of her answers at all, that they were only trying to add to their vocabulary like Indy had been doing when he'd asked her to read the passing billboards. And sometimes she couldn't figure out where the questions had come from, like when the head of cabbage scrolled, "SHOW HONOR."

"Honor?" she said. When had she mentioned honor? "It means trying to do what's right. Like Indy trying to help get me to a wedding. And us trying to help Indy find Srennom. You're not doing it for money or personal gain, you're doing it because it's your duty. It's the right thing to do."

"HIRE SERVANT DO RIGHT THING?"

"Servant?" she said bewilderedly.

"SERVANT," the head of cabbage scrolled. "MAID."

"*Maid*?" Francie repeated, utterly lost. "Oh, you're talking about my being Serena's maid of honor. A maid of honor isn't a servant. It's a bride's attendant. The bride asks a woman to be her maid of honor to say she's special to her. That's what the 'honor' part means. It's a . . ." She flailed around, trying to think of the right word. "It's a sign of what she means to her, a tribute."

"SHOW TRIBUTE," the ball of twine scrolled.

"SHOW SIGN," the yucca scrolled.

"MAID OF HONOR NO TRY DO WHATS RIGHT?" the cabbage scrolled.

"No, she does. That's why she tells the bride she'll be her maid of honor, because she has a duty to her . . ."

"SHOW DUTY," all three of them scrolled.

She was intensely grateful when Wade appeared and saved her from answering. He asked the three aliens if he could speak to Francie alone for a minute.

They scrolled, "YES YES YES," and rolled out, and Wade came over to the operating table.

"What's happening?" Francie asked him, climbing down off it. "How much trouble are Indy and Srennom in?"

"A lot," he said grimly. "But it's not just them, it's all the Hosbitaii."

"Hosbitaii? I thought they were the Yohwataah."

"No, apparently that's the name for all the aliens in the galaxy. The people of this particular planet are Hosbitaii, but they're also part of some kind of interplanetary alliance or commonwealth."

"Lyle's Galactic Federation," Francie said.

"Yeah, and that's whose laws they've broken. From what we've been able to figure out so far, they're the equivalent of federal laws, and Indy and Srennom—and by extension all the Hosbitaii—broke a bunch of those laws by coming here, and more by making contact with us," he said. "Look, I need to know what all happened before you picked me up. Did anybody see you get abducted by Indy?"

"No."

"You're sure?"

"Yes. I looked all around for someone I could call to for help, but the street was completely empty."

"How about as you drove through town and on the highway? Did anybody pass you?"

She shook her head. "No. The only vehicle I saw was a pickup truck ahead of us."

"And there's no chance they could have seen Indy?"

"No, the pickup was a long way ahead of us."

"What about the next morning before you picked me up? Did you encounter anybody else on the road?"

"No."

"How about at the wedding chapel after I left?" he asked. "Reverend Murray didn't see him, did he, or Cheree? Or one of the Dracula or Harley-Davidson wedding people?"

"No," she said, and he looked relieved.

"And you're sure there wasn't anyone else who might have seen him? Somebody at the Thunderbird Trading Post or the Tropicana? The Showgirl Spin guy, maybe?"

"No."

"You're sure?" he said, and when she nodded, he breathed, "Thank goodness! That means there've only been six fourth-level interface violations, which puts it under the limit that would make it come under Yohwataah jurisdiction."

"Fourth-level interfaces?"

"Yeah. The Yohwataah've got a system like Lyle's close encounter levels for alien contacts, only more complicated. A first-level interface is seeing, a second-level's touching, a third-level's interacting, a fourth-level's communicating, a fifth-level's forcing them to do something or go somewhere, and all of them are illegal."

A spurt of laughter escaped her. "Abduction's against the *law*?"

"Yes, but it's not funny. Indy's in serious trouble."

"I know," she said repentantly. "I was just thinking about Lyle. He'll die when he finds out aliens *can't* abduct people. How *much* trouble is Indy in?"

"Not as much as if he'd had seven interface violations. Then it'd be out of the Hosbitaii's hands, and they'd have no choice but to turn it over to the Yohwataah for adjudication."

"Adjudication? You mean putting Indy on trial? And stringing him up? You heard what they said."

"Calm down. Any number of violations under seven can be handled locally between the two planets involved, through negotiations and atonement by the offenders."

"What about Indy?"

Wade looked grim. "I don't know. I'm hoping we can negotiate his and Srennom's release, or at least a lessening of their sentence. Or make it a condition of the atonement."

"What does that mean, atonement?"

"We're not sure yet. We think it means redress to the victims."

"Redress?"

"Damages of some kind, and personal apologies. That's why the aliens want to meet with Eula Mae and Joseph and Lyle."

"*Lyle?*" Francie said. "Is that a good idea?"

"Probably not, but it wasn't a request. It was an order."

She thought of something. "Wait, Indy only abducted five of us. Who's the sixth? Did Indy try to abduct somebody else before he found me? Or is it somebody Srennom came in contact with?"

"Neither. You were the first earthling Indy saw, and Srennom had a surface vehicle with some sort of cloaking device—Lyle will be overjoyed to find that out—and has spent the past week by himself in the desert looking for thunderstorms."

"Then who's the sixth? That guard Indy lassoed when we were trying to escape? He wasn't the only person Indy 'interfaced' with when we were in custody. How many of your people interrogated him at Area 51 or wherever we were?"

"It doesn't matter. We've convinced the Hosbitaii that because the agents are government employees, they're part of the official delegation sent to respond to the Hosbitaii's violations—and, because they're bound to secrecy by the classified nature of the situation, they don't count as contacts."

"But if they don't count, then who's the sixth contact?"

"The rattlesnake who tried to bite you."

"Oh." She shuddered. "They don't want to meet with it, too, do they?"

"No. We convinced them that an apology wouldn't be an appropriate form of atonement and sending it some mice would."

"Oh, good," she said. "But, wait, Indy threw two more rattlesnakes out into the field. Don't they count as contacts, too?"

"I didn't tell the Hosbitaii about them, and you can't, either. That would put them over the seven-interface limit, and Indy would *really* be in the soup. You haven't said anything about them, have you?" he asked anxiously.

"No," she said. "But if rattlesnakes count as contacts, then what about all the sagebrush and yucca and mesquite bushes he came in contact with?"

Wade shook his head. "Even though our biologists think the Hosbitaii may have originally evolved from plants, they don't consider our plant life as having consciousness. Apparently the Hosbitaii attempted to communicate with a prickly pear when they first landed, with predictably bad results, and Indy apparently spent a half hour trying to convince a Joshua tree to drive him to a *tsurrispoinis* before he abducted you, so the Hosbitaii have decided that plants are too far down the evolutionary scale to count. I got the idea they're annoyed by that, as if their own side had let them down."

"So does this mean the Hosbitaii themselves aren't in trouble, if Indy's under the critical number of contacts?"

"It's hard to tell," he said. "They seem to have their own local system of laws regarding interactions with other planets as well as the interplanetary ones, or maybe it's all linked, I don't know. Our linguists are doing their best to sort it all out, but . . ." He shook his head. "The only thing that's clear is that the Hosbitaii don't blame any of this on us."

"Which means they blame Indy," she said. "Did you tell them it's not his fault, that he was just trying to help Srennom?"

"I tried, but that argument didn't cut any ice with them. But at least this is a local matter. I got the feeling that the Galactic Federation court or tribunal or whatever it is doesn't take *any* mitigating factors into account," he said, and leaned close to her, so close her heart began to pound. "So if you think of any other close encounters," he whispered in her ear, "keep them to yourself."

He pulled away. "I've got to go tell the Hosbitaii about the number of contacts," he said, and squeezed her hand. "Try not to worry. You're doing great."

That's what you think, she thought, watching him leave.

The moment he was gone, the aliens rolled back in and put her back up on the table. "I know you think Indy abducted me, but he didn't," she told them. "He was just trying to get me to take him to Srennom, and he didn't speak my language, so he didn't know how to ask me, and I wouldn't have understood him if he *had* asked. All he could do was make me get in the car and point where he wanted to go. It wasn't an abduction, so he shouldn't get in trouble."

"VIOLATION INTERFERE HUMAN ACTIVITIES," the head of cabbage scrolled. "WEDDING."

"If you mean Wade's and my wedding, we didn't really get married. It was just a ceremony. And if you mean Serena's wedding, Indy didn't stop it. She didn't need me there to get married."

"SERENA MARRIED?"

"Yes," Francie said, even though she didn't know that for sure. And wished it wasn't true. "Serena had her wedding. There wasn't any interference, so there was no violation."

The three aliens conferred among themselves for several minutes and then the head of cabbage scrolled, "INDY LYING SIDE-WINDER."

"What?" Francie said.

"INDY SAY FRANCIE SAY I NEED GO WEDDING INDY LYING SIDEWINDER."

"No, Indy wasn't lying. I did tell him I needed to go to the wedding, but not because Serena needed me there to be able to get married. It was because I owed it to her to be there."

"SHOW OWED."

"It means I had an obligation to her," Francie said, and because she knew that next they were going to ask, "SHOW OBLIGATION," she added, "A responsibility, a commitment. A duty," and was immediately sorry. She was going to have to define "duty" after all.

"BBHBINIITS?" the head of cabbage scrolled.

Indy had used that word when he was talking about Srennom. "Yes, *bbhbiniits*," she said. "I had a duty to Serena."

"MAID OF HONOR."

"No, not because I was her maid of honor. It was the other way around. Serena asked me to be her maid of honor because we're friends. She was my roommate in college," and then Francie could have kicked herself. Now they'd want to know what a roommate was. And college.

But instead the yucca scrolled, "SHOW FRIENDS."

"It means when two people know and like each other and want to keep each other from harm. Like Indy and me. He saved my life. If he hadn't picked up that rattlesnake and thrown it out into the field, it would have bitten me and killed me."

There was a flurry of scrolling among the three, and Francie hoped she'd finally said something that would help Indy, but after a minute the ball of twine scrolled, "INDY LYING SIDEWINDER INDY SAY FRANCIE SAVE LIFE."

"He's right," she said. "That's not a lie. I *did* save his life. I warned him about the snakes. If I hadn't, he would have rolled right onto them, and they would have bitten him. We both saved each other's lives."

That didn't impress the aliens. "INDY EXPOSE FRANCIE DANGER," the ball of twine scrolled, and that was clearly another crime he'd committed.

"But he didn't mean to," Francie protested. "He didn't know there were snakes in the rocks, and as soon as he saw there were, he protected me from them."

"INDY TOOK FRANCIE ROCKS," the head of cabbage scrolled implacably.

"No, he didn't. We stopped there because we'd run out of gas," but they clearly considered the matter closed.

"SHOW ROOMMATE," the yucca asked.

"It's a friend you live with in the same living space—"

"FRANCIE WADE."

"No," she said, though she supposed in a way they had lived together in the *Outlaw*. "Sharing living space is only part of it. Being roommates also means looking after each other and trying to help solve each other's problems and having adventures together."

"FRANCIE WADE."

"*No*," she began, and then stopped. The aliens were right. She and Wade fit that definition perfectly.

"WEDDING," the yucca scrolled wisely.

"No. I mean, roommates aren't married," she said. "That is . . ." and realized that if she said, "They can be," she'd be opening up a whole new can of worms. "Roommates are Earth humans who shared living space in *college*."

Which led to explaining "college" and then "school," but it was still better than trying to explain that some roommates were also mates, which would just cause them to say "FRANCIE WADE" again. "School's a place where young Earth humans go to learn," she said.

"SCHOOL," the yucca scrolled. "TSINIBITAI," and the others repeated it.

"No." She'd heard Indy use that word before, and she'd never mentioned roommates to him. They'd gotten the wrong idea somehow. "No," she said again, "*roommates*. You protect each other and try to keep each other from doing something stupid or dangerous."

"INDY CLOSE ENCOUNTER RATTLESNAKE."

"Yes," she said. "I had a duty to protect Indy from the rattlesnake. Because he'd saved my life."

"FRANCIE DUTY GO SERENA WEDDING."

"Yes," she said, and the three aliens began scrolling furiously to each other again for several minutes, followed by the head of cabbage scrolling in huge neon-green letters, "VIOLATION INTER-FERE BBHBINIITS."

Oh, no. All she'd accomplished by trying to explain about her duty to Serena was to get Indy accused of yet another crime, and if the size and brightness of the letters was an indication, it was a major one. "No, no, no," she said. "I had a duty to go to Serena's wedding, but I also had a duty to take Indy to the thunderstorm—the *tsurrispoinis*—to find Srennom. Because Indy'd saved me from the rattlesnake and—"

"TSURRISPOINIS TSURRISPOINIS TSURRISPOINIS," the yucca scrolled, in bright red, and when she looked at the others, they were furiously scrolling in their language.

Oh, no, she thought. *I've done it again. Don't tell me there's some interplanetary law against going to a thunderstorm.*

"SRENNOM TSURRISPOINIS WHY?" the head of cabbage scrolled.

"I—I don't know," she stammered. "He had these little silver strips, about so long." She showed them the approximate length with her hands. "And he shot them out into the storm—the *tsurrispoinis*—and when the strips came back, they were curled up, like this."

She demonstrated, which brought on a flurry of angry-looking scrolling.

"Srennom didn't have a close encounter, if that's what you're worried about. There wasn't anybody there except the four of us. And a *tsurrispoinis* isn't conscious. It isn't even alive. It's just a bunch of moisture."

They ignored her. The head of cabbage pressed a spot on the wall, and the door opened to reveal Srennom.

He rolled in, and the aliens immediately began bombarding him with questions that Srennom answered, at one point scrolling what looked like a mathematical formula for them and at another the words "SORRY SORRY SORRY."

"It *can't* have been a violation to go to a thunderstorm," Francie said. "They're not anyone's property. They're *weather*," but they paid no attention to her, continuing to demand answers from Srennom, who looked more and more terrified. The tentacles he wasn't scrolling with began to flail wildly, tangling themselves into knots.

"You're scaring him!" Francie cried, and she tried to get down off the operating table, but the ball of twine's tentacles shot out and replaced her firmly on it.

More scrolling, and the yucca suddenly shot a tentacle out and stabbed Srennom in the middle of his flailing tentacles.

"Oh, no!" Francie cried out, lunging toward them. "Don't kill him!" she begged, but it was only retrieving one of the tinsel curls.

The aliens converged on it, their scrolling as they examined it as rapid-fire as Indy's had been when they were first captured by the Hosbitaii, and then turned their attention back to Srennom, and they were obviously asking him who had helped him gather the tinsel curls.

Srennom scrolled, "TSINIBITAI KLIIHAI INDY."

Wade and I helped them, too, Francie wanted to say, but she was afraid that might get Indy and Srennom into even more trouble.

The three of them continued to scroll for a moment and then the ball of twine wrapped its tentacles around Srennom, as if it were tying up a parcel, and hustled him out of the room.

"Wait!" Francie cried, jumping off the operating table. "What are you going to do to him?" but the door had already shut behind them.

"I won't let you hurt Srennom or Indy," she said, grabbing at one of the head of cabbage's leafy tentacles to get his attention. "It's my duty to protect them, just like it was Indy's duty—*bbhbiniits*—to protect Srennom. That's all he was trying to do, find the thunderstorm, the *tsurrispoinis,* and take him home before he got in trouble."

The scrolling abruptly stopped, and the aliens rolled toward her. *Oh, no,* she thought. *What have I said now?*

The yucca thrust a swordlike tentacle at her, scrolling, "FRANCIE BBHBINIITS INDY."

"Yes," she said, trying frantically to think of something they'd understand, of something Indy might have told them in that long

recital of his. "He's my sidekick, my blood brother, my partner—
I mean, my pardner!"

"SHOW PARDNERS," the cabbage scrolled, but the yucca laid
a spear-like tentacle over his.

"CODE OF THE WEST," he scrolled, and the head of cabbage
scrolled, "PAINT YOUR WAGON."

"Yes, exactly," Francie said. "Ben Rumson and Pardner were
partners. They stood by each other and fought each other's battles.
They paid each other's debts; they kept their promises to each other.
And they stuck by each other, no matter what."

The yucca thrust out a swordlike tentacle again. "BBHBINIITS,"
it scrolled.

"Yes, *bbhbiniits,*" Francie said, and that was obviously the wrong
answer because they began rolling toward the door, which immediately opened.

"Stop! Wait!" she cried, running after them and grasping at their
tentacles. "Let me explain!" but they rolled past her as if she didn't
exist.

"Indy and Srennom didn't do anything wrong!" she cried, but
the door had already shut, vanishing into the wall without a trace.

She pounded on the spot where it had been, shouting, "Don't you
dare hurt them! I forbid it!" and "I demand to see my lawyer!" and
then went over to the wall the aliens had used and pushed on every
square inch of it, but all her effort accomplished was to slide the
window shut so she couldn't see out, and all her pushing and poking
didn't open it again.

She went back to the space where the door had been, pounded on
it some more, and then sat down against it, wondering what she'd
said to set them off.

That she'd had a duty to Indy? Was forming a bond with an alien
another violation of intergalactic law? Or had it been something else
altogether, something to do with Roswell or roommates or maids of
honor? Or Elvis Presley? *I'd have been better off telling them about
the mushroom cloud,* she thought, and the door opened behind her
and she fell over backward.

Wade helped her to her feet.

"Oh, thank goodness you're here," she said, and then stopped at the look on his face. He came into the room and the door shut instantly behind him.

"What did you say to them?" he asked accusingly.

"I don't know. What's happened?"

"They threw the linguists and me out and went into this giant huddle, scrolling like mad. The only word I caught was *tsurrispoinis*. Did you tell them about going to the thunderstorm?"

"Yes," she said miserably, "but I thought Indy'd already told them about it. He'd told them about everything else. I tried to tell them it couldn't be an interface, that thunderstorms aren't conscious."

"Did you tell them what Srennom and Indy did while they were there, about the collecting?"

"Yes. I told you, I assumed Indy'd already told them."

"Well, apparently he hadn't. Did you tell them *what* they were collecting?"

"No, because I didn't know, but I told them whatever it was, it didn't belong to anybody."

"Oh, yes, it does," Wade said. "It belongs to our planet, and it's against interplanetary law to take anything from an inhabited planet—plants, rock samples, conscious and non-conscious creatures. It's regarded as pillaging, and it's a federal crime. Which means it has to be tried by the Yohwataah." He paused, looking thoughtful. "Maybe we can say you didn't actually see them take anything, that there's no evidence they—"

Francie shook her head. "They took one of the tinsel curls from Srennom."

"Jesus," he said, and rubbed his hand across his mouth. "Now they've got proof— This is a capital offense we're talking about."

"Oh, no! What if we told them we were the ones who collected them?"

He shook his head. "You said they found one on Srennom, so even if we convince them we collected it, that would just mean he took it from us, which from what I've been able to work out is an even more serious crime."

"Then what—?"

"I want you to tell me exactly what you told them. Maybe we can find a loophole in there somewhere we can use."

She recounted the conversation, trying to remember the exact words she'd used and telling him about the whole maid-of-honor thing and the conversation about duty. "They seemed really upset about the fact that Indy'd kept me from going to Serena's wedding and that he'd interfered with my duty—they called it a *bbhbiniits*—to her."

"*Bbhbiniits*? You're sure that's the word they used?"

"Yes. Why?"

"Because according to our linguists, it doesn't just mean a duty. It means a 'holy quest,' and it's sacred in their society. It transcends all other laws, and interfering with one is the highest crime of all."

Francie went white. "So if they think Indy's interfering with my going to Serena's wedding was interfering with a sacred quest . . . But I *told* them he tried to get me to the wedding, but he just didn't understand what I meant. Surely if we explain that to them—"

"I don't think they'll give us the chance," he said. "I'm not even sure they'll let me out of here," but when he pounded on the place where the door had been, it opened, and he went out.

"I want to go with you," Francie said. "I got Indy into this mess, and I need to fix it. If I can just explain to them—" and she stopped again.

The look on his face plainly said, *I think you've done enough explaining.*

"I'm so sorry," she said, but the door had already shut behind him.

She didn't try to pound on it this time. She went back over to the operating table, climbed up on it, and waited for Wade to return.

He didn't, and neither did the head of cabbage and his buddies, not even to lead her away in the Hosbitaii equivalent of handcuffs. What seemed like hours went by, and she lay down on the table and curled up in the fetal position, almost wishing Lyle's probe-happy Grays would come in and do something awful to her. Anything would be better than this *waiting*.

But when the door finally slid open, eons later, it wasn't Grays or the Hosbitaii. It was Wade, looking pale and stunned.

CHAPTER TWENTY-THREE

Marian: Then we'll never see you again?

Shane: Never's a long time, Marian.

— *Shane*

Francie was afraid to ask what happened, but she had to. "They strung Indy and Srennom up, didn't they?" she said, her throat dry. "For what I said?"

"No," Wade said, still with that stunned look on his face.

"Then what *did* they do? Disintegrate them? Ship them off to the Yohwataah to stand trial? What did they do to them?"

"Nothing."

"What do you mean, nothing?"

"I mean, they're not in trouble anymore. In fact, they seem to have turned into the heroes of the hour. The Hosbitaii are practically carrying them around on their shoulders—if they had shoulders."

"But what about interfering with a sacred duty being punishable by death?" she asked, bewildered. "What about pillaging being a federal crime? Did we misunderstand what they were saying about that?"

"No, pillaging's definitely a federal crime, even if it's for a good cause, and Indy knew that. That's why he was so desperate to find Srennom and stop him before he got the data."

"Data?" Francie said. "I thought he was collecting water samples. If he was just collecting information on the storm, does that mean it *wasn't* pillaging?"

"No, in fact, data's worse. The Yohwataah regard the exchange of information between planets as even more dangerous than direct encounters between species, which is probably true. It would be introducing a huge variable that might cause all sorts of unforeseen consequences. So it's strictly forbidden."

"But they weren't sharing information. They were just taking it."

"It works both ways. And it's a capital crime, even if it's committed with good intentions. Which was apparently the case here. Srennom was trying to get information on storm mechanics, which was vital to his planet's survival." He made a wry face at Francie. "I know, it doesn't make any sense. They're not even allowed to try to get information that would save his planet."

"But if that's the case, how can he and Indy not be in trouble?"

"We're not completely sure, but what the situation seems to be is this: Srennom is Indy's *tsinibitai,* which means Indy had a sacred duty—a *bbhbiniits*—to help him, and—"

"Wait, you've figured out what *tsinibitai* means?"

"Yeah, as far as these things can be translated directly. Our translators say the closest equivalent seems to be 'roommate.'"

"Roommate!" Francie said. "I should have known. Only a roommate could do something so crazy you'd have to follow them out to the middle of nowhere to get them out of trouble!"

"Anyway," Wade said, "Indy had a duty to help him, and *bbhbiniitses*—sacred quests—are above the law. Which would get Indy and Srennom off the hook *except* that interfering with a sacred quest is an even worse crime than pillaging. It's up there on a level with mass murder—or treason—for the Hosbitaii."

"And they *do* think Indy interfered with my sacred duty by keeping me from being at Serena's wedding. Don't they?"

"Yeah, you were right. That's exactly what they think."

"Did you tell them he didn't mean to? That he *tried* to get me to the wedding, but he didn't understand what that meant—"

"Yeah, but it doesn't matter. Intentions don't qualify as an extenuating circumstance in Hosbitaii law, and neither does a failure to communicate. The only thing that *does* matter is that, in spite of his interfering with *your* quest, you thought you had a duty to protect Indy and get him to the *tsurrispoinis* so he could fulfill *his* sacred quest—a duty you felt you had even though he was a stranger and had endangered you, and when you explained about your duty to Serena, they realized you were talking about the same thing as their *bbhbiniitses* and that we have them, too. And that yours was more sacred than Indy's because you were willing to forgive Indy for preventing you from fulfilling your duty to a fellow human, which means it cancels out Indy's interference, his kidnapping us, and everything else that's happened, and it puts it all under the umbrella of *bbhbiniitsness,* of sacred questery."

"So what does *that* mean?"

"It means Indy and Srennom are off the hook, the Hosbitaii get to keep the data, and they're so 'mighty grateful, ma'am' they're beside themselves. They've spent the last half hour expressing their undying gratitude to us for helping Indy and Srennom and letting them have the data, and asking us how they can ever repay us." He smiled at her. "You did it. You saved the planet, just like in all those science fiction movies of Lyle's, only in this case it was Indy's planet. *And* you saved Indy."

I did, she thought, feeling weak with relief. She hadn't gotten him killed.

"They want to know what they can do to thank us," Wade said, "so you might want to come up with some suggestions."

"What about the technology you wanted for that no-gas-required car engine?" she asked. "Can you ask them for that?"

"Afraid not. Yohwataah law forbids the exchange of information, remember? And that includes technology. Especially technology. They're only allowed to give us stuff, not information."

"But can't you figure out how it worked from the *Outlaw*? Reverse-engineer it, like Lyle said they were doing at Area 51 with the UFO?"

He shook his head. "They've already switched the engine back to using diesel."

"What about"—she leaned closer to Wade and whispered— "what about Serena's car? It's still at the Thunderbird Trading Post. You could just let it stay there till they leave—"

"We already thought of that. Indy apparently switched it back before he hijacked the *Outlaw*."

"I *knew* we should have stopped and had Indy switch the engine on the Jeep on the way to the thunderstorm," she said. "Only I suppose they'd have already switched that back, too." She thought a minute. "You said they were really grateful to me. Couldn't I ask them—?"

He shook his head. "They still couldn't give it to you. I got the feeling that if there was any way to get around the law, they would— they're really grateful and want to help us—but it's out of their hands—I mean, tentacles. This is a matter of Yohwataah law, and it's completely unambiguous—and unyielding—on the subject of information sharing. It's okay, they're giving us the data from the thunderstorm, which may help us at least partly with the global warming problem, plus five hundred tons of helium, a hundred of scandium, twenty of cobalt, and a bunch of neodymium. And whatever the five of us want. Anything in particular you're hankering for? A couple of tons of diamonds maybe?"

"I want all the charges against Indy and Srennom dropped."

"They have been. I told you. They've gone from being outlaws on the run to being the heroes of the hour."

"Yes, but what if it turns out they broke some other law while they were here? I want a full pardon for both of them, in writing or whatever the Hosbitaii equivalent is, not just scrolling."

"Done," Wade said. "What else?"

"I want full pardons for them from our government, too. And for us," she said, thinking about their jailbreak and stealing the FBI van.

"Already taken care of," Wade said, "plus I got them to drop all the gambling and fraud charges against Eula Mae, and I got them to give Joseph back the *Outlaw* right away in exchange for him calling off his lawyers. A lawsuit could have proved tricky, especially if his lawyers had asked for discovery. In return, they've promised to keep our little adventure secret."

"What about Lyle? Did he agree to keep this secret, too?"

"No, but the Bureau's made it clear that all this is classified and the penalty for blabbing is life in prison."

"But is that enough to stop him? Especially since he turned out to be right about aliens landing in Roswell and the Galactic Federation and the whole operating table thing—"

"And Monument Valley," Wade said.

"What? The aliens *do* move it around?"

"No, but the linguists say there are close similarities between the Hosbitaii language and Navajo, which points to their having been in contact at some point."

"So Lyle was right about everything," she said disgustedly.

"No, remember, he was wrong about them coming here to invade us. And I'm pretty sure they're not telepathic. If they were, I'd be locked up right now for what I was thinking while we were trying to get Indy and Srennom off the hook."

"I'm serious," Francie said. "He'll be determined to tell everybody his conspiracy theories were true, prison sentence or not. You know how obsessed he is about government cover-ups."

"True," Wade said thoughtfully. "Listen, speaking of this being classified, there are a bunch of forms you need to sign—releases and Security of Information forms—and I know the Hosbitaii want to talk to you again to express their undying gratitude to you for saving their planet, but be thinking about what you want—an *Outlaw* of your own, a Rolls-Royce"—he gestured at her maid-of-honor dress—"some new clothes—"

"Very funny," she said, and after he left, she climbed back up on the operating table to wait for them, but when the door opened again it wasn't the Hosbitaii. It was Agent Sanchez.

"Agent Hastings sent me to get you," she said, and led Francie along several stainless-steel corridors and outside.

Francie was surprised to see it was still night—she felt like she'd been in that room for days. She tried to look back to see what kind of ship the Hosbitaii had, but she couldn't see a thing. The blinding white lights were still on, augmented now by an array of portable arc lights and strings of incident lights the FBI had set up. It was so bright she couldn't even see where she was going. "Watch out for the electrical cords," Agent Sanchez said after Francie'd tripped over one.

They picked their way through a crowd of vehicles and portable tents to an FBI van. Wade was standing next to its open back door. "There's somebody here who wants to talk to you," he said. "Serena."

"She's here?" Francie looked eagerly around.

"No. She doesn't know anything about this," he said, motioning to Francie to get in the back of the van and clambering in after her. "She thinks you were kidnapped by an escaped convict. And that's the story you need to stick to."

He gestured to her to sit down. "She's on Skype." He picked up a laptop and started typing. "You're calling her from FBI headquarters."

Which was apparently the reason for calling from inside the van, so Serena couldn't see any of what was going on outside. "What if she asks for details about this convict who kidnapped me?" she asked. "Shouldn't you fill me in on what she's been told?" but he had already handed her the laptop, showed her which keys to push, and left, and anyway she needn't have worried. Serena did all the talking.

"Are you okay?" she said. "I've been so worried about you! I didn't realize you were gone till almost midnight—Russell came back right after you left to go to the car and *insisted* I go with him to find the UFO, so I left a message for you with P.D., but *he* went to look for the UFO, too, and when I tried to call you, there wasn't any coverage at all out there. I told Russell he had to take me somewhere where there *was* coverage, but he refused. I had to hitch a ride with some people who were convinced the UFO had landed east of Roswell. They took me to my car, and when it wasn't there, I figured you'd taken it back to the motel, so I didn't realize you'd been kidnapped till the next morning, and when I told the police, they said I couldn't file a missing-persons report till twenty-four hours had elapsed and that you were probably somewhere at the festival or out looking for the UFO like everybody else, and I didn't know what to do!"

Serena had poured out all this in an unbroken rush, but now she hesitated, as if there was something she didn't want to tell Francie.

She went ahead and had the wedding without me, Francie thought. She'd been pretty sure this whole time that that was what had happened, and she'd thought she was resigned to it, but now she felt sick to her stomach all over again. She'd let Serena down.

"So I borrowed my uncle's car and went back out to find Russell," Serena was saying, "and when I told him what had happened, he said maybe you'd been abducted and if you had, it would be wonderful, it would *prove* all his theories about aliens were true and we'd be famous! He wanted to call the MUFON people. I couldn't believe it! What a jerk! All he cared about was his stupid UFOs! He didn't care at all about what might have happened to you. I told him I never wanted to see him again!"

Thank heavens! Francie thought. *She didn't marry him!*

"So, anyway, I couldn't get anybody to listen to me. I tried to call that FBI agent I told you about, but I couldn't get through, and I didn't know *what* to do. And then the police called me and told me you'd been kidnapped and the FBI had been put in charge of the case and they were sending over an agent to talk to me and not to tell anybody because it might jeopardize your safety. So they did— send over an agent—and I told him everything I knew, about what you were wearing and the car and everything. I've been working with him the whole time, trying to find you . . ." That uncomfortable hesitation again, and then she said, "The convict guy didn't hurt you, did he?"

"No, I'm fine," Francie said, and wondered if she should add that the convict had just been interested in escaping, but Serena might ask where he'd taken her, and she didn't know what sort of cover story they'd concocted.

While she was still debating what to say, Serena said, "Oh my God! Look at your dress! It's all dirty!"

"I'm know. I'm sorry," she began. "It—"

"That's okay. Don't worry about it," Serena said. "I'd already figured out you might need some clothes to wear, after being stuck in the same thing for days, so I brought you your bag, but they wouldn't let me in to see you. They said you couldn't have visitors till after you'd finished filing charges and giving your testimony—but Cooper said he'd see you got it."

"Cooper?"

"The agent I told you about," she said, as if Francie should know his name. But it didn't matter. She could finally get out of this disgusting dress and into some clean clothes. And not that awful tank top and shorts Wade had bought for her.

"I knew there was a reason I love you, Serena!" she exclaimed. "Only *you* would realize I'd need my clothes. Thank you!"

"What are old roommates for?" Serena said. "And really, don't worry about your dress. I think I should go with a different color anyway."

Different color? I thought you just said you never wanted to see Russell again. **Please** *don't tell me you forgave him and are going through with the wedding after all.*

"How do you feel about hot pink?" Serena was asking. "Well, heliotrope really. I found this gorgeous heliotrope maid-of-honor dress with a bustle and rows and rows of ruffles and thought it would be perfect for you."

Of course you did, Francie thought. But an ugly dress was nothing compared to the fact that Serena was still marrying Russell.

"But I thought you said—"

"That I never wanted to see Russell again? I don't. But . . ." again that odd hesitation, "you know that FBI agent I told you about that I've been working with, well, we spent a lot of time together, and I know what you're going to say, that I've only known him a few days and that's too short a time to have fallen in love with somebody, especially after I just broke up with Russell, but I realized I was never really in love with him, and sometimes when people are thrown together in a crisis, they can get really close in a really short period of time, you know?"

Yes, Francie thought. *I do know.*

"And we need to get married right away because he's been assigned to some classified project back east. I know it's asking a lot, especially after what you've been through, but do you think you could stay and be my maid of honor? It's going to be Saturday. Please say you'll come. I can't possibly get married without you."

"And I wouldn't dream of letting you," Francie said, thinking, *Well, at least this time it's someone rational, not a UFO nut.* And when Agent Cooper showed up a few minutes later, wearing a black suit and tie and carrying Francie's bag, he seemed perfectly normal.

"Here are your clothes," he said, handing her her bag.

"Thank you," she said. "Is there somewhere I could change?"

"Sure," he said. "This way," and started to lead her back across the tangle of electrical cords and cables, but within a few yards, they were intercepted by Wade, who said, "*There* you are. I've been looking for you. The Hosbitaii want to talk to you." He took Francie's bag from her and handed it to Cooper. "Hang on to this for us."

"Yes, sir," Cooper said, and walked off.

"Do you know him, Wade?" Francie asked.

"Cooper? Yeah, he's the guy I was working with out here. Why?"

"Because he and Serena are going to get married."

"You're kidding! What happened to the UFO guy?"

She told him. "Cooper's a normal person, right?" she asked. "I mean, he's an FBI agent or whatever it is you are. That means he's comparatively steady. And sane, right?"

"Depends," he said. "His nickname at the Bureau is Fox."

"Fox?"

"For Fox Mulder. You know, on *The X-Files.* 'The Truth Is Out There.'"

"Oh, no!"

"But he's a nice kind of crazy. And, face it, Serena's never going to marry anybody completely rational. Come on. The Hosbitaii are waiting." He lifted the flap to a large tent packed with Hosbitaii.

They looked like a densely planted garden. Francie recognized the head of cabbage and the yucca, though she didn't see the ball of twine. The beanstalk and the mesquite bush they'd talked to first were there, though, and so were a grapevine, a clump of pampas grass, a dozen tumbleweeds, a trailing mass of ivy, and an organ pipe cactus with spiny, ribbed arms. All of them were scrolling, "MIGHTY GRATEFUL MA'AM" and "FRANCIE FRANCIE FRANCIE!"

"I'll leave you to your fans," Wade said, and slipped out of the tent.

One of the tumbleweeds rolled forward and scrolled, "UN-TANGLE TEACH WORDS RATTLESNAKE THANKYOU THANKYOU THANKYOU," and enveloped Francie in a bear hug of branches.

This must be Indy's mother or some other family member, she thought, but the grapevine and the ivy did exactly the same thing, and she was afraid the organ pipe cactus was going to, too, but it stopped a few inches from her and scrolled, "THE WHOLE TOWNS MIGHTY GRATEFUL TO YA SHERIFF."

"I was happy to do it," Francie said. "I love Indy."

She should have known better. Every tentacle in the tent began scrolling, "SHOW LOVE," and she spent the next hour trying to define "fondness," "affection," "bond," and "tenderness."

When Wade finally came to rescue her, she was trying to explain "attachment."

"Sorry," he apologized to the ivy, "I need to borrow her for a minute," and to Francie he said, "Eula Mae wanted to tell you goodbye before they take her back to Albuquerque."

"Take her *back*?" Francie said. "I didn't even know she was here."

"The Hosbitaii insisted on them coming out here so they could thank them," Wade said. He turned to the head of cabbage. "Is it okay if I take her?"

"YES YES YES SORRY SORRY SORRY KEEP SO MANY THANK," the head of cabbage scrolled, and made a sweeping gesture with his leafy tentacle, like a bow.

So did the others. "THANK THANK THANK."

Francie bowed back. "You're very welcome," she said, and followed Wade out of the tent.

It was still dark, though there weren't as many stars, and Francie thought she could see the faintest lightening of the sky to the east beyond the glare of the lights, though not enough to make out shapes by.

"Why are they taking Eula Mae to Albuquerque?" Francie asked, following Wade. "I thought you said the FBI dropped the charges against her."

"They did. She's going straight."

"*Straight?*"

"Yeah," he said, leading her through the tangle of electrical cords to the perimeter. "I talked the Bureau into hiring her on as a consultant on gambling security. She'll be working out of our Vegas office."

The eastern sky had lightened a bit more, to a velvety blue. It still wasn't enough to be able to see the alien ship by, but she could dimly make out the shapes of the columns of the wind farm behind it, with their red aircraft warning lights.

It made her think of that first night when they'd seen the red lights and thought they were UFOs, the night Wade had woken her up to see the sunrise. "Wade—" she said.

"After you tell Eula Mae goodbye," he said, "they need you to fill out some more forms saying where you'll be and how they can get in touch with you, and then you can leave, too."

Leave?

"I had them call your boss and tell him you were helping the FBI

with an investigation and needed to stay here another week so you
don't have to go home and come back again for Serena's wedding,"
he said. "And I've arranged for Agent Wakamura to take you back
to Roswell. I'd do it, but I've got to go back to Washington to brief
them on the situation and then come back here to finalize the arrangements with the Hosbitaii so they can meet their deadline."

"Deadline?"

"Yeah, there are restrictions on how long they can remain on a
given planet as well as how many contacts with the natives they can
have. As near as we've been able to figure, given the length of their
days and ours, they've got a total of six months. And between Indy
and Srennom and this ship, the time they've been here adds up to a
little less than two months, which means there should be plenty of
time to negotiate their atonement and the transfer of gifts, but either
our calculations are wrong or we're still having language problems
because they say they need to have everything done and everybody
off the planet by Friday or they'll be in serious trouble with the Yohwataah. That's two days from now. So the deadline's really tight."

*And you want me out of the way so you can concentrate on help-
ing them meet it,* she thought. "That's okay," she said. "You don't
have to take me to Roswell. I can drive myself."

"No, you can't."

"Why not?"

"Because your Jeep's almost out of gas, and I figured you wouldn't
want to stick around till they brought some out here, that you'd be
anxious to get back to Serena and your maid-of-honor duties, so
Agent Wakamura will take you, and I'll have it brought to you later.
Or if you'd rather rent another car in Roswell, the Bureau can have
somebody take the Jeep back to Albuquerque and turn it in for you.
Whatever you want."

Whatever I want, she thought wryly. *I don't think the Hosbitaii
can give me that.*

"The Bureau will reimburse you for your expenses, including a
new phone to replace the one Indy threw out in that field. And your
dress. Tell Serena the Bureau will pay to replace it—unless you were
hoping this would get you out of wearing it."

"Serena's decided she wants different bridesmaid dresses for this wedding. Heliotrope. With ruffles," Francie said. "And a bustle."

"Ugh," he said, making a face. "Well, at least she didn't decide on a zombie wedding. Anyway, the Bureau will pay for your new dress, whatever it is. It's the least we can do after what we've put you through. And we'll reimburse you for all your rental car expenses. Including gas," he added, "which we will unfortunately continue to need."

"I'm sorry you weren't able to get the engine technology," she said.

"Yeah, well, sometimes you don't get what you want."

No, she thought, looking sadly at him, *you don't.* "Serena probably knows somebody who'll lend me a car, and if she doesn't, I'll figure out something. You don't have to worry about it."

"That's okay," he said. "I—"

"Francie!" Eula Mae cried from behind her, and when Francie turned, Eula Mae toddled forward to hug her. "I was afraid I wasn't going to get to see you before I left. I apparently just missed Lyle."

"You mean he *left*?" Francie cried.

"Yep," Joseph said, striding up. "Hightailed it out of here. They were trying to get him to sign a nondisclosure agreement, and Lyle shouted, 'I'm not going to be part of a government cover-up! The world needs to know about this!' and ran out and hopped in a car and took off."

"Oh my God!" Francie said. "We've got to stop him! Which way did he go?"

"That way," Joseph said, pointing toward the road. "But you're too late. He's already gone."

"Maybe we can catch him," Francie said. "Wade, do you have the keys to the Jeep? Come on, we've got to catch him before the police do," and realized Wade was just standing there calmly. "You let him go," she said wonderingly.

He nodded. "There was no way we were going to be able to keep him quiet, no matter what we threatened him with—"

"So you decided to let him share classified information and end up in prison?"

"No, we decided nobody's going to believe him if he does talk. I mean, what's he going to say? That he was abducted by an alien, held prisoner at Area 51, and forced to participate in a government cover-up?"

"But if he tells people what Indy or the aliens' ship looks like—"

"He can't. He didn't see it—or the Hosbitaii—and the agents debriefing him told him this place was the ley line transfer point where they'd intercepted Indy on his way to Marfa to give his over-lords the signal to begin the invasion and that, thanks to him, Indy'd been taken into custody and shipped off to Hangar 18. I can already see the title of Lyle's book: *UFO Invasion—How I Single-handedly Saved the Planet.* They also told him Indy's appearance was an illusion induced by hallucinogens in the chemtrails and crop circle spells, and that Indy's actually a Reptilian."

"And then you conveniently left the keys in the Jeep."

"No, I told you, you're nearly out of gas. I conveniently left the keys in one of the Bureau's cars." He grinned.

"Speaking of cars," Eula Mae said, "I'd better get going. Sheriff Montoya's waiting for me." She gestured vaguely toward where the police cars and FBI vans were parked.

The sky had continued to lighten as they talked. Francie still couldn't make out anything but the silhouettes of the windmills' towering pinnacles. Their red lights were no longer visible. They must be set to switch off at dawn, she thought, though it wasn't dawn yet. The aliens' blinding klieg lights were still on, but they began to click off, one by one, as the sky paled to indigo and then lavender.

"Sheriff Montoya offered to take me all the way to the airport in Albuquerque if I promised to teach him how to count cards," Eula Mae was saying, "and my flight's at noon." She glanced at her watch. "Oh, land's sake, I'm already late. If you're ever in Vegas, be sure to look me up. I'll see that you win big," and hurried off toward the cars.

"I thought she was going straight," Francie said to Wade.

"Yeah," Wade said. "That's what she told me . . ."

"I guess I'd better be headin' out, too," Joseph cut in. "They told me they've got the *Outlaw* all gassed up and ready to go, and if I start now, I should be able to make it to Gallup by suppertime."

"That's where you're going?" Francie asked. "Gallup?"

"Yep. The El Rancho Hotel where the actors stayed when they were filming *Streets of Laredo*. And then Sedona, where they filmed *Broken Arrow*, and then Monument Valley."

"Well, have a good time," Francie said. "I'll miss you," and moved to hug him, but he wasn't paying attention.

He was looking past her. "Well, I'll be goldurned," he said. "Will you get a look at that?"

"At what?" Francie said, and turned to look.

She gasped.

The sun had come up. The sky had gone from lavender to pink, but that wasn't what Joseph was looking at. He was staring at what was directly in front of them, only yards from where they stood, an impossible tableau of orange-red pinnacles and buttes and spires rising up vertically from the red sand at their bases.

"It can't be," Francie breathed, but it was. There was the stack of vermilion rock and the spire standing next to it looking exactly like a mitten, and beyond it a line of rust-colored buttes. "It's Monument Valley."

"No, it's not," Wade said. "Look," and pointed down at the red sand at their feet.

It wasn't sand. It was a reddish tile-like surface, and now that she looked more closely at the spires of rock, she could see protrusions that looked like handholds and instrument panels. It was the spaceship she'd just been in, and the mitten-shaped rocks were some sort of conning tower with a gantry beside it, and pinnacles and spires were struts and antennas. But they looked for all the world like the chimneys and buttes and mesas in that thunderstorm scene in *She Wore a Yellow Ribbon*. No wonder Indy had freaked out when he'd seen it. He'd been on the run from the authorities, and all of a sudden there they were on the screen in front of him.

For a long minute, the three of them stood there looking at it, and then Joseph said, "I'll be hornswoggled. Lyle said them aliens moved Monument Valley around, and durned if he wasn't right."

"He was *not*," Wade said. "The Hosbitaii ship just happens to look like Monument Valley."

"Or they camouflaged themselves to look like it on purpose," Francie mused. "You said your people couldn't find them. Maybe they realized looking like part of the landscape was a good way to keep from being found. And when I was at the airport that first day, somebody said the UFO had crashed near some red rocks outside of Hondo and somebody else said there *weren't* any red rocks there."

"In which case maybe they've been here before," Wade said, "and that's why they're so worried about how long Indy and Srennom have been here. And why they're in such a hurry to leave—"

"Because they used up their time quota on other visits," Francie said.

"Exactly."

She thought of something. "Does this mean they *did* crash in Roswell in 1947?" *Oh,* she thought disgustedly, *if Lyle was right about that, too—*

"No, I asked them whether they did, and they said no, that the 'crash' was a weather balloon and they knew that, and Indy told me Srennom decided that meant Roswell must have weather—and thunderstorms—and that's why he landed there."

"But if they knew it was a weather balloon, then that means they must have been here before."

"And movie scouts coulda seen their ship in Texas and southern Arizona," Joseph said, "and thought it was Monument Valley, and that's why they put it there in *Stagecoach* and *The Searchers.*"

"I doubt *that,*" Wade said, "but it might explain why there've been so many alien sightings in Monument Valley."

"Either way, I think I'd better skip Gallup and go straight on up to Monument Valley and see what I can find out," Joseph said. "Tell Lash Larue goodbye for me," he said, and took off toward his RV.

"I wanted to tell Indy goodbye, too," Francie said. "Where is he?"

"In with the Hosbitaii, being thanked some more," Wade said.

"Listen, Francie, about Agent Wakamura taking you back to Roswell, I—"

"Agent Hastings," Cooper called, coming toward them. "Sorry to interrupt, but they need you in the ship." He turned to Francie. "And Agent Wakamura needs you in the communications tent to fill out some forms." He turned back to Wade. "Agent Sanchez said to tell you it's an emergency."

"What kind of emergency?" Wade asked, instantly alert.

"She didn't say," the agent said. "Something regarding the two renegade aliens—"

"Jesus," Wade said. "Look, Francie—"

"You've got to go. I know. So do I," she said, and turned and walked quickly to the communications tent, where Agent Wakamura was already waiting for her.

"I'll take you back to town as soon as you're done here," the agent said.

"Done." That's the right word, she thought. *"Done." This is the way the world ends, not with a bang but a ride home.*

Well, and what did you think would happen? Sentimental goodbyes between you and the other stagecoach passengers, and then you and Wade would ride off into the sunset together? You're just like Lyle. You watch too many movies.

The two of you spent a few days together, you got Indy to his **tsurrispoinis,** *and you saved his planet and possibly yours,* she told herself sternly, *and now that's over, and Wade's going to go back to being a Man in Black, Indy's going to go home, and you're going to go try to talk Serena into a sensible maid-of-honor dress. And hope she's finally found the right guy.*

"I think there are some forms I'm supposed to sign?" she said to the agent.

"Yes," he said, giving her a pen and a stack of papers. She started through them, signing the Security of Information oath and a dozen other nondisclosure forms, a voucher for a new phone, and a release stating that she'd received the bag Serena had sent her. "Where *is* my bag?" she asked Agent Wakamura.

"In the van," he said. "I can bring it over if you want to change before we leave."

"Thank you," she said, and when he brought it, she ducked behind a van and changed into capri pants and the embroidered Mexican blouse Serena had given her last Christmas.

"All set?" Agent Wakamura asked her.

She nodded, and he took her bag and started out of the tent. "The van's this way."

"Wait," Francie said. "Agent Hastings said I could see Indy before I left." And when he looked blank, she explained, "The alien who abducted me. He looks like a tumbleweed."

"I'll check on that," he replied, made a call, and then said, "The alien's in a meeting with the Head and the Hosbitaii, and nobody's allowed in. Top-secret stuff. They're making arrangements to get him to his ship."

So he can get off Earth before his deadline, she thought.

"Did you need to tell him something?" the agent asked. "I might be able to get a message in to him."

"No, that's okay," she said. *I just wanted to tell him goodbye.* "It wasn't important." She managed a smile. "Where did you say your car was?"

"Van," he said. "Over there." He pointed. "I'll bet you're glad all the excitement's over so you can go home and forget it ever happened," he said, leading her toward an FBI van like the one they'd put her in outside the wedding chapel. "The last few days must have been a real nightmare for you, huh?"

"Yes," she said. *And this time the cavalry's not going to come riding in at the last minute. They've already left for Las Vegas and Monument Valley. And Washington.*

"Here we are," Agent Wakamura said, opening the back door of the van and sticking her bag in.

He shut the door, opened the front door for her, helped her in, and then went around to the driver's side and got in.

He put the key in the ignition, and Francie drew in her breath, hoping against hope a tentacle would lash out and wrap itself around his wrist to stop him. But nothing happened. Agent Wakamura turned the key and started the van.

That's because the Ringo Kid's probably already saddled up and headed for the border, she thought.

"I'll have you back to Roswell in no time," Agent Wakamura said and put the van in gear.

"Wait!" Wade called, running across the field toward them. "Francie! You can't leave!"

CHAPTER TWENTY-FOUR

Prudy: Now, why would I do that?

Jason: Because girls usually go where their husbands are.

Prudy: Oh, when you put it that way, Sheriff . . .

—Support Your Local Sheriff

"Thank God I caught you before you left," Wade said, panting. He grasped the edge of Francie's window with both hands. "We've got a problem."

Oh, no, Francie thought. *They've found out about those other rattlesnakes.* "What's happened?"

"Indy refuses to tell his people where his ship is."

"What?" Francie said, both relieved and confused. "What do you mean he won't tell them? Why would he do something like that?"

"Who knows? This is Indy we're talking about, remember?"

"But can't the Hosbitaii *make* him tell?"

"Ordinarily, yes—but since he and Srennom just saved their planet, the Hosbitaii aren't exactly in a position to order them around."

"But . . . don't the Hosbitaii have detection devices that can find it?"

"Yes, but apparently Indy camouflaged it really well, and what they don't have is time. They've got to be off-planet in two days, remember? And they need every minute of that time to work out the details of their atonement and get our gifts delivered to us. Plus, they're worried it might result in additional contacts with the natives, which they *really* want to avoid. One more, and—"

"I know, it makes it a Yohwataah case," Francie said. "So they want *me* to talk Indy into telling them where his ship is?"

"No, they want you—or, rather, us—to take him to it."

"To drive him there, you mean?"

"Yes."

"But what about your going to Washington for a briefing?"

"This is more important," Wade said. "Indy says you and I drive him, or he won't leave Earth. Which would throw the whole thing into the hands of the Yohwataah."

"But Indy knows that," Francie said, "so why would he—?" She narrowed her eyes suspiciously. "Are he and Srennom up to something? Like getting contraband data from another thunderstorm, maybe?"

"No, because Srennom already told them where his ship *and* his surface vehicle are, and they've already left to pick them up and take him to his ship. He may even be off-planet by now. No, this just seems to be something Indy came up with on his own."

"But why?"

"I don't know. He's pretty attached to us, you know. Especially to you. He may just want to spend more time with you, and put off saying goodbye as long as possible."

"If that's the case, how do we know that once we get him there, he won't refuse to leave unless we go with him back to his home planet?"

"I already asked the Hosbitaii about that," Wade said. "His ship's only big enough for one person—or alien, rather. Look, I know you're anxious to put all this behind you, that you want to get back to Roswell and talk Serena out of making you wear that fuchsia dress with the ruffles—"

"Heliotrope," Francie said.

"Heliotrope. You're a civilian, and we can't force you to do it, but it would really help us out if you'd agree to do this. And the Hosbitaii would be, in their words, 'more mighty grateful, ma'am.'"

Of course I'll do it, she thought. *Indy's not the only one around here who wants to put off saying goodbye.* "But I don't understand. If the ship's camouflaged, why can't the Hosbitaii just take Indy home in their ship and leave his here?"

"Because they can't afford even one more close encounter, and you're forgetting about the crash sightings. There are thousands of UFO nuts out there looking for it right now, and when Lyle gets done telling his story, there'll be even more. One of them's bound to stumble onto it."

"But we could run into some of those UFO nuts, too," Francie said. "Aren't the Hosbitaii worried about that?"

"Yeah, but apparently they think we're less conspicuous than a giant head of cabbage would be, especially since we can pass as UFO hunters and I can hide Indy under my shirt in a pinch. And the Jeep'll be a lot less conspicuous than Monument Valley."

"I thought you said the Jeep was nearly out of gas," she said. "Does this mean the Hosbitaii have changed their minds about giving you the no-gas-required technology?"

"Nope," he said. "It means Agent Cooper is siphoning some gas out of an FBI SUV as we speak. So you'll do it?"

"Yes," Francie said, and got out of the van. "When do we leave?"

"As soon as they finish filling your gas tank, and I change out of this." He looked her up and down. "I see you've already changed. Very pretty. But a 'UFO Chaser' tank top might be better. You don't happen to have one of those in your bag, do you?"

"No," she said, "and I am not wearing any more tank tops," but he was already loping off toward one of the tents, calling back over his shoulder, "Stay there. I'll be right back."

He was back almost immediately, driving the Jeep. He pulled it up next to the van and jumped out. "Indy's on his way."

Wade was wearing a pair of jeans and a gray-and-white baseball shirt with "51" on the front. He turned around so she could see "Roswell Aliens" on the back. "I borrowed these from Cooper," he said. "Oh, good, there he is."

Francie turned to look. Indy was rolling toward them across the tangle of electrical cords, accompanied by the head of cabbage and the ball of twine.

Francie waved at Indy, tears suddenly pricking her eyes, and she realized that, till that moment, she hadn't actually believed he was all right, that they hadn't been lying to her about not stringing him up.

The two aliens with Indy rolled up to within several feet of them, scrolling, "FRANCIE VERY MIGHTY GRATEFUL MA'AM HELP INDY SHIP," and then abruptly stopped and turned toward Indy, scrolling in bright purple, "NO NO NO AGENT HASTINGS FRANCIE NO!" followed by a flurry of neon hieroglyphics.

"What is it? What's wrong?" Wade asked, but Indy didn't answer. He was scrolling back at the two Hosbitaii in their language, obviously explaining something to them. Francie caught the English word *clo* in among the hieroglyphics.

"Oh," she said. "Wade, they don't recognize us in these clothes."

She turned to the Hosbitaii. "No, no, it's still us. Francie," she said, pointing at her chest and then at Wade's, "Agent Hastings. We're just wearing different clothes." She took hold of the wide embroidered sleeve of her blouse and held it out for them to touch. "See? Clothes," but it took several more minutes of Indy's scrolling and some exploratory touching of her blouse and Wade's shirt for them to calm down and do what they'd come to do, which was to thank Francie for helping them out by taking "INDY SHIP."

"We're happy to take him there," she said, and they all hugged her, though gingerly, as if they still didn't quite get the concept of clothes, and rolled off.

"Okay," Wade said, "let's get this show on the road," and started toward the Jeep.

Francie started after him. "Come on, Indy."

"NO NO NO," he scrolled.

"What do you mean, no?" Wade said, exasperated. "I thought

you said you wanted us to take you to your ship. Well, we're taking you. Get in the car."

"NO," Indy scrolled. He rolled over to Francie and grabbed the tail of her blouse, pulling it out of her capri pants.

"What are you *doing*?" Francie said, trying to get it away from him.

"Maybe he doesn't understand about clothes, either."

"That's ridiculous. He just explained it to the Hosbitaii. Indy, stop!" she said as he yanked the blouse up, exposing her midriff. "Wade, help me!" she exclaimed, trying to pull her blouse back down.

"Stop, Indy," Wade said, and tried to help, but Indy was determined to pull the blouse off over her head.

"NO NO NO," he scrolled continuously. "CLO WEDDING."

"Clo wedding?" Francie said. "You mean my maid-of-honor dress?"

"YES YES YES," Indy scrolled. "WHERE WHERE WHERE?"

"Don't worry, I've still got it," Francie said. "It's in the van. In my bag," and Wade ran over to the van, reached through the window for the bag, and brought it over.

"Here," he said, pulling out the dress.

Indy grabbed it and pushed it against Francie's chest like he had at the Thunderbird Trading Post, as if he could make it stick by brute force.

"I think he wants you to put it on," Wade said, and Francie glared at him.

"I know what he wants," she said, struggling with Indy and the dress. "Tell him I can't wear it, that it's too conspicuous."

"SHOW CONSPICUOUS."

"It means we don't want anyone to notice us," Wade said. "You can't have any more contacts, remember? Look, we'll take the dress with us, okay?" he said, pointing at the Jeep, and, amazingly, that seemed to satisfy Indy. He scooped the dress and Francie's bag up in his tentacles, deposited them in the back seat of the Jeep, and crawled in next to them.

"*Thank* you," Francie said to Wade, pulling her blouse back down, and got in the car. Indy immediately rolled over her to take his place on the center console.

"Where to?" Wade asked, and Indy propped his tentacle on the dashboard and pointed west.

"Just like old times," Wade said as he started the car and drove out of the perimeter the FBI had set up.

The agents had apparently been ordered to let them through because they waved them on, past a barricade of FBI vans and a large sign reading QUARANTINE AREA. NO ADMITTANCE.

"Wow, Lyle must have loved breaking out of this," Francie said. "It's just like *Close Encounters of the Third Kind.*"

"Yeah, that was what it was designed to look like," Wade said. "Cooper's idea."

"He sounds perfect for Serena," she said as they passed the last barrier.

They headed west. After only a couple of miles, Indy scrolled, "TURN TURN TURN," and pointed to a dirt road heading off through low hills.

"You're kidding," Francie said. "His ship was right under their noses?"

Indy continued to point ahead. The narrow dirt road ran straight south for half a mile and then veered sharply east behind a juniper-covered hill that cut them off from sight of the highway. "Indy, is your ship out here?" Francie asked.

Indy didn't answer, just kept pointing ahead. They went for another half mile, past the hill into a low flat area sparsely covered in weeds and beyond it some scattered brown boulders.

"STOP STOP STOP," Indy scrolled, and as soon as Wade pulled the car over, Indy opened the door and rolled out.

"You don't think *that's* his ship, do you?" Francie asked, pointing at the boulders.

"I don't know, maybe," Wade said. "Or maybe he's just trying to get his bearings. And if that's the case, he needs to stay the hell away from those boulders. We can't afford any more contacts."

"Indy, come back," Francie called, getting out of the car. "There might be rattlesnakes!"

But Indy wasn't heading for the boulders or the field. He was circling the car, tendrils waving, and after a minute, he rolled underneath it.

"What's he doing?" Francie asked.

"No idea," Wade said, squatting down, but before he could look under the car, Indy reemerged carrying a small black object, which he fiddled with for a second and then threw out into the field.

"What was that?" Francie asked.

"I'm guessing the GPS tracker the FBI put on the car," Wade said. "He apparently thinks if the Hosbitaii know which direction we're going, they'll be able to figure out where his ship is."

"SHH SHH SHH," Indy scrolled and opened the back door of the car. He rolled in, reached up to the dome light, pulled down an object, and showed it to Wade. "SHOW," he scrolled.

"Microphone," Wade said, and Indy flung it after the first object, then reached back in and moved his tentacle around the edges of the back window. He came up with a tiny round green item and handed it to Wade.

"Spycam," Wade said, and Indy took it back from him and arced it far out into the field.

"If it hits a rattlesnake, does that count as another contact?"

"Let's hope not," Wade said, and Indy rolled to the front of the car and tried to open the hood.

"He must think they've stuck a GPS device under there," Wade said, propping the hood up for Indy. Indy stuck a tentacle down behind the grill, pulled out another tracker, and threw it after the others.

"Good job," Wade said, and started to unhook the support rod and lower the hood, but Indy was poking around the engine again, winding his tentacles under and around the intake manifold, the radiator, and the engine.

"I think you got 'em all, buddy," Wade said.

"NO NO NO," Indy scrolled, and after another minute came up

holding a button-shaped silver object. He dropped it in Wade's hand.

"Whaddaya know?" Wade said, and Indy took it back from him, flung it out across the field, motioned to Wade that he could close the hood, and got back in the car.

"Okay," Wade said, getting in, "now that nobody's watching or listening, where are we going?" and Francie looked at Indy's tentacle, but he didn't scroll anything. He merely pointed back the way they'd come and, after they got to the highway, west.

"So we're going back to Roswell?" Wade said. "Is that where your ship is?"

Indy didn't answer. He just tapped the windshield.

"He must be worried that he didn't get all the spy devices," Wade said to Francie. "Okay, Indy, point the way."

Indy did, taking them west almost to Roswell, which took most of the morning, and then having them turn north on a county road and west again on a narrow dirt road. "This is the road to the J. B. Foster ranch, where the original weather balloon crash was," Wade said. "If Indy landed his ship there—"

"That would mean a UFO really *did* land there," Francie said. "Which would be pretty ironic, wouldn't it?"

" 'Ironic' is not the word I'd choose," Wade said grimly. "More like infuriating. It's a good thing Lyle thinks we're Reptilians or he'd never let us live this down," but Indy took them north again to the next county road, back east almost to Portales, and west again past Roswell.

"He must think we're still being followed and is taking some kind of evasive action," Wade said.

"Or he doesn't have any idea where his ship is, and he didn't want to admit to the Hosbitaii that he lost it," Francie said. "And that's why he was so anxious to get rid of the trackers. Indy, do you know where you're going?"

"YES YES YES," he scrolled, pointing for them to turn south at the next junction, and then, a few miles farther on, back north.

"This can't be right," Wade said. "We're getting too far west.

We've already passed Hondo and Carrizozo. What time did he abduct you?"

"I'm not sure. It was around sunset."

"Sunset was at around eight P.M.," he said. "His ship was first sighted landing a little after six. That makes it an hour and a half from then till he showed up in Roswell. He couldn't have rolled all the way from here in that time."

"Maybe he had a surface vehicle like Srennom, and he wrecked it—or lost it—and that's what he didn't want them to know."

"In which case his ship could be anywhere," Wade mused, and when, a couple of minutes later, Indy sent them heading west again, Wade said, "You don't suppose he *did* land in Monument Valley?"

"MONUMENT VALLEY?" Indy scrolled in bright red, shooting out a tentacle to look out the back window.

"No one's following us," Francie said. "You got rid of the trackers, remember? They don't know where we are," and Indy stopped scrolling and went back to pointing ahead out the windshield for the next hour.

"Any idea where we are?" Wade asked Francie when Indy showed no signs of ever stopping.

She retrieved the road map from the glove compartment and opened it out. "We're on U.S. 280, right?" she asked, and when he nodded, she said, "I think we're about five miles west of I-25 and seventy-five miles south of Albuquerque."

"That's what I was afraid of," Wade said, and pulled off to the side of the highway and stopped.

"NO NO NO," Indy scrolled. "GO."

"Not till you tell us where you're taking us," he said, switching the engine off. "Or is Francie right, and you don't know where your ship is?"

"NO NO NO INDY NOTHES."

"Then *tell* us," Wade said. "We can't just keep driving around. We'll run out of gas."

"NO NO NO," Indy scrolled. He tapped the gas gauge.

"You can't afford to have any more contacts, remember, and if we stop to buy gas—" Wade explained, but Indy continued to point at the gas gauge, tapping it insistently.

"We won't have to," Francie said. "Will we, Indy?" and when Wade looked questioningly at her, she went on, "Back there, when we thought he was looking for bugs, he was adapting the engine, just like he did on Serena's car and the *Outlaw*."

"Is Francie right?" Wade asked Indy. "Is that what you did?"

"YES YES YES."

Francie looked at Wade. "I thought you told me giving us technology was forbidden."

"It is, which is why I'd imagine he got rid of the bugs first, so they wouldn't know he'd done it. But if they find out—"

"NO NO NO," Indy scrolled. "SECRET LEAVE."

"Secret leave?" Wade said. "What's that?"

"No, not secret leave. Secret. Leave. He means the Hosbitaii will be gone in a couple of days, and all we have to do is keep it secret till they do. But, Indy, you don't know for sure that we'll be able to."

Wade nodded. "We can't risk you getting in trouble for us."

"NO NO NO," Indy scrolled. "NO TROUBLE INDY NOTHES," and tapped the windshield impatiently. "GO."

"And what does that *mean*?" Wade said. "That he knows he can outrun them?"

"Or that he knows he won't get in trouble if they do find out," Francie said.

"Because he saved their planet?"

"Maybe," she said, watching Indy scroll. "Or maybe the Hosbitaii already know about this. You said they know how the technology could save our planet, and that they'd have given it to us if their hands—I mean, tentacles—weren't tied. What if this is their way of getting around the rules?"

"And that's why they had Indy do this?" Wade said. "Indy, is that why they're having us take you to your ship?"

"YES NO," Indy scrolled.

"And what the hell does *that* mean?" Wade said.

"It means it wasn't his only reason for altering the engine," Francie said. "Indy, where are you taking us?"

"WHAT HAPPENS IN VEGAS STAYS IN VEGAS," Indy scrolled.

"So he's saying it's a secret and he won't tell us?" Wade said.

"No," Francie said grimly. "It means he's saying he's taking us to Las Vegas."

"YES YES YES," Indy scrolled, and pointed at the windshield. "GO LAS VEGAS ITS A BLAST!"

"Las *Vegas*!" Wade said.

"Indy, we can't take you to Las Vegas," Francie said. "We don't have time. It'd take us a full day to get there and another day back, and you've already wasted most of the day driving us around. You've only got two days left to get off-planet. Besides, I have to be in Roswell by tomorrow to help Serena get ready for her wedding."

"YES YES YES WEDDING," he scrolled. "GO LAS VEGAS"

"He must think all weddings are in Las Vegas, Wade," Francie said. "Yes, Indy, you're right, I have to be in Serena's wedding, but it's not in Las Vegas. It's in Roswell."

"NO NO NO SERENA," Indy scrolled. "WEDDING LAS VEGAS BBHBINIITS."

Sacred duty? Francie thought. "Indy, I don't understand—"

Wade was looking thoughtfully at the alien. "Indy, whose wedding are you talking about?"

"FRANCIE WADE."

"But we already had that wedding," Francie said. "Remember Cupid's Chapel and the bouquet and Elvis Presley?" and when he scrolled a series of "YES," she told him, "That was the wedding."

"NO NO NO DEADLINE."

"Exactly," Wade said. "You have a deadline. In two days, and if we don't get you off-planet by then—"

"NO NO NO 10 DAYS."

"*Ten* days?"

"YES YES YES," Indy scrolled in the heliotrope Serena no doubt had in mind for Francie's maid-of-honor dress. "NOT VALID" . . .

He paused. "CERTIFICATE" . . . Another pause, and then he scrolled in a different font altogether, "MUST APPEAR IN PERSON WITHIN 10 DAYS."

"Oh my gosh," Francie said, "he's talking about our marriage license. Remember Reverend Murray saying we had to go to the Marriage License Bureau and get a marriage license for the marriage to be valid."

"Within ten days," Wade said. "Indy must have heard him."

"Indy, you don't understand," Francie said. "To be able to get a marriage license you have to have the wedding ceremony certificate, and we don't have it." *And even if we did,* she thought, *Wade didn't sign his real name.*

"NO NO NO NO NO," Indy scrolled, and slid a tentacle into Wade's back pocket and pulled out a piece of paper.

"You brought it with you?" Francie said.

"Yeah. I thought if anybody stopped us and didn't buy the UFO-hunter thing, I could tell them we'd eloped."

"CERTIFICATE," Indy scrolled, and pointed at the ignition. "LAS VEGAS LICENSE."

"So, are you going to be the one to tell him the certificate's not valid or am I?" Francie asked.

"Actually," Wade said, looking uncomfortable, "it *is* valid."

"But you didn't sign your real name—"

"Yeah, I did. Reverend Murray absolutely refused to give us a certificate, and I didn't have time to argue with him with the Bureau hot on our tail. So I showed him my badge and said the ceremony was part of a government sting. Which meant he saw my name, so I had to use it on the form for the certificate."

"But during the ceremony he called you Wade—"

"I told him that was the name I was using for the sting, but it wouldn't have mattered anyway. According to Nevada law, the marriage is valid no matter what name you sign. I guess they get a lot of prospective brides and grooms giving them fake names."

"So we're *married*?"

"Not unless we get a marriage license," Wade said, and Indy

scrolled, "LAS VEGAS GO GO GO!" while he forced Wade's hand
toward the ignition.

"No, wait," Francie said. "It's not just a matter of getting a license, Indy. You need—"

"INDY NOTHES," he scrolled, and reached into the back seat
and triumphantly produced her maid-of-honor dress.

"No, no," she said, "that's not what I'm talking about. For two
people to get married, they have to be in love with each other."

"SHOW LOVE," Indy scrolled.

Oh, no, here we go again, Francie thought, trying to think what
to tell him, but he was already scrolling again.

"FRANCIE LOVE SERENA."

"Yes, I love her. She's my friend. But I'm not *in* love with her. This
is different—"

"FRANCIE IN LOVE WADE."

Yes, she thought. *But unfortunately he's not in love with me.* "I
told you, I'm not talking about friends," she said. "I'm talking
about—"

"PARDNERS," Indy scrolled.

"No, I'm not talking about partners, either. This isn't about
friends *or* partners. When two people are in love with each other,
they want to spend their whole lives together."

"TSINIBITAIS," Indy scrolled.

"*No,* not roommates. I mean two people who want to be together always, who can't bear to be parted."

"GRIZZLY?" Indy scrolled, and Francie remembered too late
that one of the Westerns Indy had watched had had a grizzly bear
tearing a prospector apart in it.

"No, not that kind of bear," she said hastily. "'Bear' means—
Wade, what are you doing?"

He was turning the key in the ignition. "I'm taking you and Indy
to Vegas," he said.

"But you can't. Indy will make us—"

"Get a marriage license. And that's just what we're going to do."

"But—"

"Look, we've only got two more days to get Indy off this planet, and at the rate you're going, it'll take you twice that long to explain what 'bear' means, let alone 'being in love.' *If* you can explain it. For all we know, the Hosbitaii *are* plants or have nine sexes or propagate some other way entirely. And even if you *do* manage to make him understand, that's no guarantee that that'll make him change his mind about getting us the license. You heard him, he considers it a *bbhbiniits*. So I say we go to Las Vegas, get the license, and get him safely off the planet and then worry about . . ." He glanced at Indy. ". . . taking care of the details later."

You mean getting an annulment, Francie thought dully. "You're right. That's the best plan," she said, making her voice matter-of-fact. "We can get it done right after he leaves." She turned to Indy and asked, "If we go to Las Vegas and get the license, do you promise to take us to your ship?"

"YES YES YES."

"With no more stalling or detours?"

"SHOW STALLING."

"You know perfectly well what stalling is," Francie said. "It's what you're doing right now. Do you promise?"

"YES YES YES."

"Okay," Wade said, and started the car and then frowned and turned off the ignition.

"NO NO NO NO," Indy scrolled. "GO LAS VEGAS."

"In a minute," Wade said. "We may not be able to . . ." He glanced meaningfully at Indy, who was trying to make him turn the key, "to take care of those details right away. I'm going to need to get this car to the Bureau so we can figure out how the no-gas thing works before they find out Indy gave it to us and swoop in to take it away."

"But I thought we decided the Hosbitaii wanted us to have it—"

"Even if they do, the Yohwataah don't. We've got to—"

"Reverse-engineer the technology, just like Lyle said."

"Yeah," he said wryly. "So until that's done we won't be able to . . . you know. And that's not the only problem. You heard Indy, getting us married is a *bbhbiniits* for him. If he found out we . . . undid it, he'd be likely to come racing back here—"

"And make us get married again."

Wade nodded. "And that would mean his violating the number-of-days restriction, to say nothing of the extra close encounters he might have in the process, which would put the whole thing in Yoh-wataah hands."

"And get Indy strung up."

"Exactly."

"So you think we should wait till after he's safely back on his home planet?" Francie said. "How long would that take?"

"I'm not sure. The Hosbitaii planet's approximately eight hundred light-years away."

"*Eight hundred years?*"

"Eight hundred *light*-years," Wade corrected, "but it wouldn't take him that long. They've obviously either got some kind of faster-than-light travel or warp drive or something. Six months, maybe a year to be on the safe side. But that's not what I'm worried about. I'm worried about him finding out even *after* he's back on his own planet."

"*What?* How?"

"Srennom knew all about us before he came. That's why he decided to come to Earth, because he knew we had thunderstorms. Remember I told you they knew that the 1947 Roswell crash wasn't a UFO? That it was a weather balloon?"

She nodded.

"Well, *how* did they know that? And how did they know we were at that thunderstorm? And taking that particular road back? It wasn't an accident they were there." He looked at her earnestly. "What if aliens are telepathic, like Lyle said, and they *do* know what we're thinking?"

"YES YES YES," Indy scrolled. "NOTHES."

"You're *telepathic*?" Francie said.

"YES YES YES WADE IN LOVE FRANCIE."

"There, you see, that proves it. He *is* telepathic." He looked suddenly serious. "I am in love with you."

"You *are*?" Francie said, and her heart began to pound.

"YES YES YES," Indy scrolled.

"Stay out of this, Indy," Wade said. "Yes. Since the moment I tried to stop your car and you nearly ran over me. How about you? Francie in love Wade?"

"YES YES YES," Indy scrolled.

"Indy, shut up," she said, and looked at Wade. "Yes yes yes."

"Thank God," he said, "because I can't—how did you put it?"

"Bear to be parted from you?"

"Exactly," he said, and leaned over to kiss her.

"NO NO NO NO," Indy scrolled. "LAS VEGAS HURRY HURRY GO."

"In a minute," Wade said. "As soon as I've finished kissing my wife."

"NO NO NO"—Indy shoved between them—"NEED LICENSE."

"No, you don't," Francie said, and proceeded to kiss Wade, and maybe Indy *was* telepathic, because he waited patiently till they came up for air, and then scrolled, "GO LAS VEGAS NOW?"

"Yes," Wade said and reached for the ignition.

"Wait," Francie said. "If they're telepathic, then why don't they know where Indy is and what he's up to? And why do they scroll at each other? Why don't they just read each other's minds?"

"NO NO NO," Indy scrolled. "VIOLATION."

"There's your answer," Wade said. "My guess is they've got a sixth level to that close-encounters list of theirs, and reading somebody's mind is really bad. Is that right, Indy?"

"YES YES YES. INTERFACE TROUBLE TROUBLE TROUBLE."

"Which doesn't seem to have kept Indy from reading ours," Francie said. "Indy, you are absolutely forbidden to read our minds, understand?"

"YES YES YES GO LAS VEGAS NOW?"

"Yes yes yes," Wade said, and started the car. "Which way, Francie?"

"Stay on this road till we reach I-25 and then turn north till you get to Albuquerque."

"Got it," Wade said. He pulled onto the road and started west, and Indy settled into his accustomed place between them and propped his tentacle on the dashboard, pointing at the windshield.

"Just like old times," Wade said.

"Yes, yes, yes," Francie said happily, looking out at the desert and the blue sky.

"Now all we have to do is get to Las Vegas and our troubles are over," Wade said. "Which way do I turn when we get to Albuquerque?"

Francie consulted the map. "I think the best route is to take I-40 to Kingman and then I-93 north like we did last time."

"NO NO NO," Indy scrolled. "I-15 NORTH SAINT GEORGE 89 WEST KANAB 160 KAYENTA."

"What?" Francie said. "I can't even find those roads on the map. Are you sure that takes us to Las Vegas?"

"NO NO NO LAS VEGAS MONUMENT VALLEY."

"Monument *Valley*?" Wade erupted, and Francie said, "We are not going to Monument Valley. You promised us no detours, remember?"

"NO NO NO."

"No, he didn't promise, or no, it isn't a detour?" Wade asked.

"I don't know," Francie said. "Indy, is Monument Valley where your ship is?"

"NO NO NO."

"Are there transfer zones there?" Wade asked. "Or a secret underground base?"

"NO NO NO."

"Then why do you want to go there?" Francie asked.

"SEE MOVE."

"*Move?*"

"YES YES YES JOSEPH SAY MONUMENT VALLEY MOVE GO LAS VEGAS THEN MONUMENT VALLEY."

"He was *kidding*," Wade said, "and we can't go to Monument

Valley. You've got two days to get off this planet. We don't have time to go to Monument Valley, too."

"YES YES YES INDY FIX," he scrolled.

"You mean you can fix the car to go faster?" Wade asked.

"NO NO NO," he scrolled. "TIME."

"No, we *don't* have time," Francie said. "You've got a deadline, and I've got to get back in time to help Serena with her wedding. I have a *bhhbiniits* to be there, and Monument Valley's four hundred miles from Las Vegas."

"INDY FIX."

"You can't *fix* it," Francie said. "I told you, Joseph was just kidding. Monument Valley doesn't move."

"NO NO NO," he scrolled, the letters orange with frustration at their not understanding. "FIX TIME!"

ACKNOWLEDGMENTS

To my husband and daughter, who went with me to Roswell,
     to my agent and editor, who displayed infinite patience with me,
     to all my friends, who ditto,
     and to Starbucks, who provided me with iced chais and any number of interesting aliens to observe while I was writing the book.

ABOUT THE AUTHOR

CONNIE WILLIS is a member of the Science Fiction Hall of Fame and a Grand Master of the Science Fiction and Fantasy Writers of America. She has received seven Nebula awards and eleven Hugo awards for her fiction; *Blackout* and *All Clear*—a novel in two parts—and *Doomsday Book* won both. Her other works include *Crosstalk, Passage, To Say Nothing of the Dog, Lincoln's Dreams, Bellwether, Impossible Things, Terra Incognita, The Best of Connie Willis,* and *A Lot Like Christmas.* Connie Willis lives with her family in Colorado, where she holed up during the pandemic and got lots done, but she sure wishes it would end. She has visited Roswell a number of times and has never seen a single alien, except on T-shirts, mugs, bumper stickers, magnets, and cookie jars. Connie is currently working on a new novel in the Oxford Time Travel series set at Tintern Abbey, Westminster Bridge, and Oxford.

conniewillis.net

ABOUT THE TYPE

This book was set in Sabon, a typeface designed by the well-known German typographer Jan Tschichold (1902–74). Sabon's design is based upon the original letter forms of sixteenth-century French type designer Claude Garamond and was created specifically to be used for three sources: foundry type for hand composition, Linotype, and Monotype. Tschichold named his typeface for the famous Frankfurt typefounder Jacques Sabon (c. 1520–80).